Lost Patrol

Lost Patrol

Morgan Hill

Sage River Books *Sisters, Oregon*

LOST PATROL
published by Sage River Books

International Standard Book Number: 1-59052-050-5

Printed in the United States of America

For information:
Sage River Books, Post Office Box 1720, Sisters, Oregon 97759

Library of Congress Cataloging-in-Publication Data

Hill, Morgan, 1933-
Lost patrol / by Morgan Hill.
p. cm.
ISBN 1-59052-050-5
1. United States--History--Civil War, 1861-1865--Fiction. 2. Apache Indians--Wars--Fiction. 3. Surveyors--Fiction. I. Title.
PS3562.A256L67 2003
813'.54--dc21 2003003866

03 04 05 06 07 08 09 — 10 9 8 7 6 5 4 3 2 1 0

CHAPTER ONE

A glaring, merciless sun hovered furnace hot in the Arizona sky, punishing the cavalry patrol as they rode along the side of a long, rocky ridge.

Lieutenant Boyd Locklin was in the lead with Sergeant Clay Harris beside him. Directly behind them, nine blue-uniformed troopers rode three abreast, with Corporals Bill Yike and Lester Dunlap bringing up the rear.

Locklin's wary eyes searched the jagged crest of the ridge as he lifted his campaign hat, wiped sweat from his brow, and riffled fingers through his thick strands of black, curly hair. Replacing the hat, he rubbed the other sleeve across his mouth, pressing the moisture from his well-trimmed mustache.

The men were experiencing the same uneasiness as their leader. Squinting against the desert's blinding glare, they cautiously studied the uneven line of the ridge, knowing Chief Pantano and his blood-hungry Apache warriors might rise up at any moment from behind the rocky crags and unleash a hail of hot lead. Each man rode in silence, gripping his .54 caliber breechloader Springfield carbine.

From the side of his mouth, Sergeant Harris said in a low tone, "Wish we could've avoided having to ride so close to that ridge. We're sitting ducks."

Locklin grinned. Pointing with his chin to the edge of the hundred-foot-deep canyon that lay twenty feet to their left, he replied, "The only way to get where we're going is to pass along here. Otherwise it would be twenty extra miles, going over those mountains behind the ridge. We could ride the bottom of the canyon, but then we'd be in this vulnerable position a whole lot longer. We'll be past the ridge in another ten minutes."

Harris was a big, blocky man, standing six-two. He was the

same height as Locklin, but outweighed him by forty pounds. Reaching into his shirt pocket, he pulled out a plug of chewing tobacco and took his eyes off the ridge long enough to extend it toward his lieutenant. "Chaw?"

Locklin's eyes were a flashing blue against the deep mahogany of his skin. Though he was only twenty-seven years of age, the six years that he had spent in the heat and the relentless dry wind of the desert had chiseled creases at the corners of his eyes. Compassion and toughness lay uneasily together. Shaking his head, he said, "You know I don't chew."

Harris shrugged his shoulders, bit off a chaw, and replaced the plug in his pocket. "Just thought maybe you'd grown up enough to take up a *man's* habit."

Boyd Locklin was not in the mood for kidding. He was concentrating on his mission. Attached to Fort Savage in southeastern Arizona Territory, he had been sent out early that morning to patrol an area not usually disturbed by the army. The fort's commandant, Colonel Brett Halloran, had received word from Fort Campbell that a small wagon train was headed west through this area against the army's advice. They were in grave danger from the Apaches, who were on the warpath.

Fort Savage was located on the San Pedro River, ten miles east of the rugged Santa Catalina Mountains. Since the California gold rush of 1849, the normal southern route to California through Arizona brought travelers from New Mexico into the Territory just south of the Peloncillo Mountains, through San Simon Valley, then northwest to the San Pedro River. When they crossed the San Pedro, they moved through Catalina Pass and headed due west across the barren wasteland to where the Gila and Colorado Rivers joined at the small settlement called Yuma. Shortly after leaving Yuma, they were in California, and proceeded on to whatever destination they had chosen for themselves.

Fort Savage had been built in 1850 at the strategic crossing of the San Pedro to give a measure of protection to travelers as they moved through the Catalinas. This was a favored spot chosen by the Indians for ambush. In 1849, Chief Pantano and his vicious Chiricahua Apaches had wiped out more than a dozen wagon trains. Since the fort had been established and the cavalry was there to escort the trains through the Catalina Pass, the Santa Catalinas had seen no more white men's blood.

The army's presence in his territory had curtailed much of Pantano's blood shedding, but not all. Filled with a malevolent hatred for the white intruders, he was still leading his warriors in attacks on wagon trains and white settlements, defying the "blue coats" to stop him.

Fort Campbell was located seventy miles east of Savage, at the foot of the Peloncillo Mountains, just fifteen miles from the New Mexico border. The dispatch received by Colonel Halloran explained that the small wagon train was being led by a Catholic priest. He was taking them to a settlement called Providence Wells near the Mexican border, just south of the Quigotoa Mountains. The priest had stubbornly refused the advice of Fort Campbell's commandant, Colonel Edgar Moffett, and left the normal trail to take a more convenient southerly route to Providence Wells. Knowing the predatory ways of the Apaches and that Pantano was camped somewhere due south of Fort Savage, Moffett had sent a dispatch, asking that Colonel Halloran send a patrol to intercept the train and escort them through the dangerous area.

Horses blew intermittently, saddle leather creaked, and the hot sun bore down as the cavalry unit moved slowly toward the end of the rocky ridge. Upon reaching it, the canyon veered off to the north and they rode out on to a broad expanse of desert. The land stretched endlessly before them, country thick with cactus and stunted brush, pocked with gullies and ridges. It was a shade of tan that looked devoid of color in the wash of the sun.

Sergeant Clay Harris breathed a sigh of relief as they left the dangerous ridge behind. He spit a brown stream and looked at his commanding officer. "If I figure right, Lieutenant, we should intercept that wagon train straight east of here within another four or five miles."

"That's the way I see it," said Locklin. Pulling rein, he signaled for the column to stop. "Watering time. We'll take ten minutes."

The men in blue watered their horses and themselves three and four at a time while the others kept watch on the desert for any sign of the wagon train or Indians. A pair of lizards sunned themselves on a flat rock nearby and a small desert rat skittered past the soldiers, diving quickly into a hole.

They were about to mount up when Corporal Bill Yike spotted a huge diamondback rattler as it slithered out from under a rock some twenty yards away. One of the horses nickered, and the snake began to hiss and coil.

Yike started to call Locklin's attention to it, but the lieutenant waved a hand. "I see him."

The snake had everybody's attention by that time. One of the young troopers raised his carbine. "I'll kill it, sir."

"No! You've got to learn, Sanders, that we don't shoot at snakes when there might be Apaches in the area. Usually they'll know when we're around, but not always. You fire that gun, and they'll have us pinpointed immediately."

"We oughtta kill it, sir," said Sanders.

Clay Harris drew his bulk up beside Sanders. "When you've been with us a little longer, sonny, you'll wait eagerly for a rattler to show up just so you can watch Lieutenant Locklin kill it."

Sanders lowered his weapon, gave the sergeant a blank look, then set his eyes on Locklin as the lieutenant bent over and picked up a fist-sized rock. The snake was coiled tight, darting its tongue in and out and swaying its head, ready to strike.

Sanders assessed the distance between his commanding officer and the deadly reptile. Chuckling, he said, "No offense, sir, but there's not one man in a thousand who could throw a rock that distance and hit that snake in the head."

"That's right," chorused three others.

The horses were showing nervousness because of the snake. Boyd Locklin gripped the rock firmly in his right hand, planted his feet, and hurled it hard. The rock flashed as it zeroed in on its target. It caught the rattler's head, shattering it with a splatter of blood.

Sanders's jaw slacked. While the other men applauded by slapping the stocks of their rifles, Sanders gasped, "If I hadn't seen it with my own eyes, I'd never have believed it!"

"Can't wait to see the next one, huh?" chortled Harris.

"That's for sure," said Sanders. "Lieutenant, where'd you learn to throw like that?"

"Back home in the Maryland woods when I was a kid. Used to hunt squirrels and various kinds of birds with rocks. Took them home to my mother and she cooked them."

Trooper Sanders was muttering to himself in amazement as the cavalry unit mounted up and continued eastward. Tawny clouds of alkali dust rose up around them. At the rear, Corporals Yike and Dunlap turned around in their saddles and scrutinized the land behind them. They saw no movement, except for the shimmering heat waves that danced over the cactus-studded sand. Some twenty miles to the west, the southern tip of the Santa Catalinas could be seen rising about the buttes and varied rock formations that jutted up from the desert floor. The Dragoons showed their rounded domes to the south, and the spires and ragged edges of the Chiricahua Mountains were barely visible straight ahead. The Chiricahuas were a main stronghold of the Apaches, but the U.S. army also knew that the vicious Pantano and his band of hard-faced killers were camped somewhere near the Dragoons.

Turning his face in that direction, Yike said, "Lester, my friend, I think one of these days Colonel Halloran is gonna line about sixty or seventy of us up and announce that we're to search that Dragoon country till we find Pantano's hideout. Our job will be to root 'em out like rodents and exterminate 'em."

Dunlap showed him a thin smile. "You think sixty or seventy of us could do it?"

"Mm-hmm. But thirty-five or forty of them desert-wise 'Paches will see us coming. If we could find some way to sneak up on them, we might have a chance with numbers like that. But ain't nobody can sneak up on them. They're too smart. Having been born in this dried-out country, they can sneak up on the likes of us without half trying. They know how to blend into the dirt and sand and rocks just like the lizards. Colonel Halloran isn't a fool. He'll keep us on the defensive. To launch a successful attack, you gotta have some element of surprise. There just ain't no way to pull that on the 'Paches."

Dunlap wiped sweat from his face and nodded. "Yeah. Guess you're right."

"But at least," said Yike with a sigh, "the army's presence in these parts has cut down on Pantano's massacres. He has a degree of respect for our fire power."

Trooper Hand Yarrow, who rode just ahead of the corporals, turned around in his saddle and said to Yike, "You're right, Corporal, the big brass will keep us on the defensive all over Indian territory for some time to come, but the handwriting is on the wall. One day the whites will swarm into this part of the country, and when we safely outnumber the savages, we'll take over and put them into subjection."

"What'll we do with them?" asked trooper Gary White.

Hunching his shoulders, Yarrow said, "I don't know. Maybe put them in prison camps."

Lieutenant Boyd Locklin spoke over his shoulder. "Won't be prison camps, gentlemen. There's talk in Washington that they'll be put on reservations. That means they'll be given a certain piece of land to live on, and that's where they'll stay. Yarrow is right. The handwriting is on the wall. It's only a matter of time."

"Don't seem right," cut in trooper Jake Ford, who rode in the middle behind Locklin. "This has been their land for who knows how long. What right have we got to come here and take it away from them?"

"It's called progress, sonny," spoke up Sergeant Clay Harris. "Some day this whole hunk of land from the Atlantic to the Pacific will be settled and civilized. Since the Indians refuse to act civil and let us share the land with them, they'll have to pay the price."

The men grew quiet again as they passed through a low spot, then began a gentle climb toward a rounded crest about two miles away. The broad expanse was scarred by shaded arroyos and cracks in the parched earth. All about them were rocks and boulders, scattered and tumbled as if some massive giant had lost his temper while playing with them and threw them in every direction. The riders found themselves weaving among stunted pinon, catclaw, nopal clusters, and mesquite bushes.

Boyd Locklin was wondering how many rattlers were nested in the clusters of sunbleached rocks and boulders when Sergeant Harris interrupted his thoughts. "We ought to catch sight of that wagon train when we top the rise, Lieutenant."

"I would think so," said Locklin, pulling a bandanna from his hip pocket. While wiping the back of his neck, he added, "If they pulled away from Fort Campbell as reported, they ought to be somewhere along in here."

Unless Pantano has already attacked them and wiped them out, thought Harris, but he was reluctant to voice it.

The unit rode in silence under the blasting ball of fire in the brassy vault overhead. The sun was beginning its westward slant as afternoon came on. The ever-present dust continued to lift from the horses' hooves, coating animals and riders, then turning to mud when it struck sweat.

As they drew near the crest of the rise, something scratched at the back of Boyd Locklin's brain. He could not give it a name, but it trailed down his spine like tiny prickling needles. Was it a forewarning of danger? Throwing up his hand, he halted the column. A slight breeze carried the dust away. As yet, they could not see over the rise.

"What is it, sir?" asked Harris.

"I don't know," replied Locklin, dismounting. "I want to take a look over the crest before we ride any further."

"I'll do it for you, sir," called Corporal Bill Yike, leaving his saddle.

The crest was about fifty yards from where they had halted. Locklin paused, then said, "I want to see for myself. You can come with me, Yike."

Yike was a short, thin man. He had to take three steps for every two of the tall lieutenant's. When they drew within ten yards of the rounded ridge, they ducked low and crept up slowly until they could see over the edge. What they saw jolted them both. Yike's face went pallid and he made a tiny intake of breath. He said something that the lieutenant could not distinguish.

There was a slight slope beyond the crest that spread out for miles, looking the same as the landscape and terrain as what lay behind them, except for myriads of sandy mounds that dotted the desert floor, most of which were laden with hunks of rock and patches of prickly pear cacti. Some sixty yards from where they stood lay the remains of the small wagon train. All eight wagons were either completely upside down or lying on their sides. Strewn about the area were the naked, bloody bodies of men, women, and children. They were grotesquely positioned, like dolls tossed down by a child who was through with them. The heads that were visible showed glistening scarlet patches where their scalps had been lifted.

In spite of the heat, Boyd Locklin felt an icy chill crawl over him—a coldness that seemed to sting his flesh. He breathed an oath, cursing the brutal Apaches.

"It's a wonder there isn't a flock of vultures around, sir," Yike said softly.

"The only reason, Corporal," replied Locklin levelly, "is that it's just been a little while since it happened. No Apaches in sight. They got out of here in a hurry."

Rising to his full height, Locklin pivoted and lifted his arm, signaling the men to come.

As they drew close, Yike said, "Brace yourself, men. It's an awful sight."

"The wagon train?" asked Harris, who was leading the lieutenant's horse. Lester Dunlap had Yike's horse.

"Yes." Locklin removed his hat to sleeve away sweat. "I figure we're about a half hour too late."

When the rest of the men had scanned the scene, Locklin said, "Well, we'll have to bury them if we can find some shovels."

All of them dismounted and slowly led their horses down the slope toward the ghastly sight. Trooper Ray Sanders said, "There aren't any horses around, Lieutenant. What would the Indians want with bulky animals that pull wagons?"

"Food," said Locklin. "Apaches love horse meat."

"Oh." Sanders was just learning the ways of the enemy.

Trooper Gary White's face matched his last name as he turned away from the others to give up what food was left in his stomach.

Every naked body had been scalped and huge blue-green flies were feasting on the bloody spots where their scalps had been.

Locklin gave an order for the men to pick up the pieces of scattered clothing and at least cover the bodies of the women and girls. As it was being done, the lieutenant moved about counting bodies, while looking in and near the wagons for shovels. He had collected two shovels when he approached a wagon that was lying upside down. The struts that held the canvas cover were shattered, so that the wagon bed lay flat against the ground. Next to the wagon lay a woman's handbag. It was partially open, exposing the tip of a small book.

Locklin leaned the shovels against a wagon wheel, bent over, and picked up the handbag. He slipped the book out and saw that it was a diary. Sergeant Clay Harris drew alongside. "Looks like somebody's diary, sir."

"Maybe we ought to keep it in case we find out where she's from. Her relatives might like to have it." Turning back the cover, Locklin said, "Let's see what her name was."

The other men drew up, encircling Locklin and Harris. Some of them kept their eyes on the surrounding desert for any sign of Indians.

"What's that, sir?" said a youthful trooper named Barry Fender.

"Diary of one of the women," replied Locklin. "Her name was Linda Lee Byrnes. The diary was presented to her by her parents for her twenty-first birthday just this year—May 2, 1858."

"Poor thing," said Harris. "Little did she know that she'd only get to write in it for a little over two months. Suppose some of these others are her parents?"

From the corner of his eye, Boyd Locklin saw a big bull rattler glide over a nearby mound between two cacti and slither into a hole. "Could be," he answered Harris. "Might be more information in her handbag, or even under this wagon—assuming this was the one she was riding in. We'll check it all out later. Right now, we'd best get to digging. I found two shovels."

"How many bodies did you count, Lieutenant?" asked Corporal Lester Dunlap.

"Nine men, eleven women, and thirteen children. Since they were stripped of their clothing, there is no way of telling which one was the priest."

"I found his garb, sir," said trooper Gary White, who still looked a bit peaked. "Robe, chain with a crucifix on it, and a prayer book."

Looking around and studying the deep gouges in the soft earth, Clay Harris said, "Looks to me like the Indians gave them a chase, then sent a second band of warriors from the opposite direction—probably over that rise we just topped—and caused them to swerve at a high speed, turning the wagons over."

"And what wagons didn't flip over from the speed, the Apaches did on their own," said Locklin. "They seem to enjoy leaving a wagon train with all the vehicles overturned." Lifting his hat and scratching his head, he said, "Funny thing. They usually burn the wagons, too. Seems like they were in a hurry this time."

"You don't suppose they had a lookout up on the crest of the rise and saw us coming, do you?" asked Corporal Bill Yike.

"It's possible," replied Locklin. "Maybe they didn't feel like a fight today."

Grinding his teeth and running his gaze over the bloody bodies that lay all around them, Sergeant Clay Harris growled, "I'd sure like to get them into a fight! Dirty savages. It'd make me happy to send every one of them to his happy hunting ground."

Locklin turned to two of the troopers. "Ford, you and Fender take your turns with the shovels first. Dig the holes over there by that farthest wagon. We'll work in shifts of ten minutes each. Can't do much more than that in this heat. I want to get this over with as soon as possible and head back to the—"

The lieutenant's words were cut off by the muffled sound of a moan coming from under the wagon. Ford and Fender were just reaching for the shovels.

Halting in his movement, Jake Ford gasped, "What was that?"

"Sounded like a female voice coming from under the wagon," said Locklin. "Let's give it a lift."

Suddenly, Clay Harris caught movement in his peripheral vision and gasped, "Lieutenant!"

The entire area seemed to explode with gunfire.

Boyd Locklin felt the heat of a bullet on his left ear as he wheeled about to see Apache warriors coming from seemingly out of nowhere, rising up like ghosts from the desert floor, rifles blazing.

CHAPTER TWO

The startled cavalrymen were frantically diving for cover and bringing their weapons to bear as some twenty-five Apaches came at them in a dust-clouded half-circle. When they had fired their single-shot rifles, the savages dropped them and drew revolvers.

It was instant bedlam.

Indians whooped and barked while their guns roared like a string of giant firecrackers. Horses screamed and bolted.

Captain Boyd Locklin instinctively dropped to the ground, whipping his revolver from its holster. He aimed a wild shot at a shape he could only half see through the blaze of sunlight and the mixed fog of dust and gun smoke. He fired again toward the charging Apaches, then crawled around the end of the upside-down wagon and rolled against its opposite side for cover.

Above the roar of the guns and the whooping of the Apaches, Locklin could hear his men crying out in pain as bullets struck them. He caught sight of another ghostly figure in the haze and fired again. He heard the Indian scream and saw him go down. Another appeared, swinging his revolver on him. Locklin got off a quick shot, hitting him in the shoulder. The Apache staggered, but did not fall. Gritting his teeth in determination to kill the white soldier, he brought his weapon up, earing back the hammer. At the same time, Locklin fired his fifth and final shot, hitting the Indian dead-center in the chest. He grunted, sagged loosely, and fell.

Locklin dropped low against the wagon and began reloading his revolver. The air was alive with the menacing thunder of guns booming and Apaches screeching.

Abruptly, one of the men in blue came stumbling out of the dust, clutching the handle of a knife that was buried to its hilt in his throat. He fell on top of Locklin, spraying him with blood. Locklin did not recognize him until he rolled him off. It was trooper Hank Yarrow. At that instant, an Apache warrior came running at Locklin, firing his gun. The bullet hissed past Locklin's shoulder, whomping into the side of the wagon.

The lieutenant's gun was not yet reloaded. Reacting instinctively, he threw it hard, hitting the Apache flush on the nose. The man fell, his momentum causing him to drop toward Locklin. Locklin gripped the handle of the knife in Yarrow's throat, yanked it free, and drove it into the throat of the Indian, who made a gagging sound, spit blood, and went limp.

A flicking glance at Yarrow told Locklin the trooper was dead. He bounded to the spot where his revolver had fallen, picked it up, and darted beside the wagon once again. In that moment of deafening noise while he punched cartridges into the cylinder, time seemed to stand still.

As a soldier, Boyd Locklin had resigned himself to the cold, hard fact that he could die young. He was well acquainted with the meager difference between living and dying in armed conflict. When the dust and smoke cleared, the lucky ones walked away or at least were carried from the scene of battle still alive. The unlucky ones lay cold, stiff, and dead.

In that strange, frozen fragment of time, the young lieutenant desperately wanted to live. At twenty-seven years of age he had not known the love and devotion of a good wife. During his four years at West Point he had met some lovely young women and even courted a couple of them seriously, but neither had proved to be the woman with whom he wanted to share the rest of his life. If he died now, his dream of finding that one woman would never be realized. There would never be children to carry on his name. Certain he was about to die, Boyd Locklin felt cheated even though the decision to be a soldier had been his own.

The wheels of time commenced to turn again for the lieutenant as he snapped the cylinder into place. Crawling to the end of the wagon, he searched for another Indian to shoot. When a slight break came amid the noise, he heard the frightened whimpering of a woman coming from beneath the bed of the overturned wagon. He then remembered the sound he and the others had heard just before the attack began. One member of the wagon train had survived!

Concentrating on the woman beneath the wagon, Locklin was not aware of the warrior who was creeping up behind him. Using the butt of his revolver, the Indian brought it down violently on the lieutenant's head. Locklin's skull seemed to explode. He slumped flat, his face settling in the dust. He was aware of the sharp pain in his head momentarily, then it began to grow dull as the earth whirled beneath him. Suddenly he was in a spinning vortex that swallowed him into a bottomless black pit.

The first sensation of life that Lieutenant Boyd Locklin felt as the vortex seemed to regurgitate him back to the earth was the intense heat that enflamed his body. Harsh sunlight was stabbing at his eyelids like red-hot irons. Blinking against the sun's brilliance, he rolled his head like a sick man on a hot pillow and tried to move his limbs. When they would not budge, panic struck him.

I'm paralyzed!

The sense of it was overwhelming, tightening his chest so that his breaths came in short gasps. His temples pulsated painfully as he forced his eyes open in spite of the sun's glare and beheld the blurred figures that stood at his feet.

There was an outburst of abrasive laughter. Blinking to clear his vision, Locklin tried again to move his arms and legs, but to no avail. Jerking his head to the right, he could see his forearm, which was stretched to the limit. His wrist was lashed to a wooden stake with rawhide cord. Whipping his head the other way, he saw that his left wrist was bound in the same manner.

The Apaches laughed again, enjoying Locklin's predicament. His vision cleared and he focused on the group of figures. It was then that he realized he was spread-eagled on the side of a mound, his wrists and ankles firmly tied to stakes that had been driven deep. The broiling early afternoon sun pressed down on him and its heat radiated up from the flat rocks that lay close by. His naked upper body was covered with a sheen of sweat.

Abruptly it all came back to him...the massacre of the small wagon train, the Apaches rising up from the desert floor like dusty specters, the blazing guns, Hank Yarrow's bloody body, the Indian he had killed with the knife from Yarrow's throat, and the empty revolver he had just reloaded.

One of the Apaches had sneaked up behind him and knocked him unconscious. Boyd Locklin was not ignorant of the Apache ways. They wanted him alive so they could torture him. An icy hand seemed to close on his spine and squeeze down hard. The awful dread of what was coming brought a sudden gush of bile to his mouth. Its bitter taste lay sticky on his tongue.

Locklin thought of his men. They must all be dead. He was grieved at that, but glad they had died in the fight. At least they would not face the hellish Apache torture that was to come to their leader.

Eight dark-skinned savages stood near Locklin's feet at the bottom of the mound. Six of them were stripped down to breechclouts, leggings, and boots stolen from the bodies of the dead cavalrymen. Their hawklike faces were daubed with paint, as were their arms and chests. The other two wore blue bullet-riddled army shirts, the tails dangling against their thighs.

Locklin's nerves and muscles were taut. He felt the pounding of his heart and the painful throb of his temples. Poised against the cobalt sky, the Apaches made barbaric figures. They were the hardest, craftiest, most merciless savages in the world. The hatred they held for white men was a living thing.

Suddenly Locklin was aware of movement behind the tightly ranked warriors, and Chief Pantano came into view as he rounded his men, ascended the mound, and halted when his body cast a shadow over his prisoner's face. Locklin knew it was Pantano. He had seen him many times from a distance. He always wore a blue coat with sergeant's stripes on it that he had taken from a soldier he had killed in a hand-to-hand knife fight four years previously.

In his early forties, Pantano was lean, muscular, and strong. His coal black hair dangled to his shoulders under a red bandanna he wore for a headband. His face was angular, chiseled in harsh, craggy lines. He had a jutting square jaw, high cheekbones, and deep set black eyes. He wore an army issue gunbelt and holster on his narrow waist. The .45 caliber revolver in the holster was once worn by an army captain.

The hot breeze toyed with Pantano's long hair as he stood over his prisoner, eyeing him dispassionately. Locklin's attention was then drawn to the Apache youth who drew up beside Pantano. He appeared to be no more then seventeen or eighteen, but bore a powerful resemblance to the chief. He wore his hair the same length under an identical bandanna. There was a large knife on his waist, along with an army Colt .45. His blue shirt was army issue and had a bullet hole in the chest just over the heart. There was a built-in sneer on his thin upper lip, a malevolent look on his face, and Locklin thought he could see a demonic fire in his black eyes.

Keeping his shadow over Locklin's sweaty face, Pantano said in a flat tone, "Your frightened men tell me you are Lieutenant Boyd Locklin. I have heard your name. You are supposed to be a great leader, Lieutenant. What shame you must feel, having led your men into my trap."

Before Locklin could reply, the voice of Jake Ford cut the air from somewhere behind the phalanx of Apaches. "They're gonna torture us, Lieutenant! He was waiting for you to come to so you could watch!"

Locklin raised his head, peering in the direction of Ford's voice. Pantano gave a command in Apache language and the eight warriors stepped aside, giving Locklin a full view of the three soldiers who were still alive. They were seated on the ground, hands behind them, shirts soaked with sweat. In the center was Ford, his terror-stricken face chalky, with sweat tracks running through powdery dust. On Ford's left was trooper Barry Fender. He had taken a bullet in the upper left arm and had his eyes squeezed shut while gritting his teeth in pain.

On Ford's other side was Sergeant Clay Harris. The big, beefy man had been shot in the right thigh. The bullet had passed through, leaving bleeding entrance and exit wounds. His pant leg was soaked with blood. The right leg was stretched out to ease the pain as much as possible, but what he was feeling was almost unbearable. He looked at Locklin with languid eyes. His heavy jaw slacked.

Swallowing hard, the lieutenant ran his gaze over the area. The bodies of the rest of his men were scattered among those of the wagon train victims. Grief washed over him like a violent ocean wave. Pantano's cutting words echoed through his mind: *"What shame you must feel, having led your men into my trap."*

Shaking them off, he told himself that no one in the army would lay the blame for this incident at his feet. The Apaches were more desert-wise than any white man would ever be, military or civilian. The army was at a great disadvantage just being in Apache territory. Any other cavalry officer—no matter how well experienced—would have moved into the area of the wagon train massacre the same as he had.

Estimating that he and his three surviving soldiers were in the hands of seventeen Apaches, Locklin wondered how many he and his men had killed. There were no Apache bodies in sight, but Locklin knew he had killed two for sure, and probably a third. At least he had put a bullet in him.

The lieutenant felt more grief for Fender, Harris, and Ford. Pantano would indeed torture them to death—unless somehow he could reason or scare him out of it. He had to try. Meshing mixed strands of inner torment into firm resolution, he looked up at the chief. "You and your men are soldiers, as we are. I am asking that we be treated as soldiers. Even if you will not spare me, I ask you to release my men and let them ride back to the fort."

Jake Ford ran his gaze between the man staked out on the mound and the man who stood over him. Harris and Fender fixed dull eyes on Pantano.

A knotted muscle rippled at Pantano's lean jaw. With a stern look flinting his black eyes, he asked, "Lieutenant, do you know who I am?"

"Yes."

Bending low, allowing the severe sunlight to strike Locklin's face, the Apache said, "Say my name."

"Pantano."

Straightening and using his body once more to shade the lieutenant's eyes, Pantano said, "Since you know who I am, white eyes leader, you ought to know that I do not consider you and your men soldiers. You are intruders! If you and your white brothers had not come to our land, no blood would have been shed, and you would not be in this predicament."

"I cannot argue on that point, Chief," said Locklin, "but since the intrusion has been made, there is nothing I can do about it personally. I am a soldier, and I take orders from my superiors. Again, as a soldier speaking to my enemy who has captured my men and me, I ask you to at least let my men go. Two of them badly need medical attention."

"Do not listen to him, Father!" cut in the youth who stood beside him. "If we were their prisoners, they would torture and kill us!"

Waving a hand at his son to quiet him, Pantano said from the side of his mouth, "I will handle this situation, Kateya. You remain silent."

Fire flashed in Kateya's eyes, but he said no more.

Running his dry tongue over equally dry lips, Locklin said, "Pantano, what your son said is not true. If you were our prisoners, we would not torture you and we would not kill you, and you know it."

Pantano's features hardened. "That is because you are civilized, right, Lieutenant? And civilized people do not murder their prisoners of war."

"Right."

"But I am a heathen. So do you not expect me to behave as a heathen?"

"You don't talk like a heathen, Pantano. You've had some education."

"You are correct. I was taught as a youth by a Methodist missionary who established a mission near the California border. He taught me Spanish and English both."

"Did he not also teach you that it is wrong to murder?"

Strong emotions showed behind the black screen of Pantano's eyes. "For a long time, the missionary taught me only the languages, but one day he began trying to persuade me that it was all right for the white people to move into Apache country and share our land. He also tried to turn me from the Apache gods to his God. This made me angry. So I cut his heart out and took his scalp. I have never trusted a white man since. I hate all of you!"

"But you know right from wrong, Pantano," reasoned the lieutenant, "and it's wrong for you to torture and kill us."

"It is right for me to protect Apache land," argued Pantano. "Since white men continue to come and seek to take our land from us, we have no choice but to kill you." Pivoting, he shouted a command in Apache.

Raising his head, Locklin looked on in horror as Ford, Harris, and Fender were flung to their backs. Harris and Fender howled in pain.

Kateya gripped his father's arm. "Let *me* kill them!"

Nodding his assent, the chief called another command, telling the warriors to hold the white men down while Kateya gave them pain.

Laughing fiendishly, the youth dashed to Clay Harris and kicked his wounded thigh, over and over again. As the sergeant screamed in agony, Boyd Locklin instinctively tugged at the rawhide cords that held him to the stakes. Jake Ford and Barry Fender looked on wide-eyed, choked with terror.

Leaving Harris's wounded leg to throb; Kateya kicked him in the mouth, breaking his teeth as mocking laughter rose gruffly from deep in Kateya's throat.

Anger ripped through Boyd Locklin. His chest heaved as the breath hissed through his nostrils. His lips were pulled thin. His voice cut the air like a whip. "Pantano! Make him stop!"

Kateya heard him. Wheeling about, he dashed up the mound, drew back his foot and slammed him in the face. Locklin's head rebounded and Kateya kicked him again. Bending over him, the youth growled, "You shut up, white eyes lieutenant! Your turn will come very soon!"

Locklin felt a cut burning his left cheek. Blood was trickling slowly down his face. Their eyes locked and held for a brief moment; then Kateya ran back to the spot where his companions were holding the three soldiers.

Clay Harris's thigh was losing blood rapidly. Kateya's attack had opened the wounds even more. The youth stood over him, grinning. "I will be back to hurt you some more, Sergeant, after I hurt your friends."

Turning to Barry Fender, he stood over him. Pulling the knife from the sheath on his waist, he showed yellow teeth in a demonic grin. "Poor bluecoat. You have a bullet in your arm. Kateya will remove it for you."

Fender struggled against the strong hands of the warriors who held him. Jake Ford looked on with unbelieving eyes, his whole body rigid. Clay Harris showed naked hatred for the vicious son of

Pantano, curling his lip over his broken teeth like a wolf.

Dropping to his knees, Kateya mirrored the sunlight off the blade of his knife, making it shine into Barry Fender's face. "No!" he gasped. "Don't touch me with that thing!"

Cocking his head, Kateya said in a pouty tone, "Now, white eyes, you are going to hurt Kateya's feelings. I only want to make you better by removing the bullet from your arm."

Pantano was still standing over Boyd Locklin. The lieutenant said, "Chief, please don't let him do it."

Sneering down at him, Pantano retorted, "You remain silent, Lieutenant, or I will have my son cut your tongue out."

A freshening shine of indignation captured Boyd Locklin's heat-flushed features. The flare of his temper made him heedless of Pantano's threat, and a heady rage was building within him. "You won't get away with this! The army will hunt you down! I'm telling you...don't let Kateya touch that man!"

A tidal sweep of anger caught Pantano's dark features. Eyes flashing, his mouth curved down into a brutal slit. "Kateya. Come and cut this white dog's tongue out!"

A hellish grin spread over the youth's face as he turned from Barry Fender to the mound. Fender began to weep. Jake Ford and Clay Harris exchanged fearful glances. The whole band of warriors shouted encouragement to the chief's son.

As Boyd Locklin watched Kateya coming toward him, his heart pumped madly in his chest. As a child he had experienced nightmares when some kind of wild beast was chasing him and his legs turned to lead, refusing to budge. He was now experiencing the same kind of fear. His legs were lashed at the stakes, as were his arms. He was totally helpless. Cold fear riffled through his sunblasted body.

Brandishing his knife, Kateya grinned at his father and straddled Locklin. Dropping to his knees, he sat on the lieutenant's midsection and laughed fiendishly, waving the knife back and forth in front of his face. Light glinted off the blade and it seemed to flare with life.

Locklin's head was hurting, a tension pounding behind his temples, but he steeled himself against what was coming. He would not give Kateya or the Apaches the satisfaction of seeing him show fear. Nor would they hear him cry out.

Locklin felt like Satan himself was looking at him through

Kateya's eyes as the youthful savage hissed, "You can make this easy or difficult, white dog. You can stick your tongue out and let me cut it off, or you can force me to gouge out your eyes and cut your throat first."

Locklin wondered how someone so young could be so completely evil. Keeping a steely look in his eyes and holding his face like granite, he grated through clenched teeth, "I'm not making anything easy for you, devil."

"Devil, am I? You will believe I am Diablo when I am through with you!"

Clamping the palm of his free hand on the lieutenant's clammy forehead, Kateya leaned hard so as to hold his head firm and pointed the ominous tip of the knife at his left eye. Still Locklin did not flinch, though inwardly his blood had turned to ice.

The Apaches cheered Kateya, urging him to gouge out the eye. Ford, Harris, and Fender looked on in horror.

Suddenly Pantano shouted, "No, Kateya! Do not take his eye. Get off him!"

Twisting around to look at his father, Kateya's brow furrowed. "What? I do not understand."

Locklin's heart was slamming his ribs violently.

"Get off him," repeated the chief. "I have not seen such courage in a white man before."

Reluctantly, the youth obeyed. He rose and stood gazing at his father as Pantano said so that all could hear, "This is a very brave man. He will not be tortured. We will leave him to die on the stakes without harming him." Looking down at Locklin, he said, "I admire your courage, Lieutenant, so I will treat you like a soldier. You are my enemy, so you must die. But I will at least let you die with a measure of dignity." Then to Kateya, "Take the bullet out of the bluecoat's arm."

Boyd Locklin strained against the rawhide cords as he watched six warriors flatten Barry Fender on the ground and hold him down. Clay Harris, whose leg was pumping blood, was in the grip of four strong warriors while Jake Ford was held by two.

Fender was dripping wet with sweat as Kateya cut away the sleeve. Fender winced and sucked air through his teeth, a look of terror on his face. His eyes bulged as the young Apache dug the tip of the knife into the bullet wound. Fender screamed and passed out.

Seconds later, Kateya rose to his feet with blood on his hands and displayed the slug between his fingers, waving it so that all could see. The warriors barked and whooped with joy.

Boyd Locklin lay on the mound, rolling his head, wishing he were in a nightmare. Wishing he could wake up and find that none of this was true. He lifted his head to look toward the center of activity once more when he heard Pantano bark a command in the Apache language. One of the warriors that had been holding Barry Fender took out his knife and quickly scalped him.

Locklin's stomach went sour as he lay his head back, gritting his teeth. How could people who call themselves human be so cruel?

Pantano joined his men and told them to scalp the big soldier next. Sergeant Clay Harris swore at them, attempting to twist free of the four strong warriors who held him.

Grinning broadly, Kateya wielded the knife that bore Barry Fender's blood and moved in on Harris. The beefy sergeant managed to jerk his good leg loose in a sudden move and kicked Kateya violently in the groin. Kateya howled, dropped the knife, and doubled over in agony.

Pantano snapped a command for his men to bring Harris under control, then leaned over his son, speaking to him in Apache. Boyd Locklin looked on, gratified at least that the heartless devil had been given some pain.

At that moment Barry Fender, who had been left lying on the ground, came to. His face was a mass of blood below the meaty spot where his forelock had been removed. His wounded arm was oozing blood and hung from his shoulder like a piece of rope as he sat up. When his good hand went to the gaping hole in his scalp, he wailed at the top of his voice and groped his way to his feet.

The Apaches laughed as Fender stumbled blindly about, thumbing the scarlet flow from his eyes. Jake Ford remained in the grasp of his captors, looking on in fear. Clay Harris fought the powerful hands that held him, swearing profusely. Boyd Locklin lay in his helpless position listening to Fender's screams. Locklin's ears were pounding and his labored breathing was a raw wheeze.

Pantano helped his son to his feet. Kateya's face was twisted in a grimace beneath the stripes of war paint. Holding himself where the pain pulsated, he set malignant black eyes on Clay Harris. The big sergeant was pinned flat on his back by seven warriors. Straightening up, Kateya moved gingerly to Harris and stood over him. When he pulled his revolver, Pantano stepped up and asked, "What are you doing?"

"He kicked me," replied Kateya. "He dies now!"

"He should suffer more first," countered the chief.

"Let him suffer in the white man's hell!" rasped the angry youth.

Easing back the hammer, he lined the muzzle between Harris's eyes. The warrior who held Harris's head let go and stood up, not wanting to be that close to the target. Kateya pulled his lips back in a savage snarl. "You die, white swine."

His features stonelike, Clay Harris closed his eyes.

The gun bucked in Kateya's hand, sending the bullet plowing through Harris's head. The roar of the shot cut the air, then beat away in hollow echoes till it died on the surrounding sunbleached hills.

The Apaches ejected a war whoop, shaking their fists at Harris's body. Kateya then pivoted slowly and put his attention on Barry Fender, who lay in a crumpled heap, bleeding to death and moaning incoherently. Cocking the gun again, he aimed it at Fender's head and fired. The trooper spasmed twice, then lay still. Again the Apaches joined in a war whoop.

All eyes then went to Jake Ford, who lay on the ground nearby, pinioned fast by the two warriors who held him. Pantano stood over him, sided by his son, then turned and looked at Boyd Locklin. His face was as ungiving as marble. "There is one left, Lieutenant. When we are finished with him, we will leave you here to die at your own pace."

Locklin knew it was useless to plead for Jake's life, but at least he would let Jake die knowing he tried. Raising his voice, he said, "Pantano, is there no pity in your heart at all? I beg you to let him live."

A sardonic smile curved the chief's mouth. "You mean let him live to fight against us again, Lieutenant? No! We will kill him so he will take no more Apache lives!"

Jake Ford's body was bathed in perspiration. His features were contorted with anguish as he trembled all over, trying to gain control of his labored breath and fight the mounting terror that clawed like a wild beast at his heart.

Producing a long-bladed knife from the sheath on his belt, Pantano bent over Ford, put his strong fingers into his hair, and cut off the forelock. Boyd Locklin shuddered as Ford screamed wildly, straining against the cords that held his hands behind his back. The men who held him let go, allowing him to squirm and wail in agony with blood covering his face and flowing into his eyes.

The rigors of shock seized Lieutenant Boyd Locklin, accompanied by a wrenching stomach. Flames of wrath surged through him, ignited by the spark of a new and fresh hatred for Apaches—especially the heartless Pantano and his diabolical son. If he lived through this, he would see to it that they paid their dues. Kateya may be only a youth, but anyone who killed like a man must face the consequences like a man.

While Jake Ford rolled on the ground wailing in pain, Pantano walked to the mound, carrying the bloody scalp. Kateya moved beside him. Standing over the lieutenant, Pantano dropped the scalp next to his head. "I will let you die looking at this."

Hatred blazed from Locklin's eyes. "What kind of animal are you? Have you no feelings at all?"

Kateya drove a hard kick into Locklin's rib cage, knocking the breath from him. "My father is not an animal, Lieutenant! You must guard your mouth!"

Streamers of pain lanced through Locklin's entire body as he sucked for air.

Leaning close, Pantano grinned evilly. "Does his torment bother you, white eyes lieutenant? You are thinking that I am totally without conscience, aren't you? Well, let me prove that you are wrong. Instead of letting your man bleed to death, I will end his suffering." Turning to Kateya, he said, "Kill him."

Laughing gleefully, Kateya ran to Ford, pulling his knife. Pouncing on him like a cougar, he drove the blade full-haft into Ford's heart. The wailing instantly stopped. While the Apaches cheered Kateya, Pantano leered at his surviving prisoner. "Now, what did I tell you? Your man suffers no more."

The hot lump in Locklin's throat kept him from speaking. He clamped his jaw so painfully tight that the bone ridges showed white.

The Apache horses were being brought up from their hiding place by two warriors Locklin had not seen as Pantano said, "You are a brave man, Lieutenant. We will see how well you do on the stakes. These hills are infested with rattlesnakes. But then, you know that, don't you? You will have no shade and the sun is very hot. You know that too. It will be interesting to see if you die from thirst or from snakebite. I will be back tomorrow to see if you are still alive."

Blinking at the sweat that rolled into his eyes, Lieutenant Boyd Locklin watched Pantano and his warriors ride away, taking all the weapons and the army horses with them. Five dead Apaches were draped over their own pintos.

The hatred that burned within Locklin toward Pantano and Kateya was akin to brimstone in the bowels of a rumbling volcano.

CHAPTER THREE

Lieutenant Boyd Locklin was staked out on the south side of the rock-strewn, cactus-dotted mound where the sun could bear down on him the rest of the day, burning his bared skin and sucking moisture from his body. By its position in the sky, Locklin estimated it was about three o'clock.

His mouth dry as a sand pit, he looked toward the upside-down wagon where he had heard the female voice earlier. It was not that of a child, but a young woman. Locklin knew she was probably paralyzed with fright, and being underneath the overturned bed, could not see what was going on. If she could get out from under the wagon, she could free him from the deeply-buried stakes.

He wanted to call to her, but not yet. The Apaches were still within earshot. Raising his head, he looked at the pillar of dust that was stirred up by the Apaches as they rode south toward the Dragoon Mountains. He would have to give it another ten minutes before calling out to tell the young woman the Apaches were gone.

A dismal thought crept its way into Locklin's mind. There was no way she could lift the wagon to free herself. It would take a very strong man to do it. Maybe...maybe she could *dig* her way out. The ground was soft in some places. Hopefully it was soft enough where the wagon had overturned.

Appraising the situation, Locklin decided to try loosening the stakes himself. Gritting his teeth, he summoned every ounce of strength in his six-foot-two-inch two-hundred-ten-pound body and pulled against the stakes. They bowed slightly, but refused to budge. He tried it twice more, but to no avail. The Apaches were masters at staking out their enemies. Pantano could ride away, confident that Locklin could never free himself.

Glancing at the dust pillar, he told himself he would give it five more minutes before calling to the woman.

All was still, except for the slight breeze that swept over the boiling desert. The lieutenant lay in silence and surveyed what he could see of the surrounding area. His heart was heavy over the deaths of his men. Pantano had left their bodies in plain view, along with the victims of the wagon train.

He thought of the men back at Fort Savage. The day had been planned so that Locklin's patrol could see the wagon train through the dangerous region and return to the fort before dark. When the unit had not shown up by dawn, Colonel Halloran would send out another patrol to find them. If Locklin had to lie in the sun as long as it might take them to find him tomorrow, he would be dead. A man's body dehydrated in a hurry in the blaze of the sun when he had no water.

Besides, he thought, *Pantano said he'd be back tomorrow. If I'm still alive when he comes, he might decide to let that devilish son of his go ahead and kill me. And then there's the woman. She has to be literally cooking under that wagon. I've got to let her know it's safe to begin digging out.*

A glance southward told him that the Apaches were now out of earshot. He was about to call toward the wagon when he caught movement on the mound from the corner of his eye. Turning his head to the right, he saw a big bull rattler slithering out of a hole no more than ten feet away. Suddenly he remembered seeing the big bull—or one like it—on that very mound earlier.

Locklin's heart quickened pace. The snake was all the way out of the hole and angling his direction. He figured it must be seven feet in length. The dark, diamond-shaped markings that ran in a neat row along its back glistened in the sun.

Abruptly it stopped, curled back a few feet, raised its wide, flat head, and observed the unfamiliar form staked out in its familiar territory. Locklin's sweaty body went cold. He dare not move a muscle or even blink an eye. He was well-experienced with the deadly reptiles. The rattler would strike at anything that moved if it felt threatened. His presence was enough to generate a threat in the snake's mind.

A stitch of mounting panic rose from deep within him. He had to breathe, and though he was now holding his breath, he couldn't hold it very long. He would take shallow breaths, moving his chest as little as possible, and hope the snake did not see or sense it. The hot breeze was drying his eyeballs. He wanted to blink, but fought off the urge.

For a long moment the big bull studied Locklin, moving its head back and forth slowly. He could feel the pressure of those shiny black elliptical eyes. He had a passing thought that they were much like Kateya's.

The rattler's mouth opened slightly and a black split tongue darted between white needle-sharp fangs, silently testing the air. The sight of it made Locklin's skin crawl.

The moment came that he had to take a breath. Cautiously he inhaled a tiny bit, allowing only a minute movement of his chest. The snake showed no sign of sensing it. The muscles in his neck were crying for relief, because of his tenseness and the fact that his head was turned to the right.

Locklin's eyes were smarting from lack of moisture. It would feel so good to blink, but to do so could bring venom-filled fangs into his face.

It was then that he heard it.

A thumping sound at the upturned wagon.

The woman was attempting to free herself. Presently there was a series of thumps, followed by a soft scraping noise.

The sounds continued, along with tiny grunting noises. She was indeed digging herself out from under the wagon.

Locklin's attention returned quickly to the snake. It was now slithering toward him, apparently feeling it was in no danger. He watched it glide silently past his face and disappear from his line of vision. With welcome relief, he closed his eyes, letting the natural moisture beneath his eyelids ease the burning sensation.

Then came a new horror.

He felt the chill of a scaly form gliding slowly and sinuously over his sweaty belly. He wanted to scream. His stomach muscles contracted and tightened. The snake stopped, feeling the movement. Locklin's heart thundered in his chest. He dare not move his head to see what the snake was doing. He could only wait for the fangs to strike or for the reptile to move on.

The scraping noises below the mound were growing louder, as

were the repeated grunts of labor. The woman was definitely making progress.

Locklin bit down hard and willed the rattler to slither away. If the woman appeared while it was on his belly, it could be enough to make it feel threatened. If it began to coil at her approach, he would have to cry out to warn her. The sudden sound coming from him could draw the fangs in a strike of death.

The snake stayed where it was, lying across the lieutenant's midsection with its body touching ground on both sides. Overhead, the sun pressed its heat down upon him until it seemed to have weight and substance. The snake's body was cold in contrast.

Nothing changed for what seemed like an eternity. The woman kept digging and grunting, and the rattler stayed. Boyd Locklin thought of all the diamondbacks he had killed in his six years on the desert. He wished he had killed more...especially this one.

His entire body was crying for movement. He ached everywhere. He pictured his hands on Pantano's throat. What a pleasure it would be to crush the windpipe with his thumbs. Any man who would stake a man out like this deserved to die. His sore ribs made him think of Kateya. If he wasn't brought into subjection by the army by the time he became a man, Kateya would deal the whites more misery than they could stand.

Locklin's attention was drawn to the sound of the woman pulling herself through the gap she had dug. The volume of her grunts and gasps told him her head was now outside the wagon. Only seconds had passed when the vocal noises stopped. She had freed herself.

Listening intently, Locklin waited for her to spot him and come his way. The snake had not moved. He dreaded what was going to happen when the woman made her approach.

All was still for a moment, then he heard her shriek, "Martha!" She burst into tears, sobbing the name repeatedly.

While the woman continued to sob, Locklin felt the snake in motion. Quickly it was off him. Relief washed over him, but caution kept him from making any sudden moves. Very carefully, he raised his head and looked for the rattler. It had slithered down the mound and was sunning itself on the hot earth near its base.

At the same moment, he noticed that the sobbing had ceased.

He saw the young woman standing over a female body that had been covered earlier by his men. She was brushing sweat-soaked auburn hair from her face and looking straight at him. She stood about twenty yards from the mound.

Lifting the skirt of her dusty dress calf-high, she started toward him at a run.

"Wait a minute, ma'am!" he called out. "There's a rattlesnake right down there at the base of the mound!"

Halting immediately, she focused on the snake, which had seen her coming and was coiling. "What should I do?"

He perused the rocks that lay on the ground. "See that big round rock over there near the husky soldier?"

It took her a moment to spot Clay Harris's lifeless bulky form, but when she did, the rock quickly drew her attention. "Yes."

"Listen carefully now, ma'am," said the lieutenant, straining his neck to see her. "You'll have to get about twenty feet from the snake and roll the rock with all your might. Understand?"

The snake was tightly coiled, watching the woman, and hissing while buzzing its rattles. "Not exactly." She gave him a puzzled look.

"Let me explain quickly. The snake sees you as a threat. That's why it is coiled and ready to fight. It will strike at anything that moves near it. The rock's weight and momentum will shatter the snake's head. Understand?"

Wiping sweat from her well-formed brow, she nodded. "I understand." She picked up the rock.

Testing it for balance, she held the cabbage-sized rock in both hands and moved toward the snake. Halting precisely twenty feet from where the reptile was coiled and hissing, she planted her feet solidly, bent over, and hurled the rock along the ground.

The snake saw it coming, drew its head back, and struck the rolling rock. Its head shattered, showering blood and scarlet matter on the sand.

"Good girl!" exclaimed the lieutenant.

Without moving, she stood looking at the snake, wide-eyed, her voice quavering. "It…it's still moving."

"Snakes do that, ma'am," Locklin responded with a note of authority in his voice. "But don't worry, it's dead."

Keeping an eye on the wriggling reptile, she gave it a wide berth while moving toward the man staked out on the mound. As she drew up, he saw that her hands were rough and bleeding. Glancing at her face, then her hands, and back to her face, he said, "You did that digging out from under the wagon, didn't you?"

"Yes. There was no other way. I couldn't budge the wagon."

"I heard you moan before the Apaches ambushed us," said the lieutenant. "So I knew someone had survived the attack on the wagon train. I also heard you whimpering while the gun battle was going on. I'm glad you were spared. My name is Boyd Locklin. Lieutenant Boyd Locklin."

Dropping to her knees beside him, she said, "I'm Linda Byrnes."

"Oh," he said with a slight smile. "Linda *Lee* Byrnes. You're twenty-one years old and your birthday is on May 2."

Linda's jaw slacked and surprise showed in her tired eyes. "How do you know all of this?"

I found your handbag over there by the wagon. Your diary was in it. I guess I dropped them when the Apaches came up out of the ground and started firing. It was just before then that we heard you moan. We were about to lift the wagon and get you out when the ambush started."

"Yes. I was unconscious until then. I...I must have hit my head awfully hard when the wagon turned over. When my head cleared there was a gun battle going on." Linda paused, looking toward the scattering of corpses. "The Apaches killed them all. Even Martha. They...scalped her, too."

Linda was fighting to keep from breaking down. Locklin looked at her with compassion and said, "I'm sorry, Miss Linda. I know this has to be very hard for you. If there's anything—"

"We can talk later," she cut in. "Right now, we've got to get you off those stakes."

While Boyd Locklin watched, the redhead rummaged about among the wagons until she found a rusty butcher knife. Within minutes she had cut him free. Sitting up, he rubbed his raw wrists to stimulate the blood circulation, then rose unsteadily to his feet.

Taking hold of his arm to steady him, Linda looked closely at his face. "Your cheek is cut. Looks like the blood has dried up, though."

"One of the Apaches kicked me," he said dryly.

"Did the Apaches say why they killed all the others but left you alive?"

"As the leader, Chief Pantano liked my courage, but he still wanted me to die. So he left me to die in the sun. It would have been that way too, if it weren't for you."

"We were both lucky," she said softly, turning to look toward the lifeless form of her friend. "Martha wasn't so lucky."

"I'm sorry," said Locklin. "Miss Linda, we need to head for Fort Savage. That's where I'm from. We're about twenty-five miles from there, maybe even thirty. There was no moon last night, so we won't have one tonight, either. I'm not sure how much we'll be able to travel in the dark. We'll have to push it as hard as possible because Chief Pantano said he'd be back tomorrow to see if I was still alive. When he finds that I've escaped, he'll ride hard to catch me. Our only refuge is the fort. We've got maybe three hours of daylight left. Let's make the best of it."

Linda ran her sorrowful gaze over the bodies that lay scattered over the area. "What about burial, Lieutenant?"

"When we get to the fort and tell Colonel Halloran what happened here, he'll send a burial detail." He scanned the cloudless sky. "So far no vultures."

Linda's hand went to her mouth. "Oh, we can't leave them here for the vultures."

"I'm afraid we don't have any choice. If Pantano catches us, we're done for. Right now, he doesn't know about you, but if we don't make it to the fort before he catches up to us, he'll do to you what he did to the other women in the train."

Biting her lower lip, she nodded slowly. "I understand. There's a canteen about half full of water under the wagon I was in, and I think I can find some beef jerky that we had in a small box."

"Good," said Locklin, running his tongue around his dry mouth. "I could use a good drink about now."

The lieutenant rolled the wagon onto its side, and while Linda Byrnes picked up the canteen and searched for the beef jerky, Locklin found his shirt next to a prickly pear cactus and slipped it on. His chest and stomach were sunburned. Buttoning it loosely, he picked up his hat, which lay nearby, and clapped it on his head. Finding Corporal Bill Yike's hat, he carried it to Linda and told her to wear it to protect her head from the hot sun. When she put it on, he grinned. "You're the prettiest corporal I've ever seen."

Linda's face tinted under the dust and sweat streaks. "I don't feel pretty at all, Lieutenant. I'm a mess."

After both had taken a good drink of water, they started walking northwestward. Locklin carried the canteen and Linda carried the small box of beef jerky.

Threading their way around boulders, cactus patches, and cracks in the ground, they moved at a good pace. The redhead finally had to ask him to slow a bit, saying his long strides were more than she could keep up with.

When they reached a spot where another few steps would remove them from within view of the overturned wagons and lifeless forms on the ground, Linda halted and looked back. Locklin paused, allowing her a moment. "You and Martha were very close friends, I take it."

"Very close. I was in the bed of the wagon when the Apaches came riding down on us. Martha was up front in the seat with Mr. and Mrs. Sterling, who owned the wagon. All the drivers put their horses to a gallop. When we reached that spot back there, another bunch of Apaches came over the ridge. Mr. Sterling swerved the wagon and it turned over. Fortunately for me, I was in the bed and ended up hidden from the Indians. I guess somehow I hit my head on something. The last thing I remember is seeing the Sterlings and Martha fly off the seat as the wagon was turning over. My next recollection is waking up and hearing a gun battle going on."

Stopping to take sips of water periodically, the couple moved on. While the sun slowly lowered toward the western horizon, Linda told Boyd Locklin her story. She had been raised in St. Joseph, Missouri, the jumping-off place for wagon trains and westward-bound travelers. Two years ago, her parents and younger sisters burned to death when the house caught fire in the middle of the night. At the time, Linda was visiting her friend Martha Lyons in Kansas City.

Martha's widowed father had gone west to Providence Wells, Arizona Territory, to marry a widow whom he had known since grammar school days in St. Joseph. He was to send for Martha once he had settled in. Martha had been staying with some neighbors until the call came for her to head west and join him.

When the letter came from her father, telling her to find a ride on a wagon train from St. Joseph, Martha had asked Linda to go with her since Linda was alone and had no family. Linda accepted the invitation. Shortly thereafter, Martha learned of a Catholic priest who was guiding a small wagon train to—of all places—Providence Wells, Arizona Territory.

The priest kindly talked to Mr. and Mrs. Sterling, asking if the two young women could ride in their wagon. The Sterlings gladly obliged, and soon Martha and Linda were on their way west. When they arrived at Fort Campbell for a two-day rest, the commandant, Colonel Moffett, had told the priest to stay on the normal trail, which led to Fort Savage, then through the Santa Cantalinas. This way, the train would have an army escort through dangerous Apache territory, then they could veer toward Providence Wells and have little fear of the Indians. The priest had argued that it would add nearly a hundred miles to take that route, and he did not want to take that long to get to his destination.

The priest assured him that God would see them through safely.

As those words came from Linda's lips, Locklin added, "I'm no theologian, but it seems to me that God gave us good sense and we should use it. What the priest did was foolish."

"I agree," said Linda, "but Martha and I had no say in the decisions. The priest conferred with the others, and they all agreed to take the shorter route."

"So what will you do now?"

Hunching her shoulders, Linda replied, "I don't know. I'll have to think on it. I have some other friends in St. Joseph, but I don't really want to ask them to give me a place to live. I...I'll just have to think it out."

"I'm sure Colonel Halloran would give you some private quarters at the fort for as long as you want to stay there. The food would be free too. There are other women at the fort, so you wouldn't be lonely. In fact, as pretty as you are, you wouldn't be lonely for male companionship, either."

Linda looked up at him. A smile made its break along her lips. "Thank you for your compliments, Lieutenant. You are very kind."

"It's not kindness, ma'am. It's just a fact."

The couple stopped to rest, sitting down on a large rock that jutted out of the desert floor. While they sipped at the canteen, the sun touched the western horizon, sending long shadows across the desert. They had entered an area that was dotted with tall, three-pronged saguaro cacti. Their lengthy shadows made a beautiful sight across the desert floor.

Capping the canteen, Locklin said, "Well, are you ready for another stretch?"

"Not really," she replied with a sigh, "but I'll do it anyway."

"You getting tired?"

"A little. I'm not used to walking like this, especially in such rugged country."

"Well, we'd better go till it gets dark, then we'll take a good rest. I'd like to push on through the night, but with no moon, it would be foolish. Too easy to step in a crack or a hole and sprain or break an ankle. We'll rest through the night and get an early start at dawn."

An hour later, though there was still ample light from the purple sky, Locklin was aware that the woman was running out of strength. Her shoulders were stooped and her feet were dragging.

"Okay, little lady, time to stop. There's a huge boulder up ahead, and it looks like pretty soft sand at its base. That'll give us a good place to spend the night."

When they reached the boulder, Linda sighed, dropped to her knees, sat down, and leaned her back against the surface. A furry little desert creature darted out from a crevice in the side of the boulder and skittered across the ground. It quickly disappeared into a patch of greasewood.

"That scare you?" asked Locklin.

"No," she said, giving him a weak smile. "If it had been a reptile of some kind, it would've. I have a deathly fear of them."

"You did all right killing that rattlesnake today."

"Only because I had to. Otherwise I would have run the other way like a scared rabbit."

Locklin sat down beside here. "Well, I guess we'd better eat supper."

Linda removed her campaign hat and laid it on the sand. Opening the little box, she attempted to put some cheer into the situation. "On the menu this evening, Lieutenant Locklin, is tasty, tantalizing, beef jerky imported from Missouri, served with warm water from the canteen. Sorry there's not some hot coffee, freshly-baked bread, and fried potatoes to go with it."

"Me too." He grinned. "But if all goes well, we'll have a good hot meal before this time tomorrow evening."

Handing him two slim slabs of jerky, she asked, "How long do you think it will take us to make the fort, leaving here at dawn?"

"Hard to say exactly. We'll have to pace ourselves because of the terrain and the heat. I'd say if we can make about the same time we've made today, we should be there by late afternoon. I just hope Pantano isn't in a hurry to check on me. If he waits at least until midafternoon, we'll be at the fort before he catches up to us. Of course, it could be that Colonel Halloran will send out a search unit to find my patrol. Maybe we'll be lucky and get a ride part of the way to the fort."

"That would be a welcome relief."

When they had eaten enough jerky to satisfy their hunger and consumed enough water to remove the salty taste, Locklin sloshed the remainder of the water in the canteen, appraising the amount left. "I'd say there's enough to see us to the fort if we go easy. I'm sure glad Pantano and his cutthroats didn't look under your wagon when they carried off the other canteens."

"Me too. For more than one reason."

"Yes," he agreed. "For more than one reason."

Linda laid her head back against the boulder, closed her eyes, and brushed a damp wisp of auburn hair from her forehead with the back of a rough, scabbed hand.

As she sat there with her eyes closed, the cavalry officer studied her profile. *Lovely woman. Perfect nose, chin, cheekbones. Beautiful emerald green eyes, white even teeth, and red lips, too.*

Eyes still closed, she said, "You've heard all about me, Lieutenant. I know very little about you."

Leaning his own head back, he said, "Not much to tell."

"I'd still like to hear it."

"Okay, where do you want me to start?"

"From the beginning."

"Way back there?"

"Mm-hmm."

"Okay. I was born in a little white house just outside of Hagerstown, Maryland, way back in the woods. It was November 12, 1830. A little arithmetic, and you'll figure out that I turn twenty-eight on my next birthday."

"I'm way ahead of you."

"My parents were John and Maybelle Locklin. My father was an attorney in Hagerstown."

"Any siblings?"

"Yes. A brother, John Jr. He was two years older than me. Drowned by falling through the ice on a pond. He was five at the time. I don't remember him."

"You said your parents *were* John and Maybelle Locklin. They are no longer living, either?"

A few seconds passed. "No. Mom died of pneumonia three months before I graduated from West Point Academy in May of 1852."

Linda opened her eyes and lifted her head from the rock. "Oh, I'm sorry. She must have been very proud to have a son graduating from West Point. Too bad she didn't live to see you graduate."

"Yes'm." Boyd nodded slowly. "Graduation day held a real mixture of emotions. At least I'm glad that Dad got to be there. It was through his connections as an attorney that I received the appointment to the academy."

Linda's dirty brow was furrowed. "When did he...pass away?"

"Eighteen months after she did. He was defending a man accused of rape and murder. When Dad got the man an acquittal, the father of the victim went berserk in the courtroom. Pulled a gun and started shooting. Hit the accused man, the judge, and Dad before he could be subdued. The judge died, too. The accused man lived. About a month later, the *real* rapist was caught after raping and killing another girl, and confessed to the crime the man Dad defended had been accused of."

"Were you still at home when your father was killed?"

"No. I was already here in Arizona. I was assigned to Fort Savage immediately after graduation."

"So you've been here a little over six years."

"Yes'm."

"You mentioned the women at the fort. Is one of them...*Mrs.* Boyd Locklin?"

Turning toward her, the lieutenant found her looking at him. "Uh...no. I'm not married."

It was growing dark, but he thought he saw a look of relief on her face.

Soon the black velvet sky was a shimmering canopy of stars. The night closed around them, cool in comparison to the heat of the day. The lonely wail of a coyote came from somewhere in the distance. Seconds later it was returned by a coyote from another direction.

"Coyote love call, eh?" Locklin chuckled dryly.

"I don't know anything about coyotes."

"They're just like everybody else. Boy needs girl...girl needs boy."

"Mm-hmm," she responded in a noncommittal hum.

"Well, I guess we'd better take a swig of water and turn in. We need to be moving at the first hint of dawn." Locklin removed the cork and handed Linda the canteen.

When both had taken their ration of water, they scooped up little mounds of sand for pillows and stretched out on the warm ground. The wind was a soft moan around the massive boulder. All had been quiet for several minutes when Locklin said, "Miss Linda?"

He thought he picked up a sniffle as she said, "Yes, Lieutenant?"

"Thank you for saving my life. I would've dehydrated and died before noon tomorrow—that is, if that rattler hadn't slithered back up there and bit me first. It just might've if you hadn't killed it."

This time there was a definite sniffle. Linda replied with a break in her voice, "You don't have to thank me, but you're welcome."

Sitting up, Locklin looked toward her dark form a few feet away. "Miss Linda, are you all right?"

He could make out the movement as she sat up. She choked back a sob. "C-could I ask you something?"

"Sure."

"Among those women at the fort, is there one you are seeing?"

The handsome lieutenant's mind ran to Colonel Halloran's daughter, Peggy. The eighteen-year-old had set her sights on him, and at times had embarrassed him in front of people in the fort by her open aggressiveness. He had explained to her repeatedly that the difference in their ages was too great, but Peggy turned a deaf ear. Only because of his respect for the colonel and Mrs. Halloran had he not sharply cut Peggy off. "No."

"Are you seeing anyone at all?"

"No. Why?"

Her sobbing intensified as she said, "I'm about to have an awful cry over Martha. I've never seen a murdered person before. Particularly one who had been scalped...and especially my own best friend. I...I need to...have you just kind of h-hold me. I...I didn't want to ask it if you were promised to...someone. It's...well, I just—"

"I believe I owe that to the lady who saved my life," cut in Locklin, moving on his knees and wrapping her in his arms. "You go ahead and cry. Get it all out."

Linda pressed her face against his muscular chest and the floodgates broke. Her agonizing wails, interspersed with deep sobs were carried across the cooling desert floor by the wind.

CHAPTER FOUR

The sun had taken its flaming dip into the western horizon nearly an hour earlier and the first blue shadows of twilight were descending over Fort Savage as Colonel Brett Halloran mounted the stairs that led to the lofty sentry post at the front gate.

Sentries Dale Roy and Chester Lykins saluted when Halloran reached the platform. Returning the salute a bit listlessly, the commandant asked, "Still nothing?"

"Nothing, sir," they said in unison.

Halloran took a deep breath and let it out slowly through his nostrils as he cast a gaze westward. Worry branded his features, etching deep lines around his eyes and mouth.

A burst of laughter carried across the compound, coming from the barracks. The colonel cast a petulant glace in that direction, then returned his gaze toward the dying light in the western sky.

"It doesn't mean the men are unconcerned, sir," spoke up Lykins. "In fact, I'd say just the opposite. That laughter has a hollow ring to it. They're just trying to ease their anxiety."

The muscles in Halloran's lean jaw corded and rippled under his skin. "I know," he replied without turning his head. "Most of them are too young and inexperienced out here to know that a late patrol nearly always means a lost patrol. If they had my experience under their belts, they couldn't even produce a laugh."

"We understand, sir," said Dale Roy. "By that, I mean we understand that we don't understand what it's like to bear your responsibility. It must be a horrible thing as commandant to send men out on that Apache-infected desert and have them never come back. But maybe it will be all right this time, sir. Lieutenant Locklin is a sharp and intelligent man. We've heard that he graduated from West Point with top honors and with the highest grades recorded at the academy for a decade before him."

"You heard right," said Halloran.

"The point I'm making, sir," proceeded Roy, "is that it would take some doing for Pantano to outfox the lieutenant."

"That's right," put in Chester Lykins. "Lieutenant Locklin is the best. It could be that the wagon train was real slow. Maybe it didn't get to the place where Locklin thought he could rendezvous with it, and he's had to push farther east to find it."

"Maybe." Halloran's voice was coated with doubt. "Not to put down the lieutenant's brilliance as an officer and leader of men, but we're not dealing in these parts with just any ordinary Apache chief. We all know that even the ordinary ones are crack military geniuses, and the whole nation of warriors are the hardest, craftiest, most merciless fighters on earth, but Pantano is head and shoulders above them all in my book. He knows the desert better than Locklin could ever know it, and he knows how to use it to his advantage. I want to be optimistic in the worst way, but I also must be realistic. Locklin's unit is late. The plan was for them to be back before dark."

Pivoting, the colonel headed toward the stairs. Over his shoulder, he said, "If Locklin's unit should show up, I want to know it immediately. Pass the word on to the men who relieve you. I mean immediately. Don't worry about getting me out of bed, either. I won't be asleep, no matter what time of the night it is."

"Yes, sir," chorused the sentries.

In the deepening shadows, Colonel Brett Halloran walked briskly toward the officers' quarters, which were located near the barracks. Walking tall, with back and head held erect, he met a few troopers along the way who asked about the late patrol. Without breaking stride, he answered their inquiries with a military snap, telling them that there was still no sign of Lieutenant Boyd Locklin and his men.

The officers' quarters were made up of six apartments, one for Captain Earl Snider and his family, and one each for Lieutenants Frank O'Brien, Warren Aulgur, Donald Nelms, and Boyd Locklin. All but Locklin were married.

At forty-nine, Halloran looked fifty-five. Such was the lot of the military leader who bore the responsibility of commanding a post in hostile territory. Having lost a great number of men in the past eight years to Apache bullets, arrows, and knives and having seen many brought in after battle still alive, but bleeding and sometimes maimed, Halloran had aged beyond his years. Recognized by his superiors in Washington as one of their best strategists, he had done an excellent job in curtailing much of the Apache killing of whites since opening the fort in 1850.

Halloran's straight dark-brown hair was streaked with gray, as was his heavy mustache. Road-map lines crisscrossed his rather handsome face, adding what his wife, Katherine, had called "lines of dignity." The first time she had given them that name, he had jokingly asked her if *dignity* was spelled "a-g-e."

Turning in at the apartment building, Halloran headed for Captain Earl Snider's door, but before he reached it, Snider emerged, putting on his campaign hat. When the captain saw his commander's form against the dim glow of the lantern that burned on a pole nearby, he closed the door behind him and said, "I was just going to the gate to see if they'd seen anything before it got dark."

"No sign of them," said the colonel. "I was coming to discuss the situation with you. If they're not here by four o'clock, I want you to lead a search squad out of here just before dawn. The regular patrols will go out as usual."

"All right, sir." Snider was a stockily built man of forty. "I don't mind telling you that I'm more than a little concerned."

"Me, too. Pantano's been rather frisky of late. He killed four settler families west of the Dragoons, you know. I think he's decided to show his strength and display some defiance. I had a queasy feeling about that wagon train taking the shortcut to Providence Wells. Still do. I just hope I'm wrong."

"Amen to that, sir. Locklin's a good man, but every time we learn one of Pantano's new tricks, he comes up with another one. If Locklin and his men are in trouble, it'll be because that crafty Apache pulled a new one on them."

"I don't even want to think about it," said Halloran, rubbing the back of his neck. "Anyway, I'll let you get back to your family. See you at four o'clock if not before."

"I hope it's before," said Snider.

Rounding the mess hall and passing the guardhouse, the

colonel moved quickly across the parade toward his house, which was situated near the stockade fence at the extreme east side of the fort. When he passed through the door, Katherine and Peggy were seated at the dining-room table, making themselves each a new dress.

They both looked up as he entered, an expectant look on their faces. Shaking his head as he moved up to the table, he said, "No sign of them."

Peggy, who was petite, blond, and quite pretty, frowned. "What do you think, Daddy?"

"I'm not sure what I think, darlin'," he replied, "but I know something's wrong."

Katherine, who would soon turn forty-three, but looked to be thirty-five, said, "Their being late might only mean the wagon train was running slow, dear. You mustn't let this upset you when you know there's a chance of something like that."

Tossing his hat on a nearby chair, the colonel rubbed the back of his neck again. "Yeah, I realize there's a chance of something like that, but there's also a chance that those thirteen men are out there being tortured to death or already have been."

Peggy's face pinched. Standing, she said with a quiver in her voice, "Don't talk like that, Daddy. Please. I can't bear the thought of anything bad happening to Boyd. He'll be all right, I'm just sure of it."

Katherine rose and looked her daughter in the eye. "Peggy, I've told you before, you are not to call Lieutenant Locklin by his first name. It isn't good manners."

A pout leaped to the teenager's mouth. "Why not? *You* call him Boyd."

"I'm older than he is," retorted Katherine. "Besides, I happen to be his commandant's wife. You are almost ten years younger than he is. You are to call him by his rank and last name unless he gives you permission to address him otherwise. You might ask him if you can call him Uncle Boyd. If he says it's all right, you can call him that."

Peggy screwed up her face. "*Uncle* Boyd! Mother, you have to be kidding! He doesn't look at me as a child. He sees me as a young woman. In fact, he sees me as a very attractive young woman."

Katherine's eyebrows arched. "Boyd has told you this?"

Tilting her chin upward and looking down her nose, Peggy said, "Yes."

The colonel's jaw squared. Fixing his daughter with a level stare, he asked, "When was this? What exactly did he say?"

Peggy felt the pressure of her father's authoritative eyes. His military mien made him hard to face. Avoiding his stare, she looked down at the cloth on the table. "Well...he...ah...didn't *say* it with words, but I can tell how he feels by the way he looks at me. And...and how he talks to me."

Her mother and father exchanged glances. They knew their daughter. Peggy had shown them a stern-willed desire to have her own way since she was very small. Since she had reached her teens, she was exhibiting a recklessness that at times overcame her common sense. There was a quickness to her that seemed to lunge at life with a rashness that ignored consequences.

Katherine said evenly, "Peggy, this is all in your imagination. The man sees you as a child, which is exactly what you are. You've got to quit this daydreaming about him and letting your imagination lead you to conclusions that are totally wrong."

Peggy kept her tone soft. "Mother, I am eighteen. That is far from being a child. You were barely my age when you married Daddy. Boyd—Lieutenant Locklin—sees me as mature for my age and I can see it in his eyes. He is attracted to me."

With exasperation showing on her face, Katherine looked at her husband. "Brett, I think you need to have a good talk with her."

"I can see that," he said. "But not tonight. Right now my mind is on thirteen men under my command who were sent out to escort a wagon train safely through an Apache danger zone and they haven't returned."

"I can appreciate that," Katherine said in a sympathetic tone. "But when Boyd returns—as I'm sure he will—it would be a good idea for you to talk to him about this so he can set Peggy straight."

"Yes," said the colonel, looking at Peggy. "That would settle it once and for all so you'd give the time of day to the young troopers at this fort who honestly do have eyes for you and are much closer to your own age."

Peggy Halloran remained silent. Sitting down, she picked up her sewing where she had left off. Deep within, she thought, *You will see, Father. When you confront Boyd with his intentions toward me, he'll come out with it. He'll tell you that he is in love with me, and that he plans one day to ask for my hand in marriage.*

Boyd Locklin awakened at the break of dawn. Clouds were gathered in the east and long banners of light were seeping through, illuminating the heavy cumulus domes. A cool breeze ruffled his hair as he sat up and looked at the small form lying next to him. In her sleep, Linda had grown cold and snuggled up close.

Rising, Locklin stretched and touched his fingertips to the cut on his cheek. It was slightly swollen, but had bled no more. He had a malevolent thought about young Kateya, then crowded it out of his mind. He had to concentrate on getting Linda to the fort before Pantano and his warriors could catch up to them.

Looking down at Linda, he hated to wake her. She had literally cried herself to sleep. His heart went out to her. She was all alone in a great big world with no one to look after her. She looked so pitiful with white splotches on her face where the tears had carried away some of the dirt.

His mind went back to the night before when he had held her in his arms while she wept. Something had happened deep inside him...and he knew what it was. From the depths of his heart, he found himself reaching out to her. He had only known her for a few hours, but he was having feelings for Linda Byrnes like he had never experienced toward another woman before. What he felt was exactly what he had known all along he would feel when he met the one woman for him. He was sure of it. He was falling in love with her.

Fixing his gaze on her lovely but dirty face, he thought, *I not only owe my life to you, Linda, but I want to spend the rest of it loving you and taking care of you. Of course I can't tell you because you'd think me an impetuous fool. Maybe...maybe you will begin having the same feelings toward me. The moment I see even a hint of it, I'll tell you what's in my heart.*

Bending down, the lieutenant stroked her soiled auburn hair. "Miss Linda...Miss Linda..."

The woman moved her head, moaned, and opened her eyes. Focusing them on the tall man in the dull light, she blinked and sat up. A tiny smile curved her lips. "Is it dawn already?"

"'Fraid so. I hated to disturb you, but we'd best eat a little jerky and get moving."

She offered him her hand and he helped her to her feet. She thanked him and ran her fingers through her hair. "I'll sure be glad to get to the fort so I can bathe."

While they ate jerky and drank a small amount of water, the sky brightened and the clouds in the east came alive with the shades of pink, red, and gold. As they started walking, Linda said, "Lieutenant, you had a bad night, didn't you?"

"What do you mean?"

"You cried out in your sleep several times."

"I did?"

"Mm-hmm."

"I didn't realize it. Sorry I disturbed you."

"That's all right. I called to you a couple of times, but you didn't respond, so I knew you were asleep. Nightmares?"

"Yes. Nightmares. I kept seeing my men being shot up by the Apaches as the ambush began yesterday. I saw it over and over and over again. But even worse, I kept reliving those horrid moments when they tortured the three men who were still alive after they had staked me out. Pantano's son was like a demon from hell. He tortured them something awful. Even scalped two of them while they were alive. I kept seeing the suffering of my men over and over."

Touching his arm, Linda said, "No wonder you were crying out. I'm so sorry."

"My suffering through it in a nightmare was nothing compared to what those poor men went through." Grinding his teeth, he added, "Someday I hope to get my hands on Kateya. That's Pantano's son. Pantano is bad enough, but that red-devil kid of his is meaner than that rattler you killed. He's got to be dealt with."

"Kid, you say? How old is he?"

"I'd say seventeen…eighteen at the most. But it's like he's got a flame of hatred inside for white men like I've never seen in an Indian. I know all the Apaches hate us, but his boy's eaten up with it. He's got a mean streak that's second to none."

An hour after leaving the spot where they had spent the night, the couple neared the place where the trail went beside the rim of the winding canyon with the jagged ridge along the opposite side. As they moved slowly through the area, Locklin explained to Linda how he and his men had expected to be ambushed there—not at the place where it happened.

The breeze was becoming a wind and growing hotter as the sun rose higher in the morning sky. When they passed the ridge and once again walked on flat, open country, the wind sent dust devils whirling like miniature tornadoes all around them. Weaving their way among cacti, desert shrubs, mesquite, and huge cracks in the ground, they moved steadily in the direction of Fort Savage to the northwest.

Linda lifted the campaign hat and wiped sweat from her brow. "Lieutenant, I don't mean to slow us up, but could we just take a small breather?"

Noting a cluster of tall monoliths up ahead, he said, "Sure. Let's stop up there at those rocks. That'll give us some shade."

"I could use some of that."

There was instant relief from the sun's blast when they sat down in the shade of the towering rocks and leaned back against them. Removing her hat, Linda rubbed away sweaty grime and wished for a tub of hot water. The wind was dying down, so she used the hat to fan her face.

Locklin laid his own hat on the sand and rested his head against the rock. "Let me know when you're ready to move on," he said quietly. "We'll take a little swig of water before we go."

"I'll only need a few minutes," she replied. "I know the danger of delay, but I don't want to collapse on you, either."

"You are very thoughtful." Locklin chuckled and closed his eyes.

The redhead gave him a smile he did not see. Her eyes clung to him. She studied his ruggedly handsome features, admiring the cut of his jaw and the way his nose was sculptured exquisitely like that of a Greek god. The man was strong, yet gentle. As long as she was with him, she felt perfectly safe in spite of the perilous situation. Boyd Locklin would get her to the fort.

Linda's admiring survey of the lieutenant went to his curly black hair, then trailed down to his broad shoulders and the deep swell of his chest. She remembered the rippling muscles in his back and shoulders that shone in the sun yesterday before he put on the shirt.

She also remembered the rock-hard, blue-veined biceps in his bulging arms. No, Linda Byrnes would never be afraid as long as she was with him.

With him. She had a passing thought that she might always like to be with him, then shook it off. She must concentrate on resting up so they could continue.

Twenty minutes later, they were once again on the move. As the morning hours passed, Locklin began looking over his shoulder periodically, wondering if Pantano had found the empty stakes on the mound yet. Once he did, the Apaches would ride hard to catch him.

Soon the sun reached its noontime zenith in the brassy sky. Its devastating rays beat down on the desert, broiling the land in a heat wave so intense that the lieutenant could smell its potency in the air. Locklin noted that there were no desert creatures in sight. Even the snakes and the lizards had fled the oven-hot rocks and sand to find shady shelter.

After a brief pause for water and rest, they resumed their wearisome vigil, Linda's feet and leg muscles turning more buttery with each step. She was sure her heels were blistering inside her shoes. Panting and sweating, she said, "Do you think a search unit will be coming for us?"

"They will unless there's more Apache trouble to deal with."

A half hour passed. Seeing that Linda was laboring in her stride once again, Locklin pointed to a cluster of huge boulders that was surrounded by a thick stand of mesquite. "We'll rest a while up there. I can tell you're about to drop."

"Getting…close," she said between gasping breaths.

As they reached the mesquite patch, Locklin halted and pointed to a shady spot. "Ladies first."

The mesquite limbs hung low. Linda bent over, making sure not to snag her hat in the branches, and dropped to her knees with a sigh. Locklin was about to follow her when he saw a movement on top of a mesa a half-mile to the northeast. Squinting against the desert's glare, he studied the spot for a moment. A rippling current of ice-cold needles ran down his spine.

Linda saw his body stiffen. Looking up at him through the mesquite branches, she asked, "What's the matter?"

"We've got company."

A feeble gasp escaped her lips. "Apaches?"

"Yes'm."

"Pantano?"

"Don't think so. Wrong direction. He'd not bother to ride around us to come from the north. Not enough to be Pantano's bunch, anyway. There are five of them."

"Have they spotted us?"

"They have."

"What are they doing?"

"Sitting on their pintos on top of the mesa, looking this way."

"They aren't riding toward us?"

"Not yet. This is one of their ugly ploys. They know there are only two of us, and they probably could make out your dress, so they know you're a woman. You never see an Apache on this desert unless he wants you to. They will work their intimidating little game for a while, then they'll come thundering at us."

Terror was very much in Linda's voice as she squeaked, "What are we going to do?"

Raising his line of sight toward the nooks and crannies of the boulders that rose above them, Locklin replied, "We're going to get you to the safest spot possible."

Taking her by the hand, the lieutenant plunged into the thick mesquite, pushing aside branches to clear the way ahead of them. When they reached the base of the nearest boulder, he peered over his shoulder through the branches toward the mesa. The Indians were no longer in sight. He knew they were now picking their way down some steep path toward the desert floor. He had to act fast.

Picking Linda up by the waist, he boosted her up to a level about five feet high. When she was on the rock securely, he scrambled up himself, then led her between two adjacent rock walls, deeper into the jumble of boulders. Once they were as deep as they could go without climbing higher, he sat her down and laid the canteen beside her. "Now, ma'am, I've got to leave you."

Voice trembling, she asked, "Where are you going?"

"I've got to lure them away from here and fight them."

"Fight them? Boyd, you can't fight those savages! You're unarmed!"

"Not completely," he said, turning to look northeast. When he couldn't see for the rounded rise of the boulder in front of him, he crawled up halfway, the heat of the rock burning his hands. Rising to his feet, he got a glimpse of the flat land between him and the mesa. The Apaches were still not in view. He was counting on it taking them some time to get off the mesa.

As he dropped back to Linda's level, she asked, "What do you mean, 'not completely'?"

"There are plenty of nice smooth rocks down there on the ground. Remember how you killed the rattler?"

"Yes."

"Indians can be killed with the same weapon. You stay here and keep quiet. Don't come out until I return for you."

"But what if—"

"If they kill me? They won't. I've got to get you safely to the fort."

"But—"

Locklin left her in a flash, bounding off the boulders and elbowing his way through the scratchy mesquite. Reaching level ground, he shot a glance in the direction of the mesa. Still there were no Apaches in sight. A half grin curved his dry lips as he hurriedly picked up four rocks the size of his fist and darted in the northeasterly direction.

Maybe I can beat them at their own game, he thought, as he found a groove just short of a patch of prickly pear cactus. He lay down in the groove, placing his head near the cactus patch and placed two rocks against each thigh. Quickly he scraped sand on top of himself until he was nearly buried. Leaving only his face exposed so he could see and breathe, he waited.

Locklin knew the five Apaches would have to ride very close to where he lay, since they were coming from the mesa. The patch of cactus would keep them from running right over the top of him.

Timing and accuracy would be everything. If he could drop one of the Apaches and get hold of his revolver, he had at least a slight chance of taking out the others. Apaches loved to wear revolvers. They used rifles and often carried bow and arrow, but they liked the feel of the revolver on their hip.

Lying there waiting, Locklin's mind ran to Linda. She was scared and had every right to be. He had to talk confidently in front of her, but he really knew his chances of overtaking five fierce, battle-wise Apaches were slim. He hated to think of Linda being murdered and scalped. He knew they wouldn't rape her unless they were some kind of renegade band. Apaches had an aversion toward adulterers. Even among their own people, adulterers and adulteresses were executed. Only the renegades had thrown off the customs of their fathers.

Gripping two rocks in each hand, he told himself he must be successful for Linda's sake. He must not let them kill her.

Suddenly the ground trembled slightly beneath him. Hardly breathing, he listened. Yes! Riders were coming at a gallop. He could hear thundering hooves. Closer and closer they came. When he heard them slow down and could make out the horses snorting and blowing, he steeled himself.

CHAPTER FIVE

Lieutenant Boyd Locklin's heart drummed his ribs as the five Apache warriors rode past him, their horses now moving at a walk. The leader was out front and the other four followed two abreast. They were looking at the jumble of boulders where they had seen the white man and woman, jabbering in their native tongue. True to form, each one carried a rifle and wore a sidearm.

When the last two were some forty feet past him, Locklin rose silently to his feet, gripping two rocks in each hand. The dirt fell from his body. Laying two rocks at his feet, he took his stance quickly. While holding a rock in his left hand, he threw the one in his right hand with great force. While it was hissing toward its target, he palmed the other rock in his right hand and hurled it even harder.

The first rock hit the Indian on Locklin's right flush on the back of the head. Instantly he began to fall from the horse. The Indian on the left turned to see what had happened a split second before the perfectly thrown rock cracked his skull and sent him reeling toward the ground.

The other three Apaches heard the *whump-whump* as their fellow warriors hit the ground. They turned around to see what had happened. They were now some ten or twelve yards ahead of the two that had fallen. The one on the right saw a deadly missile hurling toward his head. Instinctively he ducked and brought up his arm for protection at the same time. The rock glanced off his arm and struck the rump of the leader's horse, causing it to rear and bolt.

By this time Locklin had pitched the fourth rock. It slammed the Apache on the left violently, knocking him off his pinto. The lieutenant darted for the first man he had hit, who lay face-down. Grabbing the Indian's Colt .45 from its holster, he looked up to see the Apache with the bruised arm drawing a bead on him with his rifle.

Locklin dropped to the ground just as the rifle spat fire. The bullet whizzed over his head as he rolled to a prostrate position and fired, hitting the Apache dead-center in the chest. He heard a groan behind him at the same time he saw the leader bring his frightened pinto under control near the jumble of boulders.

Leaping to his feet, Locklin cocked the hammer of the Colt and ran toward the boulders. At the same time, the fourth Indian who had been hit was getting up, shaking his head, and pulling his revolver. Locklin stopped, swung the Colt on him, and dropped the hammer. The gun bucked in his hand and the Apache went down.

The lieutenant's attention went back to the leader, who raised his rifle to fire at him, then checked himself. In the same instant, Locklin knew why. He heard the rapid tattoo of footsteps and then was slammed from behind by the Apache whose gun he had taken.

The force of the blow knocked the revolver from Locklin's hand and the breath from his lungs. He was sucking for air and trying to twist from the Indian's grasp when he felt a sharp, burning sensation on his left side. He cracked the red man's jaw solidly with an elbow and rolled away from him. At the same time, he caught a glimpse of the leader moving into the mesquite thicket at the base of the boulders. The savage was looking for Linda.

Panic shot through Boyd Locklin like a bolt of lightening. He stood up and saw his immediate adversary rising to his feet, wielding a slender, wicked-looking knife. Blood glistened on the blade. The sharp pain in his side told Locklin it was his blood.

Time was of the essence. Locklin had to dispose of the Apache with the knife and stop the leader before he found Linda. The Colt .45 lay in the dust close by. He was considering making a dive for it when the Apache lunged at him, swinging the knife and ejecting a wild, animal-like cry.

Pain shot through the lieutenant's wounded side as he dodged the hissing blade, but he ignored it and seized the man's wrist with a grip of steel. The Indian was strong and nearly broke free, but Linda's danger had Locklin's adrenalin pumping. He gripped the upper arm with his other hand and brought the Apache's forearm down violently on his uplifted knee. Bone cracked and the Apache screamed, dropping the knife. Locklin quickly picked it up and drove the blade full-haft into his heart.

As the Indian collapsed with the knife buried in his chest, Locklin retrieved the Colt .45 and ran toward the boulders. While running, he broke the revolver open to check the loads. He had four unspent cartridges left. Snapping the cylinder into place, he surveyed the situation as he drew near the fringe of mesquite. The leader would find Linda any second.

He heard her scream just as he decided to climb up another way and approach Linda's position from above. Plunging recklessly through the clawing branches, he hopped onto a shoulder-high boulder and scrambled upward. He was aware of warm moisture flowing over his belt and down his pant leg, but there was not time to tend to it.

Linda was screaming repeatedly at the Apache leader as Locklin came over the rounded top of a boulder and looked down. The Indian had a grip on Linda's long hair and was dragging her toward the place in the rocks where he could take her down to the ground. He looked up to see Locklin silhouetted against the yellow sky, but it was too late to react. The Colt .45 roared four times, sending hot lead plowing through his chest. He let go of Linda's hair as he hovered there for few seconds, then slid slowly down to a sitting position, leaving a trail of blood on the rock.

Locklin eased himself down as Linda was getting to her feet. Not noticing his bleeding side, she dashed into his arms, sobbing. "Oh, Boyd, I'm so glad to see you! That…that beast knocked me down with his fist and was going to drag me all the way out of here by my hair!"

"It's all right now, Linda," he said, gritting his teeth because of the pain. "He's dead. I want you to stay here while I check on his pals. I think I killed all of them but one."

Clinging to him desperately, she gasped, "I don't want to stay here with him!" She looked down at the dead Apache leader.

"He can't hurt you now," said Locklin. "There's one I only hit in the head with a rock, and I—"

The lieutenant's words were cut off by the sound of thundering hooves. A large band of riders was pulling up. Locklin heard the metallic sound of bridle bits and the squeak of saddle leather just as a booming voice called out, "Lieutenant Locklin! We saw you climb into the rocks! Are you all right? It's Captain Earl Snider!"

Linda released a heavy sigh and leaned her head against his chest.

"I'm okay!" called out Locklin. "Be right out! Check on those Apaches out there, will you? One of them might still be alive."

"Come on, little gal," he said, looking down at the redhead. "It's all over now."

Letting go of him, Linda started to pick up the campaign hat she had been wearing when she noticed blood on her right hand. She traced it to his side. "Boyd, you're bleeding!"

"One of them got me with a knife," he said. "The men will have some bandages and antiseptic in their saddlebags."

"How deep did he stab you?"

"Don't know. Haven't had time to look at it."

Moments later, Lieutenant Boyd Locklin and Linda Byrnes emerged from the mesquite thicket with Boyd leaning on her. The other fifteen men gathered close, eager to hear what happened to Locklin's patrol, but postponed hearing the story while the wounded lieutenant was stretched out on the ground. When a corporal produced bandages and antiseptic, Linda asked if she could tend to Locklin, explaining that though she had not had formal nurse's training, she knew about wounds, cuts, and bandages.

Captain Snider gave his permission, standing by to observe. Linda found two gashes just above the beltline. Both were about an inch wide. The blade had entered and exited his side in a straight line at a depth of about an inch. As she adeptly built a compress and wrapped cloth around his slender waist to hold it, she said, "Lieutenant, these cuts are going to have to be sutured by the fort physician as soon as we can get you there. In the meantime, this will help stay the loss of blood."

"Can he ride a horse, ma'am?"

"He could, Captain," she responded, "but it will make him bleed more. The best thing would be for us to make a travois."

Snider nodded and gave a command that a few men cut branches from the mesquite trees and make poles. They would use a saddle blanket to tie between the poles and tie on the Apache pintos that stood nearby and let them pull the travois.

As the instructions were being carried out, Snider said, "Lieutenant, all four of the Indians out here are dead. Looks like you killed one by clobbering him in the head. What did you hit him with?"

"A rock," answered Locklin. "I threw rocks at four of them. I guess I must have caught that one real good, eh?"

"I'd say so. We'd have found you and the lady earlier, but we ran into a band of Apaches at sunup and had to battle it out. We killed a couple of them and lost three men in return before they ran low on ammunition and rode away. I sent four men back to the fort with the bodies."

Locklin asked what men were killed. When Snider told him, he expressed his sorrow, then asked, "Were those Apaches you fought part of Pantano's bunch?"

"I don't think so. Why?"

"Pantano is the reason you find me without my men. I'll tell you all about it, but let me say right now, you'd best keep a sharp eye out for him. He's going to be looking for me today."

"We'll do it," said Snider. "Now tell me what happened."

Locklin quickly introduced Linda Byrnes to Snider and the men who stood close, then proceeded to tell the story. He told in detail of Pantano's attack on the wagon train, his clever ambush on the patrol, and how the Apaches had staked him out on the mound to die. He went on to explain how Linda's life had been spared and how she had dug her way out from under the overturned wagon then released him from the stakes. He told how he had used the Apache's own camouflage trick by burying himself in the dirt, then rising up and throwing rocks at the ones that now lay dead.

After giving the details of how he had been stabbed while taking out three of them, then killed the leader up in the boulders, Locklin said, "So our next worry, Captain, is Pantano showing up with blood in his eye."

Snider assured him they would be watching for Pantano. He expressed his grief over the loss of Locklin's men, then commended him for the way he had taken out the five Apaches singlehandedly. "Your throwing arm is already held in awe among the men at the fort. When they hear this, you'll really be a hero."

Linda smiled as Locklin said, "Why don't we just keep it to ourselves, Captain?"

"Too late." Snider grinned and ran his gaze to the faces of the men who stood by. "These fellas admire you. They'll tell it."

Snider then told Locklin that a detail would be send out of the fort to the place of the ambush. The bodies of the wagon train victims would be buried there. The dead soldiers would be brought in for burial at the fort.

While the finishing touches were being put on the travois and a pinto was readied for pulling it, Captain Snider examined Locklin's bandage and commended Linda for a job well done. He asked how she got her experience. Linda explained that when her hometown of St. Joseph had become the jumping-off place for easterners to head west, most of them had traveled hundreds of miles by the time they reached it. There was no end of children and adults who had been injured in various and sundry ways, and needed medical care before striking out across the plains of Kansas or Nebraska. She was available, so the doctors in St. Joseph asked her to help. She had learned quickly and was kept busy except for the times she was in Kansas City visiting her friend Martha Lyons.

Linda and the lieutenant were given food and water, then with wary eyes on the lookout for Pantano, they pulled away. Locklin rode the travois behind the pinto which was led by a corporal from his saddle. One of the troopers rode another pinto, allowing Linda to ride his horse. She rode directly behind the travois so she could watch over the wounded man.

The sun beat down on them with suffocating fury. They all wiped sweat as the column moved northwest. There was a low murmur among the men as they discussed the tragic loss of Lieutenant Locklin's patrol. They spoke their sorrow over the loss of lives in the wagon train, but expressed their thankfulness that Locklin and the lovely lady had been spared.

From time to time the lieutenant looked up at Linda through a thin cloud of dust and smiled at her. When she smiled back, it made his heart quicken. There was no doubt that he was falling in love with her. She liked him. That was evident. He told himself that if he could keep her at the fort long enough, he would win her heart.

The afternoon hours seemed to drag by in the strength-sapping heat. Nerves were on edge as the men constantly scanned the desert around them, watching for Pantano and his warriors to appear.

Fort Savage came into view just as the sun touched the western horizon. Peering through the cloud of tawny dust that surrounded the column, Linda Byrnes let her line of sight trail up from the San Pedro River—which shone like a golden ribbon in the sunset—to the sharp-pointed stockade fence that surrounded the compound. The front gate faced west with its sentry tower suspended on heavy beams directly overhead. A red-white-and-blue flag waved lazily in the hot afternoon breeze above the tower.

When the column reached the south bank of the river, Lieutenant Boyd Locklin was lifted on to the horse Linda was riding so he would stay dry for the crossing. That time of year, the San Pedro was about a hundred feet wide at the spot where the fort stood on its north bank and some four feet in its center.

A shout went up from the tower as the column began crossing the muddy stream. The dual gates swung wide and the gap was filled with soldiers who were shouting excitedly. Lieutenant Boyd Locklin's name was on their lips.

Locklin sat behind Linda, his arms reaching around her as he held on to the pommel to steady himself. She struggled to veil the thrill she was experiencing with him so close to her.

There was a babble of voices as the column passed through the gate. Some were asking about the other men in Locklin's patrol, while others welcomed the lieutenant, commenting about the bandage that could be seen under his loose-hanging shirt. Still others asked where he had found the pretty lady.

Captain Earl Snider shouted above the din, telling them he would answer their questions momentarily, adding that it was imperative to get Lieutenant Locklin to the doctor. As the rest of the unit veered off toward the stables, Locklin pointed across the parade to the infirmary, telling Linda to head that way. Captain Snider stayed with them.

The excited soldiers followed. Just as they were approaching the commandant's office on their way to the infirmary, Colonel Brett Halloran appeared, stepping off the porch to intercept them. The colonel set his gaze on Locklin and smiled, but the smile drained away when he saw the bandage on his side. Halloran let his eyes flick to Linda, then looked toward the front of the compound to see if he could locate any of Locklin's men.

Snider spoke up, "The patrol was ambushed and wiped out yesterday, sir. I'm taking Lieutenant Locklin to Doc Philips. He needs attention immediately."

Nodding, the colonel walked alongside, looked at Linda again, and said to Snider, "And the lady?"

"The wagon train was also wiped out, sir. She is Miss Linda Byrnes, the only survivor. They can tell you the whole story inside the infirmary. I've got to stay out here and inform the men."

Dr. Harry Philips was standing in the open door of the infirmary as they drew up. Several of the men helped Locklin off the horse. Linda was assisted from the saddle and stayed close to the lieutenant as Colonel Halloran led them inside. Snider began telling the story to the crowd of soldiers as Philips closed the door.

Locklin introduced Linda to the colonel and the doctor as they headed for the operating table near the back of the large room, telling them that she had saved his life.

While the two men were helping Locklin onto the table, Linda said, "Actually, Lieutenant Locklin also saved my life."

Philips asked about the wound in Locklin's side as he eyed the bandage. While the lieutenant was explaining that he was stabbed by an Apache warrior, the doctor made a close inspection of the bandage. When Locklin had finished, Philips asked, "Who fixed you up?"

"Miss Byrnes did, Doc."

Smiling at the dirty, streak-faced woman, Philips said, "You've had medical training, I see."

"Not really, Doctor," she said quietly. "But I've had quite a bit of experience helping the doctors in my hometown of St. Joseph, Missouri."

"Well, ma'am," said Philips, "you did a superb job. I couldn't have done it any better myself."

"Thank you, Doctor." Linda returned the smile.

Before removing the bandage, Dr. Philips told Linda and the colonel they should take a seat. When he had finished stitching up the wounds, Halloran could talk to Locklin.

Captain Earl Snider came in just as the doctor was finishing his task. Colonel Halloran was seated across the room, but Linda was at the table assisting Philips.

"How's he doing, Doc?" asked Snider.

"He'll be as good as new in a month or so." Then Philips said to Linda, "I don't know when you're planning to leave us, ma'am, but as long as you're here, I'd sure like to have you assist me some more."

Linda glanced at the man on the table, then looked at Philips. "I'd be glad to help. I haven't had time to even think about plans to leave, yet."

I'll see if I can keep that from happening, Locklin told her in his mind.

Halloran stepped up near the table. "Miss Byrnes, you look exhausted. I've got to get a report from Lieutenant Locklin on all that's happened, but you can stay with us. We have a spare bedroom in our house. I have an eighteen-year-old daughter who is just about your size. She'll have something you can wear. I'm sure you'd like to bathe and get into some clean clothes. Mrs. Halloran and Peggy will have supper ready in about an hour. Captain Snider will take you to the house now, and I'll see you there at suppertime."

"That's very kind of you, Colonel," said Linda. Looking down at Locklin, she half-whispered, "You get some rest, Lieutenant. I'll be back to check on you when I smell better."

"You smell all right to me." He smiled.

"He'll be right over there in that bed," said Philips, pointing to a twin bed in the corner. "You're welcome to come see him anytime."

Leaving Colonel Halloran with Locklin, Captain Snider walked Linda across the compound toward the colonel's house in the fading light. The air was beginning to cool.

On the south side of the San Pedro River, a band of Apaches hunkered on the back side of a butte, peering toward the fort through the gathering darkness.

Young Kateya spoke while watching the sentries in the tower. "If we had only been a little quicker in going to check on the white eyes lieutenant, Father, we could have caught up with the bluecoats and killed them all."

"Not without plenty of time to set up another ambush, my son," said Pantano. "We do not often get opportunities to ambush the soldiers like we did at the wagon train yesterday. We will not be able to use that strategy again for a long time. The bluecoats will be watching for it. As we saw, the lieutenant even used it to surprise your Uncle Mandano and his men."

One of the warriors said, "It is hard to believe the lieutenant was able to kill all five by himself, Pantano. It must be that the soldiers arrived in time to help him."

Pantano scowled at the warrior. "You are saying that I can no longer read sign, Mingus?"

"It is not that," replied Mingus hastily, "it is just—"

"I am telling you that the Lieutenant Locklin did kill them!" Pantano snapped, cutting across Mingus's words. "And he did it by himself! He shot Mandano amid the boulders where the woman was hiding as I told you."

In the near dark, the chief's features stiffened and changed to ice. His voice trembled with cold fury as he hissed, "The Lieutenant Boyd Locklin killed my only brother. I will not rest until he is dead!"

Kateya laid a hand on his father's shoulder. "The gods will deliver him into our hands one day, Father. You will have your revenge."

Peggy Halloran was on the front porch of the log house, observing Linda Byrnes and Captain Earl Snider as they came toward her. She wore a colorful cotton dress with a bright flowery design. Her long blond hair hung in lazy swirls about her shoulders. Moving forward as the pair drew up, she said, "Lieutenant O'Brien came and told us that Boyd—ah—Lieutenant Locklin had been found, Captain. Oh, I'm so glad he's all right!"

"He'll be fine, Peggy," responded Snider. "And this is the lady who survived the wagon train massacre. Miss Linda Byrnes, this is the colonel's daughter, Peggy."

The smile on Peggy's lips seemed forced. "Oh yes, Lieutenant O'Brien did say something about a woman being brought in with Boyd." This time Peggy did not correct her familiar use of Locklin's first name, but let it hang in the air a moment. "I'm glad to make you acquaintance, Miss Byrnes," she said coolly.

"She saved the lieutenant's life, Peggy," put in Snider.

"Yes, I know." The painted-on smile was still affixed as she said, "Lieutenant O'Brien told me Boyd had been staked out and left to die by the Apaches. I'm very grateful to you for saving my favorite soldier's life, Miss Byrnes. Boyd and I...well, we're very close. So what you did means more to me than I can tell you."

Wondering what a girl so young could mean by "very close," Linda replied, "It really was no heroic feat, Peggy. The good Lord was merciful to let me live through the massacre of the people in the wagon train. I simply cut Lieutenant Locklin loose from the stakes. However, he saved my life at the risk of his own earlier today when five Apaches came riding in to kill us. One of them actually had me in his grasp and would have taken my life, but the lieutenant came to my rescue with no thought for his own safety and killed him. I will be forever in his debt."

Before Peggy could comment further, Katherine Halloran appeared at the door. "Earl, is this the young lady who was brought in with Boyd?"

"Yes'm," affirmed Snider. "The colonel told me to bring her to you. Said that she could stay in your spare bedroom. That you would let her bathe, and that since she is about Peggy's size, maybe there would be something she could wear."

"Certainly." Katherine smiled. "Come in, my dear. We'll get you all cleaned up before time for supper."

No one noticed the sour look that claimed Peggy's features.

Dr. Harry Philips was a short, stout man in his midsixties. His silver hair was thinning and a sizable paunch rode his middle. Deep lines creased his gentle face, and were emphasized by the light of the two lanterns that burned in the infirmary as he sat beside Boyd Locklin, who now sat propped up on the bed. The lieutenant had just finished eating a small portion of the meal Philips had brought him from the mess hall.

As the doctor took the tray from Locklin, he asked, "Sure you don't want some more? You've got to keep up your strength."

"Maybe tomorrow, Doc." Locklin sighed. "No more tonight. I just don't have much appetite right now."

Rising from the chair with the tray in hand, Philips smiled.

"Well, I guess I can understand that. It isn't every day you get stabbed by an Apache."

"Thank goodness for small favors," said Locklin.

Chuckling, the doctor headed toward the door. "I'll leave the lanterns burning. When you're ready to go to sleep, it won't hurt you to get up and move around to blow them out." Reaching the door, he opened it and grinned at his patient. "I have to leave the lanterns on anyway, because that pretty little redhead said she'd be back to check on you when she smelled better."

"You're so kind, Doc," Locklin replied with a crooked grin.

"Just don't want to stand in the way of romance, son."

Locklin met his gaze straight on. "Romance? Come on, Doc. We just met yesterday."

"So? I've been around for a while, boy. Been a widower for ten years, but I still remember what falling in love is like. And I can still recognize it when it shines in the eyes of a man and woman who've got such feelings for each other. I saw it real plain in both of you when you came in here."

"Get out of here, you old coot," said Locklin.

Philips laughed. "By the way, I figure some of the men will probably be coming to see you this evening, so soon's I take this tray to the mess hall, I'll hang a note on the door forbidding anyone to enter except the lady who assisted as my nurse when I patched you up. I'll write the note at the mess hall so as not to disturb you anymore. Seeing Miss Linda will be enough ado for you tonight."

When the doctor was gone, Locklin slid down in the bed, leaving his head propped up on two pillows. *"I saw it real plain in both of you..."*

The lieutenant had no doubt that what he felt for Linda had been evident in his own eyes, but had the doctor seen the same thing in Linda's eyes? He said he did. Locklin had seen compassion and concern in Linda's eyes, but had caught no more than that. He lay there hoping the doctor had seen correctly.

While he thought of Linda, Locklin's meditation was interrupted by mental recurrences of his men being killed by the Apaches. The bloody scenes came to his mind over and over again. He grieved for them as he wiped tears from his cheeks.

The lieutenant had seen many men under his command killed

in battle with Apaches during the six years he had been at Fort Savage, but only two or three at a time. To see his entire patrol wiped out in one confrontation ripped inexorably at the very core of his being.

Suddenly there were footsteps on the porch of the infirmary. Locklin quickly tried to compose himself, using the sheet to dry his face. When he heard vague scraping noises, he realized it was Dr. Philips placing the note on the door.

Hardly had ten minutes passed when Locklin became aware of male voices outside the door, followed by footsteps on the porch. He could pick up enough of the conversation to tell that several of his friends had come to see him and were unhappy to find the doctor's note forbidding their entrance. As they walked away mumbling their disappointment, Locklin smiled to himself. They were a great bunch of guys.

A half hour passed. Locklin was reliving the incident at the mesquite-fringed boulders when light footsteps met his ears. There was a slight pause, then the door opened slowly. Lieutenant Boyd Locklin's blood rose in temperature when he saw Linda's clean, shiny face in the lantern light. Stepping in, she closed the door behind her. "Hello. The note says I have the doctor's permission to see you. I smell better now. May I come in?"

CHAPTER SIX

Never had a woman stirred Boyd Locklin like Linda Byrnes. As she stood there in the glow of the lanterns, he absorbed the fullness of the picture she made with the rough log wall and the worn, unpainted door as a backdrop.

Her long auburn hair, highlighted by the soft yellow light, fell in attractive waves at the sides of her beautiful face, resting in a captivating manner on her shoulders. She wore a white cotton dress, high-necked and long-sleeved, that followed her figure till it spread gradually all the way to her ankles.

Locklin had decided, even when her hair was matted and dirty and her face was sweat-smudged, that she was the most beautiful woman he had ever seen, but the sight before him captured his breath. It took a few seconds to find his voice. Letting a wide grin spread slowly over his rugged features, he said, "Please do come in."

The redhead's exquisite mouth turned upward in a womanly way that lighted her entire countenance as she moved toward him. Locklin felt a sudden urge to open his arms and invite her for a close embrace, but he reluctantly squelched the impulse. Instead, he gingerly sat up, placed the pillows at his back, and gestured toward a nearby chair. "Please sit down."

Pulling the chair up close, Linda settled into it. "How are you feeling?"

"A little puny, ma'am. Guess it'll take a few days to get my strength back."

Touching his arm, she said, "During all the excitement out there on the desert today, you dropped the ma'am and the Miss and just called me Linda. I'd like to keep it that way."

"Come to think of it, I remember you dropping the Lieutenant too. I really liked it when you call me by my name. Let's keep it that way."

Her emerald eyes lit up as she extended her hand to shake. "It's a deal, Boyd!"

Grasping her small hand in his, Locklin squeezed it tight. "It's a deal, Linda."

Their eyes met, held, and locked as if a sudden spell had fallen over them. The force between them was like a magnet, drawing them together. It was stronger than both of them, but neither had any desire to resist. Their lips met in a soft, sweet, velvety kiss. When they parted, Boyd wrapped an arm around her neck and pulled her into the embrace he had thought about earlier.

Making it more comfortable, Linda left the chair and sat on the edge of the bed. His heart was thundering within him. Her breath fell warm on his ear as she whispered, "Can this happen in just two days?"

"I can't speak for you," he breathed, "but it did for me. In fact, I knew it yesterday."

"I believe I did, too," she said, cuddling her head into the curve of his neck. "It's...it's just all of a sudden. I've heard of it happening before, but never thought it would happen to me."

"Love is a strange thing," said Boyd, delighting in the pleasure of holding her close, and exhilarated with the knowledge that Linda had fallen for him, too. "It can leap the bounds of time. I feel like I've always loved you, yet I only found you yesterday."

"Yes, darling. I know exactly what you mean."

Silence prevailed for a long moment while Boyd held her close. "Linda..."

She pulled back and looked into his eyes. "Yes?"

"I don't want you to leave. You said you had no special place to go."

"I don't want to leave, either, but what would I do? Where would I stay? I can't take advantage of the Hallorans' hospitality. It isn't right that I interfere with their family life."

"I agree," he said, drinking in her beauty. "Let me work on it a little bit."

Linda's brow furrowed. "You need to rest. You're looking awfully tired."

"Mm-hmm." He nodded. "You need to rest, too. We've both had a rough couple of days."

They kissed again, long and lingering, then Linda stood up, flicked the hair from her eyes, and smoothed out her dress. "Anything I can do for you before I go?"

"No, thank you. I'm fine."

"All right, I'll be going now. See you in the m—"

A light tapping at the door interrupted Linda's words, followed by the door coming open instantly. Peggy Halloran crossed the threshold, held onto the doorknob, and smiled at the man. "Hello, Boyd," she chirped. "I just couldn't go to bed without coming to see if you were all right. I'd like to visit with you for a few minutes." Swerving her attention to Linda, she added crisply, "Alone."

Both Boyd and Linda were a little off-balance from the unexpected intrusion. When neither answered right away, Peggy said, "I know Doc's note said for everybody but Linda to stay out, but I figure that pertains more to the men." Leaving the door open, she moved toward the bed, saying in a throaty manner, "I'm not one of the men."

Feeling the icy wall between herself and the impudent little blond, Linda said, "I was just leaving. However, I suggest that you keep your visit to a minimum, Peggy. Lieutenant Locklin is quite exhausted. He's lost a lot of blood and needs to get a good night's rest."

Forcing another smile, Peggy looked at the redhead coldly. "I'll not stay long."

Peggy's coolness toward Linda had not gone unnoticed by Boyd Locklin. Only his respect for Colonel Halloran kept him from reprimanding her.

Smiling down at the patient, Linda said warmly, "Good night, Boyd. See you in the morning."

"I'll look forward to it." He smiled in return.

Linda crossed the room, smiled at the man she loved once more, and left quietly, closing the door behind her.

Peggy stared at the door as if Linda was still standing there until Locklin said, "Do your parents know you're here, Peggy?"

"Sort of."

"Sort of?" he echoed.

"I'm eighteen now, Boyd," she said defensively. "I don't have to ask my parents if I can take a walk around the compound after dark. Since I'm not allowed outside the walls, what could happen to me with a hundred and thirty-one soldiers around? Ah…excuse me, there are twelve fewer now. Besides, Mother and Daddy won't object. They know we're fond of each other."

"Well you're a sweet little kid. It was nice of you to come and see me. I'm doing fine, but I am really worn out. Maybe we could talk some other time."

Dropping quickly on the chair, Peggy whined, "But I want to hear all about how your patrol was wiped out by Pantano, Boyd. I want to know every detail, and all about—"

"Not tonight," cut in the weary man. "Some other time. In fact, it will be a long time before I want to talk about losing those men."

Looking hurt, Peggy stood up. "Okay. I understand. All I really wanted was to tell you that I'm glad you came back safely to me, and to spend a little time with you. How can our relationship develop if we aren't together?"

Locklin sighed. "Peggy, we've been over this before. I don't want to hurt your feelings, but we don't have a relationship. Not in the way you mean it. You're a sweet kid, and I'm fond of you, but I didn't come back to you. Like I've told you before, there's a decade of time between our ages. You need to be interested in boys your own age—like some of these young troopers."

Peggy's mouth pulled into a thin line and her eyes glinted with fire. "I'm not a little kid, Boyd! I'm a woman, and you know it! I've seen how you look at me."

"Peggy, I—"

"You know I'm too mature for those infantile troopers, Boyd. I can see it in your eyes. You love me."

Locklin closed his eyes in frustration. "Peggy, listen. You don't understand. I—"

"Oh, but I do understand. You're just afraid to declare your love for me because it would upset my father. Well, I'm willing to wait. By the time I'm twenty, I'll be old enough in Daddy's eyes for you to ask him for my hand in marriage. You won't even admit to me that you're in love with me, but I know what's in your heart, darling. I'm a woman. Women have a sixth sense about men. I know how you feel about me."

The lieutenant laid his head back on the pillow and said something under his breath that Peggy could not hear.

"What did you say?" she demanded, her features clouding.

"Nothing for your ears," the lieutenant replied. "I'm really tired, Peggy. I'd like to get some sleep."

Her countenance changed instantly. Leaning over him with a pleasant smile, she cooed, "I'll leave now so you can get your rest, my darling. Well talk some more, soon. Please know that I understand. It will all work out when I turn twenty. You'll see."

When Peggy was gone, Locklin sighed with relief, telling himself that he would have to find a way to tell Peggy they had no future together, but handle it in a manner that would not hurt his relationship with the colonel. Peggy was very headstrong and quite emotional. When the cold, hard fact finally sunk in, she would probably do something drastically theatrical to impress everyone how deeply the lieutenant had hurt her.

Moving carefully, Locklin got out of bed and doused the lanterns, feeling the weakness in his knees. Once back in bed, he soon drifted off to sleep with his mind on Linda Byrnes. The taste of her sweet lips was still with him.

Linda Byrnes lay in her bed, feeling the warmth of her few moments with the rugged, handsome lieutenant. She relived their tender embrace as they cuddled close and the sound of his voice when he said, *"Love is a strange thing. It can leap the bounds of time. I feel like I've always loved you, yet I only found you yesterday."*

Linda had never wanted a man like she wanted Boyd Locklin. Everything about him aroused her womanly senses. She had known some fine and good men in the past, but none like him. She had been fond of men, but this was not fondness. For the first time in her life she knew what it was to be in love. The thought of Boyd's kisses and the emotions that had flowed between her and the man quickened her pulse. Her small frame throbbed from the staccato beat of her heart.

The redhead's thoughts were interrupted with the sound of Peggy Halloran entering the house, followed by voices in the parlor—female voices. Katherine Halloran was asking her daughter where she had been. When Peggy replied boldly that she had been with Boyd Locklin, Katherine mildly scolded her for bothering the lieutenant while he lay in the infirmary. A few more words passed between them that Linda could not make out; then she heard Peggy come down the hall and enter her room, which was next door.

While the sound of Peggy's humming filtered through the wall, Linda thought on the girl's behavior at the infirmary. To Linda it was portentous of the trouble that lay ahead between the two of them over Boyd. The redhead would give no ground to the flippant teenager. She had found her man and no female was going to take him from her.

The sudden sound of the bugler playing reveille jerked Boyd Locklin awake. Pain lanced through the wound in his side. Wincing, he laid a hand over the bandage and opened his eyes. Dawn's gray light was pushing through the infirmary's three windows. The one on the east was brightest. He squinted, blinked a few times, then closed his eyes and waited for the bugler to finish. When the repugnant sound of reveille died out, he slowly worked his way to a sitting position and slitted his eyelids to allow a gradual adjustment for his sleepy eyes.

At the same moment, there were footsteps on the porch, followed by the door squeaking open. Familiar sounds of soldier voices coming from the open windows of the barracks rode the cool air. Dr. Harry Philips's bulky form filled the doorway as he moved inside and closed the door. Philips said in a cheerful tone, "Well, I see our patient is eager to get out of bed."

"Not terribly eager, Doc," said Locklin. "I'm still pretty weak. But after all night in a horizontal position, I thought it'd feel good to sit up for a few minutes." He paused. "What do you mean *our* patient? You have a medical mouse in your pocket?"

Philips chuckled. "No, but there's a lovely redhead waiting on the porch. She was camped outside the door of my quarters when I came out. Said she wanted to check on you this morning, but would like for me to go in first and see if you were awake. She figured the bugler probably got through to you too, but wanted to make sure before she barged in."

A slow smile worked its way across the lieutenant's features. "That lovely redhead is welcôme anytime, Doc, but before you bring her in, I want to ask you something."

"What's that?"

"Did you mean it when you told her you'd like to have her assistance some more while she's here?"

"I sure did."

"How'd you like to have her be your assistant on a permanent basis?"

"I'd love it. You think she'd stay? I'd be willing to talk the colonel into giving her regular pay. The way the men keep coming in battered, bruised, shot up, and bloody from fighting Apaches, I sure could use her."

"I feel quite sure she'd stay with an offer like that," said Locklin. "She's really got no one to go home to. I'll move into the barracks with the men and she can have my quarters."

"I don't think the colonel would go for that, son," said the physician. "I've got an extra bunk and plenty of closet space in my quarters. How about staying with me? The colonel would allow that, I'm sure."

"It's a deal, Doc," said Locklin, lying back down and covering his legs. "Tell her to come in. We'll lay the proposal before her."

The eastern horizon was ablaze in the russet and yellow glow of sunrise as Kateya and an Apache brave named Matoro knelt behind a patch of mesquite a half-mile west of Fort Savage. Using a pair of binoculars he had stolen from Sergeant Clay Harris's saddlebags, Kateya observed the mounted units as they filed through the gate to begin their routine patrols.

Colonel Brett Halloran had beefed up the patrols from thirteen men to twenty-one in an effort to thwart any more wipe-outs by Pantano and his warriors. A large wagon train had pulled in and camped on the far side of the river after dark the night before, and would be escorted that day through Catalina Pass by one of the units. The other three were fanning out in their assigned territories.

Matoro watched Kateya shift the binoculars as he watched unit leader to unit leader. "Is he not there?"

"He is not," the young warrior said with disgust. "They must be giving him a rest because of what he experienced the last two days. My father will be unhappy to learn that the Lieutenant Boyd Locklin is safe inside the fort today."

"Yes," agreed Matoro, "but soon the gods will deliver him into Pantano's hands."

Lowering the glasses, Kateya grinned evilly. "I am going to help the gods a little, my friend. I want to see the lieutenant dead as much as my father does. Devil, he called me. Yes, he shall see! This diablo will be here every morning until the Lieutenant Boyd Locklin leads a patrol. When he does, it will be his last patrol!"

CHAPTER SEVEN

Six weeks later

Beautiful Linda Byrnes had gladly accepted the doctor's offer to become his paid assistant, and Colonel Brett Halloran had been pleased to approve it. Rather than allow the physician to give up his space, Halloran insisted that Linda stay in his home until an apartment could be completed adjacent to the infirmary. It had taken only two weeks to build, and Linda was happy to be in her own home and away from the cold looks and rude treatment she received from Peggy Halloran. The blond had been careful never to let her parents see the scorn she held toward Linda.

Boyd Locklin was fully recovered from his wound, but had been barred from patrol by the colonel while he completely regained his strength. In the meantime, Locklin was training new recruits in the art of hand-to-hand combat, using knives and fists. The colonel regarded Locklin as an expert and regularly employed his talents to prepare the men for the kind of fighting they could face at any time with the Apaches.

The bond of love between Boyd and Linda grew stronger with each passing day. They had not yet shown it openly, but most of the fort personnel were silently suspicious. Peggy Halloran had seen them together many times, but refused to believe there was any romance. She still held to the belief that Locklin was in love with her, and that he would come out with it once she was old enough in the sight of her father to be married. She had not come on so boldly to the lieutenant, though she pushed her presence on him quite often. Her lack of aggressiveness had caused Locklin to feel that she was possibly getting the message.

It all changed, however, one night in mid-September.

Linda Byrnes was well-liked by Katherine Halloran and the other officers' wives. She was always included in the women's activities. A sewing bee was held regularly in the mess hall every Tuesday evening. Linda had made herself a couple of dresses, but the officers' wives decided they would all pitch in on one session and make her several dresses in order to build up her wardrobe.

Peggy attended the bee, but was not aware of the ladies' intentions for the evening until she arrived. Unable to come up with an excuse to leave, she reluctantly helped her mother with the dress she was making for Linda.

Edie O'Brien, wife of Lieutenant Frank O'Brien, and Oralee Nelms, wife of Lieutenant Donald Nelms, were working on a dress together. When they had finished it, Edie held it up. "Look, everybody, ours is done. Why don't you try it on, Linda? See if it fits all right."

Smiling, the redhead left her chair, took the dress, and went to the kitchen to change. It was a fancy, frilled dress to be worn at special social functions. When she returned to the mess hall in black-and-white, the women commented on how well it was made and how nicely it fit her.

Amy Snider, wife of Captain Earl Snider, giggled. "Lieutenant Locklin will love you in that dress, honey."

Linda's face tinted. Her emerald eyes sparkled as she said, "I hope he likes it on me."

Katherine Halloran saw her daughter's body stiffen. Peggy's features went crimson, but she said nothing.

Oralee Nelms smiled broadly. "There is something developing between you and that good-looking hunk of masculinity isn't there, Linda?"

Peggy's feral gaze flitted to Oralee, then fixed itself on Linda.

"Boyd and I have a lot in common."

Breathing hotly, Peggy rose from the table and stomped out the door, leaving her mother with her mouth agape and the ladies wondering what was wrong with the hotheaded little blond.

Outside, Peggy fumed in anger, swearing under her breath. She headed straight for Locklin's quarters and knocked on the door. When there was no answer, she knocked louder. Abruptly the door of the next apartment came open. Lieutenant Frank O'Brien appeared in the glow of the lantern that hung on a nearby pole. "If you're looking for Lieutenant Locklin, Peggy, he's in a meeting with your father and Captain Snider."

"At Daddy's office?"

"Yes."

Without another word, Peggy wheeled and darted toward the commandant's office across the parade. She could see the lantern light in the windows and a man's shadow on the glass. As she drew near, she recognized Boyd Locklin's profile. Her blood was hot as she knocked on the door. Footsteps followed, and Locklin's face greeted her as the door came open.

Colonel Halloran was on his feet behind the desk. Captain Earl Snider was seated directly in from of him. Before Locklin could speak, Halloran looked past him at his daughter. "What is it, Peggy?"

"I need to see Boyd—Lieutenant Locklin—Daddy. Now. In private."

"You'll have to wait, honey," countered Halloran. "We are discussing important matters at the moment. You'll have to see your Uncle Boyd later."

Locklin and the girl both caught the "Uncle Boyd" emphasis.

Peggy's voice had sand in it as she responded curtly, "Whatever it is, it is not as important as what I want to talk to him about. I want to talk to him right now!"

Colonel Brett Halloran's features went taut. His eyes were steely. Peggy knew she had angered him and was wishing she could call back her last statement.

The colonel's voice was deep like muffled thunder. "Listen to me, young lady! We've had five troopers killed by Apaches in the last two weeks! We are in a discussion that involves saving the lives of the rest of our men. What you have to discuss with Lieutenant Locklin is not that important! Now I will thank you to leave immediately."

Pivoting quickly to keep the men from seeing the pinch of her face, Peggy darted off the porch and disappeared in the darkness.

Locklin closed the door, wondering what that was all about, and returned to the spot where he had been standing by the window before the interruption. Halloran sank into his stuffed desk chair and swung his gaze from Snider to Locklin. "I'm sorry, gentlemen.

My daughter is quite impetuous, and every little problem in her life is an earth-shaking crisis.

Locklin smiled as Snider replied, "I'm just beginning to learn about teenage girls, sir. My Betty Lou is twelve and a half, and she's already showing like signs. I understand."

Sighing, Halloran took a cigarillo from a wooden box on his desk and stuck it between his lips. "Boyd, if you and Linda ever have children, lock them up in a closet when they turn thirteen and don't let them out till they turn twenty."

Locklin showed his crooked grin. "I'll try to remember that sage advice, sir. Ah...that is, if Linda and I ever tie the knot."

Halloran's eyebrows arched. "Well, it is in the offing, is it not?"

Snider shifted on his chair in order to get a better look at the lieutenant.

Locklin scratched the back of his neck nervously. "Well, sir, we really haven't gotten down to discussing marriage."

Halloran picked up a match from the desk, struck it, lit the cigarillo, and blowing smoke, said, "Well, don't you think it's about time the subject was broached? I mean...it will have to come from you, you know."

Boyd Locklin chuckled. *What a coincidence,* he thought. *Linda and I already have agreed to see each other after the sewing bee and nobody but the good Lord Himself knows that I am going to propose to her.* "I realize that, sir. I...well, I've just been letting her get used to army life a little before I bring up the subject."

"Mm-hmm. That makes good sense. Just don't wait too long. I have noticed the way some of the enlisted men look at her. Anytime one of them's going to ask her to take a moonlight walk with him."

"I'll keep that in mind, sir," said Locklin.

"Now where were we?" said the colonel, shifting his gaze to Snider. "Oh yes. Pantano. We've got to come up with a way to trap that filthy beast and send him to his happy hunting ground. He's getting more nervy these days. Wouldn't surprise me if he tries another ambush in Catalina Pass, no matter how many men we put in a protective unit."

"I agree," said Snider. "We've got to kill him. Once he's dead, it'll take the Chiricahuas a while to come up with another leader who can inspire them like he does."

Taking another puff on his cigarillo, Halloran said, "Okay. We're in agreement that a trap has to be set. Tomorrow morning we'll meet with the other officers, lay it before them, and put our heads together. It may take us a little while, but we'll come up with something foolproof. Pantano must be eliminated."

As the women were coming out of the mess hall chatting merrily, Linda spotted Boyd Locklin coming from the direction of the colonel's office. Carrying her four new dresses, she thanked them all for their kindness and hurried to meet the tall man.

As Locklin drew up, she said, "Oh, Boyd, just look at my new dresses!"

A lantern glowed nearby, but the light was too dim for him to see them well. "Since we're having coffee at your place, I'll examine them over there." He put an arm around her shoulders.

As they walked toward her quarters, they approached the small platform where the water barrels were kept. Three soldiers were placing empty fifty-gallon barrels in the back of a wagon. Pausing, Locklin said, "You men are working a bit late, aren't you?"

"Just wanted to load these barrels so they'll be ready to take to the river in the mornin', Lieutenant," replied one.

The normal routine was for the wagon to pass through the gate about sunup with three or four soldiers going along to fill the barrels in the San Pedro. Sentries on the wall would keep a sharp eye to make sure no Apaches came near while the barrels were being filled. So far, the Indians had never made an attempt to come that close to the fort.

"Always good to see men eager to do their work," said Locklin. "See you in the morning."

One of the others said, "Tell you what, Lieutenant..."

"What's that?"

Grinning, the man in blue said, "If you'd like to trade places with me, I'd be glad to walk Miss Linda home."

Locklin laughed. "Not tonight, Willie." As he and the redhead moved away, he called over his shoulder, "Not any other night, either!"

The soldiers laughed heartily.

At Linda's quarters, Boyd admired her new dresses, then built a fire in her small stove while she hung them up in her closet on wooden hangers. Boyd stood close as Linda filled the coffeepot and set it over the fire. She turned around to find him with open arms. Her heart throbbed as he folded her in a tight embrace. "You are without a doubt the most captivating female God ever made."

"Oh, Boyd, you are such a flatterer," she said, blushing.

"My words are not flattery, sweet lady," he said, looking deep into her eyes. "They are truth."

Linda smiled. "I'm glad you think I'm captivating. I don't care what anyone else thinks, just so you see me that way."

They melted into each other and kissed tenderly. When they broke apart, Boyd said, "I love you, Linda."

"And I love you," she half-whispered. Turning to take cups from the cupboard, she asked, "How did the meeting go?"

"As I expected. The colonel, Captain Snider, and I are in agreement. We've got to eliminate Pantano. We're grossly outnumbered by the Apaches in this country, but we're going to meet with the other officers before the patrols go out in the morning and discuss it with them. With all of us thinking on it, we're going to come up with a plan to trap Pantano and either capture him or kill him. Knowing Pantano, we're sure that taking him alive will be next to impossible so he'll have to die. One way or the other, he's got to be stopped. With him out of the way, the Chiricahuas will not be so bold. Pantano is killing more and more settlers and travelers."

"Mrs. Halloran told me tonight that you are going out on patrol in the morning."

"Yes. It's time. My strength is all the way back, and I'm ready to get back into the regular routine."

Worry showed in Linda's eyes. "You will be careful, won't you? I...I couldn't stand it if anything happened to you."

Taking both of her hands in his, Boyd towered over her, his own heart banging his ribs. Since this was the night to make his proposal, now was as good a time as any. "Linda...I...I want to ask you something."

She had been dreaming of the moment Boyd Locklin would ask her to marry him. Hoping this was the moment, she smiled. "Yes, darling?"

"Would...would it really be a big thing to you if something happened to me?"

"Oh yes!" she breathed. "You are what I live for, darling. You have become the very essence of my life. Without you I...I would have nothing to live for."

Boyd's voice cracked with emotion. "Army life carries a great deal of risk. When a man rides out into that desert to face the hostiles, there is always the possibility he might not come back. Could...could you live with that if you were married to a soldier?"

"Life itself is a risk, darling," she said, squeezing his hands. "I would rather take army life's risk and be married to the man I love than to marry the wrong man. Yes, I could live with it."

The lieutenant's heart slid up to his throat, making the next words difficult. "Linda...the ladies did a fine job making those dresses for you. Do you suppose they could make a beautiful wedding dress?"

Linda's heart fluttered, stealing her breath. Tears rimmed her eyes. "Are...are you asking me to marry you?"

Nodding, he released his crooked grin. "Yes, my sweet. In my very clumsy way, I am asking you to become my wife."

The tears spilled down her cheeks as Linda gasped, "Yes! Oh yes! I will marry you!"

They kissed lingeringly, then while they clung to each other, Linda asked, "How will we do this, Boyd? There isn't a preacher within hundreds of miles."

"No problem. Colonel Halloran has the authority to perform military weddings. I'm sure he'll be glad to tie the knot."

"Wonderful! I didn't know that. Do...do you have a date in mind?"

"As a matter of fact I do," he said. "I figure it'll take some time to make the wedding dress. And I want to give you a little time to get adjusted to the idea of becoming Mrs. Lieutenant Boyd Locklin, so I figure three weeks or so would take care of all that. I think Sunday would be the best day of the week to be married, so how about Sunday, October 10?"

"Sounds wonderful to me."

"Sorry I don't have an engagement ring to put on your finger," he said quietly, "but there aren't any jewelers within hundreds of miles, either."

"That's all right. We're just as engaged without a ring."

Fishing in his shirt pocket, Boyd produced a plain gold wedding band. "This was my mother's wedding ring, honey. She was about your size. If it fits, will you let me marry you with this ring?"

"Of course." She giggled, holding out her left hand, fingers splayed. "Try it."

Boyd slipped the gold band on her ring finger, finding that it fit snugly and comfortably.

"It's perfect! It couldn't be better if it had been sized for me!" Taking it off, she handed it back to him.

They kissed again, each telling the other how happy they were. Then they sat down at the table.

"We have a lot to talk about," Linda said, smiling, "but it can wait till tomorrow and the next day and the next. The coffee will be ready in a couple minutes. I think I should tell you about Peggy."

"Peggy?"

"Yes. She stormed out of the mess hall tonight, madder than a wet hornet."

"What about?"

"Well, when I tried on that black-and-white dress, Amy Snider commented that you would love me in it. I said I hoped you liked it on me. Since there was no engagement yet, I told them that you and I have a lot in common. It was then that Peggy made her stormy exit."

Rubbing his angular chin, Boyd said, "Hmm. That at least partially explains why she showed up at the colonel's office, demanding to talk to me immediately. It angered the colonel. He told her to leave. She did. Really mad."

"What now?"

"I'll talk to her tomorrow when we get back from patrol. Now that I can tell her you and I are engaged, it ought to settle her dream that I've got romantic feelings toward her."

"Poor little kid," said Linda. "It's going to hit her hard. She and I aren't what you'd call the best of friends, but I hate to see her hurt."

"She'll get over it," Boyd replied dryly. "I've tried my best to get it across to her, but she wouldn't listen. Our engagement will settle it."

The happy couple drank coffee and discussed a few wedding plans. Linda also told him she would like to begin fixing up his quarters, putting a woman's touch to the place. Boyd agreed wholeheartedly. It was going on eleven o'clock when they kissed goodnight and the lieutenant headed for his quarters. As he drew near, he saw a small form sitting in the shadows in front of his door.

Peggy's blond hair reflected light from the nearby lantern as she stood up. "Boyd, we need to talk."

"Peggy, it's late," he countered. "Do your parents know you're here?"

"No," she retorted. "I climbed out my window. We need to talk now."

Locklin took a deep breath and let it out through pursed lips. Knowing the answer, but feigning ignorance, he asked, "What's to talk about at this late hour?"

"Us!"

"Keep it down, Peggy," he said firmly. "You'll wake everybody in the fort."

Peggy's eyes bulged with anger. "If you don't want everybody awake, then you'd better take me inside!"

Keeping his own voice low, Locklin said, "I'm not taking a teenage girl into my apartment. We'll have to talk right here, but if you don't quiet down, the conversation is over. Understand?"

A pout worked its way on to her mouth. "All right."

"Okay. Now, let me tell you one more time. There is no us. I am a grown man, almost twenty-eight years old. You are a child, still in your teens. I don't want to hurt you, Peggy, and that's why I haven't just flat told you to leave me alone. You've got to unders—"

"But I love you, Boyd! And you love me!"

"I love you like an uncle loves his niece, Peggy, but I am not in love with you."

"Liar!" she screamed. "I've seen it in your eyes! I know how a man looks at the woman he loves!"

Locklin hissed, "I told you to quiet down!"

Suppressing her voice, Peggy said, "Okay, I'm sorry, but I know you are just as much in love with me as I am with you!"

"That's all in your imagination, girl," Locklin said levelly. "You've got to understand that. You're very pretty, and when you want to you can be a very sweet person. Somewhere along the line, when you grow up, there'll be a fine young man your own age who'll walk into your life and sweep you off your feet."

"When I grow up? I am grown up, Boyd! I'm far more mature than these baby-faced troopers who keep trying to play up to me."

At his wits' end, Locklin said, "Okay, okay. You're mature. But that doesn't change the fact that I am not in love with you, Peggy."

"But you are! I know you are! I've known it for a long time."

"Have I ever told you that I'm in love with you?"

"No, but I realize why. You are waiting until I'm old enough in Daddy's eyes. Then you'll come out with it and ask him if you can marry me."

"Listen to me, child," said Locklin. "How can I—"

"Don't call me a child!"

"You're getting loud again."

Gritting her teeth, she said, "You're upsetting me, Boyd. I'm not a child."

"Then quit acting like one. As I started to say, how can I be in love with two women at the same time?"

"You can't."

"Exactly."

Giving him a straight-pushing glare, she snapped, "Don't tell me you're infatuated with that redhead!"

"Not infatuated, Peggy. I'm head-over-heels in love with Linda."

Peggy's eyes bulged. "You can't be!"

"But I am. So much in love that less than an hour ago I asked her to marry me. We're going to be married on October 10."

Sudden shock flashed across Peggy's face, draining it of color. Her mouth went dry. "Th-this can't b-be true. Tell me you're kidding!"

"I am not kidding, Peggy," the tall man said in a solemn tone. "It is true. I've tried to tell you all along that I had no romantic feelings toward you, but you acted like you were deaf. It is not my intention to hurt you, but you have to face the facts. Linda and I are in love, and we are going to become husband and wife on October 10."

Peggy's features went from white to beet red. Her eyes smoldered, glaring at him like a pair of deadly daggers. Her lips curled over her teeth, exposing them like fangs. "I hate you!" Leaping at him and beating his chest with both fists, she screamed, "I hate you! I hate you! I hate you!"

Defending himself, Locklin grasped her wrists. She ejected a wild wail, demanding he let go of her. When he did, she turned and ran, screaming a string of profane words, calling him the worst names she could think of. Her voice quickly trailed off into the silence.

Locklin turned to enter his quarters when lantern light showed in the front window of the adjacent apartment. The door came open and Lieutenant Frank O'Brien appeared, carrying a lantern. "Something wrong out here, Boyd? We heard the voice of a frantic female."

"Just Peggy, Frank," responded Locklin. "She's had some far-fetched idea that I was in love with her. I've been trying to tell her for a long time that she was wrong. I just got the message through to her, and she took it pretty hard."

"You mean she hasn't seen what all the rest of us have seen since Linda first came here? It's as plain as a black wart on the face of an albino cat. You and Linda had it for each other from day one."

"She blinded herself to it," said Locklin. "I proposed to Linda tonight and she accepted. We're getting married in about three weeks. Peggy was waiting here when I came from Linda's apartment. I told her plain and straight that I'm in love with Linda, and that we're getting married. She went crazy."

O'Brien chuckled. "She's just a kid, Boyd. She'll be over it by morning." Extending his hand, he smiled and said, "Congratulations, pal! I'm really happy for you. Anybody can see that you and that redhead were made for each other."

Locklin shook his hand and grinned. "Thanks, pal. I feel like the luckiest man in the world."

"Well, I'll have to differ with you there, Boyd. I'm the one that got Edie. You're the second luckiest man in the world."

"I'd bust your nose if you felt any other way about it," said Locklin. "Time to turn in. I guess you know there's an officers' meeting right after breakfast."

"Yep. See you then."

"Okay. Good night," replied Locklin, entering his apartment and closing the door.

Peggy Halloran hurried to her house and climbed through her window. She was breathing hotly and whimpering at the same time. Murderous thoughts toward Boyd Locklin and Linda Byrnes were burning through her mind. She sat down on the edge of the bed, thinking through the adverse situation that had developed. There was only one thing to do. She could not stay in the fort and watch Boyd marry that woman. Boyd didn't care whether she lived or died, and neither did her parents. Nobody loved her. She would show all of them. Peggy Halloran would leave Fort Savage and cast herself on the mercy of the desert. Anything would be better than having to watch those two making eyes at each other all the time, knowing that they were married.

With grim determination, she made her plans. Many a morning she had risen at reveille and gone to the sentries' tower at the front gate to watch the water wagon make its way to the river. Peggy knew that there were always six or seven barrels in the bed of the wagon, and that three or four soldiers went along on horseback to help fill the barrels. They rode horses so if Indians should suddenly come riding down on them, the driver could hop on behind one of the riders and they could get back inside the fort in a hurry.

The riders always went in front of the wagon to scout along the riverbank and make sure it was safe before the wagon arrived. Peggy would climb into the wagon just before dawn and hide in one of the barrels. At just the right moment, she would jump from the wagon and dash into the surrounding brush. If luck was with her, the sentries in the tower would be scanning the surrounding desert and not see her.

Shedding her dress, Peggy put on a blouse and slipped into her riding britches. Very quietly, she struck a match and lit a candle. By its dim light, she scratched out a message on a piece of paper and left it lying on the bed. By the time her mother found the note, she would be long gone.

CHAPTER EIGHT

The eastern horizon blushed pink above the hills as two bronze faces peered toward the fort from a mesquite thicket near the San Pedro to the west.

Kateya and his friend Matoro saw three riders emerge through the gate, followed by the water wagon. They had seen the same thing every day since taking up their vigil six weeks previously. Ordinarily the daily patrols would follow within five to ten minutes.

Matoro said, "Kateya, I am really wondering if we are not wasting our time. It seems to me that the Lieutenant Boyd Locklin is no longer at the fort. Maybe he has been assigned somewhere else."

"No," said Kateya. "We have watched the fort these many weeks. He has not come out."

"But maybe he traveled at night."

"The army does not travel at night. I am telling you that he is still in there. I know it in my heart. I can feel it in my bones. The hatred toward him that burns in me tells me he is behind those walls. We will watch the fort every day until he—"

Kateya's words were cut off when he saw a strange sight. A blond young woman popped up from inside one of the barrels in the bed of the wagon as it neared the bank of the river. Unnoticed by the driver, she slipped from the wagon and dashed for the nearby brush that grew along the river. Even the men on horses did not see her.

The Indians exchanged glances. When Kateya smiled, Matoro smiled back.

"I do not know what the girl is doing out there," said Kateya, "but she must be going somewhere and does not want the bluecoats to know. She will probably hide there until the patrols have gone out, then head for wherever she is going."

Twenty minutes later, the barrels were full and the soldiers headed back toward the fort. When they neared the gate, Peggy left her hiding spot and scurried southward along the bank of the river. Periodically she hunkered in the brush, checking to make sure the sentries in the tower had not seen her. Soon she was out of sight from the fort, running hard.

Kateya watched her go, then looked back toward the fort. "Something is different today, Matoro. The patrols should have come out by now."

Matoro noted the gates swinging shut behind the wagon and nodded. "Yes. It seems they are not ready to come out yet."

"Then we have time to catch the girl!" exclaimed Kateya. "We will take her to my father. I know what he will do. He will send a couple of warriors to the fort bearing a white flag. They will offer to exchange the girl for the Lieutenant Boyd Locklin. Come! Let us catch her!"

During breakfast in the mess hall, Lieutenant Frank O'Brien had spread the news of the engagement. As the fort's officers were gathering in Colonel Halloran's office for their scheduled meeting, they were congratulating Boyd Locklin, each man saying that the engagement was no surprise.

Halloran moved behind his desk and grinned at Locklin. "You took my advice in a hurry, didn't you?"

"Well, sir, I have to be honest with you. I had already planned to propose last night before you urged me to get on with it."

The colonel laughed. "Okay. Main thing is that it's done. I'm happy for both of you. You're a lucky man, Lieutenant. She is one fine woman."

"I know, sir. Thank you."

Sitting down, Halloran ran his gaze over the five officers and said, "All right, gentlemen. Take your seats. It is time for us to talk about the capture or demise of Pantano. Personally, I prefer the latter, and I think Mr. Pantano will force us to make it his demise. I doubt it is possible to take him alive."

"As the rest of you know, I have discussed this with Captain Snider and with Lieutenant Locklin, because he is the senior lieutenant here. We have agreed that the six of us should put our heads together and come up with a foolproof plan to trap that bloody snake-in-the-grass and bring his career to an end. Once Pantano is eliminated, it will take the starch out of the rest of his bunch. It'll take them a while to come up with a new leader who can inspire them like Pantano has. In the meantime, we'll launch an offense and bring them to their knees. These horrible massacres have got to stop."

As the men were voicing their agreement in unison, the door burst open. Katherine Halloran entered, her face ghostly white. Gasping for breath, she stumbled toward her husband's desk. "Brett, Peggy's gone!"

All eyes were on her as Halloran rose. "What do you mean, gone?"

"You remember that when she didn't come out of her room to eat breakfast with us, we decided to let her sleep?"

"Yes."

"Well, after a while, I got to thinking that maybe she was sick. So I went in to check on her. Her bed hadn't been slept in, and I found this."

Katherine produced the note from her apron pocket and handed it to him. The colonel's voice strained as he read it aloud.

> Since nobody in this house really cares about me, and since the man I once loved and now hate is marrying that redhead, I have nothing to live for. I want to die. I'll do my dying alone, out in the desert.
>
> Regretfully, Peggy Ann Halloran

"There is no way she could have gotten out of the fort, sir," spoke up Lieutenant Warren Aulgur. "She certainly couldn't climb the stockade."

"She couldn't climb the stockade, I agree," responded Halloran, "but I know my daughter. She's outside the fort, all right. The only time the gate has been open since sunset was this morning when the water wagon went out. She was probably in one of the barrels."

Tears filled Katherine's eyes. "Brett, you've got to do something!"

Before Halloran could reply, Boyd Locklin was on his feet, heading for the door. Over his shoulder he said, "This is my fault. I've got to find her before the Apaches do!"

The colonel called after him, telling him to wait, but Locklin was in a run toward the stables. To the officers, he said, "Get all but forty men mounted! We can't leave the fort unprotected. I'm going too."

"But, sir," argued Lieutenant Donald Nelms, "this could result in a bloody battle. It is against army regulations for the commandant to engage in combat!"

"To blazes with army regulations!" bellowed Halloran. "That's my daughter out there!"

Fort Savage was an instant beehive of activity as soldiers scrambled about, picking extra ammunition and darting to the stables.

Just as Boyd Locklin was trotting his horse past the infirmary, Linda ran through the door, calling his name. Reining in, he looked down at her. "Peggy's running away, honey. She's somewhere out on the desert. I've got to find her before Pantano does."

Linda asked, "Is it because of our engagement?"

"Yes. She was waiting at my apartment door when I left you last night. I told her that I had just asked you to marry me, and she went berserk. Katherine found a note in her room. I've got to go now. I love you."

"I love you, too!" she called after him as he spurred his horse toward the gate. "Be careful, darling!"

The sentries at the gate saw Locklin coming at a gallop and heard him shouting at them to open it. He had to pause but briefly when he reached the gate. When the opening was wide enough, he gouged the animal's sides, putting it into a full gallop.

Remembering what Halloran had said about Peggy riding out in a barrel, he made for the river. It took him only a few seconds to find her footprints where she had left the wagon and hurried into the brush on the bank. He followed her trail for several hundred yards, then drew rein where it stopped. Reading sign, he quickly saw that two riders on horses without shoes had picked her up.

Locklin's pulse pounded in his temples as he headed west, following the trail of the riders. For some reason, two Apaches had been near the river. They were now taking Peggy to their camp. Determined to catch up to them before it was too late, he clenched his teeth and gouged the horse's sides once again.

The warming wind whistled in his ears as he pushed the animal to the limit. In his haste, he had not taken time to pick up a rifle. All he had to fight with was the army issue Colt .45 on his hip and a knife with a ten-inch blade in his saddlebags. The main task would be to take out the two Apaches without getting Peggy hurt or killed.

Peggy Halloran sat on a large flat rock in the insufficient shade of a paloverde tree at the crest of a long sweeping rise. The area was strewn with sunbleached slab rock, threaded thickets of catclaw, and a hundred more paloverde trees.

Knowing she was in the hands of the wicked Pantano, and guarded by four half-naked savages, Peggy was in a state of absolute terror. Her whole body shook violently as her breath came in rapid, irregular rasps. Her long blond hair was disheveled and hanging partially over her fear-filled eyes. She listened to the Apache chief explaining to his men that she would be held for ransom. That ransom would be Boyd Locklin.

Peggy learned that Pantano and some sixty painted-up warriors had gathered at this spot a few miles west of Fort Savage at dawn every morning for six weeks. While Kateya and Matoro hid themselves close to the fort and watched for Locklin to lead a patrol out, Pantano and his men waited to hear that Locklin was once again on patrol duty. The war party would then ambush the patrol and kill every bluecoat but Locklin. Pantano was intent on killing the lieutenant with his own two hands.

The fierce Chiricahua chief had frightened Peggy into telling him that Locklin was indeed at the fort. Her heart pumping madly and her hands clenched in tight knots, she had also revealed that the lieutenant's absence from patrol duty was due to a severe wound he had suffered while fighting Apaches the day he returned to the fort, bringing Linda Byrnes with him.

Peggy lashed herself for her impetuous, foolish act. Believing that Pantano would trick the army into giving him Locklin and simply keeping her to kill her, Peggy realized that she did not really want to die. She yearned to be in the safety of her home with her parents, and she no longer hated Boyd Locklin. She didn't even hate Linda Byrnes. She just wanted to go back to the fort.

Peggy listened as Pantano gave instructions to two warriors as they wiped the war paint from their faces. They were to ride up to the gate of Fort Savage bearing a white flag and ask to speak to Colonel Halloran. They were to tell him that Pantano had his daughter, and if he wanted to see her alive again, he was to send Lieutenant Boyd Locklin with them. If they were not back in an hour with Locklin, the girl would die. She would be kept a while longer to make sure the soldiers did not come with fighting in mind. If Halloran gave him Locklin and sent no soldiers to retaliate, the girl would be released unharmed.

One of the two warriors said to Pantano, "What if the Colonel Brett Halloran does not believe we have his daughter? Maybe he will think we lie."

Pantano grunted something Peggy could not understand as he turned and walked toward her, pulling his knife. Troubled lines etched themselves on the girl's brow and she cried, "What are you going to do?"

Grinning wickedly, Pantano said, "I am not going to hurt you." Taking hold of the ends of her hair, he cut off a thick lock and handed it to the warrior. "Show this to the Colonel Brett Halloran if he doubts you. He will recognize it."

The other messenger was tying a white cloth to the tip of his rifle barrel when another warrior pointed eastward. "Pantano! A rider is coming!"

All eyes turned in that direction. A column of dust rose up behind the man on the army bay. He was coming at a full gallop.

Moving to Pantano's side, Kateya said, "One rider comes to the girl's rescue?"

Peggy could not see for the close-knit group of Indians. Was someone really coming from the fort?

Pointing beyond the rider, Pantano said, "He does not come alone, my son. Look!"

Several hundred yards behind the oncoming man in blue was a huge cloud of dust, fronted by a large number of riders. Fort Savage's soldiers were coming in full force.

"Father, we must go to those rock formations to the south and make ready to fight!"

Raising a steady hand, Pantano kept his eyes eastward. "There is no need to take cover. There will be no gunfire. We have the girl with sunshine hair. They will not put her in danger." Turning toward the warriors who guarded Peggy, he barked, "Bring her to me!"

Peggy whimpered in fright as she was ushered to Pantano. Looking eastward, she saw the rider rein the bay to a halt in a tawny fog of dust. He was two hundred yards from her, but when the breeze blew the dust away, she could tell by the way he sat his horse it was Boyd Locklin. Tears filled her eyes.

With rough hands, Pantano seized Peggy, locked her neck in the crook of his left arm, and placed the muzzle of his revolver to her temple. An icy trickle of terror went down Peggy's spine.

"Do not try to free yourself, girl," warned Pantano, "or you will be very sorry. When the white eyes soldiers get here, they will learn that the only way they can save you is to bring me the Lieutenant Boyd Locklin."

Shading his eyes against the sun with one hand, Kateya focused on the lone rider. "Father, I think the gods have already brought you the man you want. I cannot be absolutely sure, but I believe the man who looks at us at this moment from the back of his horse is the Lieutenant Boyd Locklin."

Peggy's whimpering grew louder as Pantano squinted at the rider. "Yes! That is him! I am sure of it! Today he dies!"

When Boyd Locklin spotted the band of Apaches at the crest of the gentle rise, he quickly drew rein. The trail led straight to that spot. He was too late. The murderous fiends had Peggy. There was no way to rescue her. As the dust cloud around him drifted away on the breeze, he saw the savages looking at him. He thought of Linda. He would never see her again. There was no way he could escape the blood-hungry Indians. They would now mount up and chase him down.

He was wondering why they were not already heading for their horses when a sound met his ears. Thunder? No. The sky was clear. It was coming from behind him. Hipping around in the saddle, he saw the massive dust cloud and the blue uniformed riders coming toward him. *Colonel Halloran put that bunch together in a hurry.*

Turning toward the Indians again, he saw Peggy's blond hair

catch the sunlight. One of the Apaches had her in his grip and was holding a gun to her head. It was Pantano. Locklin knew what was coming. The savage beast would use her to protect himself and his men from the soldiers. If the warriors Locklin could see were all that Pantano had with him, they were going to be outnumbered by the soldiers who were bearing down from behind.

Locklin positioned his mount so he could easily look both directions. He wanted to keep an eye on Peggy, but at the same time be able to gauge the arrival of his companions. Pantano did not move, nor did his men. It was obvious that they felt secure with Peggy in their hands. And they were right. Fort Savage's fighting men would not engage in a gun battle with the colonel's daughter in the middle of it.

In less than ten minutes the thundering horde arrived, hauling up in their massive dust cloud. Locklin was not surprised to see Colonel Halloran leading them. All eyes were fixed on the Apaches at the top of the rise as Locklin moved up to meet his commandant. Captain Earl Snider flanked the colonel. Halloran's horse blew as Locklin said, "They've got Peggy, Colonel. That's Pantano holding the gun to her head."

"I see that," said Halloran grimly. "Any idea how many warriors he's got up there?"

"Unless some are hiding, sir," responded Locklin, "I'd say somewhere around fifty-five or sixty." Running his gaze over the mounted men in blue, he asked, "How many have we got?"

"A hundred and thirty-four, including you."

"We've got them more than doubled," put in Snider. "Pantano's smart enough to know he can't possibly come out of this one in good shape if he makes a fight of it."

"He's not planning on making a fight of it, Captain," said Halloran. "He doesn't need to. He's holding all the cards, and it's his deal."

"Too bad he's got Peggy," spoke up Lieutenant Warren Aulgur, nudging his horse a bit closer. "Otherwise this would be our golden opportunity to lay hands on the filthy beast."

"Yeah," said Lieutenant Donald Nelms, "if he doesn't have a bunch more warriors hiding close by."

"He doesn't," the colonel said, "or he wouldn't need to put a gun to Peggy's head. We've got them outnumbered more than two to one all right, but like I said, he's holding all the cards, and it's his deal."

"All we can do now, sir," said Locklin, "is go up there and see if we can't talk him into letting us have her. It's hard to reason with a savage, but he's got to know we're not going to just ride away and let him keep her."

"He does," said Halloran. "But he's got something in mind, or he would've high-tailed it out of here with her when he first saw us coming." Twisting in the saddle, he lifted his voice. "Men! You see the situation. We're going up there and try to reason with Pantano. We've got him well outnumbered, but as you can see, he's got a gun to Peggy's head. We can't bluff a bloody warrior like Pantano, so we've got to go see if we can negotiate with him. He wants something, or they'd already be miles away. Have your guns ready, but there'll be no shooting unless I give the order."

The soldiers understood. They gave a unified vocal assent to the colonel's words.

Boyd Locklin pivoted his horse around and fell in beside the colonel as Halloran led the column forward. Captain Earl Snider rode on the colonel's other side.

As they neared the summit of the gentle rise, Halloran took note that the Apache warriors who stood behind their chief in a half circle were wearing war paint. They had definitely planned on fighting somebody that day. Silent signals were made by Lieutenants Aulgur and Nelms, directing the men in blue to fan out in both directions, indicating that they were ready to fight if necessary and that they would be in an advantageous position to do so. The Apaches held their rifles ready and watched them with wary eyes.

Peggy broke into pitiful sobs as her father drew up within twenty feet of the spot where Pantano held her. "Daddy, make him let me go!" she wailed.

"Just calm down, honey," Halloran replied evenly, attempting to keep his voice steady. "Everything's going to be all right."

Pantano's fierce black eyes were fixed on Boyd Locklin, burning like hot coals. Locklin gave him a passive stare. The chief then tore his gaze from the lieutenant and looked at Halloran. The breeze ruffled his long, straight hair. Yellow war paint rode his brow beneath the dirty red bandanna and a crimson smear went from cheekbone to cheekbone across his humped nose, glistening blood-like in the morning sun. "This girl tells me she is your daughter," he said through his teeth.

"She is," the colonel replied coldly, his face a stony mask. "I have come to take her home."

There was a wolfish growl in Pantano's voice. "That can be done without bloodshed if you meet my demand." Snapping back the hammer of the revolver and pressing it more firmly against Peggy's temple, he added, "If you do not, she dies!"

Her body stiff with fear, Peggy screamed, "Daddy, help me-e-e!" She broke into uncontrollable sobs.

Before Halloran could speak, rage welled up in Boyd Locklin. His hand went swiftly to the butt of his service revolver. "You kill her, savage, and you'll get the first bullet! Right through the head!"

Pantano's hellish eyes reached Locklin once again, showing a sullen, sallow flash of hatred. "I am not going to kill her if the Colonel Brett Halloran meets my demand!"

Both groups of men tensed.

Above Peggy's sobbing, Halloran said, "What is this demand?"

"I want you to leave the Lieutenant Boyd Locklin with me and ride away."

Sharp creases sprang along the colonel's forehead. His features darkened. "You know I won't do that!"

Spacing his words deliberately, Pantano hissed, "Then…your…daughter…dies!"

Peggy wailed.

Locklin gave the chief a dead, stony look.

Halloran did not reply for a long moment. Peggy's terror was ripping at his heart, but he had to handle the situation slowly, with utmost care. Collecting one by one the exact words he wanted to use, they finally came out of him. "You would trade your son's life for my daughter's?"

Kateya's head bobbed at the threat of his own death.

Before Pantano could respond, Halloran said, "We've got you outnumbered better than two to one, Chief. If you fire that gun, my men are receiving orders right now to immediately riddle your son's body with bullets while Lieutenant Locklin blows your head off."

A suppressed fury became evident in Pantano's granite features. There was a barbaric glint in his eyes. "Kateya is not afraid to die! And neither is Pantano! You think if you open fire that you and your men can cut my warriors down and remain unscathed?"

"Of course not," came the colonel's brusque reply. "We'll have our casualties. But you will have more."

The barbaric glint grew stronger. "If a gun battle begins," Pantano said threateningly, "my warriors are receiving orders right now to cut you and the Lieutenant Boyd Locklin down first! They will accomplish it, I assure you!"

Halloran's angular jaw jutted. "Nobody's blood has to be shed, Chief, if you just let my daughter go, get on your horses, and ride."

Shaking his head vigorously, the determined Apache leader bellowed, "No! I have a personal matter to settle with the Lieutenant Boyd Locklin! Take your daughter, Colonel Brett Halloran, and you ride away. All I want right now is to settle a matter with the Lieutenant Boyd Locklin."

Locklin frowned, mumbled something under his breath, and swung his leg over the saddle. Touching ground, he pushed his hat to the back of his head and moved toward the spot where Pantano held Peggy. Halting about fifteen feet from them, he said, "What's eating at your guts, Pantano? Did it bother you so much that you left me to bake to death in the sun and I got away?"

"It is not that!" said Pantano. "You killed my only brother, Mandano! I must now kill you!"

Shrugging his wide shoulders, Locklin said, "I didn't even know you had a brother. You never mentioned it at the time you staked me out, so it had to have happened the next day, when I killed those five Apaches near that pile of boulders. Which one was he?"

Eyes blazing, Pantano hissed, "The one you shot up in the boulders! For that you must die!"

"Hey, pal," responded Locklin, "your brother was going to kill the woman who rescued me from your stakeout. I had no choice but to kill him."

Pantano's face went thunder black. A demented look captured his eyes. "You are intruders here! We have a right to kill all of you! And unless the bluecoats ride away and leave you with me, this girl will die!"

Locklin saw Pantano's finger tighten on the trigger. Peggy was pallid with terror, trembling all over, and whining in a low tone. The demented look in the chief's eyes told Locklin the man was about to go over the edge of reason.

Sensing that violence was about to explode, the soldiers all dismounted, holding their weapons ready. The dark-skinned warriors waited, nerves tight.

Breathing heavily, Pantano growled, "I am weary of all this talk. Colonel Brett Halloran, you have till the count of ten to say that you will ride away and leave this man with me. If you do not, the first blood shed will be your daughter's. One…two..."

"Wait a minute!" cut in Locklin. As the chief paused in his count, Locklin turned to Halloran, who was now standing a few feet behind him. "Colonel, he's not bluffing. I can see it in his eyes. Back me on what I'm about to do, okay?"

Halloran glanced at Captain Earl Snider, who stood a half-step behind him to his left, then looked at Locklin. "You know I trust your judgment. Yes, I'll back you."

Leveling the chief with a hard glare, Locklin said with grit in his voice, "Is the great Pantano willing to meet me on the field of honor for a fight to the death?"

Pantano's grip on Peggy relaxed slightly. "I would like nothing better."

"Then here are the terms," said the lieutenant. "You release the girl and let her go to her father. We will do battle right now. My commanding officer will give you his word that if you kill me, he and his men will take the girl and ride away. There will be no retaliation for my death on his part. By the same token, I want you to make your warriors agree that if I kill you, there will be no retaliation for your death on their part. I want their word on it."

"Their word will not be necessary, white eyes soldier swine!" boomed Kateya, his face flushed with hatred. "My father will cut you into little pieces!"

Pantano turned and frowned at his son. "When you become a man, Kateya, you will learn that there are times when it is wise to remain silent. For you this is one of those times."

The virile youth evaded his father's glare, looking only at the ground.

To the colonel, Pantano said, "I have your word as stated by the Lieutenant Boyd Locklin?"

A mixture of emotions churned wildly within Colonel Brett Halloran. He wanted Peggy safe in his arms, but he feared for Locklin's life. Boyd was the best at hand-to-hand combat at Fort Savage, but Pantano was known as the deadliest knife fighter among all Apaches everywhere. Locklin, however, had cast the die. All Halloran could do was back him. Nodding, he replied, "You have my word, Chief."

The men in blue exchanged fearful glances. They, too, had doubts that Boyd Locklin could win.

Taking the gun from Peggy's head, Pantano released her. The girl stumbled toward her father, who rushed forward and embraced her. Walking her slowly into he midst of the soldiers, he talked to her in quiet tones.

Pantano then turned and spoke to his warriors in the Apache language. In unison they nodded silently.

Lieutenant Warren Aulgur spoke up. "Wait a minute! How do we know what he said to them? We don't know what they're nodding about!"

Pantano gave him a mirthless smile. "If I can trust your commanding officer, white eyes soldier, you can trust me."

"It's all right, Lieutenant," said Halloran.

"Then we will prepare for battle, Lieutenant Boyd Locklin," the chief said firmly.

"Won't take me but a minute," nodded Locklin, wheeling and heading toward his horse.

CHAPTER NINE

A cold finger of fear was probing at Boyd Locklin's heart as he made his way to his horse. He knew Pantano's reputation as a fighter. He was fast, strong, deadly, and ruthless. He would probably attempt to cut Boyd, intending to make him a bloody spectacle before killing him.

Fighting the coldness in his chest, Locklin made up his mind he would not let himself be intimidated by Pantano's past accomplishments. The savage had killed many a bluecoat in hand-to-hand combat, but he was only a mortal. He, too, would bleed when cut, and a knife blade stuck in the right place would end his life.

Commanding his men to keep an eye on the Apaches, Colonel Halloran kept his arm around his trembling daughter and walked her to where Locklin was removing his gun and holster. He was laying them on his saddle when the colonel drew up behind him.

"Boyd, I hate this," Halloran said in a low tone.

Removing his hat and placing it over the holster, Locklin said, "I do too, sir, but it was the only way to save Peggy's life."

Peggy sniffled, clinging to her father, but did not look up to meet Locklin's gaze.

Peeling his shirt off, Locklin laid it over the saddle, then opened the left saddlebag. Reaching inside, he produced his shiny, long-bladed knife. Gripping the handle till his knuckles turned white, he turned to Halloran. "Colonel, if he wins, will you tell Linda that I love her with all my heart and that I'm sorry things worked out this way?"

Peggy's sniffling grew louder.

Laying his free hand on Locklin's bare shoulder, Halloran held his voice steady. "He's not going to kill you, son. It's Pantano's woman who'll get bad news today, not yours."

"Thanks for the vote of confidence, sir," said Locklin, trying to smile, "but I think you know the odds are on his side."

"No, I don't! You have Linda to live for. That's why I know you're going to be the victor."

Locklin looked deep into Halloran's eyes. This time managing a smile, he said, "I believe you've got something there, sir."

As he started to turn away, Peggy whispered, "Uncle Boyd?"

"Yes?" He looked down at her.

Face pinched and white, she said, "I'm sorry. This whole thing is my fault. I...I just want to thank you for being willing to gamble your own life to save mine. Especially...especially when I told you that I hated you."

"I know you didn't really mean it, kid." He reached out to stroke her tearstained cheek.

"I didn't! I could never hate you. I was just...just terribly upset."

"I understand."

"I...I don't dislike Miss Linda, either," said Peggy. "I realize she's exactly what you need. I'm sorry for the way I treated her. I hope she will forgive me."

"Knowing Linda as I do, she'll forgive you, Peggy. Don't worry about that." Taking a deep breath, he looked at Halloran. "Well, guess I'd better get this over with."

"We'll ride home together, son," Halloran said, forcing a note of confidence into his voice.

His face set in grim lines, Lieutenant Boyd Locklin nodded silently, then turned and headed for the spot where Pantano waited for him.

Locklin's fellow soldiers looked on him with the utmost admiration, realizing he was willing to pay the supreme sacrifice to save Peggy Halloran's life. He was tall, straight-backed, and physically hard. From a small, firm waistline his upper body spread upward in a V-shape, topping out with broad shoulders and a solid neck. His chest was deep and his arms were rock-hard with heavy veins riding the center of his biceps.

Though Locklin was only twenty-seven, there was a seasoned completeness about him. Men were willing to follow him because there was a driving energy that came out of him, even when standing still. As he walked toward the place of battle, the muscles in his arms and back rippled under his skin like living things. The men knew there was going to be a real fight, but they had confidence their man would be the victor.

Chief Pantano was powerfully built and was reputed to have the strength of an ox. However, as the Apaches beheld the lieutenant approaching with his physique uncovered, they were quick to silently acknowledge that their chief was going to have reason to remember this battle.

Pantano stood, legs spread, hands empty, watching his opponent drawing near. He still wore his blue sergeant's coat. It was unbuttoned and hung loosely about his middle. When Locklin stopped with some fifteen feet between them, the chief riveted him with a primitive abhorrence that was almost a tangible thing. Holding Locklin's gaze, he made a show of removing the blue coat with the sergeant's stripes and tossing it aside. The brilliant sunlight danced on the surface of his muscles.

Slowly his right hand crossed his bronzed body as he reached for the knife that rode his left hip. He whipped it out quickly and held it in a ready position. Sunlight glinted off the shiny blade. There was conviction in his voice. "I am going to kill you for taking the life of my brother, white eyes soldier."

Locklin could feel the rhythm of his heart pulsate in his temples, but he wore a facade that masked his apprehension. He would show no intimidation to the man who intended to kill him. "I took the life of your brother to save the life of a helpless woman he was manhandling, Pantano. He was going to kill her because she was white. I have nothing but contempt for a man who stoops so low as to use his brute strength to overpower a woman, then kills her for the sake of killing. No...you are not going to kill me for taking the life of your brother. I am going to kill you for what you did to three of my men six weeks ago. Since your people and mine are at war, I can accept the ambush that you put on us. I can even overlook the fact that you left me staked out in the broiling sun amid a bed of rattlesnakes, but the way you tortured and murdered those three men who survived the ambush is inhuman, inexcusable, and unforgivable. For that, I am going to kill you."

A deep scowl etched itself on Pantano's features, the blood of fury rushing up to darken them. His murderous stare remained a fixed pressure against Locklin as he shook the knife in his hand. "You talk tough, Lieutenant Boyd Locklin! Let's see how you fight!"

Locklin's mouth went dry as Pantano loosed a wild war cry and sprang toward him, wielding the deadly knife. He bent his knees, putting his weight on the balls of his feet, and timing his move, leaped aside to avoid the blade in the Indian's hand. In the brief instant it took Pantano to halt his momentum and turn back, Locklin moved in and lashed out with his own knife. The blade bit into flesh on Pantano's right shoulder.

There was an undercurrent of moans among the Apaches at the sight of their leader's blood. The men in blue exchanged glances of pleasure.

The wound was little more than a scratch, but it angered Pantano for letting the white man draw first blood. He lunged at Locklin, swinging the knife in a wide arc. The lieutenant dodged, took another swipe at his enemy, but missed also.

Pantano was fast on his feet. He came again quickly, the sun glinting off the blade of his knife. At the same time, Locklin braced himself, preparing once again to avoid the deadly weapon. Pantano surprised him by suddenly rolling on the ground and kicking his legs out from under him. The white man went down hard and instantly the Indian was on top of him, raising the knife. Locklin's jitters had passed and his natural reflexes were taking over. Twisting quickly, he threw Pantano off him and leaped to his feet.

Angered at his opponent's strength and agility, Pantano came at him again, swinging the knife. Locklin avoided the onslaught, stabbed at Pantano, and missed, then they came together in a bone-rattling collision and fell to the ground. Dust clouds billowed as they rolled over and over, mashing bristly clumps of catclaw, and finally slamming into a paloverde tree.

As Locklin rolled away, sucking for breath, Pantano lashed at him violently, but missed. The Apache gained his feet only to find that his enemy was up first. Locklin seized the opportunity to send a hard, piston-style punch to Pantano's nose. The Indian's head snapped back and the nose seemed to burst like a ripe tomato, gushing blood. Screeching insanely, Pantano countered by swinging his knife toward Locklin's throat as the lieutenant was coming in. Locklin reared back, making him miss, and lunged at him again.

Enraged by the sight of more of his own blood, the Indian evaded Locklin's blade and kicked him savagely in the groin. Locklin doubled over, the pain weakening his knees. In a flash, Pantano came back, bringing his weapon down. Before Locklin could get himself in motion, the deadly blade slashed his upper left arm.

Though it felt like a red-hot iron was burning his groin and waves of nausea were washing over him, Locklin jumped back to avoid the second swing. Pantano kept coming, showing his teeth like fangs.

The Apaches began to chant, repeating Pantano's name over and over. At the same time, Captain Earl Snider countered by doing the same thing. Instantly the men in blue were shouting, "Locklin! Locklin! Locklin!"

Boyd had successfully dodged another lunge, and now the two men were circling each other cautiously, both sucking hard for air. Both of them kept their feet wide apart, holding their knives at ready, waiting for the right moment to attack once more. Pantano's nose was streaming blood and his eyes were watery. Seeking to take advantage of it, Locklin feinted like a boxer, making it look like he was coming in hard to Pantano's left, then quickly changed his momentum and lunged at him from the right.

Pantano had it figured and met him head-on. Locklin felt the burn of the Apache knife along the left side of his rib cage and retaliated speedily by sending a powerful punch to the Indian's jaw. Surprised, Pantano went down, dazed and shaking his head. Locklin wanted to pounce on him and kill him right then, but the nausea he was experiencing was fierce, and he had to pause and let it pass. He took a second to check the wound in his side. It wasn't deep, but blood was issuing from the four-inch gash.

Pantano was up, shaking his head, breathing hard. The sight of Locklin's bleeding side gave him encouragement. The lieutenant had already proven to be a worthy opponent, but Pantano was confident he would be the victor. His normal method was to cut up his enemy before going for the kill, but Boyd Locklin's strength and adeptness were too great. He must make the kill now.

Wailing like a banshee, Pantano charged.

The sickening sensation was passing from Locklin as Pantano came at him. Ignoring the pain of his groin and the two wounds, he sidestepped the man and chopped him hard on the back of the neck as he passed. Pantano hit the ground, roared like a mad beast, and rolled over just as his enemy was coming down on him, knife poised. In a flash, he threw up a foot and caught Locklin's knife hand. The weapon flew from his grasp and landed on a flat rock a dozen feet away. Locklin's momentum dropped him on top of the Apache...but he was now without a knife.

Grappling, the two men rolled over and over, coming to a stop near the rock where Locklin's knife lay. This time Pantano came up on top. He raised his knife and brought it down, but the experienced soldier caught the wrist midair. Gritting his teeth, the Indian tried to force the knife downward. The blade quivered as they met each other strength for strength.

Peggy Halloran dug her fingernails into her father's sleeve while the men in blue shouted encouragement to their fellow soldier.

As blood from Pantano's nose dripped into his face, Locklin had a flashing thought of Linda. Her beautiful features lodged for an instant on the screen of his mind. He must return to her. They deserved to have a life together. No savage Indian was going to rob them of it.

Fresh adrenaline surged through Locklin's body, sending strength into the arm that held the blade at bay. Surprise showed on Pantano's face as his opponent began pushing the tip of the knife further from his body. Then the Indian did exactly what Locklin hoped he would. In order to put more of his weight on the knife hand, he pushed himself forward. Instantly, Locklin brought both knees up against his rump, sending him head over heels. Locklin kept his grip on the wrist, however, and using his other hand to help, twisted the knife from Pantano's grasp.

When the knife hit the dirt, Locklin grasped it. Pantano quickly whirled his body around and kicked Locklin's legs out from under him. While the lieutenant was getting up, the Indian seized the knife on the rock and laughed wickedly. "I will kill you with your own knife, white eyes!"

Leaping at Locklin, he swung the knife in a mighty arc with the intent of disemboweling him. Locklin withdrew his midsection in time to escape the hissing blade. Catching Pantano off balance, he slammed his jaw with a rock-hard fist, sending him staggering backward. Stumbling on the flat rock, the Apache landed on his back, the breath gushing out of him.

Screaming an obscenity at Locklin in the Apache language, Pantano was up on his knees before the lieutenant reached him, but too late he saw the glimmer of steel as it lashed at his face. The blade of Pantano's own knife ripped flesh and blood spattered the top of the flat rock. Shock showed in his eyes. This young lieutenant was stronger and more agile than any white man the Apache chief had ever fought. Blood welled between his fingers as he laid his free hand against the wound.

Panic struck Pantano. He must kill Locklin this instant or be killed himself. As he was rising to his feet, a powerful fist knocked him flat. He felt the sting of the knife tip as it slashed his face a second time.

The Apaches showed their horror with gasps and moans. Kateya blinked twice, swallowing hard, unable to believe his eyes. He had watched his father fight many a white man, but never had one given him this kind of battle.

Boyd Locklin could hear his fellow soldiers shouting for him to end it. One voice, louder than the others, was bellowing, "Cut him into little pieces, Lieutenant! Cut him up good!"

In desperation, Pantano rolled to his feet and bolted toward his enemy, shrieking wildly. His adrenaline still surging, Locklin attempted to evade the wicked blade, but stumbled slightly and took a nick on the upper chest. Lashing back, he cut the Indian's chest almost in the same place, then knocked him to his knees. From his kneeling position, Pantano lunged and drove his knife into Locklin's left thigh.

The lieutenant winced, sucking air through his teeth. His knees buckled as the Apache yanked the knife out, ready to stab him again. Countering quickly, Locklin bent over and whipped the bloody knife across Pantano's face, slicing through the bandanna. The tip of the blade gouged into his right eye. A scream escaped his lips. The bandanna clung to his long hair for an instant, then fell to the ground. His face was a mass of shiny crimson.

The Apache warriors were beside themselves, their horror growing, but they dared not interfere. The bluecoats, who outnumbered them more than two to one, would open fire. Not only that, but they knew Pantano would rather die in honor than live in dishonor because his warriors had had to rescue him.

Pantano wiped blood from his good eye and stood swaying, ready to meet the onslaught that was surely coming. His back was toward his own men, but everyone on the U.S.-army side saw the hideous bright-red furrow running from the scalp line on the left side of his head, across his brow, to the tip of the ear, leaving a gory, blood-filled crater where his right eye had been.

In a frenzy, Kateya was shaking both fists, screaming at the top of his voice, "Kill him, Father! Kill the white eyes swine! Kill him! Kill him! Kill him!"

Pantano was breathing hard, bent forward like he was leaning into a heavy wind. Mortal hatred burned like brimstone within him toward Boyd Locklin. The despicable white man had not only killed his brother, but now he had taken Pantano's right eye. His mouth curved down into brutal lines, and there was a terrible intensity in his remaining eye. No man had ever come near to besting him in hand-to-hand combat. Lieutenant Boyd Locklin must die.

Locklin was limping toward him, knife ready. Summoning every ounce of his remaining strength, Pantano charged forward to meet the hated white soldier, hoping the leg wound would render him vulnerable enough to be overpowered. All the Apache chief wanted was the chance to drive Locklin's knife into his heart.

Both men swung their knives and missed.

As Pantano was steadying himself for another thrust, Locklin quickly took advantage of him now having a blind side and chopped him with a left hook. Pantano staggered, swinging the knife in his hand blindly, hoping to strike flesh.

As he avoided the dangerous blade, Locklin saw an opening. Ignoring the fiery pangs in his wounded leg, he moved in and rammed the knife through the bicep of Pantano's left arm all the way to the hilt. Six inches of the blade appeared on the other side. The Apache leader wailed in agony. Blood spurted from the wound as Locklin jerked the knife out.

Ejecting a scream like a cornered beast, the Apache took another blind swing with the knife. Determined to end it quickly, Locklin dodged the blood-smeared weapon and unleashed another left hook, dropping Pantano flat on his back.

A loud babble of voices filled the air from both sides. The Apaches were cursing Locklin by their gods and the army people were erupting with vociferous shouts as they smelled the sweet aroma of victory.

Spitting blood and gasping for breath, Pantano looked up at his hated enemy. Locklin was standing over him, mouth hanging open, breathing raggedly. Naked determination glinted in his eyes.

Pantano struggled to rise, knowing that for him hope was an island about to be overcome by the tides of reality. His white eyes opponent was the better man and was going to kill him.

The knife in Pantano's hand felt like it weighed a ton. Gripping it tight, but knowing he had not the strength to use it, he came to a kneeling position, swaying dizzily. Pride toward his conqueror would drive him to stand up and face him at this moment.

Boyd Locklin hovered over the Apache chief, favoring his wounded leg. He observed Pantano as he groped his way to a standing position, his left arm hanging limply from the shoulder like a bloody piece of rope.

It was time.

Locklin limped two steps and thrust Pantano's knife into his belly full-haft, growling with a hiss, "This is for Clay Harris!"

The Apache jerked, blinking his eye and gritting his teeth. His knees buckled and he started to go down. Locklin locked his neck in the crook of his free arm, holding him up. He felt the warm wetness of the Indian's blood flowing over the hand that held the knife. Yanking the blade out, he plunged it in a second time. "This is for Barry Fender!"

The Apaches were in shock and had gone silent. To an Apache, his war chief was almost a god, a man invincible. The core of their great fighting prowess was the outward courage and charisma of their leader. Without such a man, their will to engage war fell to a low ebb.

A pink foam appeared at the corners of Pantano's mouth and his body was going limp. Quickly, Locklin pulled the knife out and thrust it in the belly a third time. "This is for Jake Ford!"

Pantano's single eye was turning to glass. Jerking the knife out again, Locklin breathed heatedly, "And this is for me!" With one powerful thrust, he drove the full length of the blade straight into

Pantano's heart and let him fall. He went down like a rag doll, collapsing in a heap. He was dead.

A rousing cheer went up from the men in blue.

Lieutenant Boyd Locklin's mouth was as dry as the sand he stood on. His chest was heaving as though he could find no room in his lungs for the air he needed. His wounds burned like fire while an enormous weariness flowed its cold way through his muscles. Leaning over, he pried the handle of his knife from the dead Indian's fingers, then thought of lovely Linda as he limped toward his fellow soldiers.

The stunned warriors stood in silence, waiting for Locklin to put distance between himself and Pantano's lifeless form. Kateya observed the painful movements of Boyd Locklin as he limped toward the other soldiers, who had not broken rank. They would wait for the lieutenant to come to them. Kateya's face was rigid and black with rage and his nostrils flared rhythmically. There was a demonic look in his eyes as he whipped out his knife, released a primal wail, and charged at Locklin.

Peggy Halloran screamed, "Uncle Boyd, look out!"

Pain lanced his wounded leg as Locklin wheeled to meet his attacker. He saw the devil in Kateya's eyes. Bracing himself, he let the relatively inexperienced youth come at him full charge, then timing it perfectly, eluded the knife thrust and banged Kateya's forearm with his left fist. The blow was hard enough to knock the knife out of his hand. Howling with pain and shaking his arm, Kateya cursed Locklin. The urgency for reprisal still having its way with him, the maddened youth reached down, scooped up the knife, and lunged at Locklin again.

Though Kateya was like a demon, Locklin was not willing to kill someone so young. Switching his own weapon to his left hand, he made a fist with his right. It hurt his bad leg to do it, but he sidestepped Kateya, dodged the knife, and unloaded a potent haymaker on his jaw. The young warrior went down like a dead tree in a high wind and lay still. He was out cold.

Leaving Kateya for his companions to worry about, Locklin limped to the men in blue. Peggy ran to him, embraced him, and wept as she expressed her relief that he was still alive. The men joined in, offering their congratulations. When Peggy stepped away to stand beside her father, Locklin looked at Captain Earl Snider. "Since you've got the medical supplies, Captain, see what you can do to patch me up till somebody a lot prettier than you can work on me."

Lieutenant Donald Nelms laughed. "This is only my opinion, Lieutenant Locklin, but I don't think Doc Philips is any prettier than our esteemed captain!"

There was a round of laughter as Snider went to his saddlebags, shaking his head.

The sun hung at its zenith in a faultless cobalt sky as Linda Byrnes left the mess hall carrying a meal tray. She glanced toward the gate as if her willing it would bring the large unit of blue uniformed riders in from the desert.

Entering the infirmary, she carried the tray to a small table beside the bed occupied by young trooper Wally Frye, who had broken his ankle that morning. "How's the cast, Wally?"

"Feels fine, ma'am," replied Frye. "Doc Philips did a good job. The ankle doesn't hurt so much now."

"Well, maybe it'll feel even better when you get some of this split pea soup in your tummy." She handed him a napkin.

"Tummy!" he echoed, chuckling. "I haven't heard that word since I was a kid. Ma always called it my tummy."

"I guess mothers have a vocabulary all their own."

"But you're not a mother yet."

"Guess I'm just practicing." She smiled and handed him a spoon and the steaming bowl of soup.

Thanking her, Frye said, "Guess you're practicing on how to worry like a mother too, huh? At least that's how it is with Ma. She worries a lot over me. Kinda...kinda like you're worrying over Lieutenant Locklin right now."

Brushing a lock of deep red hair from her forehead, she said, "Am I that obvious?"

"Mm-hmm."

"You understand, Wally, I'm worried about Peggy too."

"Of course, ma'am," he replied, dipping the spoon into the soup. He blew on the spoonful, then put it in his mouth. "I think it's just great about you and the lieutenant getting engaged. Even though there's a lot of worrying goes with being a soldier's wife, I think you'll do just fine, ma'am. I can tell...you've got what it takes."

"I sure hope so. I love that man an awful lot. I just don't know what I'd do if anything happened to him."

"He'll be all right, ma'am." Wally grinned, taking another spoonful of soup. "Men like Lieutenant Locklin have a certain something about them. He's a survivor." Downing the soup, he said, "Yep, he's a survivor. Just like my dad."

"Is your father in the military?" asked Linda.

"Mm-hmm. He's captain at Fort Butler up north. Been through all kinds of scrapes, fights, and battles with the Apaches but he always comes through them. Ma worries herself silly, but I've told her never to despair when Pa's out fighting Indians. They may draw some of his blood, but Pa will always come riding back to the fort. Yep, Lieutenant Locklin's just like Pa. He's a survivor."

Linda knew there were some men like that. They seemed to lead a charmed life. It was as though the Lord above had a special reason for letting them live through untold dangers and close scrapes with death, when it appeared impossible for survival. She prayed it would be so with the soldier she was going to marry.

Linda's thoughts were interrupted when the infirmary door came open. Lieutenant Frank O'Brien said, "Miss Linda, you wanted me to let you know when the troops were coming back. They're about a mile out."

Her brow pinched. "Can you tell anything yet?"

"Yes'm. With binoculars we can make out Peggy's blond hair."

"Oh, that's wonderful! You can't tell—"

"No, ma'am. But we'll be able to shortly. Let's go."

Seeing the fear in his nurse's eyes, Wally Frye said, "He'll be with them, Miss Linda. Alive. I'm sure of it. Like I told you...Boyd Locklin is a survivor."

Linda looked at Frank O'Brien. "Wally's right, ma'am. You should get Boyd to tell you all about his narrow escapes in the six years he's been here. You saw a couple of them yourself. He's a survivor, all right."

Linda excused herself to her patient and hurried out the door in front of O'Brien. They hurried to the west side of the fort and found that the sentries had already opened the gates. Dashing up to the opening she stopped and focused on the cluster of men and horses that were coming toward the fort. She could already make out Peggy Halloran's blond hair shining in the midday sun. As she shaded her eyes and squinted to look for the lieutenant, a sentry in the tower called down, "He's with them, ma'am."

Swinging her gaze up to the sentry, she saw a pair of binoculars in his hand. "You're sure?"

"Yes, ma'am. He...ah...he is not sitting his horse like normal. Seems to be hunched over. I'd say he's been wounded."

Tears filled Linda's eyes. "The main thing is that he's alive! And...and if he can ride at all, it can't be too bad."

Pacing back and forth between the gateposts while the column drew nearer, the redhead kept repeating, "The main thing is that he's alive."

When they were a hundred yards out, Linda could see that Boyd rode between Colonel Halloran—who had Peggy on his horse in front of him—and Captain Earl Snider. She was unaware of Katherine Halloran approaching from behind her as she lifted her skirt calf-high and began running toward the column. She could see Boyd looking at her. When he lifted his hand to wave, she cried, "Boyd! Oh, Boyd! You're alive! I love you! I love you!"

CHAPTER TEN

Lieutenant Boyd Locklin's wounds were efficiently treated by Dr. Harry Philips, and soon he was on the mend. The excellent care he received from Linda Byrnes expedited his healing.

The two were wed on Sunday, October 10, 1858, with Colonel Brett Halloran officiating and the entire population of Fort Savage attending. Peggy Halloran was maid of honor at Linda's request, and Captain Earl Snider stood up as best man.

Lieutenant and Mrs. Locklin were superbly happy, falling deeper in love with each passing day.

In the months that followed Pantano's death, his band of bloodthirsty warriors seemed to have disappeared from the face of the earth. Other bands of Chiricahuas kept Fort Savage's men busy as they attacked travelers and settlers, making life miserable for white people in Arizona Territory. When the men brought up the subject of Pantano's warriors around the fort, Colonel Halloran told them that the vicious band was no doubt holed up somewhere, and would surface when they came up with a new leader.

Much of Colonel Halloran's attention was centered on news of developments back east, where the slavery issue was becoming a sharp point of division between the northern and southern states. The matter was becoming serious and Halloran discussed each bit of news that came on the subject with his officers.

When a newspaper from Washington, D.C., arrived, quoting one politician as saying that the slavery issue could bring on a "second American Revolution," there was cause for alarm among every man and woman in the fort. Many of the soldiers did not understand the issues, and asked for an explanation from Colonel Halloran. At an evening meeting in the mess hall—with only the necessary sentries missing—Halloran stood before the crowd and gave an informal address on the entire subject, allowing his hearers to interrupt him with questions.

Halloran began by pointing out that the United States of America was beginning to be looked upon by other nations as a world power, that in their eyes it was the epitome of democratic ideals. Indications of prosperity were abundant. Well-to-do families in the larger cities were installing indoor privies; plans were in the works for a railroad all the way to California; and the United States would soon build a transatlantic cable to Europe. The growing threat of a rift in the Union over the slavery controversy was putting the country's progress in jeopardy.

When asked about slavery's beginnings in the United States, the colonel pointed out that it developed slowly in the late eighteenth century as the country found itself following divergent paths due to geography and climate. These two factors began shaping radically different economic and social patterns in the North and in the South. In the upper Atlantic regions, the terrain was rocky and laden with rough, uneven land. The interior was heavily forested and difficult to access. The winters were long and often quite severe, making agriculture a task for only the very hardy. These conditions tended to build up large bodies of population along the coast with many northern settlers becoming seamen, fishermen, ship builders, merchants, and most of all, industrialists.

In the South, the terrain and climate favored the agrarian way of life. Level land, rich of soil, was plentiful and accessible because the coastal plain extended well inland and the rivers were navigable year-round. The warm weather, the long growing seasons, and the great stretches of flat terrain were perfect for the plantation system—a method of large-scale farming that employed great numbers of unskilled workers. Cotton, tobacco, rice, and sugarcane plantations were in abundance and needed workers in order to function.

As the nineteenth century came, plantation owners saw too much of their profit being devoured by the money they paid the laborers, though the scale was quite low. They learned of slave traders who would bring in slaves from Africa and the West Indies. Once the plantation owners had made the initial investment, there would be little output. The slaves could be fed and housed quite cheaply. Since in other countries of the world slavery was regarded as a legitimate means of maintaining a low overhead, and the Constitution of the United States recognized slaves as a form of chattel, they knew it would work in this country. Thousands of Negroes were brought in on ships from Africa and the West Indies.

As black slavery spread in the South during the early years of the nineteenth century, opposition to it spread in the North. By mid-century Washington politicians who feared a split between the North and the South fashioned careful compromises to resolve sectional disputes. However, the plain fact of the matter was that Northerners and Southerners had become so different—so stubbornly incompatible and antagonistic—that no amount of political ingenuity could avail.

So it was that the United States in late 1858 was sitting on the proverbial powder keg. In spite of the Southern plantation owners issuing heartrending statements that they could not stay in business without slave labor, opposition to slavery prevailed in the North. The Northerners called it "degrading and immoral," caring nothing about the plantation owners' plight.

In the South, the commitment to slavery was now inalterable. It did not matter that only one-fourth of the families actually owned slaves. Southern white people were firmly convinced that their own livelihood, their Southern traditions, and indeed their own personal safety amid four million Negroes all depended on preserving and extending the use of slave labor.

And now to make matters worse, a fanatical abolitionist named John Brown was commanding a band of men who were going about, freeing slaves in Kansas. President James Buchanan had mildly called for Brown's arrest, but Northerners could see through it. Buchanan's weak-kneed compromise last April in calling for Congress to give Kansas statehood, though the territory was proslavery, had resulted in the Democratic Party being split. As a result, the Republican Party had been born.

Congress was in a cold war with itself. Heated debates over John Brown's actions were taking place daily in the assembly. Tempers were flaring and Congressmen on both sides of the issue were swearing at each other, almost coming to blows. Matters grew worse when in October it was learned that Senator Henry Wilson of Massachusetts and Senator William Seward of New York knew of a scheme by Brown to raid the U.S. arsenal at Harpers Ferry, Virginia, and had done nothing to stop it. Though the raid never took place, Congressmen from the South wanted the senators thrown out of office. When it did not happen, a broader wedge was driven between the two sides of Congress.

The latest newspaper from Washington, D.C., that had come into Halloran's hands reported that John Brown had taken his militia into Missouri and was freeing slaves there. Though President Buchanan assured the proslavery men of Congress that he was trying to stop Brown, they refused to believe him. There was even talk of Southern states seceding from the Union.

When asked by his men what all of this could mean, Colonel Halloran's eyes grew misty as he declared his fears that a civil war could very well be in the making.

In early January 1859, Dr. Harry Philips confirmed to Boyd and Linda Locklin that Linda was with child. The baby would be born about the first week of September. The Locklins were elated. The news added even more spark to their marriage and their love grew ever stronger and deeper.

On September 6, 1859, Steven Boyd Locklin was born, adding more joy to the Locklin household.

There were continued skirmishes between the men of Fort Savage and the Chiricahua Apaches because of the Indians' attacks on white settlers and travelers, but as yet nothing had been seen of Pantano's vicious warriors.

In early November, Colonel Halloran received an eastern newspaper that carried the story of John Brown's raid on Harpers Ferry with his small army on October 16. After reading the entire paper, Halloran called the occupants of Fort Savage together and brought them up to date. United States marines had been called to Harpers Ferry to put down Brown's attempted seizure of the town, and after the marines had killed all but four of his men, they stormed the building where Brown was holed up and captured him. The marine commander was Lieutenant Colonel Robert E. Lee of the Second United States Cavalry.

In January 1860, Halloran gathered his people together once

more and read them the newspaper account of John Brown's hanging. In Charles Town, Virginia, on December 2, 1859, Brown was taken from his cell to the place of execution as a great crowd looked on. On the way to the scaffold, he handed a guard a final note which read, "I, John Brown, am now quite certain that the crimes of this guilty land—making slaves of human beings—will never be purged away but with blood."

With a somber look on his face, Colonel Halloran spoke his conviction that Brown's words seemed to be prophetic. A civil war could hardly be avoided. A cloud of gloom hung over Fort Savage in the days that followed.

News of ominous national trouble continued to find its way to Arizona Territory. On February 27, 1860, an up-and-coming Republican politician from Illinois spoke to a large crowd of New York Republicans in New York City. He was lecturing to the cream of the state's intellectual and political society, men of power and financial means. Addressing slavery as a moral issue, the tall, slender, self-educated man denounced the practice, saying it was dreadfully wrong, a denial of American principle that all men were created equal.

"The South," declared Lincoln, "will only be satisfied when the free states recognize slavery as being right. Can we cast our votes with their view, and against our own? If sense of duty forbids this, then let us stand by our duty fearlessly and effectively. Let us have faith that right makes might, and in that faith, let us, to the end, dare to do our duty as we understand it."

Lincoln received a standing ovation for his speech. In the months that followed, his popularity among Northerners snowballed, and in October, he won the Republican nomination. Abraham Lincoln seemed destined for the White House.

Southern newspapers braced the people for the anticipated victory of Lincoln, sounding the secessionist battle cry. An Atlanta journal declared, "We regard every man an enemy to the institutions of the South who does not boldly state that he believes African slavery to be a social, moral, and political blessing."

The *Charleston Mercury*, in a vitriolic attack on Lincoln, branded him "the beau ideal of a relentless, dogged, free-soil Border Ruffian, a vulgar mobocrat and a Southern hater."

Another southern newspaper proclaimed with burning words, "Rather than submit to such humiliation and degradation as the inauguration of Abraham Lincoln, the South will see the Potomac River crimsoned in human gore, and Pennsylvania Avenue paved ten fathoms deep with mangled bodies."

Charleston, South Carolina, was becoming the hot spot of the South. Election Day was set for Tuesday, November 6. On Monday, November 5, the *Charleston Courier* came out with the eye-catching headline: "IF LINCOLN IS ELECTED, SOUTH CAROLINA WILL LEAD BOLDLY FOR A SOUTHERN CONFEDERACY!"

Though outpolled in the popular vote by over 900,000 votes, Abraham Lincoln won the electoral vote by carrying all the highly populated northern states except New Jersey. Secession of the southern states was inevitable. On December 20, 1860, Charleston was overflowing with enthusiastic Southern patriots as the entire government of South Carolina gathered for a secession convention. At 1:15 P.M. on that day, South Carolina voted unanimously to secede from the Union. The state's elected officials signed an ordinance reading:

> *We the people of the State of South Carolina, in Convention assembled, do declare and ordain that the union now subsisting between South Carolina and other States, under the name of The United States of America, is hereby dissolved.*

Thus, Charleston needed only one spark to explode into war...one spark in a city loaded with firebrands.

On February 26, 1861, Lieutenant Boyd Locklin was playing with his son on the floor of the apartment while Linda was washing dishes. Little Stevie, who would soon be a year-and-a-half old, was giggling and squealing as his father held him down, tickling him playfully. Linda looked on and smiled, happy that her two men enjoyed each other so much.

Laughing with the little tyke, Boyd grasped him with both hands, rolled onto his back, and held Stevie above him, rocking him back and forth vigorously. Suddenly Stevie burped, spraying Boyd with a small amount of the food he had swallowed only moments earlier.

As Boyd set him down and wiped at the food, Linda said, "Maybe you boys should not be so vigorous so soon after supper."

The lieutenant chuckled. "Yes, Mother."

The redhead looked down at her son. "Boyd, I declare, that boy is you all over again. I see it more every day. Not only does he have your blue eyes, your skin texture, your dark curly hair, and your facial features—he also has your little idiosyncrasies."

"You're making me angry, telling me all these things," Boyd said, releasing his crooked grin. "What do you mean, he's got my little idiosyncrasies?"

"He laughs like you do. He's developing that slanted, mischievous grin like yours, and he's ticklish just like you are."

"Well, in that last idiosyncrasy, he takes after you too."

Placing her hands on her hips, she threw her head back. "Oh no, he doesn't! I'm not ticklish."

Bending over and ruffling Stevie's hair, Boyd said, "You hear that, son? Your mother says she's not ticklish. Let me show you that she doesn't always speak the truth."

With that, Boyd lunged and seized Linda with both hands. She laughed while he wrapped one arm around her, holding her tight, then began tickling her rib cage with the other. Stevie giggled, clapping his hands and enjoying it while his mother squirmed and laughed.

Suddenly the tickling stopped and so did Linda's laughter. The lieutenant and his wife were looking into each other's eyes. Stevie wasn't surprised when they kissed over and over again. He was used to it. He saw it happen many times whenever his father was home.

There was an abrupt knock at the door. Still holding Linda tight, Boyd sighed, "Always something to interrupt my love life."

The knock was repeated quickly.

"We'll take up where we left off when we get rid of whoever this is."

Opening the door, the lieutenant was surprised to see Colonel Brett Halloran. Removing his campaign hat, the colonel smiled. "I need to see you, Boyd. Official business."

"Yes, sir," said Locklin. "We can go over to your office."

"I can talk to you here."

Picking Stevie up, Linda said, "I'll take the baby into the bedroom so you two can talk."

"Oh no," spoke up Halloran. "I…ah…I need to talk to both of you."

"Oh? Well, Boyd, invite the colonel in."

Grinning and shaking his head, Locklin said, "I'm sorry, sir. Please come in."

While the men sat down at the kitchen table, Linda took her son to the bedroom and closed the door. The bedroom was well-supplied with homemade wooden toys donated by the soldiers who ran the fort's wood shop.

When she returned, both men stood while she took her seat, then sat down. Halloran was at one end of the table and Locklin at the other. Linda sat between them.

"Well, sir," said Locklin, "what is this official business?"

Extracting an official-looking brown envelope from his coat pocket, Halloran replied, "I have orders from Washington to leave Fort Savage and report to army headquarters there by April 1. An army dispatcher just arrived with these twenty minutes ago."

Boyd and Linda exchanged sorrowful glances, then Boyd looked at Halloran. "I don't like this, sir. Life won't be the same here at Savage without you. Why do they want you in Washington? It's not this war thing, is it?"

"Afraid so," said the colonel. "Letter here says Jefferson Davis was sworn in as president of the Confederate States of America on February 18. It is definite that the Southerners are gathering arms. Lincoln is to be sworn in on March 4. The top military men in Washington are expecting that the Confederates will declare war anytime after that. They're inducting men into the Federal Army all over the northern states. My orders are to report to General Winfield Scott, whom you know is general-in-chief. I'll be taking Katherine and Peggy with me. They will stay with some of Katherine's relatives in St. Louis."

Face pinched, Linda said, "I hate this, Colonel. Both your ladies have become my closest friends."

The colonel sighed. "That's the way military life is, dear." Turning his attention back to Boyd, he said, "Actually, I've been corresponding with Washington on this matter for six months, but I haven't told anyone in the fort about it because there was really nothing definite to tell. But with these recent developments, there's no question this country's in for a civil war. So, of course, these orders are no surprise. I've been given a brevet promotion to brigadier-general in the Union Army of the Potomac. They don't really expect the war to last very long, but there's a chance I'll keep the rank when it's over."

"Congratulations, sir."

Linda echoed the same words, wondering what was coming next. Halloran had some good reason why he wanted her in on the conversation.

Pulling the folded papers from the envelope, the colonel said, "Earl Snider is being promoted to colonel and will be commandant here."

"I'm glad for that, sir. Captain Snider deserves it."

Adjusting himself on the chair, Halloran cleared his throat. "There's more here, Boyd. Your name is included in these orders." As he spoke, the colonel unfolded the papers, flattening them out on the table.

"My name, sir?" said Locklin, glancing at his wife.

Linda smiled and silently mouthed, *Promotion! Captain!*

Boyd grinned broadly, then turned back to Halloran.

"Yes. You are also to receive a promotion."

Linda smiled with pride.

Her thoughts jumbled when she heard the colonel say, "You will soon be Major Boyd Locklin."

Boyd's jaw slacked and his head bobbed. It took him a few seconds to find his voice. "Major? But sir, the army hasn't been assigning majors to these western forts. I don't understand."

Linda waited for Halloran's next words.

"Excuse me, Boyd," said the colonel, "I should have said brevet major. You see, by my request, you are going with me. I'll be heading up a division in the Army of the Potomac, and you'll serve under me as commander of a brigade. As you know, brigades are headed up by both majors and colonels. I have told you before that I like your style. I have the utmost confidence in your fighting ability and the way you lead men. I told this to the big brass in Washington, and they granted my request." Shuffling through the papers, he extracted a sheet and handed it to Locklin. "Here, see for yourself."

As Boyd took the sheet, Linda left her chair and stood behind him, looking over his shoulder. While they read it silently, Halloran said, "See? You will be given the promotion the day you report to General Scott's office in Washington."

"I see that, sir," said Locklin, handing the paper back to the colonel. "But isn't this highly irregular? I mean, a man has to be a captain before he can be a major."

"Not in wartime," said Halloran. "The army won't have an abundance of capable officers. We've got to work with what we've got. As you just read, General Scott has taken my suggestion and agreed to make you a brevet major because you've got the experience in combat. You're the best, and I'll be mighty proud to have you as a leader in my division."

"Thank you, sir."

Linda laid her hands on Boyd's wide shoulders. He felt a slight trembling in them. The thought of her husband being away from her an undetermined amount of time was objectionable. "But, Colonel Halloran," she said, her voice tight, "I don't want to stay here with Boyd gone…and your family gone, too."

"You won't have to," Halloran replied quietly. "You can go with Boyd and live somewhere close by. Even though his promotion is brevet, the government will pay for your housing. Our command base is near Washington, but it could get pretty dangerous around there. I would suggest you make your home a bit farther north. I understand that some army officers are putting their families in York, Pennsylvania. I suggest the same for the Locklins. You and Stevie would be safe there, yet close enough that Boyd could come and see you periodically. And like I said, they really don't expect the war to last very long."

Reaching back and grasping Linda's hands in his own, Boyd squeezed them firmly. "We can handle that, sir. I'm very honored that you think this much of me." Turning to look at his wife, he added, "And I'm sure Linda feels this way, too."

"Yes, of course. It will be much better if Stevie and I are near Boyd. And I thank you for your confidence in my husband, Colonel."

Halloran ran his fingers over his mustache. "Look at it this way, too. There's a very good chance that when the war is over, the brevet will be dropped, Boyd, and you'll remain a major at a major's pay. That'd be okay, wouldn't it?"

"Sure would, sir," responded Locklin. "Again…thank you."

"You're quite welcome. I'm looking forward to having you command a brigade in my division. I hope there'll be more men just like you leading the troops."

"You'll never find another man quite like Boyd, sir," said Linda with conviction. "Of course, this is his wife speaking. So when do we head east?"

"Within a week," came the reply. "We'll have an army escort all the way to St. Louis. I'll leave my family there, and the rest of us will take a train to Washington. You and Stevie can stay in a hotel for the first couple of days while Boyd is commissioned and briefed, then he can take you to York. He can get you settled in your home, then he'll need to be back in Washington to help train the enlisted men."

Colonel Halloran thanked Linda for being a good army wife and left. The Locklins embraced, each sharing their mixed emotions. They were happy at Fort Savage and did not want to leave, but they were also excited about Boyd's chance to hold the rank of major permanently.

CHAPTER ELEVEN

On Friday, April 5, 1861, a horse-drawn army wagon rounded the corner of Sixth and Mulberry Streets in York, Pennsylvania. Two men in dark blue uniforms were in the seat. The corporal, who held the reins, said, "It's supposed to be 631 Mulberry, Sergeant."

"Yeah. That's right over there...the small white one between those two big two-story ones."

Inside the small white house, Linda Locklin finished packing her husband's large canvas bag and tied it at the top with leather thongs. As she turned to leave the room, her eyes went to the framed photograph of her husband. On his second day in Washington, the army had taken the photograph of Boyd in his major's uniform for their records. A copy had been given to Linda, which she quickly put in a frame.

Linda picked up the frame, looked at the handsome face in the photograph, and held it close to her breast. After a long moment, she set the picture down, wiped away the tears that brimmed up in her eyes, and left the room.

Major Boyd Locklin had just finished polishing his boots at the kitchen table and was pulling on the second one as Linda walked in. Stevie was in his high chair, eating a home-baked cookie.

Rising from the chair, the major looked at the woman he loved. "It's almost noon. They'll be here any minute. You know how the army is—always on time."

Linda closed the gap between them and Boyd folded her in his arms. They kissed; then she laid her head against his chest. "Oh, darling, if I only knew when you'd walk through that door again. Being separated from you is hard enough, but the real tough part is not knowing when you'll be back."

"Shouldn't be too long. If the Confederates don't start the war shortly, I'm sure I'll be able to come home soon."

At that moment the rattle of a wagon met their ears as it rolled to a halt in front of the house. He kissed Linda's forehead. "That'll be my chariot. I'll be back as soon as possible, sweetheart."

"Hopefully the experts are right and this whole thing will be over soon."

"It will," he replied grimly. "As far as I'm concerned, the sooner the better. The quicker it starts, the quicker it'll end."

There was a knock at the screen door. Releasing Linda, Boyd hurried to the door. Noting the stripes on the man's sleeve, he said, "Just about ready to go, Sergeant. Wait right here."

"Yes, sir," came the sergeant's snappy response.

Linda leaned on the frame of the kitchen door and watched her husband dash into the bedroom and return with the canvas bag. He handed it to the sergeant, telling him he would be out in a moment; then gathered Linda into his arms again. Tears glistened on her cheeks. They kissed several times. "I'll miss you and Stevie like fire, honey."

"We'll miss you, too," she responded, sniffling. "Please take care of yourself. I need you. Your son needs you."

"I will." He hurried into the kitchen and lifted his little son from the high chair. He hugged him tight, told him he loved him and to be a good boy. Setting him back in the high chair, he returned to his wife. They kissed again, long and sweetly, then he was out the door.

The sergeant had placed himself in the bed of the wagon, leaving the seat next to the driver for the major. Boyd Locklin climbed in and looked back as the wagon did a complete turn in the street and headed in the direction from which it had come. Linda stood on the porch, holding Stevie. Her face shining with tears, she told Stevie to wave to his daddy and waved herself.

Major Boyd Locklin, rough and rugged officer in the Union Army of the Potomac, struggled to swallow the hot lump that burned his throat and fought tears as he waved back.

On Thursday night, April 11, 1861, Major Robert Anderson stood behind the parapet on the west wall of Fort Sumter, South Carolina, and looked toward Charleston, some three miles across the harbor.

His meager force of sixty men stood with him. Through the thin mists that curled and twisted over the water like silky ghosts, they looked at the orange light reflecting off the low-hanging clouds. Many huge bonfires were burning all over Charleston, casting dancing shadows on the buildings and throwing light toward the sky. The excitement and patriotic passions that had been building up since secession in December were now at a fevered pitch. Noisy parades snaked through the city's streets, drums rolled, bands played, and people shouted. Anderson and his handful of Union soldiers were trapped on the tiny island, and every one of the excited Southerners in Charleston knew it.

A proper and taciturn man in his late forties, Anderson had been appointed as commander of three Federal forts in Charleston Harbor the day after Abraham Lincoln's election in early November, 1860—Fort Moultrie, Fort Castle Pickney, and Fort Sumter. United States Secretary of War, John B. Floyd, had appointed Anderson to the post because of the determination and devotion to duty that he had shown as an officer in the Mexican War.

Anderson and his sixty men had arrived in Charleston in late November. The major soon saw that his force was spread too thin to protect the Federal forts from Confederate invasion. He sent a message to Secretary Floyd immediately, asking for more men. When the return message told him there were no men to spare, that he would have to make his defense with the forces that he had, Anderson had only one sensible course of action. He must move all his men and as much equipment as possible on to one island and abandon the others. Since Fort Sumter was best situated for defense and by far better equipped for fighting, he would fortify there.

Under cover of darkness on December 26, the Union soldiers ferried their gear to Sumter. At sunrise the next morning, the crowds in Charleston saw smoke rising from the two abandoned islands. Major Anderson's men had burned all the wooden gun carriages, leaving the cannons inoperable for Confederate use. When the secessionists saw the Stars and Stripes being raised on the mast atop Sumter's ramparts, they realized that the fort was then fully garrisoned.

Major Robert Anderson's situation was brought to the attention of President Abraham Lincoln, who was made to realize that the men in Fort Sumter would need supplies. Lincoln sent a messenger with a letter to South Carolina's governor, explaining that he was sending a ship to his men at Fort Sumter with supplies, stressing the peaceful intent of the mission.

The governor, expecting treachery, contacted President Jefferson Davis in Montgomery, Alabama, asking what he should do. Davis sent a message back, saying he would send Brigadier General P. G. T. Beauregard to take command of the Charleston post. The decision whether to allow the supply ship to deliver goods to Fort Sumter would lie with Beauregard.

When Beauregard arrived and learned that the commander at Fort Sumter was Major Robert Anderson, he made allowance for one small boat to be sent if the ship would remain outside the harbor. Anderson had been Beauregard's artillery instructor twenty years earlier at West Point. The two had become friends in later years and it grieved Beauregard that Anderson was now his adversary. Anderson, however, was unaware that his old friend was now Confederate commander at Charleston.

Though he allowed the small boat to carry food and supplies to Fort Sumter periodically, Beauregard worked feverishly to complete his artillery buildup. By early April he had brought overwhelming strength to bear on Fort Sumter. Long range cannons and high trajectory howitzers had been set up at Fort Moultrie on Sullivan's Island, at Fort Johnson on nearby James Island, and at Cummings Point on Morris Island. Sumter was surrounded with massive artillery power.

On April 10, the Confederate secretary of war telegraphed Beauregard that he was to demand Fort Sumter's immediate evacuation. If Anderson did not comply, Beauregard was to take appropriate military action.

As Major Anderson and his men saw the sights and heard the sound coming from Charleston, one of the soldiers stepped close to Anderson. "Sir, I think some kind of aggression is about to begin. We've watched the Southerners load those three islands with artillery for over a week. Nothing more has been shipped in since yesterday. With what's going on in Charleston right now, it seems to me whatever those Rebels have got planned is about to take place."

The others turned their attention to their commander as Anderson nodded slowly. "I've been thinking the same thing, Hobbs."

"What are we going to do, sir?"

"Our duty," said Anderson. "We were sent here to hold on to Union property. We had no choice but to abandon Moultrie and Castle Pinckney, and now we have no choice but to defend Sumter and the flag that flies over our heads."

Another soldier swallowed with difficulty. "I think I know how Travis, Bowie, Crockett, and those other men felt at the Alamo."

No one commented, but all remembered the hopeless situation of the gallant men at the Alamo who died under the guns and bayonets of the Mexican army almost twenty-five years ago.

Anderson's men tried not to show their fear, but it was so strong, it permeated the cool night air around them. Trepidation was gripping the heart of the commander, but for the sake of his men, he masked it.

Turning to his captain, Anderson asked, "What time is it?"

The captain produced his pocket watch, struck a match, and used the glow of the flame to read it. "Twenty minutes after nine, sir."

Thanking him, the major mused a moment, then said to them all, "The usual time in war to launch an attack is at dawn. If the Confederates are ready to begin hostilities and they hold to tradition, we've got about seven hours to wait. However, if they decide to break tradition, they—"

"Boat coming!" cried one of the soldiers, pointing west.

The eighteen-foot Confederate boat was rounding James Island, which stood between Fort Sumter and Charleston, and bearing directly toward them.

"Shall we man the guns, sir?" asked a youthful corporal.

"No need. When they're ready to unleash on us, it won't be from a harmless craft like that one. Apparently someone wants to talk."

Leaving fifty-seven men in the fort and taking his three officers with him, Anderson walked down to the wharf by the orange glow and met the boat as it drew up. There were seven Confederate soldiers aboard. Two manned oars at the bow and two at the stern. In the center sat three officers.

"Good evening, gentlemen," Anderson said in a friendly tone. "To what do we owe this visit?"

The oldest officer stood up in the bobbing boat. "I am Colonel James Chesnut, serving under Brigadier General Pierre Gustave Toutant Beauregard, Confederate commander at Charleston. And you are Major Anderson, I assume?"

Surprise showed on Anderson's face. "Pierre Beauregard? I know him well. We are old friends. Yes, I am Anderson."

"The general told me you were his artillery instructor at West Point," Chesnut replied. He then introduced the colonel and captain who accompanied him.

Anderson introduced his captain and two lieutenants. "I still don't know why you gentlemen are here."

Chesnut asked his two officers to help him onto the wharf, then as they stood beside him, he withdrew an envelope from his coat. "I have been instructed by General Beauregard to deliver this message to you."

Anderson asked his captain to strike a match so he could read the message. It took him only seconds to read it. As he folded the paper and placed it back in the envelope, the captain inquired, "What does it say, sir?"

"It's an ultimatum. We must leave the fort at once or be fired upon."

"I must have your answer, major," spoke up Chesnut.

Face set in a grim mask, Anderson replied, "The answer is a flat negative, sir. We have been sent here by our superiors to hold what is Union property. We gave up Moultrie and Castle Pinckney reluctantly, but we will not leave Sumter."

Indignation darkened Chesnut's features. There was a sudden heat in his voice. "You had better think this over, Major! A stubborn, foolish act on your part could catapult this divided land of ours into a civil war!"

"Not unless you people fire the first shot!" Anderson bit back. "President Lincoln has solemnly declared that if there is war, you Southern boys will have to start it."

"Do you want it written down in history that Major Robert Anderson's foolishness brought on a bloody war between the states?"

"Foolishness?" echoed Anderson. "You are a soldier, Colonel! You are telling me it is foolishness to obey orders and refuse to surrender property that belongs to the Union?"

Chesnut stood silent for a long moment, obviously unable to answer Anderson's question. Wiping a palm over his face, he said, "All right, I need your reply in writing. Please put it on the back of General Beauregard's letter."

Nodding silently, Anderson took a pencil stub from his coat pocket, removed the letter from the envelope, and hastily wrote his reply. He signed it, "Your friend, Robert."

Anderson and his officers stood on the wharf and watched the Confederates row the boat toward Charleston. When they were out of earshot, the captain asked, "What do you think, Major? Will they bombard us?"

"I think they will, eventually. Maybe not yet, but they want a war. Sooner or later they will fire the first shot."

The major and his officers returned to the fort and satisfied the curiosity of the rest of the men. They were noticeably nervous about the situation. One of the soldiers asked, "Major, is there not some way to preserve our honor, yet not have to die? If they bombard us, certainly we will all be killed."

Anderson bent his head and rubbed the back of his neck wearily. "We are soldiers, Corporal. When we are given orders, it is our duty to obey them. My orders are to avoid a clash if honor permits. If not, I am to defend this enclave by strength of arms." Pausing a moment, he ran his gaze over the dim faces of his men. "I think Colonel Chesnut will be back. If I know my old friend Beauregard like I think I do, he will give me one more chance to bend under his pressure. If I don't, at least he can tell himself and the whole world that he was as long-suffering as a man in his position should have been. This would throw heavier blame on us if the war is started here."

The captain queried, "Are you going to do something different if he comes back, sir?"

"Yes. It could be that Secretary Floyd, who gave me my orders, might change his mind if I get a message to him, telling him that surrendering Sumter to the Confederates would put no blight on our honor if it postpones the inevitable bloodshed for a while. I'll need a couple of days. We'll just have to wait and see if Chesnut comes back, and if Beauregard will give me the time I need."

About half of the men were sleeping when in the wee hours of the night, the Confederate boat was seen coming again. This time, Major Anderson sent his captain and two enlisted men to the wharf with instructions to invite Colonel Chesnut and his men inside the fort. The men at the oars remained in the boat as Colonel James Chesnut, along with the same officers who had been with him before, entered the fort.

Major Anderson and his lieutenant sat at a large round table in the stone-walled room that served as the fort's mess hall. A lantern glowed at the center of the table. When Chesnut and his companions were ushered in, the Union officers stood. Anderson gestured toward the chairs that surrounded the table, telling them to be seated.

Anderson and Chesnut sat opposite from each other, their weary faces showing the strain they were under. Chesnut leaned his elbows on the table. "General Beauregard sent me with his authority to tell you that he will give you this final opportunity to evacuate the fort. You've had some time to think it over. I am asking you again...will you comply?"

"I cannot disobey my orders, Colonel," came the level reply. "However, if General Beauregard will give me time to communicate with the secretary of war, I will see if he will change the orders. I will need until the fifteenth. In the meantime, we will not fire our guns unless fired upon, or unless I detect some other act of hostile intent that would endanger the fort. Those are my terms."

Below a neatly trimmed mustache, Chesnut's lips made a long, firm line. "I, also, have orders, Major. If you do not agree to load your men in your boats and follow us to shore immediately, I am to issue you a solemn message."

"I need time, Colonel," insisted Anderson, his eyes holding Chesnut's gaze.

The Colonel's features hardened. His voice was stern. "You cannot have the time, Major."

Anderson's officers felt the grim reality of the moment when they saw the resolute look in his eyes and the tight, uncompromising set of his jaw. An embittered sense of futility flattened his words. "Then I must tell you that we are staying to defend this fort, Colonel James Chesnut."

The colonel pushed his chair back and stood up. Immediately

the rest of the men rose to their feet. The lantern light cast shadows on the upper part of Chesnut's face, making his eyes dark pits. "Very well. Then by the authority of General Beauregard, I have the honor to hereby notify you that our Confederate batteries will open fire on Fort Sumter in one hour." Looking at his pocket watch, he added, "It is now three-thirty."

Anderson rounded the table and extended his hand to Chesnut. As the colonel met his grip, Anderson said, "If we never meet in this world again, Colonel, God grant that we may meet in the next."

Sixty-one Union soldiers stood at the ramparts and watched the Confederate boat skim across the dark water and disappear. At four o'clock they heard the bells of St. Michael's church in Charleston peal out the time.

At 4:25 there was a slight hint of gray breaking on the eastern horizon. Major Anderson stood under the Stars and Stripes at the flag pole. "All right, Union soldiers: man your guns."

It was precisely 4:30 A.M. when the boom of a big gun rocked the harbor. Instantly the men at Fort Sumter tracked the shell by its burning fuse as it rose upward from Fort Moultrie, arcing toward Sumter.

One of the Union soldiers, who stood ready to fire his own cannon, said to the major, "It looks like a giant firefly, sir."

CHAPTER TWELVE

The dreaded Civil War was now a reality.

The Confederates had fired on Union property and had drawn first blood. The newly inaugurated president of the United States reacted swiftly. The Union army had only 15,000 men. Lincoln published a proclamation calling on the northern states to furnish 75,000 volunteers immediately. Throughout the North, men responded quickly to the president's call with wild enthusiasm. During the next few weeks, militiamen mustered, patriotic rallies were held, and the North prepared for conflict.

War fever also swept the South. People were crying for an attack on Washington, D.C., and the extermination of "Black Republican" government. Southerners, elated by the easy victory at Fort Sumter, hailed General P. G. T. Beauregard as their first national hero.

In Virginia, an army was building speedily under the capable leadership of Major-General Robert E. Lee, who until April 18 had been a colonel in the Union army.

As the weeks passed, and the number of eager fighting men swelled, Lee soon divided his Confederate Army of Northern Virginia into two powerful units: the Army of the Potomac, under Brigadier General P. G. T. Beauregard, and the Army of Shenandoah, under General Joseph E. Johnston.

In the three months that followed the attack on Fort Sumter, there were skirmishes all over northern Virginia, especially in the western part of the state. A few hundred men were killed on both sides, and many hundreds wounded. Military leaders of both the Union and Confederacy knew that there were large battles in the offing, wherein thousands would be killed and wounded in single encounters. Just where and when the first big one would take place, no one was sure.

By mid-July, Abraham Lincoln's call for volunteers had produced an army of well over 150,000 troops. The Union army, under the leadership of General Winfield Scott, was being set up in three fighting units: the Union Army of the Potomac, the Union Army of the Tennessee, and the Union Army of the Ohio.

The Union Army of the Potomac was divided into two units: one under General Scott himself, and the other under Major General Irvin McDowell. Scott's troops, numbering some forty thousand, were camped on the Maryland side of the Potomac just outside Washington. McDowell's unit of thirty thousand men was situated in the hills of northern Virginia, high in the hills known as Virginia Heights, overlooking Bull Run Creek.

Federal spies reported to General Scott that Lee's army was still growing, but they had no idea how many men he had. Scott was sure the Confederates had at least as many men as the Union did, and feared that they might have a good many more. Expectations that the war was going to be short were fading fast.

General Winfield Scott, a hard and tough seventy-seven-year-old veteran of the Mexican War, divided his unit of the army into six corps, numbered One, Two, Five, Six, Nine, and Twelve. Major General William B. Franklin headed up Six Corps, of which the Third Division was under the command of Brigadier General Brett Halloran. *A* Brigade in Third Division was commanded by Major Boyd Locklin.

Locklin worked several hours every day training the new recruits in hand-to-hand combat, using bayonets, knives, and fists. He even taught them the art of rock-throwing in case the need should arise.

On July 18, 1861, Locklin ate supper with the other officers of Third Division, then excused himself, saying he needed to write a letter to his wife. Going to his private tent, which stood next to General Halloran's, he paused outside for a moment and let his gaze travel the length of the camp. White canvas tents stood in long, even rows in the open meadows, some even running into the wooded areas a hundred yards from the bank of the Potomac.

The western sky was purple and fading as the dying day gave way to the night. Small fires winked in the gathering darkness where soldiers were heating water in galvanized tubs to wash their clothes.

It was a warm evening, and innumerable crickets were tuning up for their nightly concert.

A group of young recruits some thirty yards away were doing their wash together and telling jokes. Locklin felt a cold, icy ball settle in his stomach. *Enjoy yourselves now, boys,* he thought. *There'll be no joking when you're watching each other bleed and die in battle.*

Entering the tent, Locklin removed his campaign hat, tossed it on the cot, and fired a lantern. Sitting down at a small table that General Halloran had procured, he took paper and envelope from a large brown folder and picked up a pencil. His heart was heavy with loneliness as he placed the date at the top of the sheet and wrote:

My darling Linda,

I received your sweet letter of July 2 this morning. I suppose it is taking my mail just as long to get to you. I am glad you and "Little Boyd"—as you call him—are doing well. There are no words to tell how very much I miss you both. My hopes for being able to come home before this war breaks into big battles have been dashed. Lee is pushing more and more troops into Virginia, and we all know things are going to get hot soon.

I'm still occupied every day, teaching these boys (and I do mean boys!) how to handle themselves in man-to-man fighting. Some of them are not much more than children.

We know now that it will take longer to end this war than President Lincoln first thought. I'll be so glad when it's over and we can get back to our normal lives. I will no doubt be assigned to a western fort again, since I am an experienced Indian fighter. At least I can come home to you every night again.

Take care of yourself and our little son. My love for you grows stronger each day. Remember, you are the very heartbeat of my life.

Yours always,
Boyd

Locklin was addressing the envelope when a familiar voice called his name from outside the tent.

"Yes, General, please come in."

Brett Halloran stepped inside, holding the flap. "Big powwow, Boyd. General Franklin wants to meet with the two of us in his tent pronto."

Standing, Locklin licked the envelope and sealed it. Picking up his hat, he said, "Let's not keep the big brass waiting."

On the way to Franklin's tent, Locklin posted his letter with the sergeant in charge of mail, telling him jokingly to see that it got to his wife before Christmas.

Major General William B. Franklin was a lean and somewhat handsome man in his early fifties. Though his thick head of hair and bushy mustache were once quite dark, they were now almost totally white, contrasting pleasantly with his dark blue uniform. Greeting both men with a warm smile, he invited them to sit down in front of his crude field operations desk. He seated himself behind it. Two lanterns lighted the tent, hanging on vertical poles.

Leaning on the desk, Franklin set his eyes on Locklin. "Major, I have been observing your work with the men. You're doing a great job. I like the way you carry yourself. Your friend General Halloran here keeps telling me of your adept handling of the Indian situations that you faced in Arizona."

Releasing his crooked grin, Locklin glanced briefly at Halloran. "The general sometimes adds a little flourish to his stories, sir."

"I doubt that." A serious look framed his features as he said, "I've got a job for you, Major. It will also involve a few of your choicest men. There'll be some risk, but by orders of General Scott, the job must be done."

"I figure risk goes with being a soldier, sir."

"That's the kind of attitude I expected from you. You're the man for this job, all right. I wanted General Halloran here for this, since he is commander of your division."

"I appreciate your confidence in me, sir," said Locklin. "What's the job?"

"As you know, I pointed out in a briefing last week that Lee has placed twenty thousand men on the Potomac about twenty-five miles south of Washington and he has also put about twelve thousand troops in the lower Shenandoah Valley."

"Yes, sir. General Beauregard heads up the Potomac division and General Johnston is commander of the Shenandoah division."

"Correct." Franklin nodded, pulling a map from the desk drawer. "I understand you were born and raised in these parts."

"Right here in Maryland, sir. Over by Hagerstown."

"You acquainted with the Manassas area in Virginia?"

"Somewhat. I never got over there very much."

Placing the map on top of the desk so it was right-side-up to Locklin and Halloran, Franklin used a pencil tip as a pointer. "Right here at Manassas Junction is where Beauregard is bivouacked. He has all twenty thousand out in the open on purpose. It's a show of strength."

"Yes, sir."

"See the railroad markings there?"

"Mm-hmm."

"It's called Manassas Junction because the Manassas Gap Railroad from Shenandoah Valley meets the Orange and Alexandria Railroad from Gordonsville. Beauregard's forces are right there on Bull Run Creek where the tracks intersect. He's positioned there because the railroad is strategic for the Confederates. You know that General McDowell has his thirty thousand men in the hills overlooking the area. General Scott believes that our first big battle could take place right there, and I agree with him."

"Since there's so much manpower—both Union and Confederate collected right there," said Halloran.

"That's it," said Franklin. "Now here's what General Scott is thinking. If we do get into a battle at Manassas Junction and if we can manage to defeat Beauregard there, the first thing Lee will do is load his forces in the lower Shenandoah on the trains and come at us with guns blazing. We will have been in battle, but the Rebels from the Valley will be fresh. It could be our undoing."

Locklin ran his finger across the map, tracing the railroad line from its starting point at Manassas Gap along its thirty-mile stretch eastward to Manassas Junction. Without looking up, he said, "I know what my job is, sir."

Franklin winked at Halloran. "Tell me."

"I see several streams crisscrossing the land between these points.

Every one of them has to have a bridge where the railroad crosses it." He looked up at Franklin. "I think General Scott wants some bridge work done."

Franklin eased back in his chair and smiled. "You are quite correct. The general figures only one has to be knocked out."

Locklin grinned. "The biggest one, right? The one that spans the Rappahannock River just east of Manassas Gap."

"Good thinking, Major," said Franklin. "What we have to do quickly is to come up with the best plan to destroy the bridge. I like dynamite. We have some here in the camp. Take as many men as you think you'll need and blow the bridge to smithereens."

Locklin put the tips of his fingers to both temples, thinking. After a brief silence, he said, "General, that could be dangerous. We know Johnston's got his army somewhere in that area. The noise could bring a thousand angry Rebels on us before we could get out of there. I don't want my men getting killed."

"You have a better idea?"

"Yes, sir. Why don't I take a dozen men in on horseback in the dead of night? We'll use axes and saws and just weaken the struts so the bridge will collapse the first time they run a train on it. If it's loaded with troops, so much the better. We'll get a whole bunch of birds with one stone, so to speak."

Smiling, Franklin looked at Halloran. "What do you think of this kid? He's got some smarts. Chances are that the Confederates are camped close enough to hear dynamite explode, but far enough away that they'll never hear axes and saws."

"He'll probably make colonel before this war's over," said Halloran with a smile. "That is good thinking."

"How soon does General Scott want this done, sir?" queried Locklin.

"Tomorrow night. Take the dozen men you choose and ride out of here at daybreak. You're looking at forty to forty-five miles from here to the bridge. You'll have to keep to the lowlands and stay below the ridges. Traveling like that, it'll take you till dark to get there. Once you're in the area, use the darkness to check for an enemy camp. If you find one too close, follow the track eastward and weaken the next bridge. Just be sure you're a long way out of the area before dawn. Understand?"

"Yes, sir," snapped Locklin, military style.

"I will expect a report the minute you get back."

"You'll have it, sir."

As the sun was setting on the afternoon of July 18, Linda Locklin carried Stevie out the front door of the house and walked across the neighbor's yard to the north. Seventy-year-old widow Maude Stillwell was sitting in her rocking chair on the front porch of the large two-story house. When Stevie spotted the gray-haired woman, he pointed and jabbered indistinguishable words excitedly.

Mrs. Stillwell smiled from ear to ear, clapped her hands, and rose from the chair. "Oh, there's Granny Maude's boy! Let me have him."

Stevie gladly went to the widow, hugging her neck. To Linda she said, "I suppose it's too near suppertime for my boy to have a C-O-O-K-I-E."

Linda laughed. "You grandmas! If we mothers didn't watch you close, you'd spoil our children rotten! Yes, Granny Maude, it is too near suppertime for your boy to have a you-know-what. But supper is why I'm here. I noticed day before yesterday that a young woman moved in with you. Is she an army wife?"

"Yes," said Maude, carrying Stevie to her chair and sitting down. Gesturing to an identical rocker next to her, she said, "Take a seat, dearie."

Linda obeyed. "Where's she from?"

"Albany, New York. Her name's Anna Nelson. Her husband is in the war, just like yours."

"They don't have any children?"

"No. Anna works as sort of a nurse, taking care of that rich banker, Harvey King. He's retired now, but he still owns controlling stock in the Penn Bank and Trust here in York. He needs special care, and for that matter, his wife Althea isn't too well either. Mr. King's all stove up with arthritis. Althea's still able to get about, but time's gonna catch her one of these days. She'll soon be eighty-four." After a pause, she added, "You said supper is why you're here. I don't understand."

"Well," replied Linda, brushing a fallen lock from her forehead,

"I noticed yesterday evening that your new tenant came home about this time and I thought I'd come over and invite the two of you for supper. I'd like to meet her since we both have army husbands and army loneliness in common."

Maude grinned. "That's very thoughtful of you, dearie. I'm sure Anna will appreciate that. She does talk a lot about missing her husband. But you two girls don't want an old widow boring you. I can fix my own supper."

Linda reached over and patted Maude's arm. "Now we'll hear no more talk like that. Stevie and I want Granny Maude for supper, too."

At that moment, Linda saw the pretty brunette coming along the street. "There she is now."

Maude introduced the two young women and they liked each other immediately. Maude explained to Anna why Linda was there, and Anna quickly volunteered to help her cook supper. Maude said she would keep Stevie with her and bring him over when supper was ready.

After freshening up a bit, Anna entered the Locklin house and pitched in with supper preparations. While they were working, Linda asked, "Where is your husband stationed, Anna?"

"Ken is in northern Virginia. He's with the Eleventh New York Fire Zouaves. You know, the bunch with the bright-colored uniforms."

"I've hear about them."

"The Zouaves have been assigned to the Union Army of the Potomac unit commanded by General Irvin McDowell. So all I know is they're in northern Virginia. Where is your husband?"

"Boyd is in the Union Army of the Potomac also. As a major, he commands a regiment under General Winfield Scott in Maryland."

After discussing their husbands, the tragedy of the country in a civil war, and the fears they shared about becoming widows, Linda said, "Granny Maude tells me you're a nurse."

"Not exactly," replied Anna. "I've had a little training in medicine, but I'm not a real nurse. I was lucky to land the job taking care of Mr. King. I've offered to cook for them also, but dear Mrs. King wants to do it as long as she's able. I really can't blame her. Getting old has to be hard."

Linda told Anna of her own experience in medicine, also without the benefit of a nurse's degree. Their interest in each other deepened immediately, finding they had even more in common.

When supper was over, Maude Stillwell went home to retire for the night. After the dishes were done and the kitchen was cleaned up, Stevie was put to bed. The young army wives sat up and talked till late. Finally, Anna said, "Honey, I've got to get home or I'll meet myself coming out of the house at sunrise, heading for work."

Linda accompanied her to the front porch, asking how far she had to walk to work. Anna replied that the King house was in the snooty neighborhood five blocks east.

Just before leaving, the brunette thanked Linda for inviting her for supper, then embraced her, saying she wanted to become good friends. Linda agreed, remarking that they needed each other.

The full moon was clear-edged and silver-white against the deep blackness of the night.

Major Boyd Locklin and eight of his twelve men huddled in tall grass at the top of a small hill, overlooking the railroad bridge that spanned the Rappahannock. The river wended its way southeastward, looking like a silver ribbon in the moonlight.

Locklin glanced at the dozen and one horses they had tied to bushes at the bottom of the hill, then looked back at the bridge, which stood a hundred and fifty yards away. He turned to Lieutenant Avery Baird. "The shadows are so heavy under the bridge that I can't tell how thick the struts are, but from here I'd say we need to work on the beams and struts in the middle. I'd say the bridge is about seventy feet across, wouldn't you?"

"Yes, sir," said Baird. "If we can weaken it so it collapses when the engine is halfway across, it'll drop the rest of the train in the river."

"Wish I could be here to watch it go," said trooper Jerry Kuhns.

"Would be fun," said trooper Cy Henderson.

"Hey! Here come Weymouth and Lynch!"

All eyes turned eastward to watch two figures running across a grassy meadow. When they were still a hundred yards away, someone said, "Major, Casey and Yarrow are on their way, too."

Locklin ran his gaze due west to see Corporal Hal Casey and trooper Pete Yarrow threading their way swiftly down a steep slope, moving in and out of the shadows of the trees.

Sergeant Dan Weymouth and trooper Stan Lynch arrived first. Puffing, Weymouth said, "No Confederate camps in that direction, Major."

"Good." Locklin turned his attention back to the two men coming from the west.

The major knew there were no enemy camps to the north, for they had come from that direction. The long, sweeping valley to the south was open country and revealed no Rebels for as far as the eye could see in the bright moonlight. There was a high, treelined ridge to the west. Locklin would know about it in a few moments.

Bending low as they left the trees and came into open meadow, Casey and Yarrow ran hard and soon drew up. Casey said, "Major, there's a large Rebel camp on the other side of the ridge about three quarters of a mile."

"We figure, sir," gasped Yarrow, "it's a good half-mile from the top of the ridge to the bridge. That puts the camp better than a mile away. They'd sure hear dynamite explodin', but they ain't gonna hear us choppin' and sawin' from that distance...especially with all those trees in between to soak up the sound."

Locklin took out his pocket watch, angling it toward the moon. "Okay, men, it's 11:20. Let's set our goal to do the necessary damage by 2:00. That'll get us out of enemy territory by sunup. Let's go."

Major Boyd Locklin and Lieutenant Avery Baird each carried an ax and wore his sidearm. The rest of them carried an ax or saw in one hand and a .52 caliber Sharps single-shot breech-loading carbine in the other.

The rippling waters of the river met their ears as they reached the bottom of the slope. They were within thirty yards of the wooden structure when a voice underneath it shouted, "It's Yankees!"

Suddenly guns roared, flashing orange in the deep shadows under the bridge. Locklin was commanding his men to get down when he heard Pete Yarrow grunt and saw him fall. Hal Casey was directly in front of Locklin. A slug plowed through Casey's head, spraying the major's face with blood just as he was whipping out his

Colt .44 service revolver and starting to belly down.

Casey flopped flat on his back as if someone had struck him violently in the face with a club. Wiping the dead corporal's blood from his eyes, Locklin triggered a shot. Bullets were buzzing like angry bees and striking sod all around them as the surprised Union soldiers flattened themselves and returned fire, aiming at the powder flashes in the black void beneath the bridge. Across the moonlit distance a man screamed and staggered into view, toppling in a heap.

While firing his revolver rapidly, Boyd Locklin realized that the Confederate leaders had thought of the bridge too, and had sent men to protect it from sabotage. He hoped they were few in number.

The deadly Confederate volley lasted only until every weapon had been fired. There was an abrupt silence under the bridge, but some of Locklin's men had already reloaded their carbines and were firing their second round. It was evident that the Rebels had muzzle-loading muskets, and were in the comparatively lengthy process of reloading. Locklin knew that was the time to attack, but hesitated because he couldn't see his enemies in the inky shadows. "Keep shooting!" he shouted to his men while breaking the Colt open and punching out empty shells. "They've got muzzle loaders!"

Suddenly there was a Rebel yell, and eight men in gray came charging into the moonlight, wielding muskets fitted with bayonets. Hearing Locklin's words, they would not waste further time ramrodding the muskets. They would attack the Yankees with cold steel.

Three Rebels went down under Union fire, then all the shooting ceased. Boyd Locklin was not finished reloading, and now would be denied the time to do it. Dropping the revolver in the grass, he grabbed the ax he had been carrying and stood up. From the corner of his eye, he saw Lieutenant Avery Baird lying face-down and still on the ground a few feet to his right.

The other Federals, realizing there was not even time to reload their single-shots, leaped to their feet. Some had axes and others gripped the barrels of their carbines to use the weapons as clubs. As they braced themselves for the bayonet onslaught, fortune was with them. They outnumbered the men in gray more than two to one.

The clash was fierce as the enemies came together. Confederate bayonets licked hungrily for Yankee blood and moonlight glinted off

Union ax blades as they hissed in wide arcs, chopping into Rebel flesh.

One wiry Rebel lunged straight at Locklin, his sharp-pointed bayonet thrust forward; his eyes live as coals; his teeth showing in a grimace of determination. The major could hear the clatter of weapons, the grunting and cries of soldiers in mortal combat as he skillfully dodged the bayonet. The Rebel skidded to a halt, cursed, and came at Locklin again; eyes narrowed against the little devil points of light shining out of them. "You die, Yankee!" He lunged full-speed.

Locklin could still feel the wetness of Hal Casey's blood on his face, and the thought of it pulsed adrenaline through his veins. Timing his move by past battle experience, he evaded the hungry bayonet and swung his ax savagely as the Rebel stumbled past him, driving the heavy blade into his left shoulder. The rebel screamed, dropped the rifle, and fell. Locklin pulled the ax free, turned the blunt end forward and brought it down full force against the man's head. It made a sickening sodden, meaty sound, crushing the skull.

The major's attention went quickly to the conflict around him. He heard a blood-curdling scream and saw that a Confederate had trooper Stan Lynch pinned to the ground with his bayonet through Lynch's shoulder. It was Lynch who was screaming. Locklin darted at the Rebel, swung his ax, and caught him flush in the rib cage. The ax head buried itself deep. The Rebel ejected a cry and collapsed. Leaving the ax in his body, the major turned his attention to Lynch, who lay on his back with his free hand gripping the musket, attempting to remove the bayonet from his shoulder.

Locklin was vaguely aware that there were no more battle sounds as he said, "Here, Stan, let me have it." With an abrupt jerk, he pulled the bayonet free, then looked around to see that all the Rebels lay on the ground. Breathing hard, his men looked at him. Some of them had nicks and cuts, and their uniforms were ragged.

Speaking to Sergeant Dan Weymouth, Locklin said, "Take care of Stan, will you?" Even as he spoke, he was counting those on their feet and searching for his own men among the fallen.

There were four Yankees down besides Stan Lynch: Lieutenant Avery Baird, trooper Pete Yarrow, Corporal Hal Casey, and a trooper named Wally Teeter. As he knelt beside Avery Baird, who lay face-down, he said to the others, "Make sure every one of those Rebels is dead. Check under the bridge."

As Locklin turned Baird over, the lieutenant's hat fell off. The dead man's face was an alabaster mask in the moonlight. He had taken a slug through the right side of his forehead. His eyes were open and empty, like those of a fish on an iced slab. The night breeze ruffled his hair, blowing wisps across his pale brow.

Locklin thought of the men who had died under his command in Arizona Territory. A nauseous feeling washed over him. He would never get used to losing his men.

There was a sudden cry from the deep shadows under the bridge. "Major! Rebels coming from the camp!"

One of the other men swore as Locklin swung his gaze westward to see a swarm of gray uniforms topping the tree-lined ridge in the moonlight and barreling down the steep slope toward them. The sound of gunfire had alerted the Confederate camp. He saw no horses. They were all on foot.

Scooping up his revolver and holstering it, Locklin shouted, "Head for the horses! We can make it! They're all afoot!"

Dashing quickly to where Sergeant Dan Weymouth was using a dead Rebel's shirt to bandage Stan Lynch, the major said, "That'll have to do, Sergeant. I'll carry him."

"Let's both carry, sir," suggested Weymouth. "It'll be faster that way."

"Okay," nodded Locklin, looking around to make sure the rest of his men were heading northward. As they picked up Lynch cradlestyle, Locklin said, "I hate to leave those bodies behind, but we don't have a choice."

"You're right about that!" agreed Weymouth as they headed up the slope, bearing their wounded comrade.

When they reached the crest of the hill, Locklin looked back. The wild, yelling Rebels were almost to the river. Some were stopping and firing their muskets. Hot lead balls were plowing into the hill just below where Locklin and Weymouth stood, but the muskets lacked the range to find their targets.

Hurriedly they bore the bleeding Lynch down the slope to the bushes where the horses were tied. The other men were already mounted. Weymouth hoisted Lynch onto his horse and swung up behind him, telling him to hold on.

Locklin leaped into his saddle and led his men at a full gallop across meadows strewn with wildflowers, through moon-shaded woods, and over grassy fields toward Maryland and the Potomac.

CHAPTER THIRTEEN

The late afternoon sun was casting long shadows across the lazy Potomac on July 20 when Major Boyd Locklin and his weary, bedraggled men rode into the Union camp. They were surprised to see that Six Corps' twenty-six hundred men were busy packing up, getting ready to move out.

As Locklin's group halted at the hospital tent to turn the wounded Stan Lynch over to the medical staff, Locklin saw General Brett Halloran hastening toward him. Leaving his saddle, Locklin told his men to get something to eat, then go to their tents for some much needed sleep.

"What do you suppose is going on with our corps packing up, Major?" asked Cy Henderson.

"General Halloran's coming," said Locklin. "He'll tell us."

Drawing up, Halloran ran his gaze over the ragged group and looked close to see who was being carried into the hospital tent. "How'd it go, Major?"

"Why is our bunch moving out, sir?" asked Locklin, his curiosity high.

"I'll explain in a minute," responded Halloran, "but first I want to know about the bridge. General Franklin is anxious to know, too."

"We didn't get to sabotage the bridge, sir," Locklin replied glumly. "Confederates had a unit there to protect it. We couldn't see them. They were hiding in a pocket of darkness under the bridge. We had scouted and found a large Confederate camp about a mile-and-a-quarter due west over a ridge. Knowing they were too far away to hear us work on the bridge, we left our horses in a thicket and headed for it. Rebels underneath opened fire on us. We fought them and killed them all, but the sound of the gunfire brought a horde of them down on us from the camp. We had to get out of there in a hurry."

Halloran swept his gaze over the others. "How many men did you lose?"

"Four, sir. Lieutenant Baird, Corporal Casey, and troopers Yarrow and Teeter."

"How serious is Lynch?"

"He took a bayonet in the shoulder. He'll be all right, I'm sure. General, I'm sorry we didn't get the job done."

"Hey." Halloran gripped Locklin's arm. "How were you to know the Rebs were thinking ahead of us? Don't blame yourself. You did all that could be expected of you. I'll accompany you for your report to General Franklin in a minute, but let me explain about Six Corps moving out."

Locklin's seven men huddled close as Halloran explained that a big battle was pending at Manassas Junction. Some of General Irvin McDowell's unit had been in skirmishes with Confederates, and it was known that General Beauregard had sent a message to General Johnston to send forces from Shenandoah Valley. Learning this, McDowell had wired General Scott to send help. Expecting that Lee might be planning an attack on Washington, Scott was reluctant to cut his Potomac forces too low, so he was sending Six Corps in response to McDowell's plea.

"How soon are we moving out, sir?" asked Locklin.

"When night falls, so we can move under cover of darkness. I was planning on assigning another man to lead your brigade if you weren't back in time. I know you haven't had any sleep. Maybe I ought to go ahead and do that."

"Oh no, sir!" responded Locklin, shaking his head. "I'm all right. I can do it."

Locklin's seven men quickly spoke up; assuring Halloran they could make the march also. They wanted to be in on the big battle. They would get something to eat; then begin packing up. Appreciating their enthusiasm, the general consented. Halloran and Locklin then went to General Franklin's tent so the major could make his report.

Franklin was disappointed that the bridge was still intact, but commended Locklin for the efforts of him and his men in their attempt. He also expressed his sorrow in the loss of the four men.

General William B. Franklin's Six Corps pulled out of the camp when darkness had fully settled in and waded across the Potomac on to Virginia soil. Thankful for a cloud cover, they marched until two A.M., then bedded down for a three-hour sleep. Dawn was breaking when they continued the march after gulping down their breakfast rations. Only the officers who led the divisions, the brigades, and the regiments rode horseback.

Keeping their eyes peeled for Confederate troops, the men in blue pressed southward in their fifty-mile trek to meet up with General Irvin McDowell's forces. It was late afternoon when they topped the hills of Virginia Heights and were welcomed by McDowell and his men. McDowell informed General Franklin that they were going to launch an attack on the Confederates at six-thirty the next morning. After supper, McDowell was calling a meeting of all officers for a council of war.

While the weary Six Corps sat down to rest among the trees, General McDowell took Franklin and his officers to the edge of the wooded area and showed them the valley below. There they saw the Confederate troops clustered around the intersection of railroad track on the banks of Bull Run Creek.

Passing around a crudely drawn map of the area, McDowell pointed out strategic landmarks that would be involved in the battle. There were several houses that were scattered over the area, which had been vacated by their occupants. There was also Sudley Springs Ford, Blackburn's Ford, Bald Hill, and Stone Bridge, which spanned Bull Run Creek.

McDowell assigned Franklin's corps to beeline from Virginia Heights to Stone Bridge the instant his cannons started bombardment at six-thirty in the morning. Once they had secured the bridge, they were to leave a hundred men there to guard it while the others proceeded southwest toward Manassas-Sudley Road, capturing and holding the houses along the way. They would be joined by the New York Fire Zouaves at the road and would head due south for Bald Hill, where the Rebels were dug in solid. A brigade from Major General Ambrose Burnside's Nine Corps would also converge at Bald Hill.

Later that evening, the council of war was held. There, Boyd Locklin learned that some six hours after he and his men had ridden away from the bridge over the Rappahannock, Confederate General Joseph E. Johnston had sent General Thomas Jackson's Virginia Brigade of nearly three thousand men from Winchester to the railroad tracks where they boarded a Manassas Gap train and were quickly transported to Bull Run Creek to prepare for battle. Gritting his teeth, Locklin wished he had been able to sabotage the bridge.

At six-thirty the next morning, a special unit of McDowell's division gathered around a six-thousand–pound Parrott cannon that was strategically placed in the hills above Stone Bridge. The huge army of men in blue waited with great anticipation, hearts pounding. The Parrott was aimed at the Confederate troops who were clustered near the bridge.

Brigadier General D. T. Tyler, who commanded the special unit, jerked the lanyard on the huge gun. It thundered, and seconds later the big ball exploded in the midst of the Rebels, throwing bodies in every direction…and the battle had begun.

Yankees whooped and Rebels yelled as the two armies clashed amid booming cannons, roaring howitzers, and the crack of rifles and muskets. The entire bowl-shaped valley rocked with ear-splitting thunder.

General William B. Franklin's Six Corps spread out on the grassy slopes and worked their way toward the bridge. The Confederates, though temporarily stunned by the assault of the Parrott, were determined to hold their position. While the battle waged hot and heavy all over the area, Six Corps concentrated on Stone Bridge.

Remaining on top of the hill under the trees, General Franklin observed the fierce conflict, flanked by the commanders of his three divisions, Major General Henry Slocum of First Division, Major General William F. Smith of Second Division, and Major General Brett Halloran of Third Division. Six corporals stood nearby, alert and ready to carry orders to the officers amid the battle.

Franklin swerved his binoculars to the west for a moment, looking at General McDowell's forces, who were swarming the Confederates on that side of the battlefield. The whole valley was alive with clouds of powder smoke, drifting endlessly on the morning breeze.

Down on the level where guns roared and bullets whined, Major Boyd Locklin was bellied in the grass with his men, firing his service revolver at the enemy. The fighting had been in progress for nearly an hour when a corporal flopped down beside Locklin and told him that the generals were sending messages to the other brigade commanders to make a circle around the bridge, surrounding the Rebels. Locklin and his men were to stay on their present parallel and keep pushing forward.

The major quickly sent the message along the line to his men. Within another hour, the Confederates at Stone Bridge saw that they were almost surrounded. Suddenly they left their protective places and ran toward the cluster of houses, which lay southwest about two hundred yards.

The Yankees jumped to their feet, shouting exultantly and firing at the fleeing enemy soldiers. Locklin counted off a hundred men in his brigade, commanding them to remain at the bridge and hold it. He was aware that he had already lost at least forty men, who lay dead or wounded on the hillside.

As the Federal troops closed in from all sides on the area where the houses were clustered, they saw the Rebels taking refuge inside them and in adjacent barns and sheds. Soon the men in gray were firing from windows and doors.

Major Boyd Locklin was charging toward the houses with a dozen men flanking him. They were coming up on a two-story house, which was sided by a large barn. Suddenly the barn door flew open, and they found themselves looking down the ominous black bore of a howitzer on wheels. It was evident that the Confederates had placed it there earlier, the result of a backup plan.

The cannon boomed just as Locklin shouted for them to hit the dirt. It was too late for six of them. The shell struck to Locklin's right, just as he bellied down, exploding in a ball of fire. While deadly shrapnel ripped into their bodies, it lifted the hapless Union soldiers off their feet. One of them landed on Locklin.

Pushing the lifeless form off him, the major bounded to his feet, shot at the Rebels who were already reloading the howitzer, and shouted at the other six, "Get 'em!"

Locklin was aware of howitzers roaring at the other houses as he led his men in a dead-heat run, firing at the cannon crew at the same time. Two of the crew went down and the others disappeared into the dark gloom of the barn.

Abruptly musket barrels appeared at knotholes, belching fire. The small double doors in the loft overhead came open and more guns blazed.

A hot lead ball hummed past Locklin's left ear, and by reflex, he ducked to the right. Unwittingly he saved his life by ducking, for another slug split air where his head had been a fraction of a second before. Two of Locklin's men were hit and went down spurting blood. Three of the others made a mad dash from the line of fire, diving between the barn and a small shed next to it. Locklin darted behind a hay wagon and was followed by trooper Cy Henderson.

The major and Henderson saw their three comrades disappear around the corner of the barn. "I think they're going to go in from the back," Locklin said in a low tone, shooting toward the opening in the loft.

There was a howl, followed by a man in gray peeling out the loft door and hitting the ground like a sack of meal. Sunlight glinted off the tip of a musket barrel as it pushed through a knothole on ground level. Henderson took quick aim with his .52 caliber Sharps carbine and put a slug just above the knothole. He know he had hit his target when the musket pointed skyward, roared, then slipped from sight.

At the same time, another musket fired from the same level about six feet to the left. The bullet chewed into the hay wagon inches from Henderson's face, splattering him with splinters. Locklin zeroed in on the spot and fired. A painful scream followed.

Suddenly three shots clattered rapidly from inside the barn, echoing loudly through the wide doorway. Locklin knew his men had entered the structure from the rear. A gray uniform appeared at the loft opening, behind a musket. Locklin brought his revolver up quickly and dropped the hammer. It made a loud, hollow click. In the excitement he had forgotten to count his shots. The Rebel's gun spit fire, sending a bullet into the wagon bed inches from Locklin's face. Henderson had just snapped another bullet into the breech of his Sharps. In the same instant, he reacted to the major's predicament, firing at the Rebel in the loft before he could remove himself from view. The Rebel took the .52 caliber slug in his chest and disappeared.

More shots came from the barn, followed by grunting sounds and clattering noises. Three Yankees were in hand-to-hand combat with an unknown number of determined Confederate soldiers. Both Locklin and Henderson started to reload their guns in preparation to dash into the barn, but were stopped short when two Rebels bolted from inside, brandishing muskets with fixed bayonets. They had been watching the Yankees behind the wagon, and without time to reload their muskets, they decided to attack before Locklin and Henderson could get bullets into their guns.

Locklin had noticed several potato-sized rocks lying around. Gasping the word, "Rocks!" he jammed his revolver into its holster, bent over, and picked up two round-edged ones. While Henderson dropped the carbine and went for two just like them, the major stepped out from behind the wagon and hurled his first rock at the charging Rebel who was about four steps in front of his companion. The rock caught the man flush on the nose. While he was going down, Locklin unleashed his second stony missile. It smacked the Rebel square between the eyes, stopping him in his tracks less than twenty feet away.

Henderson stood poised with no target while the major dashed to the first one, who was rolling his head with blood bubbling from his nose. Locklin picked up the musket and drove the man's own bayonet through his heart. He turned to see Henderson standing over the other one. The Rebel lay still, his sightless eyes staring vacantly toward the hazy Virginia sky.

Sounds of the battle filled the air all around them.

"You killed him with that rock, Major!" said the young trooper, amazement showing on his face. "I'd never have believed it if I hadn't seen it for myself!"

"Grab his musket, Cy," said Locklin, taking off for the barn.

With Henderson twenty yards behind him, the major held the Rebel's musket with the bayonet poised and bowled through the barn door. Though the interior was dark compared to the sunlit yard outside, he could see one of his men lying bloody on the dirt floor. The other two were battling it out with three Rebels, fighting off bayonets by using their carbines as clubs.

Clenching his teeth, Locklin lunged across the barn and drove fourteen inches of cold steel into the rib cage of a Rebel. The man screamed and buckled. As Locklin was withdrawing the bayonet, Cy Henderson barged through the door, and without breaking stride, shot across the barn and thrust the bayonet into the back of one of the other Confederates. As the man's shriek cut the air, Locklin headed for the last one, who had a Yankee cornered and was about to finish him off with his bayonet.

When the Rebel saw Locklin coming, he quickly threw down his musket and raised his hands. "I surrender! I surrender!"

"Go on and kill him, Major!" implored the Yankee in the corner. "Kill him!"

Locklin shook his head. "Can't do it, Wilson. He has surrendered and disarmed himself. If I killed him now, it would be murder."

Frank Wilson knew his commander was right. Without speaking, he bent over and picked up the Rebel's musket.

"We're taking you as our prisoner, Reb," Locklin said. "What's your name?"

"Billy Joe Moore," said the Southerner, still holding his hands high.

To the other Yankee, Locklin said, "Search him, Hanford, then find something to tie his hands with behind his back."

While Frank Wilson held the bayonet aimed at Moore's back, Delbert Hanford began searching him. At the same time, the major walked past three more dead Rebels and knelt down beside the wounded man in blue who lay near the door. It was trooper Jerry Kuhns.

Eyeing the blood-soaked shirt, Locklin could see that Kuhns had been shot in the chest. He was breathing shallowly and death's pallor was on his face.

The battle still raged outside as Locklin laid a hand on Kuhns's brow. "We'll get you out of here as soon as we can, Jerry. Probably have to wait till dark. I've got to get back to my men out there. We have to take all these houses."

Kuhns raised a trembling hand and took hold of Locklin's arm. There was terror in his eyes as he squeaked, "Please don't leave me, Major! Please! I'm scared! Help me! I don't want to die!"

Locklin knew the young trooper would be dead shortly. Patting the hand, he said, "I won't leave you, Jerry. Just relax. You're going to be okay."

While Locklin knelt beside the dying man and Delbert Hanford was searching for a piece of cord or rope to tie up the prisoner, Billy Joe Moore's eyes caught the butt of Locklin's revolver. He figured he could spring away from the bayonet at his back and have the gun in his hand before anyone could stop him.

Moving with the swiftness of a cat, Moore made his play. It took everyone by surprise, for he had the gun out of Locklin's holster before anyone could move. His eyes were wild as he cocked the weapon, holding it with both hands and waving it threateningly. "Now I'm leavin' here, bluebellies! But before I do, I'm sendin' you to bluebelly hell!"

Knowing the revolver was empty, Locklin stood up slowly, ready to pounce on him.

Moore aimed the gun at Locklin's head and squeezed the trigger. Trooper Frank Wilson was already in motion when the hammer snapped on the spent shell. Moore's face showed surprise and fear at the same time. He swung the muzzle at the charging Wilson and it clicked hollowly again a split second before Wilson's bayonet pierced his chest. He went down hard, dropping the revolver to grasp the barrel of the musket. The horrid knowledge of death showed in his eyes. Blood spread on his shirt around the blade of the bayonet. He grunted, worked his jaw soundlessly, and died.

Delbert Hanford stepped up with a length of rope in his hand. "Guess we won't need this."

Pulling the bayonet out, Wilson looked at Locklin. "I'm sorry, sir. He moved so fast. If…if your gun had been loaded, he'd have killed you, and it'd been my fault."

Picking up his revolver, Locklin smiled. "It's all right, soldier. Nobody can expect you to react like a veteran until you are one. You still did all right."

Relief showed on Wilson's face. "Thank you, sir."

Holding the gun loosely in his hand, the major turned back to Jerry Kuhns. Henderson, Hanford, and Wilson gathered close.

Locklin saw the glassy eyes, staring straight ahead, seeing nothing. Bending over, he pressed the eyelids down. "He's gone, fellas."

The sounds of war were outside, but the interior of the barn was quiet as a tomb. Major Boyd Locklin was once again feeling the awful effects of losing men under his command. Breaking the silence with only the sound of reloading his revolver, he did it slowly and methodically, blinking back the moisture in his eyes. Snapping the cylinder in place, he took a deep breath. "Load your carbines, soldiers. Let's get back to the war."

The battle at Bull Run Creek raged on. It seemed that victory would be in the hands of the Union until early afternoon. General McDowell made some grave tactical errors at midday, and the tide turned swiftly for the Confederates. Especially effective was the Confederate brigade led by Brigadier General Thomas Jackson. It was Jackson's calm courage in the thick of the battle that inspired his men to beat back Union charges until the Virginia Brigade had the Yankees in retreat.

Amid the fiercest action, a Confederate officer was heard to cry, "There stands Jackson like a stone wall!" The words were like magic. Immediately the nickname stuck and the Confederates drove the Union army northward, shouting the praises of "Stonewall" Jackson.

The battle ended at four o'clock, when the Union army, outsmarted because of McDowell's miscalculations, began to disintegrate. Victory had eluded them. Mercifully, there was no Confederate pursuit. By that time, the Rebels were too exhausted to fight and were glad to see the men in blue disappear over the hills to the north.

General William B. Franklin's Six Corps suffered many casualties, as did McDowell's regular army, along with its special units. Brigadier General Brett Halloran and Major Boyd Locklin rode side by side on the long journey back to the Potomac, both keenly feeling the loss of many good men.

Arriving at the camp on July 24, General Irvin McDowell made his report to General-in-Chief Winfield Scott, accompanied by the commanders of his six divisions. Displeased with McDowell's display of poor judgment in Bull Run, Scott relieved him of his command. On July 26, McDowell's army received a new commander, General George B. McClellan.

Within two days of their arrival at the Union camp, the battle-weary men who had fought at Bull Run posted letters to their families, wanting to let them know as soon as possible that they had survived the battle. Included in the thousands of letters was one addressed to Mrs. Linda Locklin, 631 Mulberry Street, York, Pennsylvania.

CHAPTER FOURTEEN

On Monday, August 5, 1861, Linda Locklin left York's city market carrying a bag of groceries and headed in the direction of Mulberry Street. It was her custom every weekday to go to the post office in case a letter had come from Boyd. Since she needed groceries, she had passed the post office on her way to the market, intending to stop on the way back.

The broiling sun beat down on her as she made her way along the street. Her face was shiny with sweat as she entered the post office, and she could feel a wet trickle running down her back. The postmaster, an aging man with little meat on his bones, was busy with a customer. Linda set the grocery bag on a small table, removed a hanky from her purse, and mopped her face.

A moment later the customer turned and walked toward the door. When the postmaster saw Linda, he smiled. "Guess what, Mrs. Locklin. That letter you've been looking for is here!" As he spoke, he reached into a cubbyhole behind him and produced the envelope.

Linda's heart drummed her ribs. "Oh, thank you, Mr. Peabody!" She took it from his hand. "I'll force myself to wait till I get home to read it."

Grinning, Peabody said, "I can understand that. Sort of want to do your crying in private."

"Yes." She smiled. "Something like that."

"Have you seen the paper?" he asked, picking up the York Courier and flashing the front page at her.

"No."

"It's got some facts and figures about that awful battle at Bull Run. You said your husband wouldn't have been in it, didn't you, ma'am?"

"That's right." The redhead wiped sweat again. "He's with General Scott at Washington. But my friend Anna Nelson—the one you gave me a letter for last week—her husband is with the special forces from New York who are with General McDowell in northern Virginia. Ever since we heard about the Bull Run battle, she's been on pins and needles."

"I'll bet." Laying the paper out flat on the counter, Peabody ran a bony finger down a column and stopped halfway down the page. "Listen to this. Government authorities say we had thirty-five thousand men in that battle. They figure the Confederates had about that many. Says here we had nearly five hundred killed, over eleven hundred wounded, and some thirteen hundred men are missing."

"Terrible, isn't it?"

"Yes'm. I read here somewhere that General McDowell's men are now back at Washington. He was put out as commander, and General McClellan's got his job."

Linda was interested in knowing all she could about the war. "Do you have another copy of the paper, Mr. Peabody?"

Scratching his head, the postmaster said, "Not really, but tell you what. I just put one in the cubbyhole for old Mrs. Shettleton this morning. Heard about twenty minutes ago that she died last night. She won't need it. You can have her copy."

Linda expressed her sorrow; then folded the newspaper and put it in the grocery bag. Eager to read Boyd's letter, she walked briskly in spite of the heat and was home shortly. Stevie was taking his nap at Granny Maude's house, which gave her time to read the letter with no interruptions.

Her fingers were shaking as she sat down at the kitchen table and tore the envelope open. Tears came as she read the words written by her husband on July 18. When she had read it the fourth time, she broke into sobs, clutching it to her breast.

That evening after putting Stevie to bed, Linda sat down at the table, and by lantern light, read the letter again. She cried some more, then laid out the newspaper and started reading. When she reached the second column and read that General William B. Franklin's Six Corps had gone south and fought at Bull Run, her heart pounded so hard, it took her breath away. She was just getting control when she heard a voice at the screen door.

"Linda? Anna. May I come in?"

"Yes, of course!"

When the brunette saw Linda's ashen face, she said, "Honey, what's the matter?"

Clasping her hands to keep them from trembling, Linda replied, "I just read in the *Courier* that General Franklin's Six Corps was sent to Bull Run to bolster McDowell's army. Boyd is with them."

Wrapping her arms around the smaller woman, Anna said, "Now we both have to wait for word from our men. Oh, I wish there was some way we could know right now that they're okay."

"Me, too. But we play the good old army game. I went through this same type of thing when Boyd was fighting Indians in Arizona. Sometimes when his patrol was late getting in, I thought I'd lose my mind."

"Sometimes we have to be tougher than the men, don't we?" Anna sighed.

"Grittier, at least. Would you like some coffee?"

"I sure would. More than anything, I just need to talk. I'm sure glad we have each other."

"Me, too." Linda wiped a tear from her eye.

On Tuesday, August 13, Maude Stillwell was sitting on her front porch rocking and fanning herself while watching little Steven Locklin at play. The sun was lowering in the western sky, but the heat had not yet begun to subside. Keeping an eye on Stevie, who played near her feet, she kept the other on the street, looking for Linda, who had gone to the post office.

Moments later, Linda rounded the corner a half-block away; she was smiling and waving an envelope. Maude was relieved. Linda had received a letter from Boyd and he was all right.

When Linda approached the porch, the older woman stood up. "It's from Boyd and he's okay, right?"

"Right!" Linda laughed and wiped tears. "He was in the thick of the fight at Bull Run, but thank God he didn't get a scratch!"

"Wonderful!" Maude clapped her hands together. "But no letter for Anna, I guess."

"No, but I'm sure she'll hear from Ken soon."

Linda picked her son up. "Your daddy's all right, Stevie. He's all right. Can you say Daddy?"

Boyd Locklin's likeness looked his mother in the eye and said, "Da-a-a-ddy."

"Did Boyd say anything about more fighting, honey?" queried Maude.

The smile on Linda's lips faded. "Yes. He said they would be back in battle soon, he was sure. But...but I know he'll be all right, Granny Maude. I just know it. One of his friends at Fort Savage once called him a survivor. I have to believe that and hold on to it. My husband is a survivor."

Maude started to comment, but looked down the street to see Anna Nelson coming home from work. "There's Anna. She'll be glad to know about Boyd."

When the brunette reached the porch, Linda showed her the letter and they both cried together. Trying to encourage her friend, Linda told her she would hear from Ken soon. Linda was about to take Stevie home when a young man on horseback rode up, checked the number of Maude's house, and dismounted. The three women noticed he was carrying a yellow envelope.

"Good afternoon, ladies. I'm from the York Telegraph Service. I have a telegram here for Mrs. Anna Nelson."

Something cold slid next to Anna's spine. She knew that all public telegraph service from the war zone had been suspended. Only messages within the military were being sent. Her voice was strained as she said, "I'm Mrs. Nelson."

The messenger had her sign a slip of paper confirming she had received the telegram, then hurried to his horse and trotted away.

Maude and Linda looked on silently as Anna ripped the envelope open and began reading the message. They saw her face pinch and lose color. She started crying before she had even finished reading it.

When Linda saw her knees buckle, she stood Stevie on the porch and took Anna in her arms. First there was a wordless wail, then Anna sucked in a long breath. "He's dead! Ken's dead! He was killed at Bull Run!"

Speaking in low, soothing tones, Linda sat her down on the step.

While Anna sobbed incoherently, Linda took the telegram from her hand and read it. "It's from the office of the secretary of war. Ken was killed July 21 at Bull Run. One of his officers saw him shot, and confirmed that he was dead before they retreated back to Washington. They assume he was buried in a common grave with other Union soldiers by the Confederates."

"Let's get inside," said Maude. "I've got some powders that will help her settle down."

On August 26, Linda received another letter from Boyd, informing her that he had been in many skirmishes in the woods and fields of northern Virginia, but was unscathed. He wanted desperately to be there for Stevie's second birthday, September 6, but knew it was impossible. Linda cried herself to sleep that night, clutching the letter to her heart.

The war kept Boyd and Linda apart as it raged hot and heavy. He was kept busy fighting in northern and western Virginia, and was not able to send letters except when he pulled back into Maryland on the Potomac for rest—which came only three times in the next year. Each time, there were many letters from Linda waiting for him, which he read many times over.

Linda kept up with the war as best she could by reading the *York Courier* and talking to a few wounded Union soldiers who had been sent home to York.

On Saturday, September 6, 1862, Maude Stillwell was busy in her kitchen, baking a birthday cake for her favorite little boy. She had invited Linda and Stevie for supper and was surprising them with the cake. She had also secretly made some clothes for the three-year-old and had wrapped them in pretty paper.

For her age Maude had good ears, and when she heard the sound of heavy hooves and the rattle of harness as a wagon hauled to a stop next door, she hurried to the front of the house and stepped out on the porch. She was stunned to see an army wagon at the Locklin house and the major alighting from the seat. The corporal who was driving the wagon was on the ground, lifting Locklin's heavy canvas bag from the bed.

Locklin saw the gray-haired woman the instant she appeared and headed toward her, smiling. "Hello, Granny Maude! You're just as pretty as ever."

Blushing, Maude accepted his embrace. "Boyd Locklin, how did you arrange this?"

"Pulled a few strings with General Scott. I can only stay a couple of days. If I got it right from Linda's letters, she gets home from work in about half an hour."

"That's right." Maude giggled. "Boy howdy, is she gonna be surprised! You know, I guess, that the Kings allow Linda to keep Stevie with her while she's at their house during the day."

"Yes'm. She wrote and told me all about Anna Nelson, and that when Anna went back to New York, the Kings offered her Anna's job. From what I can tell, it sounds like the job has been good for Linda. Keeps her from being so lonely with me gone."

"That it does," said the widow. "She's happy just to be able to take care of someone, too. It's born in her."

"How well I know," Boyd said.

"Excuse me, Major," said the corporal, who had crossed the yard to speak to him, "I put your bag on the porch. I'll be going now."

"Thank you, Matson. See you Monday about noon."

"Right, sir. Have a nice time with your family."

"I'm going to do that," Locklin assured him.

As the wagon pulled away, the tall man said, "Well, Granny Maude, guess I'll go on over to the house. See you later."

"You sure will. I've already invited Linda and Stevie for supper. Think I've got an extra plate somewheres in the cupboard. So you're invited too. We're having a little birthday party for Granny Maude's boy. I think it's wonderful that you can be here for his birthday."

"Me, too," Boyd said, heading toward his house. "See you later."

Maude Stillwell wiped tears as she watched the handsome major cross the yard, pick up his canvas bag, and enter the house. She could hardly wait for Linda to come home. Returning to the kitchen, she made further preparations for supper, then hurried back to the front porch. She had hardly sat down on her rocker when she saw Linda coming down the street, holding Stevie's hand. Her auburn hair reflected the light of the lowering sun.

As was her custom since going to work for Harvey and Althea King, Linda turned into Maude's yard for a brief chat. Maude cast a glance at the Locklin house. The front door was open, but Boyd was not in sight. Her heart raced as Linda said, "Well, Granny Maude, what have you been doing today?"

The widow rose from the rocker, unable to mask the excitement she was feeling inside. "Oh, just puttering around the kitchen."

Frowning, Linda tilted her head. "Are you all right, honey?"

"Oh, just fine."

"You seem a bit nervous or something."

Flicking a glace at the Locklin house again, Maude said, "Nervous? Oh no. I'm just excited."

A broad smile captured Linda's face. "Oh yes. Of course. Stevie's birthday dinner."

Another glance showed Maude the major standing on his porch. Taking a couple of short breaths, she said, "I…ah…I'm excited about the dinner, but—"

At that instant, Linda finally noticed the widow looking toward her house. Her emerald eyes trailed that way slowly and beheld the magnificent man in the dark blue uniform.

Maude's heart was in her throat.

Boyd was smiling as he stepped off the porch. Linda stood transfixed, unable to move, not believing her eyes. Stevie raced toward the porch, squealing as he recognized the man from the picture his mother was always kissing.

Suddenly Linda found her feet and dashed toward Boyd, sobbing, "Boyd, darling! Boyd! You're home! I love you! I love you!"

The reunion was tearful for both husband and wife as they kissed, embraced, and kissed again. Stevie cried as he reached Boyd, "Daddy! Daddy!"

"Here's your big boy, darling," said Linda, shedding more tears.

Laughing and taking Stevie from the ground, Boyd hugged him and said to Linda, "He knows me! There's no way he can remember—"

"He knows your picture, darling! He sees it every day of his life."

While the Locklins were in the house getting ready to go to Granny Maude's for supper and the birthday party, Boyd explained to Linda how he learned that Major General Henry Slocum, commander of First Division, Six Corps was making a trip by wagon to York in order to attend a close friend's wedding. Boyd was in camp for a few days of rest. He asked General Slocum if he could ride along, providing he could obtain permission from General Franklin to make the trip. Franklin gladly obliged. The wedding would be on Sunday afternoon. General Slocum and Corporal Matson would be by to pick him up at noon on Monday.

Linda expressed her wish that they could have longer together, but said they would make the most of what time they had.

Saturday night and Sunday were wonderful for the Locklins, but passed all too quickly. Maude Stillwell filled in at the King home to let Linda have every precious minute with her husband.

It was noon Monday and the army wagon was right on time. Boyd introduced General Slocum and Corporal Matson to Linda and proudly showed off his son. Corporal Matson tossed the major's canvas bag in the wagon and climbed in the seat.

Boyd took his wife and son back inside the house for a private moment. He hugged and kissed Stevie, telling him he would be back as soon as possible. Folding Linda in his arms, he kissed her and held her close. "I'll be back, sweetheart. I love you more than human language can express. Don't ever forget that."

"Forget?" she said shakily. "How could I forget? I love you exactly the same way. Your love is my very lifeline. You are my life, darling."

Boyd climbed into the bed of the wagon, sat on his canvas bag, and waved at his family as the wagon pulled away. He could hardly see the tears on Linda's cheeks for the moisture in his own eyes.

Locklin blinked at the moisture and kept his eyes on Linda and Stevie until the wagon rounded the corner at the end of the block.

Knowing he was having a hard time, General Slocum let him compose himself, then turned around on the seat. "Major, I received a wire from General McClellan about an hour ago. On Thursday, Lee marched his army to the Potomac and began crossing into Maryland."

Surprise registered on Locklin's features. "He what?"

"You heard me correctly. Took him until last night to get them all across. He's got a massive force in Yankee territory. They crossed at White's Ford and are camped at Frederick."

"Did General McClellan say what General Scott is going to do?"

"It's not Scott anymore. President Lincoln has made McClellan general-in-chief."

"Scott's age?"

"I'm sure it is. The old man is almost eighty. I'm sure he's glad to let McClellan have it."

"All right, so did General McClellan say what he's doing?"

"Yes. Late Friday, he started to march the bulk of the army from Virginia and our own Maryland camp toward Antietam Creek. He left two corps at Washington to protect it and is moving eighty-four thousand troops to meet Lee. We're supposed to hurry and get to Antietam as soon as possible. Six Corps is already there."

At that moment they were pulling out of York. General Slocum told the corporal to put the horses to a gallop.

As the wagon bounced along the road, Locklin raised his voice above the rumble of the hooves and rattle of the wagon. "Why do you suppose Lee is pulling this bold move?"

"I can only guess," came the general's ready reply. "For one thing, I think he simply wants to harass us on our own soil. For another, he'll feed his army and animals on Maryland's rich autumn harvest and give the Virginia farmers a chance to bring in what remains of their crops, unmolested by Union troops."

Lockin removed his campaign hat and ran splayed fingers through his thick, curly hair. "Sir, this may be shaping up to be the worst battle yet."

"Has all the potential." Slocum sighed.

"Have we ever gotten the official figures on the battle we fought at Gaines's Mill, sir?" Corporal Matson asked Slocum.

The wagon hit a rut, jarring all three men. Slocum adjusted himself on the seat. "In round figures, we had nine hundred killed, thirty-one hundred wounded, and twenty-eight hundred missing or captured. Our spies tell us the Confederates really took a licking. They had fourteen hundred killed and sixty-five hundred wounded. They've issued no figures as of yet on how many turned up missing. We know we captured about two hundred."

"So far," put in Locklin, "the biggest battle was the one at

Shiloh. General Halloran told me that General Grant reported over seventeen hundred killed, eighty-four hundred wounded, and twenty-nine hundred missing or captured. If I remember correctly, he said our spies reported almost exactly the same number of Rebels killed and about an even eight thousand wounded. We captured about six hundred."

Matson slowed the horses to cross a shallow brook. As they splashed across, he said to both officers, "Do we know where they're taking our men when they capture them?"

"We know of a few places," said Slocum. "Some are being kept in southern Virginia, some in Tennessee, and we suspect, but can't say for sure, that they're even taking some down into the swamps of Georgia."

"Don't you think, sir, that most of those we list as missing or captured are actually captured?"

"Probably."

"How can there be very many missing? I would think when a battlefield is cleaned up, they'd find all the bodies."

"Many a man gets his face blown off under cannon fire, Corporal," said the general. "When we can't prove who he was, his name will automatically appear on the 'missing or captured' list. Of course, we know that some men run away during a battle, and then when we're fighting beside a stream, often men are shot and fall in. Their bodies float downstream and are never recovered."

Matson nodded. "I see. Thank you, sir. That makes sense."

General Slocum, Major Locklin, and Corporal Matson drew near Antietam Creek at sundown. As they pulled out of a thick stand of trees, they saw Six Corps' banner on a tall pole, waving in the breeze beneath the Stars and Stripes. As usual, the white tents were lined up in straight lines with men in blue uniforms scurrying about.

Slocum and Locklin were immediately ushered inside General McClellan's tent for a briefing. Generals Franklin and Halloran happened to be in the tent at the time. Halloran quickly asked Boyd about Linda and Stevie, then McClellan shook hands with both Slocum and Locklin, telling them to sit down.

McClellan, a short, stocky man, got down to business by informing Slocum and Locklin that he had apportioned his eighty-four thousand troops into fifteen divisions, and assembled the divisions into three wings. All three would march toward Lee's forces camped at Frederick on parallel roads. McClellan would ride in the center wing with Major General Edwin Sumner along National Road, which ran in a beeline toward Frederick. The right wing, under Major General Ambrose Burnside, would take a route near the Baltimore and Ohio Railroad. The left wing, under Major General William B. Franklin, would hug the Maryland shore of the Potomac River. Burnside's Nine Corps would have fourteen thousand men, Franklin's Six Corps, twelve thousand, with some fifty-eight thousand bulking up the center wing.

This enabled the Union Army of the Potomac to advance on a twenty-five-mile–wide front that covered the approaches to both Washington and Baltimore. McClellan would move his troops very slow, realizing that General Robert E. Lee could have a trick up his sleeve—namely a swing north to invade Pennsylvania. When Major Locklin heard this, he thought of Linda and Stevie. How safe were they?

McClellan pointed out that his slow move would provide the necessary concentration of troops in case they had to make a sudden turn toward Pennsylvania.

The march began on Wednesday, September 10. As the Union Army of the Potomac neared Frederick at twilight on September 11, General McClellan received reliable reports that Lee had withdrawn from the town. On Friday, September 12, McClellan stopped the center and left wings, and sent Burnside and his Nine Corps to check it out. When a rider returned, confirming that the Confederates had indeed pulled out, McClellan sent word to Franklin to remain on the bank of the Potomac and rode into Fredrick on Saturday morning, September 13. He was given a warm welcome by the people.

Later that day, a strange thing happened.

McClellan was setting up his headquarters at the edge of Frederick and was conferring with a delegation of Frederick businessmen, when General Samuel E. Pittman of the Twenty-Seventh Indiana brigade stood outside McClellan's tent and asked permission to see him immediately. When McClellan told him to wait a few minutes, Pittman insisted that his message was of extreme importance.

The businessmen excused themselves and left.

His eyes wild with excitement, Pittman handed McClellan a Confederate document that two of his men had just found in the woods outside Frederick. Some Rebel messenger had unwittingly dropped it. McClellan was amazed to see that it was addressed to Confederate General Daniel H. Hill and bore the heading: *Special Orders N. 191, Headquarters, Army of Northern Virginia.*

McClellan unfolded the paper and read it with rising excitement. There, spelled out in detail in the handwriting of Robert E. Lee's adjutant general, were the whereabouts and objectives of each command in Lee's army. Lee had divided his army. One wing was pushing toward the Pennsylvania line for invasion into that state, and the other was circling around northwest to come at McClellan's army by surprise from the rear.

At first, the general could hardly believe his stroke of luck. He shared with Pittman his fear that the document might not be authentic. Pittman smiled and assured him it was absolutely authentic. Pittman and Lee's adjutant general, Robert H. Chilton, had been close comrades in the prewar army. The handwriting, without a doubt, was Chilton's. Elated, McClellan threw up his arms, exclaiming that he could now set a trap for Lee's divided army.

McClellan sent messages to each of his commanders, advising them of their good fortune in finding the Confederate document and issuing orders where each one was to take his units to set the trap for the swarm of Rebels.

On the north bank of the Potomac, Franklin's Six Corps received orders to head due east to South Mountain, where they would be joined by other units to head off the Confederate wing that was headed for Pennsylvania. There was to be one brigade of Six Corps left behind. Franklin could choose which brigade. It would be their task to dig in on the bank of the Potomac at the spot where Antietam Creek flowed into the Potomac. This was strategic, for they would be halfway between Sharpsburg to the north and Harpers Ferry to the south. McClellan was sending huge numbers of men toward Sharpsburg to meet the Confederates coming in from the northwest, and another large number to take control of Harpers Ferry. Any unexpected move by the enemy up or down the Potomac was to be quickly reported to McClellan by that brigade.

General Franklin immediately called together the commanders of his three divisions: General Slocum, General Smith, and General Halloran. He needed their advice as to which brigade should be left on the Potomac. Several were suggested, but as they discussed the leaders of the brigades and the fact that the lone brigade might be called upon to engage the enemy, their minds went toward *A* Brigade of Third Division. All agreed that Major Boyd Locklin was the man to leave in charge of such an important assignment. He commanded a tough outfit of men, and the brigade was now four hundred strong.

Locklin was called in and given his orders. He would be given four howitzers to defend the campsite. Patrols must move up and down the Potomac day and night without ceasing in order to spot any movement of the Confederates along the river. General McClellan would keep his headquarters at Frederick and must be notified as soon as possible if Lee's troops were moving either direction on the Potomac. Two horses would be provided, one for Locklin and another for his messenger to ride if word was to be sent to McClellan.

When the orders had been given to Locklin, Franklin said, "General McClellan is depending on you, Major. Your job is a vital one. Any questions?"

"Only one, sir."

"Yes?"

"When are the rest of you pulling out?"

"At dawn tomorrow. You'll move to your position upriver at the same time." Franklin paused a moment, then said to them all, "Gentlemen, the handwriting is on the wall. There's a big battle in the making. From what I read in General McClellan's personal note to me, he is greatly encouraged by having Lee's orders in his hands. He smells victory, and so do I."

"I hope so," put in Locklin. "Those Rebels heading for Pennsylvania have me worried. My wife and son are in York. They've got to be stopped."

"They will be," said General Brett Halloran, laying a hand on Boyd's shoulder. "They will be."

CHAPTER FIFTEEN

On Sunday, September 14, Major Boyd Locklin established his camp on the Maryland bank of the Potomac where Antietam Creek emptied its waters into the broad river. He assigned Lieutenants Jake Bolger and Alfred Mansfield to set up the patrols. There would be fifty men in each patrol, with the entire brigade rotating. Three hundred would be at the camp at all times, with a patrol of fifty going south and a patrol of fifty going north. Patrolling would go on around the clock.

The four howitzers were positioned so as to defend the camp on all four sides. The Potomac was low at that time of the year, averaging some four-and-a-half feet in depth. If the Rebels tried wading across from the Virginia side, they would be vulnerable to the howitzer that was aimed toward the river. At that spot, the Potomac was about a hundred yards wide, with heavy thicket on the opposite bank.

When Bolger and Mansfield were not leading patrols, there were six sergeants who would do it, including Locklin's close friend, Sergeant Dan Weymouth. Corporal Bob Lee, who was kidded a great deal about his name, would be the messenger on horseback, should Locklin send a message to General McClellan.

On the same day, Federals and Confederates clashed at South Mountain, some ten miles east of Locklin's camp. The Confederates took a beating, and the push toward Pennsylvania was thwarted. General Robert E. Lee was with his men at South Mountain, and led them to retreat into the heavily-wooded area westward. While that battle was going on, there was hot conflict at Harpers Ferry, about six miles south of Locklin. There, the Union took a beating, and had to withdraw, leaving the town in Rebel hands.

On Monday morning, September 15, General Robert E. Lee

led his troops from the fields and meadows west of South Mountain across the meandering Antietam Creek and approached the little Maryland town of Sharpsburg, which was situated some four miles across undulating land from Boyd Locklin's camp. Because of the hills that lay between them, Locklin could not see Sharpsburg. Lee imbedded his army in a rolling ridge of hills just south of the town.

At the Potomac, Locklin's brigade was keeping up its vigil, patrolling the river some four miles in each direction. Unknown to them, General Stonewall Jackson arrived at Sharpsburg from Harpers Ferry on Monday night, bringing three divisions with him.

At dawn on Tuesday morning, Major Boyd Locklin's two patrols converged at the camp site, reporting that they had seen nothing. As the sun rose brightly in the Maryland sky, General George B. McClellan was putting the final touches on his battle plan. He began issuing orders for an attack at dawn on Wednesday. He was pulling all of his troops toward Sharpsburg.

Late in the afternoon, dark, ominous clouds began filling the sky, and the smell of rain was in the air. Sergeant Dan Weymouth was leading the patrol north of the camp. When they reached the four-mile point and turned around to head back, one of the troopers ran to Weymouth and pointed northeastward. "Sarge, look up there among the trees. See those figures in the shadows?"

The distance from the river bank to the treelined ridge the trooper was indicating was about four hundred yards. The darkening sky made the shadows heavy. Squinting, Weymouth focused on the dense stand of trees. "I can't make any figures out. It's too dark up there."

By this time, the rest of the men were scanning the ridge for figures, but no one could make out anything unusual. "I think you're spooked, Riley," spoke up a corporal. "There's nobody up there."

"I'm not blind, Corporal," Riley countered defensively. "I saw men up there, but they've disappeared now. Probably because they saw us looking their way."

Another trooper chuckled. "They have on gray uniforms, Riley?"

"I couldn't tell that, pal," replied Riley, "but I've got a feeling they were Rebels. We'd best get back to camp and report this to Major Locklin."

"Report what? The rest of us didn't see little men up there."

Weymouth said, "We'll tell the major what Riley saw, anyhow. C'mon. Let's head back."

While following Sergeant Weymouth at a trot, trooper Bart Riley kept an eye to the east. Twice more he thought he saw a small group of men following along, their heads appearing from behind the tops of the rolling hills. Both times, he started to call Weymouth's attention to them, but they vanished quickly, so he decided to keep it to himself.

When the camp came into view and the huffing, puffing soldiers slowed down, Riley was sure he saw figures dart between trees some two hundred yards to the east. The next patrol, which would be led by Lieutenant Jake Bolger, was not ready to go. They were not expecting Weymouth's patrol to be back so soon. As Bolger commanded them to make ready, one of his patrol asked Weymouth why they had come back out of breath. Weymouth replied that one of the men thought he saw some Rebels watching them. It needed to be reported to the major speedily.

Word spread quickly, and every man in the camp gathered around to hear trooper Bart Riley tell what he had seen. Still a little short of breath, Riley told his story to Major Boyd Locklin, including the sightings while they were running back to camp.

The other men in the patrol spoke up to assure Locklin they had seen nothing of the kind. The major thanked Riley for his report and immediately sent a fifty-man detail to the hills eastward. If they spotted Rebels, they were to hurry back without engaging in battle unless forced to it.

Nearly two hours later, the detail returned, saying they had seen no sign of the enemy. Riley's only comment was that the Rebels had had time to get away before the detail got near them. Locklin was about to comment on the situation when a voice at the edge of the camp shouted, "Major, rider coming in!"

Darkness was almost upon them and tiny drops of rain were falling as the rider skidded to a halt in the midst of the camp. Dismounting, he introduced himself as adjutant corporal to General McClellan. Major Locklin was handed an envelope. The corporal followed him into his tent, where Locklin lit a lantern and read McClellan's orders. When he had finished, he folded the paper and replaced it in the envelope. "Tell General McClellan we will move from this position in the morning so as to be exactly where he wants us at five o'clock. Our howitzers will be in place, and our men will be ready to attack the Rebel fortification at the designated signal."

The corporal rode away and Locklin gathered his men around to explain McClellan's orders. The rain was falling harder as Locklin said, "Men, General McClellan informs me that Lee has situated a massive force just south of Sharpsburg, and he is with them."

"Sharpsburg!" exclaimed a trooper. "Major, that's only four miles from here!"

"Correct."

"See there!" said Riley. "They're practically breathing down our necks! You guys still want to tell me I was seeing spooks this afternoon?"

Nobody answered.

Locklin went on to explain that they were to pull away from the campsite in time to dig in about five hundred yards west of Lee's positions by 5:00 A.M. McClellan had his army ready to attack from every direction. *A* Brigade would be flanked by other divisions of General Franklin's Six Corps. The signal to attack would be when one of the big six-thousand pound Parrot guns launched a shell into the middle of Lee's fortification at precisely 5:30.

The rain continued to fall. After supper, the men of *A* Brigade headed for their tents, excited about taking the fight to Robert E. Lee himself. By midnight the rain had dwindled to a soft drizzle.

Lying on the cot in his tent fully clothed, Major Boyd Locklin listened to the patter above him and thought of Linda and Stevie. His heart ached to fold the beautiful redhead in his arms and kiss her. He had never known he could love a woman so much. And then there was that bright-eyed little facsimile of himself: Steven Boyd Locklin. What a blessing to the Locklin home. He hoped Stevie would grow up to be a doctor or a lawyer. Though Stevie's father was a born soldier, he wanted something better for his son.

Boyd's thoughts then ran to the big battle that would take place the next morning. How many of his men would be killed? How many maimed, crippled, and disfigured? He fell asleep thinking of his family once again.

A Brigade was up at 3:30 A.M. The rain had stopped and little tendrils of mist rose from the damp ground as the men ate breakfast by firelight. Every man checked his weapon and made sure his powder was dry.

Major Boyd Locklin finished giving last-minute instructions to Lieutenants Bolger and Mansfield, then turned to Corporal Bob Lee, telling him to saddle both horses and take them to the river for a nice long drink. As Lee was walking away, Locklin turned to see the bulky form of Sergeant Dan Weymouth drawing up. Locklin grinned at him in the dim gray light that came from the eastern sky. "You ready to go, Dan?"

"Yes, sir. I...ah...I just wanted to say something, sir."

"Yes?"

"Well, sir...we all know this is gonna be a big one. I just want to...well, I just want to tell you that in case...in case I shouldn't come through this one, it's been a pleasure to serve under you."

"Hey, Sergeant," said Boyd, cuffing him on the shoulder and releasing his crooked grin, "don't talk like that. You're going to come through it okay. We'll get together after this war is over and talk about old times. Got it?"

Grinning weakly, the man nodded. "Sure. Sure we will."

Lifting his voice to make it heard by all, the major bellowed, "All right, men! It's time to go give those Confederates what's coming to them!"

There were shouts of agreement as Locklin turned and made his way to the spot at the riverbank where Corporal Bob Lee was watering the horses.

"All finished, sir," said Lee, handing Locklin the reins. Saddle leather creaked as Lee mounted up.

Locklin's horse was facing downstream. The major looked over the animal's broad back at the muddy Potomac and put his left foot in the stirrup.

Suddenly there was a staccato of cannon fire from the heavy brush across the river. Locklin saw the fire flashes and heard the instant shriek of shells as they arced over the Potomac. He was already swinging toward the saddle and stopped with his right leg in midair. Before he could touch ground, the first shell struck directly behind Corporal Bob Lee's horse, exploding in a wicked spray of canister and grape. The blast knocked Lee from the saddle. Three troopers were caught by the shrapnel and died instantly.

Three more shells struck almost as one, as the men of *A* Brigade scattered for cover. Another hit the bank directly below Boyd Locklin's horse. The sudden impact of the explosion lifted the horse off the ground, ripping its belly open. The horse screamed and toppled into the muddy water. Musket fire followed.

Sergeant Dan Weymouth was just bellying down with his Sharps carbine in hand when he saw the explosion under Locklin's horse. The shock of it jolted him, automatically making his eyes go shut. When he opened them, there was a cloud of smoke where the major and his horse had been, and as it quickly drifted away, Weymouth could see the horse in the river, surrounded by bloody water, but there was no sign of Locklin.

There was a break in the Confederate cannon fire, and Weymouth could hear Lieutenant Jake Bolger shouting for the men to bring over the howitzers. Other Union men were bellied down and firing back with their rifles.

The disappearance of Locklin had a nightmarish effect on Sergeant Dan Weymouth. The major had to be in the river. Tiny needles danced down his spine as he stood up.

"Major-r-r!" Weymouth dropped the rifle and dashed toward the river.

Diving in, Weymouth came up seconds later and cast his gaze downstream, wiping the dirty water from his eyes. The early morning air shivered with gunfire. Locklin's dead horse was being carried away slowly by the drift of the river. Searching the surface desperately, he looked for the major but he was nowhere to be seen.

Abruptly, lead balls were hitting water all around him. The Rebels had seen him go in the river and were determined to keep him from getting out. Plunging beneath the surface, Weymouth made for the bank, feeling sick about the loss of Major Locklin. Keeping his eyes closed to protect them from the mud in the water, he reached forward until he felt the rough edge of the bank. He sprang up and lunged for solid ground, clawing at the brush. There was a sudden sharp pain is his upper left shoulder. Desperate, he crawled up the bank with hot lead striking ground on both sides of him.

Collapsing in a low spot, Weymouth sucked hard for breath and wept for the major. Howitzers, muskets, and rifles were spitting death in the smoke of battle on both sides of the Potomac. Clouds of smoke drifted on the humid air while both sides fought tenaciously, with many dying amid cries of pain and horror.

While the conflict continued at the river, bombardment began on schedule at Sharpsburg on the bank of Antietam Creek.

It was Friday morning, September 19, 1862. Harvey King sat in his wheelchair at the breakfast table, struggling to hold the fork with his twisted, arthritic hands. Seated directly across from him, Althea looked on with pity while finishing her own breakfast. She would offer to help him, but the old man had a stubborn streak, and would feed himself as long as he could grasp a fork.

They heard the door open at the front of the house and smiled at each other. Both of them had grown to love Linda Locklin and her little son.

"It's us!" called Linda, and seconds later, she and Stevie entered the kitchen.

Stevie ran to the open arms of "Grandma" Althea, and both of the Kings saw the gray pallor on Linda's face.

"What's the matter, honey?" queried the old man.

Linda held a copy of the *York Courier* in her trembling hand. She unfolded it. "There's been an awful battle at Antietam Creek. Paper says it's the worst since the war began. Franklin's Six Corps was in the middle of it."

"Let me see," said Harvey, extending twisted fingers toward her.

Handing it to him, Linda sat down at the table, rubbing her temples nervously. Althea held Stevie with one hand and patted Linda's arm with the other. "Now, honey, don't think the worst. I'm sure that man of yours is alive and well."

The redhead reached for Althea's hand and patted it in the same manner. Tears glistened in her emerald eyes. "He has to be, Althea. He just has to be. I can't live without him."

Shoving his plate and coffee cup aside, Harvey spread the paper before him, adjusted his half-moon glasses on the end of his nose, and started reading silently. Shaking his head, he mumbled, "Awful. Awful."

"How about sharing it?" asked Althea.

"*Courier* reporter was in Hagerstown Wednesday when the battle took place. He went on down to Sharpsburg yesterday morning. Says—have you read this, Linda?"

"No. Only the headlines and the roster on page three that lists the fighting units that were involved in the battle."

Nodding, King proceeded. "Says there were so many bodies strewn over the battlefield, a man could hardly walk across it and keep his feet on sod."

Althea said, "Linda, why don't you take Stevie and go to the parlor? You don't need to hear this."

Linda drew a shuddering breath. "No. No, facts are facts. I might as well know what happened."

Clearing his throat, the old man said, "According to General McClellan himself, our side had eighty-seven thousand men in the battle. He estimates that the Confederates had only about forty thousand...yet our losses were greater. Says here that we had two thousand one hundred killed, nine thousand five hundred wounded, and some seven hundred fifty or so missing. They figure most of those were captured."

"What are the Confederate figures?" asked Althea.

"Same reporter says he talked to one of Lee's generals, who had been wounded. They had about fifteen hundred killed. Not quite eight thousand wounded. Considerably less than our side, that's for sure. Does say, though, that the Rebels are missing almost nineteen hundred men. Nothing said here about how many of those we might have captured."

"I suppose the army doesn't let that out so the Confederates won't really know, wouldn't you say?" put in Althea.

"Makes sense. Says that late yesterday General Lee led his survivors across the Potomac at Shepardstown, taking them back into Virginia. So looks to me like though we had the greater losses, we still won the fight. Ol' Bobby Lee went running home with his tail between his legs." Harvey read a little farther and laughed. "Listen to this. Says when the Rebels started crossing the Potomac, their band struck up playing, 'Maryland, My Maryland.' The tattered soldiers cursed at them, telling them the only song they wanted to hear was 'Dixie.'"

"I wonder what will happen now," said Linda. "Do you suppose they'll keep on fighting?"

"Have to, honey," responded Harvey, looking at her over the tops of his glasses. "Nobody's surrendered yet. There'll be war until somebody surrenders. I can tell you right now, it isn't going to be the Union surrendering."

That night, Linda lay in her bed, weeping. Twenty-one hundred Union soldiers killed. Was Boyd lying out there in a common grave at Antietam Creek? She thought of the day the messenger brought the yellow envelope to Anna Nelson. Dread filled her heart. Would the same thing happen to her?

When dawn came the next morning, Linda had not been to sleep. Only after three nights of anguish did she become so exhausted that she slept the whole night through.

Daily, she went to the post office to see if there was any word from Boyd, and daily she lived with the fear that the telegraph messenger would show up with a yellow envelope.

Two weeks passed with no word of any kind. The Kings were kind and compassionate, showing understanding when Linda's work failed to measure up to her normal standard.

It was almost noon on Saturday, October 4, when Maude Stillwell heard a knock at her front door as she was cleaning shelves in the pantry. Moving quickly, she dusted off her hands and went to the door. She opened it and saw two men in blue uniforms. She recognized the sergeant stripes on the coat of the husky man whose left arm rode a sling, but could not read the rank of the tall, slender man who stood with him. She could tell by his mien that he was an officer.

Touching his campaign hat, the tall man said, "Good morning, ma'am. We are looking for Mrs. Locklin, who lives next door. She doesn't seem to be home. Would you happen to know where we might find her?"

A stab of fear touched the elderly woman's mind. "Oh, dear, has something happened to Major Locklin?"

Reluctant to divulge Boyd Locklin's fate to a neighbor before giving the bad news to Linda, General Brett Halloran said, "We need to see Mrs. Locklin, ma'am. I'm General Halloran of the Union Army of the Potomac, and this is Sergeant Dan Weymouth."

Weymouth touched the bill of his cap. "Ma'am."

Maude was troubled that the general did not answer her question. Her wrinkled face pinched as she said, "I can tell you where to find Mrs. Locklin, General, but if you bear bad news, it is best you not go there to deliver it. Is it bad news?"

Halloran saw that he was going to have to tell the woman about Locklin. "What…ah….is your name, ma'am?"

"Maude Stillwell. I'm a widow."

"I see. Do you…ah…do you know Mrs. Locklin well?"

"We are very close friends, yes. I often take care of little Stevie, the major's son. The child and I are very close, also. If something has happened to Boyd, you can tell me."

Halloran flicked a glance at Weymouth, then said, "Well, Mrs. Stillwell, the news we bear is bad. Major Locklin was in the battle at Sharpsburg, Maryland, on September 17. Sergeant Weymouth here was under the major's command. He saw the major and his horse take a cannon ball blast and fall into the Potomac River. Major Locklin never surfaced. Since his body has never been found, he is listed as missing."

Maude began to cry. "Oh, I'm so sorry. Poor, poor little Linda. This is going to devastate her. And poor little Stevie. He hardly knew his daddy."

"You say you know where Mrs. Locklin is, ma'am?" asked Halloran.

"Yes. She works as day housekeeper for Mr. and Mrs. Harvey King over in the fancy part of town. Mr. King is a banker, and quite wealthy. They let Linda keep Stevie with her while she works. I…I think it would be best if you could wait till she comes home this afternoon, gentlemen. I would like to be with her when she hears the news, especially since she has to hear it from strangers."

"I am not a stranger to Linda, ma'am," said Halloran. "I was Major Locklin's commander at Fort Savage in Arizona when he and Linda met. In fact, it was I who performed their wedding ceremony."

Maude's eyes lit up. "Oh yes! Halloran. Now I remember Linda telling me about you. This is good. I'm sure it will help Linda when she hears about Boyd, to hear it from you."

"Yes, ma'am. Linda did not know Sergeant Weymouth, of course, but Boyd and the sergeant were good friends. I thought it would help her some to have Sergeant Weymouth with me."

"I'm sure it will. Would you gentlemen like to wait here in my house until Linda gets home? She usually arrives at about five-thirty."

"Thank you, ma'am," said Halloran, "but we have a room at the York Hotel. We'll go back there and return at five-thirty, or just a little after."

Maude watched the two soldiers mount their horses and ride away, then collapsed on her couch and wept hard.

The October air was too crisp for Maude Stillwell to sit on her porch, but she watched the street from her parlor window, starting at five-fifteen. Her heart was heavy. Ten minutes later, she saw Linda round the corner. Since the weather had cooled and Maude was not on her porch when mother and son arrived home in the evenings, Linda had not been stopping. Maude hoped she would not stop today. She would rather let General Halloran break the news. If Maude saw Linda first, she would not be able to hide the sorrow she was feeling. Linda would detect immediately that something serious was wrong, and Maude would be forced to tell her about Boyd. She did not want that responsibility.

Watching through the curtains so Linda couldn't see her, Maude sighed with relief when the redhead passed her house, only glancing at the window. When mother and son had entered the Locklin house, Maude watched for the army officers. They rode up some five or six minutes after Linda had arrived home. Maude would give them time to break the news, then head across the yard to be as much comfort to Linda as possible.

Linda Locklin removed Stevie's coat and cap and let him run to the toys in the parlor that he had not seen since early morning. While he amused himself, she went to the bedroom, hung her coat and scarf in the closet, and picked up Boyd's photograph from the dresser. Tears misted in her eyes. With a sigh, she kissed the picture. "I love you, Major Boyd Locklin, you handsome hunk of masculinity. Please let me hear from you. I must know that you're all right."

Kissing the picture again, she set it down and went to the kitchen. She was about to call Stevie to her and ask what he wanted for supper when she heard a knock at the front door.

Smiling at the little boy as he made horsy noises while trotting a small wooden horse across the floor, Linda opened the door. She was surprised to see the face of General Brett Halloran. Instinctively she knew something was wrong.

Giving Halloran's companion a swift glance, she said, "Hello, General. How nice to see you." As she spoke, she gave him a sisterly embrace.

"It's good to see you, too," said Halloran, looking through the door at Stevie, who had just taken note of him.

Spotting the blue uniform, the little boy ran toward Halloran. "Daddy! Daddy!"

Linda picked him up. "No, it's not Daddy, honey. Daddy will be coming home soon, though." Then she said to the men in blue, "Please come in."

The soldiers removed their hats and entered the parlor. Linda's heart pounded in her breast. "May I take your coats? Please sit down."

Halloran said, "This is Sergeant Dan Weymouth, Linda."

The redhead forced a smile and nodded. "Happy to meet you, Sergeant. I see your arm is in a sling. Were you in that awful battle at Sharpsburg?"

"Yes'm," replied the sergeant. "Took a bullet in my shoulder. I...ah...I'll just leave my coat on, ma'am. Too much hassle to mess with this sling."

Linda put Stevie down, telling him to take his horse and go play in his room. He obeyed immediately. Taking Weymouth's cap, along with Halloran's coat and hat, Linda began hanging them on a nearby coat tree. The two men moved to the couch and stood in front of it, exchanging glances.

Keeping her back to them, Linda pondered the solemn look on their faces. They had bad news. She was sure of it. Her mouth went dry and she felt fear rising from deep within her like a bubble searching for the surface. Before turning around, she asked cautiously, "What brings you to York, General?"

"Why don't you come and sit down, Linda?" said Halloran.

She knew what it was by Halloran's evasion of her question. Slowly turning to face them, her voice trembled as she said, "It's Boyd, isn't it? Something has happened to him."

Weymouth bit down hard on his lip.

The ache in Halloran's chest spread all over his body. His features tightened. Gesturing toward an overstuffed chair that faced the couch six feet away, he said shakily, "I think it would be best if you sit down."

Linda stepped close and looked him in the eye. "Tell me what happened to my husband."

Halloran was pale and stone faced. "Boyd took a cannon ball on the bank of the Potomac, Linda. He and his horse went into the river. Boyd's body never surfaced."

An icy dagger of pain lanced through Linda's chest, piercing her throat. Her voice came out a strangled croak. "He...he's dead?"

Halloran took her hands in his, feeling them tremble. "There is a remote chance that he's still alive, honey." He tried to force a tone of encouragement in his voice. "Since his body hasn't been found, the army has listed him as missing. It...it could be that somehow he survived the explosion of the cannon ball, and was only wounded. He might have emerged from the river downstream and been captured. The Confederates may have him in one of their prison camps. I brought Sergeant Weymouth because he was just a few yards from Boyd when he and the horse were hit. He was under Boyd's command. They were also very close friends."

"Oh...yes," she nodded, making her way to the overstuffed chair. Halloran helped her sit as she said, "I....I'm sorry, Sergeant. I should have remembered your name immediately. When...when Boyd was here last month, he spoke of you often. He always called you 'Dan,' though. The last name just didn't register."

"I understand, ma'am," Weymouth replied.

The typical military wife, Linda Locklin held her poise and fought back the rush of emotion that was struggling to burst within her and said to Weymouth, "You actually saw Boyd get hit?"

"I wasn't actually looking at him when the shell struck and exploded, ma'am. I was getting in position to use my carbine. The major was about to mount his horse just before that bombardment started. The next thing I knew, the shell hit and exploded. There was a big cloud of smoke. When it drifted away, the horse was in the river."

"Was it dead?"

"Yes."

"Not just stunned?"

"No, ma'am. It...it...well, the ball tore its belly open real bad. There was...lots of blood in the water."

"But you saw nothing of Boyd?"

"No. Immediately I ran and dived in to see if I could find him. It had rained all night, and the river was real muddy. I couldn't see anything below the surface, and the major...the major didn't come up. I was looking for him when the Rebels opened up on me with their muskets. That's when I took a slug in my shoulder. I crawled up on the bank, found what shelter I could, and waited for help. It didn't come until after dark that night."

There was a light tap at the front door.

"I'll get it," said the general, heading that way.

Maude Stillwell looked up at him. "Does she know yet?"

"Yes. Please come in."

Hurrying past Halloran, the woman went to Linda, weeping. The sudden appearance of her dear friend, and the tears that were flowing, broke the floodgates for Linda. As the two women embraced, Linda realized that the soldiers had talked to Maude earlier and told her about Boyd.

Halloran and Weymouth stood by and waited while Linda cried her heart out, clinging to the gray-haired woman. Stevie appeared, having heard the commotion. Linda took him with one arm while keeping her hold on Maude with the other. The child began to cry because his mother was crying. After a few minutes, Linda gained control of herself and calmed her son, telling him she was all right. Holding him to her breast, she looked up at Halloran. "How do I explain this to a three-year-old?"

"I don't think you can, honey," responded the general. "Best thing, I think, is to tell him you're upset because his daddy isn't coming home as soon as you'd hoped. Hold on to the hope that somehow Boyd survived the explosion of the cannon ball, drifted downriver, and was captured. If that's the case...when the war's over, he'll come home."

The word survived stuck in Linda's thoughts. Suddenly her mind flashed back to that day Boyd had risked his life to go after the runaway Peggy Halloran and seemed so long in returning. It was in Fort Savage's infirmary that Wally Frye said, "He'll be all right, ma'am. Men like Lieutenant Locklin have a certain something about them. He's a survivor."

Somehow Wally's words lit a candle of hope in Linda's heart. It was barely more than a thread to cling to, but she would not give up. She would believe that Boyd was alive in a Confederate prison camp somewhere. Someday…someday when the war was over, he would come home to her.

Halloran rose from the couch and Weymouth followed suit as the general said, "We must be going, Linda. Mrs. Stillwell, you'll stay with her, won't you?"

"Of course." Maude rose as well. "I'll stay just as long as she needs me."

Linda handed Stevie to Maude and said to Halloran, "Thank you for coming to tell me."

"I wouldn't have it any other way," he said tenderly. "I just couldn't let you learn of it by a cold, unfeeling telegram."

Linda embraced him, telling him to greet Katherine and Peggy whenever he saw them. She then embraced the sergeant, thanking him for trying to save Boyd and for coming along with the general. Halloran expressed his hope that one day when the war was over, the Locklins and the Hallorans could get together. Then the two men were gone.

Maude stayed and fixed a light supper, urging Linda to eat though she had no appetite. When bedtime came, Linda assured her that she would be all right. Maude could go home and get to bed.

Later, after Stevie was asleep, Linda lay in her bed, praying that Boyd would one day come home. Tears stained her pillow as she thought back to the last time she saw him. She remembered the tenderness of his kiss and his words echoed through her mind: *"I'll be back, sweetheart. I love you more than human language can express. Don't ever forget that."*

Sinking her fingernails deep into the pillow, she sobbed, "Oh my darling, I love you so! You must come back to me! You must!"

CHAPTER SIXTEEN

In early November, Linda Locklin discovered that she was with child, a result of Boyd's having been home in September. She was elated, telling herself if Boyd was alive, they would have another child to enjoy together. If her hopes were unfounded and he was dead, she would at least have another part of him to live on, like little Stevie.

Linda battled her fears and prayed hard as months passed with no word from the government about her husband. Rebecca Lynne Locklin was born June 2, 1863. The family savings was running low, and Linda knew that she could not afford the house rent on her small salary. When she discussed it with the Kings, they invited her to become a live-in housekeeper. The house was large. Linda and her two children would have ample room and a good degree of privacy. She was also given a generous raise in salary that assured she and the children would have everything they needed.

Maude Stillwell often had visits from Linda, Stevie, and Rebecca. The tiny girl had auburn hair exactly like Linda's, and Maude spoke repeatedly of how much she resembled her mother.

Twice in 1863 and three times in 1864, Linda received letters from General Halloran, informing her that nothing had changed in the army records. Major Boyd Locklin was still listed as missing. In January 1865, the *York Courier* carried the story of a battle in southern Virginia, where two generals of the Union Army of the Potomac were killed on the same day. One of them was General Brett Halloran. Linda grieved over his death and sent a letter to Katherine Halloran, St. Louis, Missouri, hoping the post office there would know where she was and deliver it. The letter expressed her deepest sympathy and her love.

On Monday morning, April 10, 1865, Linda was carrying

Harvey King's breakfast tray up the winding staircase when she heard gunshots and cheerful shouting on the street. Harvey was bedfast now and needed special care. The noise continued as she propped him up in the bed. He still insisted on feeding himself, so she left him, saying she wanted to see what was causing the jubilation.

When she reached the bottom of the stairs, Althea and the children were coming from the kitchen, excited about the noise. Rebecca had egg all over the front of her dress. Linda ran ahead of them, saying they should stay inside.

Leaving the old woman and the children at the door, she left the porch and walked toward a wild group of young people who were shouting joyfully and dancing about. She was about to ask the reason for the celebration when she heard a young man shout, "The war is over! The war is over! We won! Grant defeated Lee!"

Elbowing her way through the crowd to the young man, she asked, "How do you know this?"

"Hey, lady," he said, "it came to the *York Courier* office by wire a half hour ago! There'll be a special edition off the press before noon." Pivoting, he ran down the street, waving his arms. "Wahoo-o-o-o! The war is over! My dad can come home now! Wahooo-o-o!"

Elated, Linda lifted her skirts and ran back to the big house. Althea and the children were on the porch steps, waiting for her. "Did you hear that, Althea? The war is over! Lee surrendered to Grant! We won!"

"Yes! That's wonderful!"

Five-and-a-half-year-old Steven took hold of his mother's sleeve and asked, "Will our daddy be coming home like that boy's, Mommy?"

A cold hand seemed to clutch Linda's spine. Smiling, she knelt down and gathered both children in her arms. "It shouldn't be very long now and your daddy will be coming home!"

Linda tried to ignore the look of doubt that framed Althea's wrinkled face and fought back the fears that were stabbing at her own heart by reminding herself of Wally Frye's words, "He'll be all right, ma'am. Men like Lieutenant Locklin have a certain something about them. He's a survivor."

Just before noon, Linda put some money in the hand of a

neighbor boy and sent him to the *Courier* office to buy a paper. When he returned, Linda let him keep the change and hurried into the house with the paper. Althea followed and the children gathered at the big kitchen table as Linda spread it out and began reading aloud.

There was a lilt in Linda's voice as she read to them that the Confederate army, grossly outnumbered by the Federals, had begun to crumble on April 6. By April 8, it was done. On Sunday, April 9, General Robert E. Lee capitulated to save further Confederate losses. With General Ulysses S. Grant looking on, Lee signed the documents of surrender at Appomattox Court House, Virginia. Moments later, Lee rode away on his dappled horse with 12,000 weeping men following on foot. The article closed off with words from President Abraham Lincoln, urging the people of the North to treat the defeated Southerners with charity, rather than hatred.

On Thursday, April 13, there was a message on the front page of the *Courier* from the U.S. Army to all Northerners who had their men reported as missing during the war. Contact with Confederate officials revealed that all Union prisoners of war would be released by April 15. Because of General Lee's generous terms of surrender, the prisoners would be transported north on trains. They would be back with their families shortly.

Inside of a week from the surrender, the nation was shocked by the brutal assassination of President Abraham Lincoln. Linda Locklin carried the sadness of Lincoln's death for the next few weeks as she hoped and prayed for Boyd's return. Her hopes weakened as soldiers from York began returning from the southern prison camps, but there was no tall, handsome major at her doorstep.

Harvey and Althea King did their best to encourage Linda, as did Maude Stillwell during Linda's visits.

The summer came and went, and when Boyd still had not appeared, Linda's hopes were fading like the green was fading from the grass of the King lawn.

On a cold day in January 1866, Linda walked Stevie to school, then returned home to begin a day of house cleaning. Two-year-old Rebecca played happily in her room with her dolls while Linda worked.

At two-thirty in the afternoon, Linda found Althea in the

library, asleep in a large overstuffed chair with an open book in her lap. Already in her coat and scarf, she touched Althea's shoulder and spoke her name softly. The woman awoke with a start.

"I'm sorry to bother you, Althea," said Linda, "but I'm going after Stevie now, and I wanted you to know that Rebecca is taking her nap."

"It's all right, honey." Althea stretched her arms. "I just haven't slept good for a couple of nights. I haven't said anything about it, but Harvey's pain is getting worse, and he's been keeping me awake, rubbing his arms and legs."

"Why didn't you wake me?" asked Linda. "I would do that for you."

"No, dear," she said, patting her hand. "I...I know he probably won't be with me much longer. I want to do all I can while he's still alive."

"I understand." Linda walked from the room, saying, "I'll be back with Stevie in half an hour. Rebecca will no doubt stay asleep while I'm gone."

Linda met her son when he came out of the one-room schoolhouse. Both wearing mittens, they held hands and chatted as they headed for home. The King house was situated on a large lot in the middle of the block on Castle Avenue between Oak and Poplar Streets. The schoolhouse was on Poplar, five blocks east of Castle Avenue. When they turned the corner at Poplar and Castle, Linda noticed a buggy parked in front of the King place. The vehicle was unfamiliar. As they drew closer, she saw a tall, broad-shouldered man in a dark blue uniform standing at the door, apparently waiting for an answer to his knock. He was turned slightly, showing Linda only his back. She wondered if Althea had gone back to sleep.

A few more steps, and the redhead was focusing on the campaign hat. The man was an officer. And he had dark hair. Suddenly she stopped, swallowing hard, her eyes wide. Stevie looked up at her, frowning. "What's the matter, Mommy?"

Linda's heart thundered in her breast. Her feet seemed frozen to the ground. Her breath was visible as it emerged from her open mouth in short gasps, chilled by the cold air.

"It's your daddy, Stevie!" Letting go of his hand, she bolted toward the house, crying, "Boyd, Boyd, darling! You're home! I knew it! I knew—"

As Linda was running toward him, shouting, the officer turned to face her. When she saw his features, the breath left her, and she collapsed in a heap.

The man darted to Linda and knelt beside her. Stevie skidded to a halt. "You're not my daddy."

"No, son," said the officer. "I can tell you're Steven Locklin, though."

Linda was blinking her eyes, trying to focus on him.

"Mrs. Locklin, are you all right?"

She licked her lips and shook her head to clear it. "I…I think so."

"Here, let me help you to sit up," said the soldier, raising her to a sitting position. "I'm sorry about this. You…you mistook me for your husband, didn't you?"

Placing trembling fingers to her forehead, she nodded. "Yes. You're…you're built exactly like him. I think I can stand."

He helped her to her feet. "I'm Captain Jake Bolger, ma'am. I served as a lieutenant in *A* Brigade under the major. I was with him when—I was with him the day he went in the river. I have something for you."

Bolger walked Linda to the porch with Stevie following. There was a large paper bag on the porch floor. Opening the door, Linda invited him in. Bolger picked up the bag, entered behind mother and son, and closed the door. Telling Stevie to tiptoe into the library and see if "Grandma" Althea was awake—and not to disturb her if she was asleep—Linda sat down in the small receiving room just off the entryway and asked Captain Bolger to take off his coat and be seated.

Removing only his hat, he said, "I really don't have very long, Mrs. Locklin. I lost a little time finding you after I talked to Mrs. Stillwell."

He was opening the paper bag when Stevie returned, informing his mother that Grandma was indeed asleep. When the boy sat down beside Linda, Bolger produced an officer's campaign hat, which she recognized instantly. "That's my husband's hat," she said in a whisper.

"Yes, ma'am," said Bolger, handing it to her. "After the Sharpsburg battle, I went back to the spot where the major took the shell and went into the river. Just...just wanted to spend a few minutes there. He meant an awful lot to me, ma'am—to all of us."

Tears glistened in Linda's eyes. "I can understand that," she responded softly.

"While I was standing there," proceeded Bolger, "I noticed his hat in the bushes. I picked it up, planning to bring it to you whenever I had the time to do it. I'm on leave right now, and I only live a couple of hours' ride from here, across the Maryland line, so I thought I'd bring it to you. Sorry I've been so long in getting it done."

Clutching Boyd's hat close to her heart, Linda said, "Don't apologize for that, Captain. I just appreciate your thoughtfulness. Thank you so much. Maybe one day Boyd can thank you, too."

Bolger's brow furrowed. "Ma'am?"

"I mean, if he's alive and has been in a Confederate prison camp...and just hasn't been able to get home yet."

Bolger's features tightened. "Mrs. Locklin," he said with difficulty, "all the prisoners were released by the Confederates within a week after the war ended. The War Department listed all our soldiers who hadn't returned by July 1 as dead. Didn't they notify you?"

Linda's heart went cold. "No," she replied weakly.

"Oh, ma'am, I really am sorry. I hate to be the one to break this to you. They should have notified you of it months ago. I'm really sorry."

"Please don't feel bad, Captain. It is certainly no fault of yours. It was very kind and thoughtful of you to bring Boyd's hat to me. Thank you."

Stevie's face pinched as he took hold of his mother's hand. "Daddy's dead, isn't he, Mommy?"

Linda wrapped him in her arms and held him tight, pressing her cheek against the top of his head. A hot lump was in her throat, constricting it.

The captain knelt on one knee and laid a hand on the boy's shoulder. "Stevie, your daddy was one of the finest men I have ever known. He was strong and brave and he loved you and your mother very much. He talked a lot about both of you. He's...he's gone now, and you'll have to be the man of the family. Your mother will need to lean on you real hard sometimes. You be brave and strong like your daddy and help her, okay?"

Lip quivering and tears spilling, Steven Boyd Locklin nodded.

Bolger stood up. "I must be going, Mrs. Locklin. I can show myself out. You stay right here with Stevie. It has been a genuine pleasure to meet you."

Linda forced a smile and extended him her right hand. "Thank you, Captain. God bless you."

Holding her hand and squeezing gently, the army officer said, "The major told me you were the most beautiful woman in all the world, ma'am. May I say that I agree with him?"

Linda's face flushed. "You are very kind."

Releasing her hand, Bolger replied, "It's not kindness, ma'am. Just clear eyesight and good judgment." Pivoting, he walked to the door, laid his hand on the knob, and turned to face her. "Good-bye, ma'am," he said gently.

"Good-bye, Captain. Maybe we'll meet again sometime."

"I would really like that," he replied with feeling. "But it will be a while. The reason I'm on leave right now is because I'm being transferred to a fort out west—New Mexico or Arizona. The army gave me a few days to visit my parents before heading west."

"You aren't married, Captain?"

"No. Just haven't found the right gal yet." He paused, then added, "If I'd met you before you and the major were married, I'll say this: I would have given him some earnest competition for your hand."

Linda blushed. "Aren't you the flatterer, though?"

Opening the door and placing the campaign hat on his head, the captain said, "When I do return to Maryland to see my parents, maybe I'll swing by York again."

"You would be quite welcome," Linda assured him.

"Good-bye again, ma'am." He smiled and was gone.

That night, Linda sat before her mirror in her nightgown and brushed her long, auburn hair by lantern light. Stevie was in the next room asleep. Laying the brush down, she looked at her reflection. Tears filled her eyes and lines creased her brow. "You're a widow, Linda. Your husband is dead. Boyd won't be coming back."

Bursting into uncontrollable sobs, she threw herself across the bed and cried herself to sleep.

In March 1866, Harvey King died. In late June, Althea slipped and fell down the spiral staircase in her house and broke her hip. Four days later, she lay at the point of death in York's City Hospital, her lungs filling with fluid.

Having left Stevie and Rebecca with Maude Stillwell, Linda sat on a chair in the hall outside Althea's room, waiting for Dr. Clarence Wood to emerge. Wood was the physician who had cared for Linda during her pregnancy with Rebecca and had delivered her. He had also been Harvey King's physician.

Presently the door came open. A nurse appeared, followed by the doctor. Wood was grim. When Linda stood and looked at him, he shook his head. "She's gone, Linda. The pneumonia was too much for her."

Linda wept as the doctor took her down the hall to a small room. He let her cry it out, then asked quietly, "What are you going to do now?"

"I don't know," she replied, dabbing at her eyes with a hanky. "I suppose the children and I could move in with Mrs. Stillwell, at least temporarily. I'll have to find another job."

"I know how pleased the Kings were with your work, dear," said Wood. "From what they told me, you handled Harvey's problems better than most qualified nurses could have done. If you had the formal education, I would see to it that you had a job right here at the hospital."

"But I don't."

"I know, but I do have an idea. I've been thinking about it ever since Althea began to show pneumonia. It was almost certain that her aged, tired body would never make it."

"What's the idea?"

"I have a very close friend whose wife is an invalid. She needs the kind of care you can give her. My friend has been looking for someone to live in and do just about exactly the same thing you've been doing since you moved in with the Kings. He'll treat you right, I know." Taking a deep breath, he said, "There are a couple of drawbacks, though. And because of those, you may not want the job."

"Well, tell me."

"My friend is an army colonel. I figure that since you are an army widow, you might have had enough of the military."

"That wouldn't bother me, doctor," Linda replied evenly. "What's the other drawback?"

Wood rubbed the back of his neck. "Well, the colonel is commandant at Fort Sumner, New Mexico, and that's a long way from here."

Happy for the opportunity, Linda assured the doctor that moving to New Mexico would be no problem. She had to provide for her children one way or another.

Wood immediately wired Colonel Wayne Stover, and by the next day, Linda had the job. After a tearful good-bye with Maude Stillwell, Linda and the children boarded a train westward. From St. Louis, Missouri, they rode hot, dusty stagecoaches and arrived at Fort Sumner on August 3, 1866. The fort was located in eastern New Mexico on the Pecos River.

They were given comfortable quarters and immediately felt at home in the military surroundings. Colonel Stover, in his early sixties, had fought in the Civil War under General Ulysses S. Grant and had heard of Major Boyd Locklin.

Linda immediately fell in love with fifty-eight-year-old Cora Stover, who was confined to a wheelchair due to a horseback riding accident some twenty years previously. Stevie and Rebecca adjusted quickly, finding friends among the other military children.

A short time after arriving at Sumner, Linda found several of the soldiers showing interest in her. She was kind to them but kept them at bay, explaining when necessary that she still deeply cherished the memory of her husband, and might never be interested in another man.

In December 1866, during supper in the Stover house, Cora looked across the table and said, "Wayne, don't you think it's time to tell Linda?"

The colonel was mopping gravy from his plate with a piece of bread. "I was going to wait till after supper, honey, but I guess now's as good a time as any."

Linda was putting a second helping of mashed potatoes on Stevie's plate. Setting the bowl down, she asked, "Tell me what?"

"I received word today that I'm being transferred to Fort Grant, over in Arizona. The commandant was killed last week by Apaches, and they need a new man."

"We'll be taking you with us, dear," spoke up Cora. "You won't mind moving to Arizona, will you?"

"Of course not. Where is Fort Grant?"

"Southeastern part," said Stover. "About thirty-five miles due west of the Peloncillo Mountains."

"Hmm. Must be fairly new. That would put it about halfway between Fort Savage and Fort Campbell. I know it wasn't there when Boyd and I were at Savage."

The colonel cleared his throat. "Well, Linda," he said nervously, "Fort Grant was built two years ago after Fort Savage was burned down. You've always spoken with such sentimentality about Savage that I didn't want to tell you about it."

"Did Apaches burn it?"

"Yes. There's one band of Chiricahua Apaches that is wreaking havoc all over that area. Have been for about two years. They're led by a self-styled murderous cutthroat who calls himself Diablo."

"Diablo? That's the Spanish word for devil, isn't it?"

"Yes, and they tell me the name fits him perfectly. He is one bloody hellion. In fact it is Diablo who killed Colonel Paul Emery, the man I am to replace. Caught him riding with a cavalry escort while on his way north to Fort Apache and ambushed the escort. Two men were wounded and left for dead. They made it back to Fort Grant and told the story. Diablo had Emery personally marked as his own victim. Tortured him to death."

Stover poured more gravy on his plate and picked up another slice of bread.

Cora said, "You'd best tell her the rest of it, dear. She really should know."

Curious, Linda set her gaze on the colonel.

"Well, there was a letter that came with my order of transfer. Big brass wanted to fill me in on this Diablo character. Seems he had a smoldering hatred toward your husband. Boyd had killed his father, Chief Pantano."

"Kateya!" gasped Linda. "That's Kateya! He was only a teenager when Boyd killed Pantano. So he calls himself Diablo now."

"That's him. The letter says that Boyd once called him devil. He didn't like it then, but later must have decided it was all right. Two years ago he showed up leading a vicious pack of Apache killers. White people were being massacred by the dozens. One day he waylaid a cavalry patrol, outnumbering them three to one, and took them captive. He sent two of his warriors to Fort Savage under a white flag, carrying personal effects of the men in the patrol to prove they had them, and demanded they turn Lieutenant Boyd Locklin over to Diablo. If they refused, the entire patrol would be massacred. When the warriors were told that Lieutenant Locklin was no longer at the fort, they rode away in anger. Two days later, Diablo led a huge force of Apaches against the fort and burned it down. The men in the patrol were never seen again."

"So Kateya grew up and became their leader. I suppose somebody will have to kill him just like Boyd killed his father."

"She may be wondering about the safety of her children at Fort Grant, dear," said Cora.

"Yes. They're strengthening the number of troops at Grant, Linda. Shouldn't be any more risk there than you have right here."

"We're not afraid," spoke up Stevie. "Our daddy was a brave soldier. We're brave just like him, huh, Becky?"

Rebecca nodded, chewing a mouthful of potatoes.

"When are we going to Fort Grant, Colonel?" asked Linda.

"Have to report January 7."

"Then January 7 it is," she said with spirit.

CHAPTER SEVENTEEN

The noonday Arizona sun was the color of a polished bugle as it bore down unmercifully on the twenty-man detail out of Fort Grant.

It was late June 1867, and the men in sweaty, dust-filmed uniforms rode double file, carbines leaning forward. In the lead of the dual column was Captain William Coe, whose red-rimmed eyes kept a steady vigil on the desert around them. Riding beside Coe was Lieutenant Price Wesson, a sandy-haired son of the South, who had graduated from West Point less than a year before the Civil War began, and had fought on the Confederate side under General Stonewall Jackson.

Coe, who had fought as a lieutenant in the Union Army of the Tennessee under General Ulysses S. Grant, was promoted to captain two weeks before the war ended. In May 1865 he was appointed to Fort Savage and learned quickly that fighting Apaches was totally different than fighting Rebels. He had been in several battles where the young charismatic Apache leader, Diablo, was present, and though he hated the Indian for his cruel ways, he had learned to respect him for his fighting prowess.

When Diablo led a giant force of Apaches against Fort Savage because they failed to produce Lieutenant Boyd Locklin for his bloodlust, the demonic madman burned it to the ground. Coe's wife and two young sons came dangerously close to dying in the fire. His closest friend and commandant of the fort, Colonel Earl Snider, had died of multiple burns. In his wrath, Coe had sworn to one day kill Diablo.

The captain had then become good friends with Colonel Paul Emery, who replaced Snider. A scheme by the wicked Apache leader put Emery in his hands. Showing no mercy, Diablo tortured him to death, which intensified Coe's commitment to personally kill him.

Though he had not yet been close enough in battle to single out Diablo, Coe still lived for the moment he could send the devil to the flames of perdition where he belonged.

Even now, as Coe led his patrol across the burning sands, he thought of Diablo. Was he out there somewhere among the sandy hills, rock formations, or crevices watching and waiting with another of his ambush schemes? Coe was aware that the nefarious Apache leader had somehow learned of his vow to get him. After a recent ambush on a cavalry patrol, Diablo held two men captive. He tortured and killed one of them while making his companion watch; then sent the survivor back to Fort Grant as a messenger. The soldier rode into the fort with the front of his shirt soaked with blood. Diablo had carved his name on the man's chest and gave him a message for Captain William Coe. One day the two of them would meet face-to-face, and Diablo would kill him and carve his name in Coe's chest.

Lieutenant Price Wesson broke into Coe's thoughts. "Apaches are strange creatures, Captain."

"I know that," replied Coe, "but I'm not sure what you mean by calling them strange."

"I mean, they're so rotten sneaky. In the war, you bluebellies at least had the guts to come at us head-on. No hiding like little children and springing on you from ambush. I'd just like to meet those shifty-eyed savages head-on, right out in the open."

"They'd still be a plenty tough bunch to reckon with."

"Well, I wish they'd just come at us like white men and fight. This isn't war. It's only a stretched out string of skirmishes. There aren't any big battles."

Coe was silent for a moment; then he said, "In my estimation, even a skirmish is big if it calls for a man to put his life on the line—and ours do. We've seen many men killed in them."

"I know, but give me huge battles like Shiloh and Chickamauga. Now that was real war."

Coe was in no mood for wrangling with Wesson on the subject. The lieutenant was not his favorite person, anyhow. Wesson was a handsome man of sorts, with his pale blue eyes, sandy hair, and sleek, carefully trimmed mustache, but he carried an eternal arrogant, churlish look on his face. Of course, it fit his warped personality. Coe knew from army records that while in the Civil War, Wesson's hot temper, impetuosity, and egotistical attitude had kept him from making the rank of captain. He figured it must have been displayed to the extreme, because the Confederates were running low on captains the last year of the war.

Coe also knew that Wesson envied his captain's bars. It showed up in conversation quite often and was backed by the look in his eyes. Many of the men at Fort Grant had reported privately to Coe that Wesson was saying snide things about him behind his back. One often-repeated crack was that in order to be made a captain at thirty years of age, Coe had licked the boots of the brass in Washington. Wesson had just turned thirty-six.

Another thing that bothered William Coe was the way Wesson had gotten to lovely Linda Locklin through her children. He had played up to them, giving them money and presents to win their affection. When he felt secure enough, he convinced Linda that Steven and Rebecca desperately needed a father figure in their lives. It was obvious to many at the fort that Linda cared deeply for her children, and Wesson had used her concern for them to persuade her to let him become their stepfather. The wedding was set for Sunday, August 11.

Coe's wife, Alice, had become a close friend to Linda, and shared with him that she wanted to warn Linda about marrying Wesson, but had felt it might ruin their friendship. So far, she had said nothing, hoping that Linda would see the man for what he really was before it was too late.

With the incessant squeak of saddle leather and the rhythmic clop of hooves, Lieutenant Price Wesson left off conversation with the captain and thought of beautiful Linda. As a native of Knoxville, Tennessee, Wesson had a slight southern accent and knew how to put on the charm of a southern gentleman. He had been at Fort Grant eight months when Linda and her children arrived with Colonel Stover and his wife.

Wesson had fallen in love with the gorgeous widow the first time he laid eyes on her. Several of the single men began calling on her, but she was still strongly attached to the memory of her dead husband and politely turned them away. Wesson, who was a bit more cunning than the others, decided to get close to her by making friends with Steven and Rebecca. Once that relationship was established, it was a smooth road to Linda. She was naturally quite lonely, and since he was welcome at their quarters because of the children's affection for him, he took advantage of her loneliness, showering her with kindness and affection.

Wesson could be a real charmer when he wanted to, and with the captivating redhead, he wanted to. Just two weeks ago, she had accepted his marriage proposal. Of course, she had explained that she was not in love with him, but this was no deterrent. In time, he would make her forget the dead major and he would win her heart.

The double column hit bottom in a deep draw, climbed out, and found a trail running irregularly through a vast plain dotted with various rock formations, cactus patches, greasewood, yucca, and a spindle tracery of ocotillo. Following the trail, they came upon a thicket of mesquite, which offered a measure of shade.

Captain William Coe raised his hand in a signal to halt and called out over his shoulder, "Let's take a break, men."

Leaving their saddles to the blast of the sun, the soldiers carried their canteens into the thicket, sat down, and popped corks. Under Coe's orders, Sergeants Bifford Caley and Harold Timms walked the perimeter of the shade and studied the surrounding desert. A couple of desert hawks circled in the cloudless sky to the south, and a few small creatures skittered about on the hot sand, but there was no sign of Indians.

After twenty minutes, Captain Coe stood to his feet and wiped sweat from his brow with a bandanna. "Okay, Uncle Sam's fine, fit, and fiery men of war, let's saddle up."

Amid a jocose rumble of complaints against the heat, the men rose and headed for their horses. Suddenly, Sergeant Bifford Caley touched Coe's arm and pointed with the other hand. "Captain, take a look up there."

"Hold it, men," ordered Coe as he followed Caley's extended finger and set his gaze on the bold figure of an Apache standing atop a tall rock some sixty yards to the west.

"Diablo!" gasped one of them.

The audacious young Apache chief stood flagrantly silhouetted against the sky, his long black hair flying in the wind. He held a nickel-plated carbine challengingly above his head, the sun glistening from its shiny barrel. He wore army pants tucked into knee-high moccasins that were turned down at the top. Naked above his waist, his chest was crisscrossed with a pair of cartridge bandoliers. His copper-colored, muscular body shone in the brilliant light.

While the cavalrymen were gasping Diablo's name, Lieutenant Price Wesson said to Coe, "Standing up there all high and mighty. Let's go get him!"

Perturbed at Wesson's outburst, Coe said, "You fool! Can't you see that's exactly what he wants us to do? He's got warriors ready to jump us."

Wesson's face darkened. A thick vein at the side of his forehead throbbed noticeably. "I can't agree with your tactics, Coe! You want that monster dead, don't you? So he's got warriors hidden in those rocks! Let's draw them out in the open by heading toward him and make a real battle out of this!"

Raking Wesson with a hot glare, Coe growled, "You're flirting with a court martial, mister! You'd best—"

"Captain!" cut in Sergeant Harold Timms. "Here they come!"

A dozen Apaches were coming from behind the rock formation, firing their carbines while running toward them.

"Quick!" shouted Coe. "Back into the thicket!"

As the soldiers wheeled and plunged into the heavy stand of mesquite, they saw two more bands of red men running toward them from the east and the north, guns blazing. They returned fire with hot lead hissing into the thicket, splintering mesquite, ricocheting off rocks within the thicket. One man bellowed with pain and another let out a yelp as Apache lead struck white flesh.

The area was alive with gunfire. Dirt spouted up where army bullets struck all around the racing Apaches.

Captain Coe had grabbed his rifle from its scabbard on his saddle while dashing for cover. When he flopped down, he looked toward the top of the rock to see Diablo kneeling and watching him. Taking careful aim, Coe sent a bullet hungrily seeking Diablo. It chewed rock at the hated Apache's feet, causing him to jump backward and disappear.

The Apaches were now flattened on the desert floor, taking shelter behind stumpy rocks and in crevices.

Lieutenant Price Wesson lay six feet from Coe, still angry for the tongue-lashing Coe had given him. Keeping his head down while reloading his revolver, Wesson gave the captain a malignant stare. When Coe glared back, Wesson rasped, "I don't like being called a fool!"

"A man talks like a fool, he is a fool!" countered Coe. "If we'd headed for those rocks, they'd have caught us flat-footed in the open. You're not fighting Federals now, Wesson. You're up against the fiercest men of war in the world. If you live through this one, keep that in mind."

The army horses stood in a cluster a hundred yards from the thicket, having fled only seconds after the firing had started. As the battle wore on, the Apaches crawled slowly toward the thicket while firing intermittently. Their objective was to engage the white men in hand-to-hand conflict. They carried less ammunition than the soldiers and would rather use knives.

Shouting a warning to his men that the Apaches were trying to get in close, Coe drew a bead on one just as he raised up his head from a crevice and squeezed the trigger. The carbine barked into the heat-laden air and the Indian's face mushroomed red. The whiplash of the bullet's impact threw him back into the crevice.

Jacking another cartridge into the chamber, Coe looked around to see that his men were expertly keeping the savages pinned down, forcing them to fight back with their guns, using up precious, limited ammunition. They remembered well what he had taught them during the sessions at the fort. Coe's quick glance also showed him four men in blue, lying still, their faces in the dirt.

Just as the captain turned back to the business at hand, he saw a grinning enemy bent low and heading toward himself and Wesson as fast as he could run. Wesson had already seen him and dropped the hammer of his revolver. It made a dead click. Coe, expecting the lieutenant to get him, was not prepared. Firing instinctively, he hit the charging brave in the thigh. The determined savage stumbled and fell, but rolled to his feet and kept coming, though limping heavily. His black eyes were aflame with hatred and determination as he came at Coe, wielding a long-bladed knife. It all happened so fast that Coe didn't have time to lever in another cartridge. Leaping to his feet, he met the Indian head-on, dodging the deadly blade and driving the butt of the carbine at him with full force. The solid wood made a meaty smack as it caved in the man's head.

Smoke and dust were boiling around the thicket. Peering into it, Coe worked the lever. "You need to learn to count your shots, Wesson!"

The lieutenant was swearing, but not at Coe. His fingers were dug into the cartridge pouch on his belt, finding that he only had two left.

The captain was about to drop down again when a ghostly figure plunged through the cloud of dust and smoke, eyes wild. It was Diablo. There was a maniacal look in his eyes as he fired the nickel-plated carbine in his hands. The slug hit Coe in the chest like a sledgehammer.

Price Wesson froze, his fingers holding the last two cartridges. He saw that Diablo's attention was strictly on the man who had vowed to kill him. Thinking fast, Wesson dropped his face in the dirt and played dead.

Mesquite branches clawed at Coe as he fell flat on his back. His chest was numb, and he could barely breathe. The threatening shape of Diablo towered over him as the rest of his men blasted away at the Apaches, unaware of what was happening at the spot occupied by the captain and lieutenant. Coe saw the cold, dark shine of the Indian's eyes; the grinning, sensual trap of his mouth; the vicious hawklike features behind the bore of the carbine that was lined on his face.

It was William Coe's time to die.

"You lose, Captain," hissed Diablo, and squeezed the trigger.

Captain William Coe, U.S. Army, never heard the shot that killed him.

Price Wesson lay still, his heart drumming his ribs. Not until he heard Diablo at a distance shouting at his warriors did Wesson look up. The Apache chief had accomplished his desired objective by killing Coe. Knowing his warriors were low on ammunition, he was calling for them to forsake the fight.

Wesson rose up on one knee and saw the Apaches working their way toward the tall rocks while firing over their shoulders into the thicket. Intent on gunning down as many Apaches as possible before they reached the rocks, the soldiers were blasting away at them. Thinking fast, Wesson smashed himself across the left cheekbone with the barrel of his revolver, splitting the skin. Blood spurted. Jamming the gun in its holster, he picked up the carbine and emptied it in the direction of the Indians just as the last one disappeared behind the rocks.

Instantly the men quit firing and started checking on their comrades. Standing over Coe's body, Wesson shouted, "The captain's dead, men! I'm in charge now!"

At that instant, the Apaches were seen on horseback, galloping full-speed across the rock-strewn desert.

Letting the blood flow freely down his cheek, Wesson faced the men who were coming at him through the thicket. "Get the horses! They're low on ammunition. Let's go after them!"

Sergeant Biff Caley elbowed his way to Wesson and knelt beside the captain's body, removing his hat. The others drew up in a circle, pushing mesquite branches aside as they beheld their dead leader.

Perturbed that no one had headed for the horses, Wesson flared angrily, "Did you men hear me? I said get the horses! We're going after those bloody savages!"

Sergeant Harold Timms drew up and knelt next to Caley, showing his sorrow at Coe's death. Still no one jumped at the lieutenant's order. Caley stood up and asked, "How'd it happen, Lieutenant?"

"We'll talk about it later," replied Wesson, hoping they would all notice his bleeding face. "Right now I want all of us who are able to mount up and go after Diablo!"

Caley shook his head. "That would be a foolish thing to do, Lieutenant."

Remembering what Coe had said, Wesson bristled at the word *foolish.* "Aren't you forgetting something, Sergeant? I'm the only officer here. Who are you to tell me what is foolish?"

"The voice of experience," replied Caley evenly. "We're low on ammunition, ourselves. With the head start the Apaches have on us, we'd never catch them before they reach their secret lair. They'd send some more of their pals out after us and wipe us out."

Timms stood up. "Biff's right, Lieutenant. If we got close to wherever they're hiding out, we'd be dead in our tracks."

Although he hated to admit that these men were much more experienced in fighting Indians than he was, Wesson realized the foolishness of his impetuous order. Pulling a bandanna to wipe the blood from his face, he nodded. "All right. We'll get Diablo another time."

"I asked how the captain got it, Lieutenant," said Caley.

"It was Diablo, himself," replied Wesson. "He came out of the dust and smoke, looking for Coe. It was evident because he beelined for him. I was in the process of loading my revolver and wasn't in a position to fire at him. Seeing that he was after Coe, I jumped between them, using my body as a shield. Instead of shooting me, Diablo cracked me with his carbine. I don't know exactly what happened then, because I fell. I heard two shots. The first one must have been the one in the captain's chest, and the second shot, the one in his head."

In addition to Captain Coe, six other men in the detail were dead. Three others were wounded, but none seriously. Sadly, the soldiers picked up their dead, draping them over their horses' backs, helped the wounded men into their saddles, and rode for the fort.

As they moved slowly in that direction, Lieutenant Price Wesson rode in the lead. Happy inside that Coe had been killed, Wesson told himself this would be his golden opportunity. By rights, he should be the man to take Coe's place. This would mean that long-awaited promotion to captain. Just to be sure it fell his way, Wesson would talk to Colonel Stover about it.

CHAPTER EIGHTEEN

The lowering sun cast long shadows across the floor of Colonel Wayne Stover's parlor as Cora sat in her wheelchair, sipping a cup of hot tea. Seated beside her on the overstuffed sofa was Linda Locklin. Opposite them on a love seat was Alice Coe. Several children could be heard laughing and squealing in the small yard behind the house.

Alice Coe had an ulterior motive in dropping by for late afternoon tea. She had to find the courage to express her feelings to Linda about Price Wesson. Alice could not let her friend enter the marriage tie with the repugnant lieutenant without at least making an attempt to stop it. She had been there for a half hour and was on her third cup of tea, but had not yet been daring enough to broach the subject.

The three women had discussed several topics since sitting down for tea, but the upcoming wedding had not come up, nor had the name of Price Wesson.

A lull finally came in the conversation, and Cora made an opening for Alice by saying, "Linda, Wayne and I will miss having you and the children right here in the house when you and Lieutenant Wesson get married. I'm so glad, however, that you'll still be here every day to take care of me."

Linda and Wesson had argued about her staying on as Cora's housekeeper and nurse once she was his wife. Linda had finally convinced him that it made her happy to care for Cora, and insisted that she could both keep up their home and see to Cora's needs. Though Price had agreed, she wondered if he wouldn't try to stop her once they were married. She had told Cora nothing of Price's objections.

"I'm glad for the privilege," said Linda.

Alice's heart was pounding. She was about to speak up when

Cora asked, "How many days until the wedding, honey?"

Linda took a sip of tea then set the cup in the saucer on her lap. "Well, let's see…today is almost gone, so we'll start with tomorrow, which is June 28. That would make it…ah…forty-five days."

Alice decided it was now or never. "Linda, could I ask you something?"

"Of course."

"Are you…are you really excited about marrying Price?"

Linda's smile waned. "Well, I can't say that it's anything like the way I felt when I was engaged to Boyd. But—"

"Are you really in love with him?" Having broken the ice, Alice found her courage growing. When Linda frowned, Alice said, "I know I'm sticking my nose in, but I'm your friend, and I care about you."

"I appreciate that," Linda said, her face flushing slightly. "I've told Price that I'm not in love with him…that I'm…well, still in love with the memory of a wonderful man. He's willing to take me on that basis. He says he'll be so good to me that I'll forget Boyd and learn to love him. I don't really think it'll happen like that, but as Price says, my children need a daddy."

Cora Stover wanted to speak up, but Alice was handling the subject so well that she let her continue without interruption.

"At risk of making you angry at me, Linda, I'll just come right out with it. I don't think the man will make you a good husband. We've all seen his bad temper, and we know how he has embarrassed you time and again with his public fits of jealousy when you so much as smile at another one of the soldiers. If he's like this now, what'll he be like once you wear his ring and his name?"

Linda's features tinted again. "Price loves Steven and Rebecca, and they love him. That counts for a lot. And he's right. They do need a father's hand."

Deciding to put a word in, Cora cleared her throat and said, "Certainly you are aware, honey, that Price is not well liked by his fellow soldiers. This could be a detriment to your happiness."

Linda was silent a moment. "I haven't said anything about this to either of you, but the day is not too far off when Price and I will leave Fort Grant. I think the men here have become prejudiced against him because of his temperament."

Cora frowned. "Why would you be leaving here, honey?"

"Well, Price says he's already past due for promotion. He's expecting it any time. Since these western forts are only allowed one captain apiece—and William is that man here—Price will no doubt be transferred to another fort. Perhaps he can make the people there like him better."

Cora and Alice exchanged furtive glances.

"Honey, I wouldn't hurt you for the world," Alice said. "You know that. But I have to say this. Price Wesson isn't going to be liked no matter where he goes."

"And he's not up for promotion either, Linda," put in Cora. "Wayne has discussed him with me, and he has also discussed the idea of promotion with Alice and William. According to Wayne and William, Price is not captain material. He is too impetuous, cocky, and hot-tempered to be a captain. They don't even think he should be a lieutenant, but Washington sent him here, and they're trying to make the best of it."

Linda Locklin sat in silence, chewing on her lower lip. Her stomach was churning. Though she knew Price had those detrimental traits, she had tried to dwell on his good qualities. Hard pressed for further words of defense for Wesson, she stood up and said, "The patrols should be coming in. You probably want to get home so you can put supper on the stove, Alice."

"You're right. William will be hungry as a bear." Alice rose from the love seat. "Linda, I...I hope you aren't angry with me."

"Of course not," smiled the redhead, embracing her. "I deeply appreciate your concern for my happiness. I—"

Linda's words were cut off by the sound of boots on the porch, followed by the door coming open. The formidable figure of Colonel Wayne Stover appeared, his face ashen gray. Closing the door, he ran a dismal gaze over the faces of the women, letting it settle on Alice.

Reading her husband's doleful countenance, Cora spoke before the colonel could say anything to Alice. "Wayne, something's happened. What is it?"

"Bad news. Please sit down, Alice."

Captain William Coe's wife took the news of her husband's death hard. While she sobbed, Linda embraced her, saying that she understood her grief. She had lost a husband in battle, too.

When Alice grew calm, she spoke words of hatred for the vile Diablo, who had taken William's life as he had vowed to do. The colonel, trying to give any consolation possible, told Alice that even though Diablo had killed William as he had said, at least he was deprived of carving his name in William's chest.

Alice's sons were called in from the backyard and told of their father's death. Steven Locklin tried to comfort his friends, saying that though he was only three years old when his father was killed, he at least partially understood their grief.

The colonel spoke his words of condolence, then left Alice and her sons in the care of Linda and Cora and headed for his office.

As Stover crossed the compound, he was stopped several times by the soldiers, asking for details on the deaths of Captain Coe and the other men of the patrol. When he finally drew up to the office, which was located on the dusty parade, he saw Lieutenant Price Wesson sitting on a bench near the door, waiting for him.

Wesson rose and saluted. "Colonel, I need to talk to you."

"Right now?" responded Stover, walking past him and opening the office door. "I'm quite busy, Lieutenant."

"I realize that, sir," nodded the sandy-haired man, "but this is an urgent matter."

"All right, come in." Removing his hat and sitting down behind his desk, Stover motioned for Wesson to take a chair. "Now what is this urgent matter?"

Holding his campaign hat in his hands, Wesson said, "Well, sir, with Captain Coe dead, now the fort will need another captain. Since the next rank above lieutenant is captain, I would like to ask you to recommend to Washington that I receive a promotion and take Coe's place."

Shaking his head, Stover said firmly, "I'll do nothing of the kind."

An icy wave of frustration rippled through Wesson. Holding his voice level, he said, "I don't understand."

"I think you do. You've not shown me that you're captain material. You have proven yourself to be immature, egotistical to a fault, hair-triggered with your temper, and quite often indifferent to the feelings of others. Until I can see definite improvement in these areas, there will be no talk of promotion. Understand?"

Stover's words twisted into Wesson's gut. Hot streamers of wrath lanced through him. He wanted to leap over the desk and strangle the old man's life from him, but he forced himself to show an outward coolness. "Yes, sir. I understand. You will soon find reason to recommend me for promotion. I guarantee it."

"Fine," said Stover, "now if you'll excuse me, I have work to do."

Later that evening, Price Wesson knocked on the door of the Coe apartment. When one of the boys responded, Wesson said, "I was told that Mrs. Locklin is here. May I see her?"

Linda appeared, stepping onto the porch and pulling the door shut behind her. She saw the tightness on Wesson's face and waited for him to speak.

"What are you doing here?" he demanded curtly. "You knew I was coming to your quarters to take you for a walk. We agreed on that before I rode out his morning."

Linda felt resentment rise within. Her voice was coated with ire. "Price, that was before Captain Coe was killed! Alice is one of my best friends. Right now, she's in an awful state of grief. She needs me, so I'm here. I forgot all about our date for a walk."

"Forgot? Is that all I mean to you, Linda? I was out there in that battle today, myself. Maybe I need some soothing from the woman I am soon to marry. How about me?"

She let his words ride the air for a short moment. "You? You got back without a scratch, for which I am thankful, but William Coe's body lies in the infirmary tonight with a bullet between his eyes and the back of his head missing. He was a fellow officer. Don't you feel anything for him, or for his widow and sons?"

"Of course," lied Wesson, "but we can't let our world fall apart, either. Fighting Apaches is tough business, and I need my woman to lean on after I've stared death in the face."

"I'm sorry I can't be in two places at one, Price, but right now Alice needs me more than you do."

"All right," he sighed back. "I'll go now. How about at least giving me a kiss?"

Relinquishing, Linda puckered and gave him a short peck.

Looking as if she had just slapped his face, he asked, "You call that a kiss?"

"It's the best I can do right now, Price. Now please, I must get back to Alice."

Wesson pursed his lips and set his jaw angrily. He wheeled without a word and stomped away in the darkness.

Linda turned slowly toward the door, feeling sick inside. Earlier in the day, Alice Coe had unwittingly worded exactly how Linda had been feeling. She had been having genuine doubts that Price would make her a good husband, but could not bring herself to tell him so.

On July 1, Price Wesson was leading a routine patrol of a dozen men in an area some five miles north of Fort Grant. As they rode in the dust and heat, watching for Indians, Wesson was alone in his thoughts. He hated Colonel Wayne Stover for pointing out his faults, but he hated him even more because Stover had never trusted him to lead an assault on the Apaches. He was always relegated to simple patrols that seldom even led to a skirmish. Other lieutenants in the fort were assigned to lead the cavalry into fierce, planned conflict, and they were younger and less experienced than he.

From there Wesson's thoughts ran to Linda and the coolness he had been feeling from her the past few days. Last night he had come right out and asked her if she had found another man, saying that it wouldn't be hard to see him on the sly with all the dark corners in the fort. Linda hadn't seemed too shaken at his question, but insisted there was not another man. Not quite believing her, Wesson had gripped her shoulders until she winced with pain, saying if she ever left him for another man, she would never become the man's wife because he would kill him. All his life he had looked for a woman like her, and he would not give her up to anybody.

Laughing within himself, Wesson remembered the frightened look on Linda's face at that moment. He was sure what he had said would do the trick. If she was seeing one of the other soldiers, she'd break it off now.

Sergeant Bifford Caley rode beside Wesson. Lieutenant Wesson was not aware of it, but Colonel Stover had sent Caley on the patrol to keep things level and under control in case they met up with hostiles.

The troopers behind Wesson and Caley were conversing about

the fine burial sermon Colonel Stover had given for Captain William Coe. Irritated at the reminder that he would not succeed Coe, Price Wesson swore under his breath and tilted the brim of his hat lower over his face against the beating glare of tawny earth and metal yellow sky. Sweat was running into his eyes and trickling down his back.

The conversation about Coe broke off when one of the troopers called from the column behind, "Lieutenant, word is that a new captain is being sent to us shortly. Who is he? Where's he from?"

Hipping around in the saddle, Wesson squinted harshly at him. "I don't know who's spreading that kind of stuff. Could be one of us lieutenants will get a promotion and take Coe's place."

"Why would you say that, Lieutenant?" queried Caley. "Colonel Stover told me about the new captain. Didn't he tell you?"

The concentrated malevolence Wesson was carrying toward Stover instantly grew stronger. He shuddered with anger, clenched his jaw, and said through his teeth, "Stover told me nothing. What do you know that I don't?"

"Only that the colonel wired Washington, explaining about Coe's death, and requested a new captain. Washington wired back two days ago, saying they were working on it. The western forts are short on captains, but Grant's location is strategic, and they would be sending a man from either a New Mexico fort or one here in Arizona."

Sitting like a statue on his horse, Wesson looked like he had just taken a shot between the eyes with a poleax. His mouth clamped shut and his face flamed.

Caley waited for an outburst of temper, but it did not come. The lieutenant was visibly angered.

Wesson held the sergeant with riveting blue eyes. "Do the other four lieutenants at Grant know about this?"

"Yeah, I think so. Seems they've each talked to me about it. Everybody's curious as to who the new captain might be."

A sardonic expression twisted Wesson's thin lips. The words came out like a snake's hiss. "Why does a mere sergeant have this privileged information, but I, as one of five lieutenants, have not been informed?"

Caley wanted to bite back at Wesson's use of the word *mere,* but checked the urge. "I don't know. You'll have to ask the colonel."

Wesson lifted his hat and wiped sweat from his brow. "Hotshot new captain, eh? Probably send us some dud who's been riding a desk for the last five years."

"He'll be a man of special choice," said Caley. "I guess you know that Colonel Stover will be retiring in another three years or so. Whoever they pick will no doubt go to major in a year or two, then be made colonel when he succeeds him as commandant of Fort Grant."

The anger inside Price Wesson was volcanic. Something else he hadn't been told: Stover was planning to retire in three years. He did not let on to Caley that this was also a surprise, but rode in silence. His mind froze as a deadly, wicked embryonic scheme began to take form in his thoughts.

Somehow Wesson would find a way to get in the colonel's good graces—maybe even doing something heroic while fighting the Apaches. Once he was secure in that respect, he would wrangle a spot in a patrol or an attack detail with the new captain. In the heat of battle, he would position himself so as to put a bullet in the new captain's heart. Who would know that it wasn't an Apache bullet?

Once this was done, Wesson would be made captain. From there he would make major, no matter who he had to step on or squash, and finally he would be named commandant of Fort Grant and be promoted to colonel. Linda would be plenty proud to call him her husband then.

During the next week Linda tried to find a way to tell Wesson that she did not feel at peace to go on with the wedding plans, but when he showed loving attention to Steven and Rebecca, she found it impossible. When the two of them were alone together, she noticed that he was preoccupied. When she asked about it, he told her he was merely loaded down with his official duties. Linda would never know of his scheme to become commandant of the fort. It was on his mind continuously.

On July 8, the setting sun made a slow explosion of color on the long-fingered clouds that hovered on the western horizon. Colonel Wayne Stover stood at the open gate of the fort and gazed longingly across the vivid desert floor as it reflected the fiery sunset. At sunrise that morning, he had sent out five patrols as usual. They were always to return to the fort no later than an hour before the sun touched the distant mountains to the west. Lieutenant Harry Miller's patrol had not returned.

An hour later, as the purple sky was darkening, there was still no patrol. Gathering the other four lieutenants around him at the gate, Stover gave orders that every patrol would join the search party the next morning.

"None of us saw Diablo today, Colonel," said Lieutenant John Frame. "I hate to say this, but maybe Miller did. As you know, Diablo doesn't always attack when he lets himself be seen. Much of the time, he just likes to rattle our nerves by playing cat and mouse. I just hope today wasn't his time to spring on the mouse."

"Twenty-one mice to be exact," Stover said bleakly.

Commanding the sentries to let him know immediately should the patrol or any part of it return, the colonel dismissed his officers, left the gate, and walked to Lieutenant Harry Miller's quarters to try to encourage Miller's wife. While she held her two children close to her with a look of despair on her face, Stover spoke words that he didn't even believe himself. He told Opal Miller that many unexpected things could have happened other than the patrol meeting up with Apaches. They may still come riding in at any time.

The colonel went home. He shared his fear that the patrol was lost with Cora and Linda Locklin. While they discussed the situation, there was a knock at the door. Opening it, Stover saw the grim face of one of the sentries. "Colonel," he said in a dismal tone, "we have something to show you at the gate."

"Has it to do with the late patrol?"

"Yes, sir."

"Can't you bring it here?"

Looking past the colonel toward Cora and Linda, the sentry replied, "It would be best if I didn't, sir."

"I understand," said Stover. Telling Cora he would return shortly, he hastened to the gate with the sentry.

Arriving at the gate, he found Sergeant Bifford Caley with two other sentries. They were standing by a burlap sack that lay on the ground just inside the gate. The two sentries held kerosene lanterns.

Looking down at the sack, Stover asked, "So what is this?"

"We haven't opened it, sir," said the sentry who had come to get him. "As you can see, there's blood soaking through. We thought you should be present when it was opened."

"So how did we get it?" asked Stover.

One of the other sentries said, "A lone rider came galloping by in the darkness and tossed it over the stockade. He was here and gone before we could even catch a glimpse of him or his horse."

Motioning with his hand toward the bloody sack, Stover said, "Open it, Sergeant."

The neck of the burlap sack was tied with rawhide cord. Caley quickly untied it and turned the sack upside down, dumping its contents on the ground. One of the sentries gagged at the sight of the crimson scalps, turned and ran into the shadows, losing his supper.

Colonel Wayne Stover mumbled an indistinguishable oath and Sergeant Caley swore vehemently as he began separating the scalps so he could count them. When he was done, he stood at full height. "Twenty-one, sir. The Apaches scalped every man in Lieutenant Miller's patrol."

"Diablo," murmured Stover, the name tasting sour on his tongue.

"Has to be," agreed one of the sentries. "Bad as the Apaches are on the whole, most of them aren't so wicked as to do a thing like this."

"Wiping out the entire patrol is bad enough," said Caley, "but to rub it in our faces like this is totally barbaric."

"Demonic is a better word for it. See that the scalps are buried, will you, Sergeant? I've got to go break this to Opal Miller."

Dawn was breaking on the eastern horizon when troopers Hank Ketcham and Darrell DeFoe climbed the steps to the tower at the front gate of Fort Grant to relieve the sentries who had been on duty since midnight. When the sun peeked over the earth's edge, Darrell DeFoe said, "When the sun came up yesterday morning, I ate breakfast with three of the men who were in Lieutenant Miller's patrol. And now...now they're gone. They'll never see another sunrise."

"Tough way to make a living, this army life," commented Ketcham. "You just get to know a fella well, and boom, he's gone."

"Yeah. Sure makes you hate them dirty redskins," DeFoe said. "'Specially that beast Diablo. One of these days he'll get what's—"

DeFoe's words died on his lips as he squinted across the desert while reaching for a pair of binoculars that lay on a small shelf.

"What is it?" asked Ketcham, looking in the same direction.

Holding the binoculars to his eyes and turning the focus wheel, DeFoe said, "Riders. See them?"

"I can make out a bunch of horses, anyway."

"Oh no," gasped DeFoe.

"What?"

"I said riders, but they aren't riders in the usual sense."

"What do you mean?"

"They're dead riders. It's Miller's patrol. There's a body draped over every horse. Better get word to the colonel."

Soldiers were moving about the compound, getting ready for the new day. Hank Ketcham turned, cupped hands to his mouth, and shouted, "Hey, fellas! Somebody go get Colonel Stover! Quick!"

Moments later, Colonel Stover stood at the open gate with a large cluster of men around him, including his four lieutenants: John Frame, Cort Whitney, Al Zimmerman, and Price Wesson.

Sergeants Bifford Caley and Harold Timms stood closest to the colonel as the twenty-one horses drew up, each bearing a half-naked soldier over its back. The wrists and ankles of the dead men were lashed together underneath the horses' bellies. Meaty red patches were visible where their forelocks had been lifted.

There were gasps and curses heard among the men. Sick at heart, Colonel Stover blinked at the excess moisture in his eyes and told the men to lead the horses to the stables. The bodies would be removed there, placed in wagons, and covered until they could be buried. The entire group gathered by the wagons at the stables, ready to remove the bodies from the horses' backs.

Colonel Stover stepped up to the animal that bore the lifeless form of Lieutenant Harry Miller and ordered it removed first. When Miller's chest was exposed, Stover ejected a loud oath. Diablo had carved his name in Miller's chest with a dull knife. It was soon discovered that the same thing had been done to every soldier's chest.

Colonel Stover's eyes were narrow slits of fire. The words hissed out of him: "I'd love to lead an assault on that red devil and fill him so full of lead they'd have to use a team of horses to drag him to his grave."

"I wish you could lead such an assault, Colonel," spoke up Lieutenant Al Zimmerman. "Mad as you are right now, I think you'd plow through a hundred screeching Apaches to get to Diablo."

Every man at Fort Grant knew the army's regulations, which forbade a fort's commandant to engage in field combat. Lieutenant Cort Whitney stepped close to Stover. "Sir, I've had the most experience in Indian fighting of your lieutenants. How about letting me take a hundred and fifty men, find Diablo's secret lair, and storm the place?"

"It wouldn't be that simple," replied the colonel. "Bad as I want that demon's hide, I'll have to wait till our new captain gets here. He and I will make plans, and he will lead the assault."

Whitney said, "If the new captain does do Diablo in, he'll be some kind of hero, that's for sure."

The others agreed.

Cort Whitney's words burned like static fire in Price Wesson's mind. This was the key to gaining favor with Stover. Lieutenant Price Wesson must be the man to kill Diablo!

Late the next afternoon, the bodies of the twenty-one soldiers were buried in the fort's cemetery a quarter-mile west of the compound. Except for three sentries in the tower above the front gate, the entire populace of Fort Grant was at the burial. There was a small range of low hills between the fort and the cemetery, blocking the view of one place to the other.

In the tower, the sentries discussed the fact that Linda Locklin rode in the wagon that bore Opal Miller, holding her in her arms and speaking soothingly as the funeral procession had left the fort for the cemetery some twenty minutes earlier. Along with everyone else at Fort Grant, they deeply admired the widow. One sentry, a trooper named Ollie Chance, said to the others, "It sure bothers me to see that beautiful lady being taken in by Wesson. She's far too good for the likes of him."

"I agree," said trooper Nate Burt. "She deserves a lot better than him. Woman like that oughtta have a real man."

"You mean like you, pal?" asked trooper Ben Halverson.

Burt shrugged. "Well, she could do worse."

"Yeah," said Chance with a grin, "but not much worse."

At that moment, the sentries saw a platoon of riders coming toward them from the east. They were about a mile away.

"Well, I'll swan," said Chance, looking though the binoculars, "we're about to have company."

"Couldn't be the new replacements for Miller's patrol this soon," observed Halverson.

"Not hardly," said Burt. "I'll bet it's our new captain."

As the platoon rounded the corner of the stockade and headed for the gate, Halverson said, "That must be him in the middle, there in the lead with two lieutenants flanking him."

"I would say so," said Chance.

Hastening down the steps and opening the gate, the sentries stood in the entrance way as the column of seventeen men drew to a halt. The officer sat tall in the saddle, the gold braid around his hatbrim glistening in the sun. He had dark hair and a well-trimmed mustache. His eyes were a flashing blue against his skin.

Saluting, trooper Ollie Chance said, "Welcome to Fort Grant, sir. From where do you come?"

"Fort Butler, New Mexico, soldier," replied the officer. "I am to report to Colonel Wayne Stover as your new second man here. My escort will need food and lodging for the night, and they'll be on their way back to Fort Butler in the morning."

Chance noted the maple leaves on the officer's shoulders. "Excuse me, sir, but I believe the colonel is expecting a captain."

"Didn't work out. Right now, we're a little short of captains here in the Southwest. Since Colonel Stover is slated to retire in approximately three years, the army sent me, instead. They have me in mind to replace the colonel when he retires."

"I see, sir. And may I ask your name, please?"

The tall, broad-shouldered man smiled. "Of course. I am Major Boyd Locklin."

CHAPTER NINETEEN

Everyone at Fort Grant knew Linda Locklin's story. The shock of learning that her husband was alive frayed Ollie Chance's nerves, sending a crawling sensation over his entire body.

He wanted to look at his partners, but could only hope they realized the situation also. If Major Boyd Locklin knew his wife and children were at the fort, he would have mentioned them first. Whatever happened to him during the Civil War when he came up missing had resulted in his losing track of his family. It was not for Ollie Chance or the other two sentries to break the news to him.

"May I be the first to welcome you as our new major, sir? And I'm sure I speak for my trooper friends Ben Halverson and Nate Burt, also."

"Right," said Halverson, saluting.

"Yes, sir!" snapped Burt.

"I must point out, Major," said Chance, "that we're the only ones here at the moment. We had an entire patrol massacred two days ago. They're being buried at the cemetery just behind those hills. Everyone in the fort but us is attending the burial. They should be back within a half hour or so. I'm sure the colonel would want you to wait in his office. I'll take you there. The rest of these men can take the horses to the stables and make themselves at home in barracks number three. There'll be supper tonight and a hearty breakfast in the morning."

When the funeral procession returned to the fort, the wagon carrying Opal Miller, Linda Locklin, and their children came through the gate first. Colonel Stover's wagon would be last because the soldiers who attended Cora in her wheelchair had waited until the other wagons were pulling away from the cemetery to load her up.

As the Miller wagon rolled past them, the sentries smiled and waved, knowing that Linda Locklin was in for a pleasant shock. Price Wesson was on horseback, riding beside the wagon. The sentries know Wesson was in for a shock too, but it would be far from pleasant. Exchanging glances, the sentries smiled at each other.

At the Miller apartment, Price Wesson made a date with Linda for a stroll after the evening meal. As she walked Opal toward the apartment door, Linda told herself that tonight's stroll would give her the opportunity to inform Price that the wedding date was off. Not wanting to hurt him, she would simply say that she just needed more time before taking such a big step.

When the wagon carrying the Stovers approached the gate, trooper Ollie Chance waved them to a halt. A corporal was driving, and the colonel sat in the seat beside him. A trooper rode in the back, steadying Cora's wheelchair.

"Colonel, sir," said Chance, stepping up to the wagon, "a platoon just arrived from Fort Butler, bringing the captain you've been expecting. I took the captain to your office, and sent the others to barracks number three."

"Good!" said Stover. "I'm glad he's here. What's his name?"

Chance would not drop the bomb in front of others. Scratching at the side of his head, he said, "Ah, sir, could I talk to you in private? It is really imperative that I do. I mean right now."

Eyeing him questioningly, Stover said, "Of course," and slid to the ground. Telling the two soldiers to take Cora to the house, he stepped aside with Chance out of earshot from the others. "Now what's all the mystery about?"

"Well, sir…ah…it's just that the captain you were expecting is not a captain. He's a major."

Stover's heavy eyebrows arched. "A major?"

"Yes, sir. When I told him you were expecting a captain, he said the army is short of captains in the Southwest right now and that they had sent him instead. He added that the big brass have him in mind to replace you when you retire."

The colonel rubbed his jaw. "I see. What did you say his name is?"

"I…ah…I didn't sir. He's from Fort Butler. You are going to be shocked when I tell you his name."

"Oh? I can't imagine who he could be that I would be shocked to hear his name."

"You're right about that, sir. You never would have imagined it."

"Well? Out with it. What's his name?"

"Major Boyd Locklin."

The colonel's eyes bugged out and his mouth dropped open. For a moment, he just stared at the sentry. "L-Locklin? The Major B-Boyd Locklin?"

"Yes, sir. He didn't say anything at all about his family being here, Colonel, so I assume he's not aware of it. I didn't tell him a thing. I figured you'd want to handle that."

Rubbing his chin once more, Stover nodded. "Yes. Yes, I'll handle it. You say you took him to my office?"

"Yes, sir. He's waiting for you there."

Looking around to be sure no one was within earshot, the colonel said, "Ollie, I assume Burt and Halverson were in on this reception."

"Yes, sir."

"Anyone else?"

"No."

"All right. You tell them to keep it absolutely to themselves. The major's identity must be kept secret until I can talk to Locklin and present him to Linda. Get word to those men from Fort Butler too. I'm holding you responsible to see that none of this gets out until the Locklins have seen each other. I'll let you know when that is."

"Yes, sir." Chance saluted. "I'll handle it, sir."

Butterflies were flittering in Colonel Wayne Stover's stomach when he moved through the door of his office. The major rose from a straight-backed chair, smiling. Stover recognized the man instantly, remembering the photograph Linda kept of him in her quarters.

Gripping Locklin's hand, Stover introduced himself. "Trooper Chance explained why the army sent you—a major—instead of a captain."

"Yes, sir," said Locklin, pulling an official-looking envelope from a folder in his hand. "Here are the papers from Washington."

Locklin noticed the colonel's hand was trembling as he accepted the envelope and thanked him. Recalling that the commandant had just buried an entire patrol of his men, he said, "Colonel, the sentry told me about the burial at the cemetery. I was sorry to hear about the massacre."

"Yes," replied Stover solemnly. "It was bad. We'll talk about the serious Apache problem we're having a little later, Major, but right now, there is something of utmost importance I need to discuss with you."

Bidding Locklin to sit in the chair facing his desk, Stover took his seat behind the desk and leaned on it with his elbows. "I know quite a bit about you, Major."

Surprise showed on Lockin's features. "You do?"

"Mm-hmm. I know you fought in the Civil War under General William B. Franklin in Six Corps, Union Army of the Potomac. I also know that you were reported missing after the battle at Sharpsburg."

Amazement showed in the major's eyes. "That's all in those papers I gave you, sir...but how do you know this about me?"

"I'll get to that in a moment. But first I would like to know what happened when you took the cannon ball on the bank of the Potomac."

Eyes wide, the major said, "You even know about that! I know. You've got somebody here who was with me at Sharpsburg in Six Corps. But he...or they...don't know that I was captured and taken to a stinking Confederate prison camp in southern Georgia."

Stover was eager to tell Locklin about his family being at the fort, but only if there was some genuine good reason why he had not made contact with Linda since the war was over. Easing back in his chair, he said, "My source of information is not someone who was with you at Sharpsburg. Tell me, please, about your capture and what you've been doing in the twenty-seven months since the war has been over."

Locklin quickly explained that when the surprise bombardment came from across the Potomac on September 17, 1862, he was just mounting his horse. When the cannon ball hit the bank and exploded, the horse's big body took most of the shrapnel. Locklin's foot was hung up in the stirrup and he went in the river with the horse. The animal rolled on top of him in the water and the current began taking both of them downriver. While holding his breath till it felt like his lungs would burst, he struggled to get his foot free.

When he got loose, he surfaced, took a deep breath of air, and tried to swim to the bank. He hadn't realized until then that he had taken a hunk of shrapnel in the calf of his right leg. He was going into shock. He made it to the bank, which at that spot was covered with heavy brush. He managed to get the bulk of his body into the brush before he passed out. The next thing he knew, he was in Confederate hands at Harpers Ferry.

A Confederate doctor removed the shrapnel from his leg, and when he was able to travel, he was taken—along with several hundred other captured Federals—to a prison camp a few miles west of Chattanooga, Tennessee. During the next year, a problem developed between Locklin and the Confederate captain who was in charge of the camp. When the captain struck Locklin, Locklin hit him back, breaking his nose. Then the captain sent Locklin to a prison camp located in the swamps of southern Georgia. It was a punishment camp for Union Soldiers who had failed to knuckle under to Confederate authorities in the other camps all over the South.

When the war was over, the Rebel officers in charge of the punishment camp decided to defy Robert E. Lee's surrender agreement regarding the release of prisoners and secretly kept fourteen Yankee officers, whom they hated with a passion. Locklin was one of them. It was not until April 1866 that Locklin and his fellow prisoners managed to escape. It took them a month to get to Washington.

"So as you can imagine, Colonel," said Locklin, "I don't have a lot of love for Rebels."

"I can imagine," said Stover, pulling at his droopy mustache. "So what has happened since May of sixty-six?"

"Well, the first thing I did after reporting to army headquarters was to head for home. My wife and son were living in York, Pennsylvania. When I got there, they were no longer in the house we were renting and there was no one who knew where they had gone. The one neighbor that my wife was closest to—an elderly woman named Maude Stillwell—had died of cancer. Had she been alive, I'm sure she would have known where my wife and son had gone. In desperation, I tried the post office. The postmaster who knew Linda—

that's my wife's name—had been killed in a hunting accident and the new postmaster knew nothing of her. One stroke of luck—"

"Yes?"

"One of the postal employees, who had been there for many years, told me that Linda had gone to New Mexico. He didn't know where or with whom. So that's all I had. New Mexico. Having retained my rank of major, I put in for duty at a fort in New Mexico—which, as you know, turned out to be Fort Butler. Using every means at my disposal, I have searched for my wife and boy all over New Mexico Territory. I mean every town, village, and hamlet. They seem to have vanished from the face of the earth. I know they're somewhere, but the army declared me dead a few months after the war was over. Linda has probably married again by now and it'll be a miracle from heaven if I ever get to see her or Steven again."

The colonel's heart was fluttering with excitement. "Do you believe in miracles from heaven, Major?"

Puzzled, Locklin replied cautiously, "I've seen a few."

"Bet you've never seen one as great as I've got for you."

"What are you talking about, sir?"

Stover leaned across the desk, his smile broadening. "Linda and Steven are right here in this fort!"

Boyd Locklin's head bobbed. He tried to speak, but his tongue seemed incapable of movement. His heart thudded in his chest.

Seeing the numbing astonishment on Locklin's face, Stover decided instantly to let Linda tell her husband about her betrothal to Price Wesson. "She's still your wife, too!"

Locklin wiped a shaky palm over his face. "Th-this is l-like a d-dream, Colonel! My family is right here in the fort? Right now?"

"Right now," said Stover. "And I guess I should go ahead and tell you this...you also have a daughter!"

Locklin's head bobbed again. "A daughter? But how—? When—?"

"She was born almost exactly nine months after you had been home in York for Steven's third birthday. Her name is Rebecca Lynne."

The major's lips were white. He felt as if the blood was draining from his body. "How...how did they end up here? I...I never thought of looking in a fort for them!"

Colonel Stover told the man how Dr. Clarence Wood in York had wired him at Fort Sumner, New Mexico, about Linda becoming housekeeper and nurse for his crippled wife, Cora, and how he had hired her, sight unseen. He went on to explain about the move to Fort Grant because of the death of the previous commandant.

Breathlessly, the major stood up and asked, "Where are they, sir?"

"They live in a private part of our house. About ninety yards from where you stand."

Locklin's words came rapid-fire. "I want to see them! Now! Is Linda still the same beautiful, vibrant personality? Does Stevie still look like me? And...how about my daughter? What's she like? Let's see, she's...ah...four years old, now. And...and Stevie. Why, he'll be eight next month. Does Linda talk about me at all? What about Stevie? Does he ever mention me? And Rebecca Lynne—that's such a pretty name—does she—"

"Hold on, Major," cut in Stover. "If I may give my opinion, I think it would be best if you meet with Linda first. Let her get over the jolt before you see the children. I think you two should have some time alone to begin with."

Putting his fingertips to his temples and looking at the floor, the major said, "Sure. Sure, sir. You're right. It's just that...well, it's been nearly five years since I've seen Linda and Stevie. And now that I have a daughter, I can hardly wait to meet her."

"I understand, Major," said Stover. "To answer those questions: I think Linda gets more beautiful every day. Becky Lynne is a sweetheart, and she looks as much like Linda as Steven looks like you. Becky's hair is exactly the same auburn shade as her mother's. Stevie isn't Stevie anymore. He prefers to be called 'Steve' or 'Steven.' Fine boy. He talks about his dad quite often, and Linda brings your name up at least a million times a day."

The major was thumbing tears from his eyes as Colonel Stover headed toward the door. "I'll send Linda over here right now. All I'm going to tell her is that someone she knows from Fort Butler is here to see her and is waiting in my office. You'll have to take it from there. Can you handle it?"

"I can handle it, sir," Locklin responded firmly.

When the door closed, the major began pacing the floor nervously.

Colonel Stover found Linda still at Opal Miller's apartment. Giving her the exact message he had intended, he left for home to tell the good news to Cora.

Leaving Steven and Rebecca with Opal, Linda hastened across the compound, wondering who was at Fort Butler, New Mexico, who knew her. She was only a few steps from the office door when her mind went back to that cold winter's day in York when she had mistaken that nice Captain Jake Bolger for Boyd. She remembered that he was going to be assigned to a fort in New Mexico or Arizona. Of course. That's who it was. Bolger had been assigned to Fort Butler. It was nice of him to stop by.

Grasping the knob, she pushed the door open and saw the tall, dark-haired officer in the blue uniform, standing with his back to her. Thinking for certain it was Bolger, she drew a breath to speak just as he turned around.

For an instant she thought her eyes were playing tricks on her. She had mistaken Bolger for Boyd once, and now she was doing it again. But no. It *was* Boyd. An older Boyd, but definitely Boyd.

Linda stopped in her tracks, her scalp prickling as if she had seen a ghost. She stood holding the doorknob for a space of time that seemed endless, still as a statue, eyes wide open, breathless.

Tears were shining in Boyd's eyes as he came toward her, seemingly in slow motion. "Linda, darling." He opened his arms.

Linda's mouth was working loosely, as though she had lost the power of speech. Suddenly her head began to swim and she felt her knees turn to water. Strong hands caught her before she fell and pulled her into a powerful embrace. She could hear him speaking to her, but the words were fuzzy.

Slowly her head cleared and she found herself looking up into the face she had only dreamed of for the past five years. The press of his arms about her told Linda this was no dream. Breathing his name, she burst into tears. "Oh my darling! You're alive! You're alive! I thought you were dead, but you're alive! You're really alive!"

At that point, she laid her head on his chest and wept wordlessly for several minutes. When she began to gain control of herself, Boyd cupped her face in his hands and kissed her lips repeatedly. When they embraced again, she drew a shuddering breath. "Darling, what happened to you? Where have you been? How did you find me?"

"Come. Sit down and I'll tell you all about it."

While facing Linda as they sat on straight-backed chairs, Boyd held her hands and told his story, bringing her up to the moment, and telling her that Colonel Stover had explained how and why she was at Fort Grant. "The colonel told me about Rebecca Lynne. I can't wait to meet her. And I guess my little Stevie isn't so little any more. He's 'Steven' now."

"Yes." She sniffled, wiping her tears with a hanky she had in her sleeve. "Or you can call him 'Steve.' He's a fine boy, Boyd. You'll be proud of him. He's done his best to be the man of this family. Oh…this is so wonderful! I can't wait for the children to see you!"

Suddenly Linda thought about Price Wesson. "Oh, Boyd. I assume Colonel Stover didn't tell you about Price Wesson."

"No. Who's he?"

Beginning with the fact that Wesson was an ex-Confederate soldier, Linda told her husband about her engagement to the lieutenant, which had come about so the children could have a father figure. She explained that Wesson knew she was not in love with him, but that he was willing to marry her anyhow. Then she quickly informed Boyd that she had planned to break off the engagement that very night because she had too many doubts about marrying him.

Holding her close, Boyd told Linda he could not blame her for wanting a husband for her and a father for the children. After all, the government had declared him dead.

The redhead kissed her husband and laughed. "It's no problem now. I'm a married woman, not a widow!"

Linda led her husband across the compound; tearfully introducing him to the soldiers they met along the way. Taking him in to the Stover house, she introduced him to Cora, then planted him in their quarters while she ran to the Miller house and brought the children. Steven and Rebecca were stunned but happy to learn that their father was alive. They both took to him warmly and lovingly, without reservation.

Later that evening, the Stovers and the Locklins were eating supper when a loud knock was heard at the door. Rising from the table,

Colonel Stover said, "I'll see who it is."

Linda thought of Wesson, but dismissed it because it was too early for him to show up.

When Stover opened the door, which was out of sight from the kitchen, he beheld a red-faced Price Wesson.

"You must have heard," Stover said calmly.

The lieutenant almost swore but checked himself. "You bet I heard! Some of the men she introduced him to were spreading it around. I want to talk to her!"

Wesson's angry voice carried to the kitchen. Boyd shoved his chair back. "I'll go talk to him."

"No, darling," said Linda, already on her feet. "Let me handle it."

"I'll go with you," Boyd insisted.

"No, please. Let me talk to him alone."

Reluctantly, Boyd allowed her to go. Colonel Stover returned, shaking his head, and sat down.

Moments later, Wesson's loud, angry voice rode the air. He was railing at Linda, demanding that she divorce Boyd and marry him as planned.

"That's enough," said the major, throwing down his napkin and rising. "I'm sorry, Colonel, Mrs. Stover, but the man's gone far enough."

"I agree, Major." Stover watched as the man bolted from the kitchen.

Wesson's voice was gaining in intensity as Locklin drew nearer the front door. Just as he stepped out onto the porch, the lieutenant was gripping Linda's shoulders and shaking her. He stopped and looked at the taller man, sneering. "Butt out, Locklin. This is between her and me."

A smoky anger burned in Locklin's eyes. "Get your hands off her!"

"What right do you have to tell me to let go of her? You haven't cared a lick for Linda or the kids all this time. Now you show up and stick your nose in where it doesn't belong. Why don't you just go back to wherever you've been all these years and crawl back under your rock?"

Locklin's eyes flinted and the hair stood up on the back of his neck. Linda saw the danger in him. To Wesson she said, "Let go of me."

The man dropped his hands, giving Locklin a defiant glare.

"Apparently you haven't heard the whole story, Price," said Linda. "Boyd was in a Confederate prison camp."

Wesson sneered. "Is that what he told you? Hmpf. The prison camps were emptied out within a week after the war was over."

"Not the one I was in."

"You're a liar! If anybody would do a thing like that, it would be you blue-bellies."

Boyd Locklin's fist lashed out with the speed of a lightning bolt, connecting solidly on Wesson's jaw. His face twisted out of shape and he hit the porch floor like a felled oak.

When Price Wesson came to, he was lying in the dirt in front of Stover's house. His head was pounding and he felt nauseous. In the shadows of dusk, he saw the colonel standing over him. As he rolled on to his knees in an attempt to get up, Stover gripped an arm and hoisted him to his feet. He felt like he had been kicked in the head by a mule.

While Wesson was trying to get his legs under himself solidly, the colonel said, "You'd best face the fact that Linda is no longer available, Lieutenant. If you make any more trouble over her, you'll only get more of what the major just dished out to you. I have papers from Washington on him. He was indeed held in a Confederate prison camp in southern Georgia until he escaped in April of last year. He tried desperately to find his family, but all the strings at York were broken. Providence has brought them back together. You'd best leave it at that. And one more thing: you'd better remember that Locklin is a major. He could press charges for the way you spoke to him tonight and have you disciplined."

Without a word, Wesson turned and shuffled toward his quarters, leaving the colonel standing there. Holding his throbbing head, he vowed to himself that he would find a way to kill Boyd Locklin. He would also be the one to kill Diablo. He would be promoted to captain, and he would also marry Linda.

At dawn the next morning, Major Boyd Locklin stood at the gate and bid the sixteen men from Fort Butler good-bye, saying he hoped to see them again one day.

After breakfast with his newly found family at the Stover house, Locklin walked with the colonel to the parade, where the entire military force—except for the sentries in the tower and the men confined in the infirmary—were assembled in perfect ranks. The moment Stover and Locklin appeared, the soldiers snapped to attention. Lieutenants John Frame, Price Wesson, Cort Whitney, and Al Zimmerman stood ahead of the enlisted men, offering a salute as they drew up. Colonel and major returned the salute, then halted and faced the men. With Locklin standing beside him, Stover gave him a formal introduction and told his story in brief.

While the colonel was speaking, Locklin observed a malignant sneer on the face of Price Wesson.

When Stover was finished, he shook hands with Locklin, welcoming him to Fort Grant, then asked him to address the men. The major gave the usual amenities, then told them of his desire to rid eastern Arizona of the plague known as Diablo. He went on to explain that Linda had told him Diablo's true identity, and that while stationed at Fort Savage before the Civil War, he had killed Apache Chief Pantano, who was Kateya's father. Locklin saw the evil in Kateya back then and had called him "devil."

Since maturing into manhood, Kateya had taken the Spanish word for "devil" as his name: Diablo. Locklin also told them that it was Diablo who had burned down Fort Savage in a fit of anger when he went there to find and take the life of the man who had killed his father, but Locklin was at the time in a Confederate prison camp.

The men—except for Price Wesson—gave the major a loud, unified welcome as they were dismissed. Moments later, Stover and Locklin stood in front of the colonel's office and watched the four lieutenants lead their patrols out of the fort, then turned and passed through the door.

Sitting down in the office, they discussed Diablo and the threat he offered to white people all over the area. Stover pointed out that the daily patrols from the fort were keeping the Apaches from shedding the blood they would like to, but still in the last two years, Diablo and his warriors had killed forty-nine soldiers from Fort Grant, plus about thirty more from other forts within a seventy-mile radius. They had massacred white settlers and travelers by the dozens. The army had killed a good number of Diablo's men in the same period of time, but he never seemed to have any problem replacing them.

Stover told Locklin that Diablo had a well-hidden camp somewhere nearby, but none of his patrols had ever been able to locate it. The colonel said he knew it was in the vicinity because Diablo could always make a strike on settlers, travelers, and sometimes patrols, yet disappear in a hurry. It would be Major Locklin's job to find the hidden lair, launch an assault against it, and rid Arizona of Diablo and his rabid, murderous pack.

The major asked, "Exactly how many men do we have here at the fort, sir?"

"One hundred and sixty-nine," came the reply. "Right now there are four men recovering from battle wounds who are unable to fight. Dr. Quitman, our fort physician, tells me two of them will be back in commission within another month. He has not predicted a recovery time for the other two."

"I assume you've requested replacements for the patrol that was wiped out?"

"Yes, but it'll be a while before we get them."

"So we have a hundred and sixty-five men who can fight."

"Plus one," said Stover. "You."

"Yes, sir. And of course there has to be a sufficient number left here at the fort at all times, so how many men do you think I could have to make up a search and destroy unit?"

"Safely a hundred."

"You have any idea how many warriors Diablo has in his camp?"

"From what I can put together, about seventy-five. I'm told that he mustered up about two hundred when he attacked and burned Fort Savage. Got the additional help from some of the camps in the Chiricahua Mountains, I think. That's probably where he's getting the replacements, too."

"Mm-hmm," mused Locklin, stroking his mustache. "So if you're correct about him having around seventy-five, I'd have at least some advantage with a force of a hundred men."

"*Some* advantage is right. The hardest part of your job won't be in locating the hidden camp, but in launching a successful attack. Sneaking up on Apaches is next to impossible."

"How well I know," said Locklin. "But it's got to be done. This bloodshedding has got to be stopped."

"I wish I had three or four hundred men to give you for the job," said Stover. "Every warrior in that camp will have to be killed."

"Not necessarily, sir."

"What do you mean?"

"From what I'm hearing, Diablo has become to his warriors exactly what his father, Pantano, was. A god. After I killed Pantano, his warriors melted away like whipped dogs, and apparently didn't surface again until Kateya—Diablo—matured enough to lead them. If we can kill Diablo, his warriors will quickly lose the will to fight—at least until they can find another god to follow."

Suddenly there was a sound of pounding hooves, a horse skidding to a halt, and boots thumping on the porch. Both officers were on their feet as a loud knock met their ears.

Stover opened the door to find Corporal Harley Carter, whom he knew had ridden out with Lieutenant Al Zimmerman. Carter's face was white. "Colonel, sir, our patrol headed east from the fort. We didn't get more than a couple miles beyond the first range of hills when we found the unit of men who were headed back to Fort Butler. They...they must've run into Diablo. Fourteen are dead and two are missing!"

CHAPTER TWENTY

Lieutenant Royce Barrett and trooper Jack Erb rode their mounts side by side with their hands tied behind them. Apaches on pintos had them hemmed in on all sides. The Diablo rode directly in front of them, twisting around periodically to give them a wicked stare.

Erb had been nicked on the left arm with a bullet when the Apaches came from seemingly out of nowhere and attacked the unit from Fort Butler. Barrett was unscathed. They knew they were the only ones to come out of the ambush alive. They saw their comrades lying dead all around them when they threw up their hands in surrender. Both had wept silently as they were hurried away from the bloody scene when one of Diablo's scouts shouted from the crest of a nearby hill that a cavalry patrol was coming that way.

Barrett and Erb had barely been snatched from the scythe of the grim reaper, but by the looks they were getting from Diablo, they wondered if it would not had been better if they had died quickly with their fellow soldiers.

Diablo and his men had spoken only in the Apache language since they took their prisoners, so Barrett and Erb could only guess what they were planning to do to them.

The morning sun was giving off more heat as it rose higher in the eastern sky. Jack Erb's surface wound had stopped bleeding, but it was stinging like he'd been bitten by a poisonous reptile.

Diablo led the group northeast, making a wide circle so as not to be seen from the tower at Fort Grant. They rode through rugged, rocky land, speckled with catclaw and mesquite bush amid tumbled rocks and boulders. At the base of one huge boulder, Erb spotted two six-foot diamondbacks sunning themselves. One was in a dormant slumber, stretched out full length. The other was moving its wide head from side to side in a half-coiled position. Erb's skin crawled at the sight of them.

About seven miles due north of Fort Grant, they splashed into a wide, shallow creek and rode its current eastward for about half a mile. At a sharp bend where mesquite, catclaw, and prickly pear clusters grew heavily on both banks, they took a right turn, squeezed between the thick patches of brush, and moved through a tangle of ridge and ravine until they came to a labyrinth of canyons that joined each other in crooked angles. The soldiers were amazed when Diablo led them into a canyon whose mouth was obscured by jumbled boulders and brush that disguised it completely. Lieutenant Royce Barrett figured the hidden canyon was about a mile from the creek they had traversed.

Within minutes they were in a flat, open area which was obviously their camp. Some thirty Apaches had accompanied Diablo in the ambush, but there were about fifty more waiting to greet them at the camp.

Leaving their hands tied, Diablo sat his prisoners on the ground near a large black spot, which was obviously where the cookfires were burned for preparing meals.

The Apaches collected in the shade at the edge of the canyon, leaving Barrett and Erb in the harsh sunlight. Sweat dampened their uniforms while they talked in low tones, each sharing his fears with the other. From time to time, Diablo would look at them with black eyes that resembled twin shotgun bores. They shuddered, knowing he was planning some kind of torture for them.

Just before noon, a fire was built and the warriors cooked themselves a meal, letting the two soldiers watch while they ate. Collecting in what little shade the canyon offered at that time of the day, the Indians talked in their own language, with some of them intermittently looking toward the sun. Barrett and Erb agreed that Diablo was waiting for time to pass. They became so tense that their muscles ached.

Sweat dripped into Erb's eyes as he said in a tight voice, from which a note of hysteria was not far absent, "Lieutenant, maybe we ought to just make a run for it, since our legs aren't tied. They might open fire and kill us quickly."

Royce Barrett's face was pale under the sheen of sweat that

drenched it. A muscle twitched spasmodically in his cheek. "No, they wouldn't. They're bent on making us die slowly. I can see it in their eyes."

At that moment, Diáblo said something to the group in Apache; then walked toward the prisoners. Several of the Indians headed to the nearby rope corral, where the horses stood in the blaze of the sun.

"Get on your feet," Diablo commanded as he drew up. There was a glitter of evil in his eyes. "You are going for a little ride."

The prisoners rode in numb silence as a dozen warriors flanked them. With Diablo in the lead, they returned to the shallow creek, and then proceeded to cross it. Climbing the bank on the opposite side, they traveled in the heat for ten minutes until a rock pit came into view. They could see that the pit was near the open desert where they had ridden into the creek bed, but was concealed by a circle of sandstone bluffs.

The sun bore down like a burning brand and heat waves danced over the pit, which was some thirty feet deep, with sheer walls that would be impossible to climb. The floor of the pit, which was a hundred feet square, was laden with huge rocks and spotted with prickly pear cactus and dried-out clumps of catclaw.

Halting the horses some fifty feet from a gentle rise that rimmed the pit, the Apaches yanked the prisoners from their saddles and led them up the rise. At its crest, they looked down a steep, stone-floored embankment that ran about thirty feet and dropped off suddenly at the pit's sheer rock wall. Being careful with their own footing on the steep embankment, the Apaches forced Barrett and Erb toward the pit's edge. When they stood at the very lip, both men felt the heat reflecting from the pit and saw dozens of sunbleached human skeletons scattered about, and a concentration of them at the base of a tall, slender rock that jutted up out of the pit's floor in the very center. Its top was some fourteen feet from its base.

It was evident that men had climbed the jagged, slightly sloped side of the rock to perch on its narrow top, then had fallen and died at its base. Or they had died, then fallen. It was hard to say which.

Barrett and Erb knew they were going in the pit. Horror gripped them. They understood then why Diablo waited. This was the hottest time of day. The pit was a virtual oven. It had to be at least

120 degrees down there. They would dehydrate and die of thirst in a matter of a few agonizing hours. Both were wondering why so many of Diablo's victims had climbed onto the tall rock.

Suddenly their question was answered as they caught sight of movement on the pit floor. At first they had not noticed the snakes because they were the same color as the bedrock over which they slithered. There was a seething mass of them—diamondback rattlers, gliding effortlessly over the hot rocks, black eyes unblinking, tongues flicking eagerly.

Abject terror seized both soldiers. Their eyes bulged and their hearts pounded violently. Royce Barrett's skin crawled. He drew his breath in short, pained gulps. "Please don't put us in there. We've done you no harm. Don't—"

"Quiet!" boomed Diablo, cutting him off. "You white eyes soldiers are supposed to be so brave! Let us see it now."

Jack Erb wanted to scream, but his throat wouldn't let him. He was frozen with fright. His entire body trembled like a leaf in a cold autumn wind to the point that his teeth were chattering.

Laughing, Diablo told his men to untie the soldiers' hands and drop them into the pit. Holding Barrett and Erb by the wrists, the Apaches clung to the steep embankment at the edge of the pit and lowered them over the lip to arm's length, then let them fall.

When their feet first touched the ground, there were no snakes close. Barrett said, "Let's get to the rock!"

As he darted in that direction, he saw four or five coiling snakes at the rock's base. Looking around he noticed multitudes of stones on the pit's floor. Leaning over, he picked up a couple of fist-sized stones and hurled them at the snakes. Instantly the reptiles hissed and separated, giving him room to dart to the rock's base and climb. Dashing for it, he was soon climbing. When he reached the top and sat down, he looked back, thinking Erb was on his heels, but he was not.

The trooper had stumbled and fallen, and three rattlers were striking at him. One caught him in the right cheek and another in the neck. The third hit his arm and its fangs snagged in the cloth of his shirt. Screaming, Erb leaped to his feet, grabbed the snake's body, yanked it loose, and threw it as far as he could. Hisses and rattles filled the hot afternoon air as the other two snakes struck again, this time hitting his boots.

Barrett looked on in horror and was halfway down the rock, extending his hand and yelling for Erb to come so he could pull him up. The trooper stumbled toward the rock, but fell again. Two more rattlers attacked him.

Standing on the steep incline at the edge of the pit, Diablo laughed and called to Barrett, "Lieutenant! You are such a brave soldier! Why don't you go help your friend?"

Snakes were coming from every direction, converging on Jack Erb. He was barely able to swing his arms as he struggled to fight them off. The venom embedded in his face and neck was taking its toll.

Diablo smiled demonically and waved as he started up the incline. Calling to Barrett over his shoulder, he said, "Stay on the rock, Lieutenant! The snakes cannot climb it!"

The sun had been down for half an hour and the purple shadows were deepening as Linda Locklin stood in the tower at the fort gate with two sentries and strained her eyes to pick up some kind of movement on the darkening desert. Worry showed on her lovely face.

Twenty minutes after Corporal Harley Carter had ridden in to report the ambush of the Fort Butler unit, Major Boyd Locklin kissed his wife, leaped into the saddle, and rode away at a gallop. Colonel Stover gave permission for Locklin to take Lieutenant Zimmerman's patrol unit and follow the tracks of the Apache horses. Hopefully Diablo would head back to his hidden camp and Locklin could locate it. Once he knew where it was, he could prepare a larger unit, return to the camp at just the right time, and make the attack.

Lieutenant Price Wesson and his patrol had arrived before sundown, as had the others.

When it was too dark to see any more, Linda left the tower and headed for the Stover house. Pole lanterns were being lit all over the compound. Just as Linda passed the infirmary, she saw a form move out of the shadows and stand in her path. She thought it looked like the shape of Price Wesson, and knew she was correct when he spoke.

"Hello, Linda, darling."

"Price, it would be best if you'd leave me alone. And I don't want you calling me 'darling.'"

Stepping so close she could feel his breath, he said, "Have you ever thought about how things would be if that so-called husband of yours had not shown up till after we were married? You'd be my wife instead of his."

"He is my husband, Price, and talking 'ifs' is a waste of time. Right now, my husband and his search party are late. I'm worried. Very worried. And I need to get home to my children. Now, will you please remove yourself so I can be on my way?"

"Only after you give me one of those luscious kisses of yours."

"You try to get one, and I'll tell my husband when he does get back. Do you want some more of what he gave you last night?"

"Won't happen this time. I'll tell him you met me here on purpose and offered it to me."

"He won't believe—"

Linda's words were stifled as Wesson grabbed her and kissed her. At the same moment, Dr. Ernest Quitman came out the door of the infirmary, carrying a lantern. He heard Linda giving off a tormented moan and swung the light in that direction. Wesson quickly let go of her, looking at the physician with wide eyes. Linda spat and wiped the back of her hand across her mouth.

Quitman moved to them, holding the lantern high so as to get a good look at the lieutenant's face. "What's going on here?"

"Well, we were just talking," said Wesson nervously.

"What I saw wasn't conversation, mister," snapped Quitman. "You were quite evidently forcing yourself on Mrs. Locklin. The sounds coming from her were not the sounds of ecstasy."

Suddenly they heard excited voices coming from the tower. The search party was coming in. Wheeling, Linda ran to the gate just as it swung open.

At the supper table in the Stover home, Boyd Locklin explained that he and his unit had followed Diablo northeastward, but lost all sign when they came to a rocky area, where the ground was so hard it was impossible to track. They had stayed in the area, searching until it was becoming too dark, then headed back for the fort. The search would be resumed in the morning.

Colonel Stover said, "I assume you were able to figure out what two men the Apaches took with them."

"Yes, sir. Lieutenant Royce Barrett and a trooper named Jack Erb. Barrett has a wife and three children. Both men are probably dead by now."

"Shame," said Stover, shaking his head. "That beast has got to be stopped."

"We'll get him, sir," Locklin said.

Later, as Boyd and Linda lay in bed talking, he said, "Sorry to worry you, honey, but time is of the essence with this Diablo. We've got to find his lair and take care of him."

Linda sighed and clung to him. "I guess all my worrying is for nothing, but I can't help it."

"For nothing? I want you to be concerned about me."

"Oh, that'll never change, but someone once told me you'd always be all right because you're a survivor."

"Oh? Who was that?"

"Remember Wally Frye at Savage?"

"Mm-hmm."

"It was him. I was taking care of him in the infirmary when you had gone to find Peggy Halloran and were late in returning. I was very worried, and Wally's words were a real help. I thought of them many times when you were reported as missing. I clung to them, but I let them slip from me when I learned that you had been declared dead. I hadn't thought of them until just now. You are a survivor, Major Boyd Locklin. I've got to keep that in mind when it appears that something has happened to you."

"You do that." He held her close. After a long moment, he said, "Honey, pardon me if I'm way off on this, but I thought I detected tonight that there was something else bothering you besides my getting in late. Am I right?"

There was a lengthy pause.

"Okay," he said softly, "no answer means yes. What is it?"

Digging her fingernails in his arm, Linda told him of meeting Price Wesson and of his kissing her and being seen by Dr. Quitman.

While she told the story, anger mounted steadily in Boyd Locklin. When she finished, a red-hot temper was driving through him. He jumped out of bed, lit a lantern, and began dressing.

"What are you doing?"

"I'm going to teach the pale-eyed lieutenant a lesson. First, I am going to get the colonel out of bed and warn him that his lieutenant is about to get the whipping of his life, so if he wants to put me on report, he can plan accordingly."

"Can't you get in trouble for manhandling a fellow officer?"

"Not as much trouble as Price Wesson is in right now," Boyd said flatly, and was gone.

Some five minutes later, as Linda lay in silence with her stomach churning, she heard loud male voices. They were coming from near the officers' quarters. Soon there were more voices, shouting and cheering. Rising from the bed, she went to the window and stuck her head out. Whatever was happening, she could tell that the crowd was enjoying it. Only three or four minutes had passed from the time she had first heard the loud voices until all was quiet.

A couple of minutes later Linda heard her husband talking to Colonel Stover. The conversation lasted for about half a minute, then the bedroom door opened and Boyd entered. Linda was sitting on the edge of the bed. By the lantern light, she saw that his knuckles were bruised, and she looked up and waited for him to speak.

Unbuttoning his shirt, he said levelly, "Mr. Wesson won't be kissing anybody for a while."

"Colonel Stover isn't going to put you on report?"

"When I talked to him before going to Wesson's quarters, he grinned and said he would put me on report only if any of the other officers complained. Then he chuckled and said that would happen the day the sun doesn't rise."

"I guess nobody in the fort likes Price."

"Judging by the attitude of the crowd that watched him get his lesson, I'd say you're right about that."

"But what if Price decides to press charges? He could even go above the colonel's head and contact the top generals in Washington."

Boyd laughed. "Yeah, he could do that, but he won't. If he made a case of it, I would be given a chance to defend myself. Wesson knows that I would tell that he kissed you against your will, and that Dr. Quitman would testify that he saw it and you were struggling to fight him off. In fact, just before Dr. Quitman took him to the infirmary to sew his mouth up, he told him that he'd testify to it if it ever came into litigation. Wesson would fry his own hide and he knows it."

"So what did Colonel Stover say after Price got his lesson?"

"Patted me on the back and said it was what any good husband would have done. Then the scalawag pulled one on me."

"What did he do?"

"Said he's going to send Wesson with me as my lieutenant in the search unit tomorrow. Wants us to develop character, he said."

Linda giggled. "The colonel does have a sense of humor, doesn't he?"

The next morning, as dawn was spreading its gray light over the desert, the sentries in the tower observed two army horses coming toward the gate. They each carried a half-naked bloated body.

Colonel Stover and Major Locklin were summoned, along with Dr. Ernest Quitman. Other soldiers collected at the gate.

Locklin quickly identified the dead men as Lieutenant Royce Barrett and trooper Jack Erb. Diablo's name had been carved in their chests, and Dr. Quitman's inspection revealed that they died of multiple rattlesnake bites. The fury that Locklin showed at the atrocity spread rapidly among the men. All agreed that Diablo must be stopped.

Just after sunrise, Major Boyd Locklin led his unit of one hundred men out of the fort and headed north. A bruised and battered Price Wesson rode beside him. Wesson's upper lip was puffy and held together with four stitches. Hatred burned within Wesson toward the major. He would find a way to kill him.

In the unit were Sergeants Bifford Caley, Harold Timms, Mike O'Hara, and Roy Mason. Returning to the spot where he had left off the day before, Locklin spread his men out in a wide swath, telling them to look for any sign that would indicate the presence of humans or horses. About noon, one of the troopers discovered horse droppings on the bank of a shallow creek that ran east and west.

When the major was summoned, he took one look at the droppings and splashed across the creek to the opposite side. When he could find no indication that a group of riders had climbed out of the creek there, he rode back to his men. "The ground is soft on the other side, men. Nobody emerged from the creek over there. These horse droppings are about twenty-four hours old. That would be about the time Barrett and Erb would have been taken to the Apache hideout. Let's split up. Lieutenant Wesson, you take half the men and ride the creek east. I'll take the other half and go west. You take Sergeants Caley and Mason. Move slow and study the banks close. If you find the spot where they climbed out of the creek, don't pursue the trail any further. Send a man back to advise me. We'll join you and follow the trail together. I'll do the same if we find where they pulled out."

Locklin did not miss the flame of hatred in Wesson's eyes as the lieutenant acknowledged his orders and led his men downstream.

Looking at Sergeants Timms and O'Hara, the major said, "Okay, hawkeyes, let's find that Apache trail."

Locklin and his men moved slowly up the creek, scrutinizing the banks for signs where men and horses had emerged to return to dry land. They had gone about half a mile when suddenly they heard gunfire erupt to the east. "Come on!" Locklin shouted, wheeling his horse in midstream. "Wesson's under attack!"

Splashing water higher than their heads, the cavalrymen galloped downstream, and within minutes, came upon a grisly scene. Several men in blue uniforms were floating face-down in blood-red water as the soldiers and Apaches were firing at each other from the thick brush on both sides of the creek. The Indians were on the north bank and the white men on the south bank. There were no dead Apaches floating in the stream. The soldiers had been taken in a surprise attack. Wesson's unit had been whittled down in a hurry.

Not wanting to lead his men into the crossfire, Locklin led them out of the creek on the south bank and made his way to the spot where Wesson and about twenty men were firing from a dense thicket.

Just as they arrived and were dismounting, the Apaches came swarming on foot across the creek, whooping and firing their carbines. Locklin was trying to estimate the number of Apaches charging across the creek when he saw another swarm about thirty yards downstream, darting out of the creek and climbing the south bank. They emerged from the thicket at the crest, finding open, rock-strewn land, and ran hard to attack from the high ground.

Locklin's unit charged up to meet them, diving for cover behind brush and opening fire. Within seconds, the whole area was alive with gunfire and clouded with powder smoke. Men were falling on both sides as the battle progressed. Soon the Apaches reverted to their age-old fighting technique of yelping and hooting as they moved in close, running in two overlapping fan-shaped lines. Limited on ammunition, they wanted to fight hand-to-hand.

Major Boyd Locklin was hunkered down behind a thick mesquite bush, firing his revolver at the elusive Indians. He noticed that Price Wesson had withdrawn from the creek bank, along with Sergeant Roy Mason. They were shooting from behind a large rock about thirty feet to his left.

Price Wesson had seen Locklin at the mesquite bush. With murder in mind, he worked his way in that direction while firing at the Indians. He had just made it to a large rock and was looking around to see if he could shoot the major without being seen. Most of the men in blue were either still in the thicket, or were firing from behind rocks beyond the spot where Locklin was situated. If Wesson could find just a second or two when nobody could see him, even in their peripheral vision, he would put a bullet through the major's head.

His plan was foiled, at least for the moment, as Sergeant Roy Mason emerged from the thicket and made a dive behind the same rock. Shouldering his rifle, Mason fired into the thicket, saying loudly, "There's more of them coming up from the creek, Lieutenant!"

Cursing Mason under his breath, Wesson nodded and fired in that direction.

Boyd Locklin had just reloaded and was firing on an Apache who was running toward him. The Indian did a nose dive into the dirt and lay still. Suddenly amid the smoke and dust, a determined warrior came at Locklin from behind, raising his knife for the kill. Roy Mason happened to see him. "Major, behind you!"

Hearing Mason's cry, Locklin pivoted and fired point blank at the charging figure. His bullet struck the Indian in the throat. He went down, gagging on a fountain of his own blood. The knife fell at Locklin's feet.

At the same moment, the major saw three warriors lunge at Mason and Wesson from the thicket that lined the creek. Mason wheeled and met them with a shot. The first one went down. The second one stumbled over the Apache, but his momentum carried him into Mason. The third was going around them, gripping his knife and heading for Wesson. Swinging his gun on him, Wesson squeezed the trigger. There was a horrible dead snap of metal against metal. The gun was empty.

Wesson froze, his pale blue eyes twin pools of terror as they beheld the flashing blade meant for his flesh. There was a loud roar and the savage dropped like a brain-shot bull, hitting the ground hard. Wesson looked toward Locklin and saw the smoking gun in his hand. The major had saved his life.

While this was going on, the Apache that stumbled into Roy Mason drove his knife into Mason's heart. He was turning toward Wesson with the bloody knife in his hand and the lieutenant didn't see him. Locklin raised his gun and fired. The bullet centered the Indian's chest, exploding his heart. As he toppled, Wesson glanced at him, then looked back at the major. Locklin had saved his life twice in a matter of seconds.

The major and the lieutenant were both reloading when a screeching Apache came running at Locklin, knife poised. Thinking fast, the major picked up a potato-sized rock and threw it hard. It struck the Indian dead-center between the eyes, stunning him. When he hit the ground, Locklin picked up the knife that had fallen at his feet earlier and plunged it into his heart.

Unknown to Boyd Locklin, Diablo observed the battle from a rocky knoll two hundred yards away, using a pair of army binoculars. The Apache chief was shocked to see the face of Locklin when it appeared in the eyes of the binoculars. Instantly the old hatred he had felt toward Locklin flamed anew in his wicked heart. Several warriors waited with Diablo, ready for orders. When he saw Locklin hit one of his choicest warriors between the eyes with a rock, then drive a knife through his heart, he screamed at the men who flanked him to go together and capture the dark-haired officer. If they could do it, they should capture the light-haired officer next to him. Both would die in the snake pit.

Lieutenant Price Wesson finished loading his revolver as Major Boyd Locklin picked up the gun he had started to load. Though the major had saved his life twice, Wesson still planned to kill him. Locklin hastened to Wesson's side, knelt beside him, and finished loading. Snapping the cylinder in place, he said breathlessly, "I've got to move along the line and see how it's going with the other men. If I can, I'll send some more to flank you here."

"Do it fast," said the lieutenant. "More Apaches could be coming up from the creek."

Locklin had a passing thought that the man should at least thank him for saving his skin, but quickly let it go. Price Wesson wasn't going to show even an ounce of decency.

Though the Apaches had found a measure of success in their hand-to-hand attack, they had also lost several warriors. Orders being shouted by a subchief named Bando had them scurrying back to their carbines. Taking cover in the thicket, they continued the fight.

The line of soldiers was in a curve, and Major Boyd Locklin could not see them all. Among those he could see, several men were down, some wounded, and others dead.

Bullets were buzzing over Locklin and Wesson's heads. Keeping his head down, Locklin noticed Sergeant Bifford Caley and a trooper named Justin Young come bounding over a sandy knoll and hit the ground behind a large rock a few yards to his right, taking a position where two soldiers had fallen. Instantly they began firing their rifles.

Wesson had seen the two dead soldiers off to the right, but did not see Caley and Young move into the position. He was ready to shoot the major in the back when he started up the line. When the Apache bullets let up for a brief moment, Locklin said, "Okay, Wesson, I'm going. Hang tough."

"Sure," nodded Wesson, ready to cut him down.

Just as Locklin pivoted to run, Wesson saw that Caley and Young had taken the nearby position. He dare not shoot the major now.

Suddenly a barrage of gunfire was unleashed by the Apaches. Locklin and Wesson ducked low, firing back at the edges of the big rock. They were unaware of Diablo's special force bursting from the thicket behind them, wielding clubs.

Seconds later, Caley and Young caught a glimpse of the Apaches dragging the limp forms of Locklin and Wesson toward the thicket, but they dared not shoot at them for fear of hitting the major and the lieutenant. The Apaches and their captives were quickly out of sight. Caley and Young turned back to the battle at hand.

The fighting went on for about five minutes, then almost as suddenly as the Apaches had attacked, they withdrew, leaving their dead behind, splashing into the creek. The men in blue stopped firing, but rose up to pursue them.

Sergeant Bifford Caley's big voice boomed, "Hold it, men! They've got Major Locklin and the lieutenant! If we make pursuit, they'll kill them and leave their bodies for us to find!"

Being the senior sergeant in the unit, Caley took charge. He gathered the men together, including the wounded, and told them that he and Young had seen the Apaches drag the unconscious forms of Locklin and Wesson into the thicket.

Some of the men were attending to the wounded. "Sarge, how do you know the major and the lieutenant were unconscious?" a wounded soldier said. "Maybe they were dead."

Shaking his head, Caley replied, "They weren't dead. Some of the bunch that took them were carrying clubs. The Apaches love to capture officers so they can torture them to death."

"With rattlesnakes, like happened to those two men from Fort Butler?"

Caley's features paled. "I hope not."

"What can we do?" asked Sergeant Mike O'Hara.

"Have to take them by surprise," came the ready reply. "The Apaches like to see their captives in mental anguish before the torture begins. Let's hope they'll be real slow about it this time. Right now, we've got to get these wounded men back to the fort. When we tell Colonel Stover what has happened, he'll have a large unit looking for the camp right away. Has to be back in that direction across the creek, somewhere."

Gathering a total of eighteen dead soldiers from the creek and dry ground, they draped them over the horses' backs, helped the eleven wounded men into their saddles, and headed for Fort Grant.

CHAPTER TWENTY-ONE

When Boyd Locklin came to consciousness, he found himself sitting on the ground with his hands tied spread-eagle to the wheel of an old wagon. The sun was low enough to cast long shadows in the hidden canyon, but he was positioned in its pitiless glare.

Sweat ran freely down his face, stinging his eyes as he focused on the dark, sinister faces of the three Apaches who sat on the ground in from of him. In the middle was Kateya, who now called himself Diablo. Mad-eyed and grinning, Diablo said, "It has taken you a long time to come around, Lieutenant Boyd Locklin. Excuse me. It is Major Boyd Locklin now. I am sure you remember me."

Locklin's mouth was dry. Working up a bit of saliva, he said, "Kateya."

The Apache's wild eyes widened with anger. "It is Diablo now! It was you who first called me 'devil,' was it not?"

Ignoring the question, Locklin asked, "Where is Lieutenant Wesson?"

"He is tied to the wheel behind you on the other side of the wagon."

"I'm here," spoke up Wesson from the opposite side.

Gesturing toward the two Indians that flanked him, Diablo said, "May I present my subchiefs, Bando and Nachise."

Locklin licked his dry lips. There was a dull center of pain on the back of his head. He did not speak to the subchiefs, but noted that they both wore their hair long and filthy like their leader. All three were clad in blue U.S. army shirts and wore red bandanna headbands. Locklin noticed also that Diablo had taken his holster and revolver and was wearing them on his own waist.

Locklin said, "So what now?"

Standing up, the Apache kicked Locklin violently in the face. "How is this to make a start?" He laughed. "You killed my father. I am going to punish you for that."

Pain throbbed where foot had met cheek, and his head pounded. "It was a fair fight."

A grimace claimed Diablo's features, peeling his thin lips back over pink gums and yellow teeth. "That does not matter, white eyes swine! The fact remains that you are the dirty bluecoat who took his life. I have been waiting a long time for this day, and I will make the most of it. I cannot tell you how good it feels to have you in my power." Leaning over, he moved so close that Locklin could feel the heat and smell the stench of his breath. "Tomorrow you die! I want you to think about it. Did you see the two bluecoats I sent back to the fort? The ones who had been with the rattlesnakes?"

"Yes," replied the major coldly. "You are a beast!"

"Oh, not a beast, Major! No! No! I am a devil!" He swung a fist, chopping Locklin hard on the jaw.

The pounding agony in Locklin's head intensified.

Diablo then sank the fingers of his left hand into Locklin's thick hair, shook his head, and hissed, "I have hundreds of diamondback friends, white eyes major! They are just waiting to sink their fangs into your pale flesh! I want you to think about it all night."

The major did not reply. His mind ran to Linda and his two wonderful children. He was in the clutches of his worst enemy. After all of his scrapes fighting Apaches before, and coming through the Civil War alive when it appeared that he was dead, was Diablo going to be the one to take his life? He could see no chance of it being otherwise.

Letting go of Locklin's hair, Diablo stood erect and placed his hands on his hips. "This lieutenant of yours doesn't think much of you, Major. He told me that you stole his wife and children. He begged me with tears to let him go to them and kill only you. I asked him why I should do that, and he said because he did not kill my father, you did. And he also said you should die because you stole his family from him."

Throwing his head back, Locklin said, "Wesson, you're even lower than I thought you were."

The lieutenant said nothing.

Diablo laughed and scratched his dirty head. "Both of you are going to die tomorrow. Is that not something special? You are enemies, but you will die together!" The Apache was still laughing as he walked away with his subchiefs.

As darkness fell, Locklin could hear Price Wesson sniffling and weeping behind him. Thinking of his family once more, he yearned for them, yearned to tell Linda again how much he loved her. And to have a few moments to talk to Steven and let him know that he loved him as much as it was possible for a father to love his son. And...little Rebecca Lynne. Such a delight to her daddy's heart. If only he could hold her tight and tell her how much he loved her.

He thought of Linda's words last night, about his being a survivor. Was he going to let her down this time? What chance would he have in this hopeless situation? He pictured the bloated, fang-speckled bodies of Royce Barrett and Jack Erb. What a horrible way to die! Dread gnawed at him like a parasite.

A deathly pallor spread over Linda Locklin's face. Her knees went watery, sweat beaded her brow, and she trembled like an aspen as the strong hands of Colonel Wayne Stover eased her onto the sofa. Steven and Rebecca quickly sat beside her, clinging to her arms. They looked up with large eyes as their mother said, "If Diablo's got him, Colonel, we'll never see him alive again. He'll send Boyd's body back with his name carved on his chest."

Stover wished for words that would ease her fears, but they did not exist. Making an attempt with what words he had, he said, "It could be like Sergeant Caley said, dear. Maybe Diablo will want to put Boyd through a great amount of mental pressure before he—before he takes out his hatred on him." The colonel had tried to break the news to Linda outside of the children's presence, but she had insisted that as army children they needed to be in on it.

Steven's face was white as he gripped Linda's arm. "Is Daddy really not coming home this time, Mommy?"

Silent tears spilled from Linda's eyes. The hot lump in her throat had her voice locked.

Cora wheeled her chair close and laid a steady hand on the lovely woman's shoulder, squeezing tight.

The colonel spoke again. "As I was saying, Linda, maybe Diablo will work his mental torture several days before he begins the physical kind. We know his hidden camp is somewhere near that spot at the creek where the battle took place today. The Indians were on foot." Kneeling down so as to look her straight in the eye, he said, "Listen to me. I am going to break army regulations and lead the assault myself. If we can just buy a little time before Diablo does his worst, there's a possibility that we can find his lair and rescue both men."

Linda knew how long the army had been attempting to locate Diablo's hiding place, and that they had never come close. Knowing her husband's unit had been fighting near it that day did little to encourage her. It had to be well-hidden and quite difficult to penetrate, or the bloody Apache chief would not be so flagrant in his attacks on white people.

Suddenly, there was something indescribable that welled up within her. Strength from deep within, that came with one word for her mind—survivor. Gritting her teeth and clenching her fists, she said, "Boyd Locklin is a survivor, Colonel. We talked about that just last night. Someone had said that about him years ago at Fort Savage. And...and you know what I said to him? I said, 'You are a survivor, Boyd Locklin. I've got to keep that in mind when it appears that something has happened to you.' And he said, 'You do that.' Well, Colonel, Cora, Steven, Becky, that's exactly the way it's going to be! We're all going to expect him to come back safely to us because we're going to remember that Major Boyd Locklin is a survivor!"

At dawn the next morning, Linda stood at the gate and watched Colonel Wayne Stover lead his force of one hundred-ten men out of the fort, leaving only twenty-six able bodied men to defend it, but all agreed that the enemy camp must be found, penetrated, and vanquished. If they could rescue Major Locklin and Lieutenant Wesson in the process, all the better.

Linda stood at the gate and watched the column of riders until they vanished over the hills to the north. Turning back, she crossed the compound, clenching her fists, and repeating to herself, "He's a survivor. Boyd Locklin will come home to me alive because he's a survivor. He's a survivor. He's a survivor. He's a survivor."

Riding army horses with their hands tied behind their backs, Major Boyd Locklin and Lieutenant Price Wesson were escorted by Diablo, Nachise, and Bando as they moved slowly out of the deeply shadowed canyon onto the trail that led to the creek and beyond. The rising sun peeked over the brush-laden hills.

Wesson was quivering at the thought of facing death by fangs. Locklin kept his mind on his family, wishing he could hold them in his arms.

Soon they crossed the creek where the battle had been fought the day before and began climbing the south bank. Locklin noted that the Apaches had picked up their dead some time during the night.

Moments later, the huge rock pit came into view, and Locklin knew this would be the place where he and Wesson would face the snakes…and death. He noted how the nearly perfectly square pit was situated so that it was concealed from the open desert by a ring of sandstone bluffs. Anyone traveling in this area would never know the pit was there.

The Apaches halted the horses on the crest above the pit and dragged the two soldiers from their saddles. Both men looked the pit over as they were ushered down the steep stone-floored embankment. When they reached the lip of the thirty-foot wall, Diablo and Nachise held guns on them while Bando untied their hands.

Bando then drew his gun and the three Apaches backed up the steep incline a few steps. The satisfaction of revenge flitted across Diablo's dark face like the shadow of a demon from hell. "Now, Major Boyd Locklin, I repay you for taking the life of my father."

While Price Wesson was fearfully gazing down at the slithering rattlesnakes amid skeletons, rocks, cactus, and clumps of catclaw in the pit, the major gave Diablo a defiant look.

Waving Locklin's own gun at him, the Apache said in a noxious voice, "You are thinking how you would like to kill me, Major. Correct? Well, come ahead. Maybe you are also thinking that if you tried and failed, at least you could die quickly from a bullet, rather than slowly from snakebite. But Diablo controls the situation. If you make a move toward me, I will not shoot to kill, only to wound. This place where we stand is so steep, that you will only fall into the pit anyhow. So because I want you to die a very slow and agonizing death, I will allow you to drop into the pit unharmed."

Price Wesson broke into tears, his whole body shaking violently. "Please, Diablo! Don't do this to me! I don't want to die! I'll join up with you. Yes! I'll become an Apache and fight against those awful white people who have invaded your land! Please! Don't make me go into that pit!"

A glimmer shone in Diablo's black eyes. Curling his lip over his yellow teeth, he snarled, "Next to the hate I feel toward the man who killed my father, Lieutenant Price Wesson, is the hatred I feel toward a man who will be a traitor to his own people. It is my pleasure to know you will die in the pit. Now both of you turn around and drop over the wall!"

Wesson's wails of terror echoed around the pit as Boyd Locklin pivoted, looked down at the snakes crawling listlessly over the rock-strewn floor below him, then bent down, gripped the ledge, and lowered his body over the jagged lip. While hanging there with his feet dangling, he looked directly below. The snake closest to the spot where he would land was about twenty feet away. Locklin had taken note of the tall rock in the center of the pit, and of the countless number of fist-sized stones that lay scattered about. All he could do would be to use his stone-throwing ability to clear a path to the tall rock. He could tell by the skeletons collected at the base that many a man had fallen from its top, dead or dying from dehydration.

Locklin had the same innate lust for life that was placed in every human being by his Creator. He was determined to make it to the rock and prolong life as long as possible.

Still wailing, Wesson lowered himself next to Locklin, and hung on to the rocky lip.

Before letting go, Locklin said, "Listen to me, Wesson. It's a long drop. Don't stiffen your legs. Bend your knees slightly. That'll cushion the fall. As soon as you hit bottom, grab up stones and start throwing them at the snakes. We need to clear a path to that tall rock over there. Got it?"

Blubbering, the lieutenant drew a shuddering breath. "Yes."

Locklin let go, hit the ground, and stayed on his feet. Pain from the sudden stop lanced through his legs all the way up his back, but he ignored it and grabbed up stones. Stuffing one in each pocket, he picked up others and sent one hissing toward the closest snake, which was now slithering toward him. The stone, directly on target, shattered the snake's head.

Wesson had hit the pit floor and fallen flat while Locklin was killing the snake. He gained his feet and was picking up stones when the major hurled a second one at a diamondback that was hissing and coiling on the path directly between the men and the tall rock. Wesson was amazed at Locklin's accuracy as he saw the head splatter.

From up above, the Apaches watched with interest as Locklin led the terrified lieutenant toward safety by killing snakes with rocks on all sides of them. Wesson did his part in throwing, but usually missed, though his stones did cause a few to slither another direction.

Leaving a trail of dead snakes, Locklin gained the rock and helped Wesson to the top. There was barely room enough for both of them to sit.

Hands on hips, Diablo laughed. "Congratulations, brave white eyes soldiers! You made it to the top! Since you are not the best of friends, it will be interesting to see if one tries to shove the other off the rock. My little diamondback pets are waiting for you. I wonder which one they will get to kill first!"

Bando laughed in the same manner as his chief. "Look, white eyes." He pointed skyward. "The sun is rising higher! It will get very hot down there before the day is over. Without water, your bodies will soon dry up. Then the snakes will have their way with you!"

"Yes!" Nachise laughed. "Like those bluecoats who lie dead below you with no meat on their bones!"

Waving in a mocking manner, Diablo started up the steep slope. "We are going to the creek to get a nice drink of cool water, then to the camp to sit in the shade. We will return later to see if either of you is still alive."

Locklin and Wesson watched the Apaches reach the crest of the rise, mount their pintos, and lead the army horses away. Within seconds they were out of sight.

Wesson's breathing was laborious. Locklin said coolly, "Better get a grip on yourself, or you'll be off this rock real quick."

Shuddering with fright, Wesson clenched his jaws tight, but said nothing.

Leaning over the edge, the major let his gaze flick over the vast floor of the pit. There were snakes everywhere. A few were content to lie in one spot, but most of them were in motion—a smooth, silent slithering.

Slowly, Locklin brought his gaze back to the base of the rock where the sunbleached skeletons lay in a jumbled heap. A close look showed that some of the skulls still had patches of hair, and here and there were pieces of blue uniform. Now he knew what had happened to many of the soldiers who had been captured by Diablo.

Movement caught Locklin's eye as a big bull rattler came sliding upward from the deep shade below, its large flat head pushing between the ribs of one of the skeletons. His mind went back to the day Pantano had staked him out on the mound and the big rattler crawled over his body.

This brought his thoughts to Linda, for it was the time and place they first met. His heart ached for her. His heart ached for Steven. His heart ached for Becky. He thought of his conversation with Linda night before last, when she called him a survivor. He had cheated death many times, but he had never been in a hopeless situation like this one. Even if he slid to the ground and somehow could kill snakes all the way to the wall, there was no way to climb it. Uniformly, it was sheer rock all around and thirty feet to the top.

The sun was beginning to make its rays felt. Soon it would be well over a hundred degrees in the pit. Raising his line of sight to the sandstone bluffs that surrounded him, Locklin told himself that no search party from Fort Grant would ever find them. From out on the desert, the bluffs looked like they were solidly connected from one side to the other.

Flies came with the heat. Most of them collected on the dead snakes, swarming on the bloody meat where the heads had been. Others found the patches of hair on the skulls, while still others buzzed around the heads of the men atop the rock.

Price Wesson's face had taken on a ghastly hue. Fear showed in his eyes as he swatted at a fly. "We're dead, aren't we?"

"Not yet. We're not done for till we are dead."

Despair made Wesson's voice tremble. "There's no way out of this. We'll dehydrate and fall to the snakes, but not before our tongues swell up in our mouths and our eyes go dry. I don't want to die this way, Locklin! I don't want to die at all!"

"So you can go home to your wife and children, eh?" said Locklin, his voice a hollow, breathy exhalation. There was anger in his dark blue eyes.

Wesson would not meet his gaze.

Locklin made a pass at a pesky fly, palmed sweat from his face, and submitted himself to the naked violence of the sun.

At Fort Grant, the officers' wives sat in the Stover parlor, having gathered to encourage and comfort Linda Locklin. Each had said a little speech she had prepared, and now Cora was saying, "You're the perfect army wife, Linda. In the few years you have been married to Boyd, you've suffered more anxiety than most army wives will know in an entire lifetime. Yet, here you are, calm and collected. Your husband is in the hands of a devil-demented man who hates him with a passion, but you sit there with your arms around your children, giving them strength and hope. I admire you, honey. I really do."

Linda tried to smile. "The calm you see is on the outside, dear Cora. I wouldn't be human and not have genuine anxiety at a time like this. But...but I've spent a sleepless night praying and as I told you last night, keeping in mind that my husband has a special something about him. He's the kind that survives when others in the same situation would not make it. Hanging on to that, and believing that the good Lord has His hand on him, I am expecting Major Boyd Locklin to come back to us alive."

It was a day of flame. As the morning dragged on, the blazing single eye of the sun looked down on the two men who huddled on the rock and it slowly sucked the moisture from their bodies. Wesson sat with his knees drawn up, leaning his sweaty face against them. Locklin was watching a rattler gliding silently across the floor of the pit, sneaking up on a desert rat that was poking its long nose curiously at the bloody end of one of the dead snakes.

The major knew there had to be a small opening of some kind in the rock wall of the pit. Diamondbacks lived on small animals. It was from their bodies that the snakes got their water. There were plenty of snakes around, so there had to be a way they could get out to find food, or the food could get in to them.

Slithering up behind the rat with its black tongue flicking the air, the rattler curled its scaly body partially and struck with lightning speed. The rat squealed, tried to fight back, but the venom paralyzed its small frame within seconds. The snake opened its wide mouth, and soon there was a telltale lump in its long, slender body.

It was coming up on noon and the heat was unbearable. Wesson's pale flesh looked like old parchment, hanging on the sharp angles of his face. Locklin thought the man had aged forty years since dawn.

Shaking his head, Wesson worked his tongue loose from the roof of his mouth, looked down at the skeletons below, and said, "It must be a horrible thing to die of snakebite."

"It's horrible, all right," said Locklin. "I've watched it happen."

Wesson's face went even whiter. "Takes a while to die?"

"Yes."

"Lot of pain?"

"Excruciating. You don't want to hear about it."

"Yes, I do. Tell me."

Shrugging, Locklin said, "The pain is like the sting of a thousand wasps. Shoots from the actual bite through the rest of your body. Horrible stomach cramps. Fever. Chills. Intestines draw up like knotted rope. Nausea. Vomiting. In the last stage, the venom works on the eyes, making everything look yellow. Then, it's over. Horrible."

Wesson looked sick.

"I told you you didn't want to hear it," said the major.

Suddenly the lieutenant's eyes fluttered. He reeled dangerously and started to fall from the rock. Quickly, Locklin grabbed his shoulders and kept him from peeling over the edge.

At that instant, laughter filled the air and echoed off the surrounding granite walls. Gripping Wesson, Locklin looked up to see

Diablo standing at the edge of the pit. Nachise and Bando stood beside him. All three wore army-issue gun belts. Diablo still had Locklin's gun on his hip.

"Now that is a sight to see!" exclaimed Diablo. "You are truly a man of valor, Major Boyd Locklin! This man lies about you, tries to get me to kill you while letting him live, and when all you have to do is let him fall, you go the trouble to spare his life for a little longer! You amaze me, killer of my father."

"We expected to find both of you at the bottom of the rock by this time, Major," spoke up Bando. "Some of you white men have more stamina than others."

"Ho!" Nachise laughed. "There are many hours of heat left. With no water, they will die before sundown."

Wesson's head lifted on a rubbery neck. He looked toward the Indians with dull eyes, but did not try to speak.

Diablo showed his ugly, stained teeth in a smile. "We will be back in a few hours, brave soldiers. Too bad you are not near the creek, so you can hear the singing of the cool waters."

With that, the Apaches climbed the slope, mounted their pintos, and rode away.

Working his tongue laboriously, Price Wesson steadied himself on the rock. "You don't need to hold on to me now, Major."

Locklin let go and tried to work up his own saliva. His shirt was drenched with sweat.

Wesson set his dull gaze on Locklin. "Diablo's right, you know. I did lie about you. I did try to get him to kill you. Why would you put yourself out to spare my life? You could have let me fall a few minutes ago."

With dry tongue, Locklin replied, "I'll be honest. One part of me wanted to let you fall, but the other part made me grab you. That's the part that says even though you forced yourself on Linda, and even though you tried to get Diablo to kill me while sparing you, I cannot kill you for it. If I had let you fall, it would be the same as killing you."

Wesson was quiet for a long moment. "Neither one of us is going to have Linda now. We're done for. Nachise is right. We'll be dead before sundown."

Locklin did not comment.

The sun reached its high point in the brassy sky, then slowly began its westerly arc downward. Shimmering heat waves rose from the pit, taking more moisture from the two men who languished atop the rock.

Colonel Wayne Stover and his one-hundred-ten-man force crossed the creek where the battle had been fought and rode toward the labyrinth of canyons that joined each other. Riding alongside Stover as a guide, Sergeant Bifford Caley said, "That Apache camp has got to be back in here somewhere, sir. I saw them head this direction when they fled with the major and Wesson."

"We'll scout out every nook and cranny," Stover said.

Unknowingly, at two o'clock in the afternoon, the army search party passed by the obscure entrance to Diablo's hidden canyon. Three hours later, after finding nothing in several box canyons, they dejectedly began to work their way back toward the creek.

About an hour from the sun touching the western horizon, Price Wesson looked at the sunburned face of Boyd Locklin. "If we make it till sundown we might survive the night, but we'll never live through tomorrow."

"Yeah." Locklin nodded, running a dry tongue over equally dry lips. He had kept Wesson from falling off the rock two more times, but wondered if he'd have the strength to do it again.

"I think my tongue is beginning to swell," said Wesson. "Is yours?"

"Might be. I'm not sure."

At that moment, both men heard a horse blow. They looked northward to see Diablo and his two henchmen dismount and ease their way down the precipitous slope to the pit's edge.

Amazed to find Locklin and Wesson still on the rock, Diablo laughed fiendishly. "You white eyes soldiers are not cooperating! My slithering pets beneath you are eager to sink their fangs into your flesh!"

Stark panic showed in Price Wesson's otherwise dull, red-rimmed eyes. "Please, Diablo, don't let us die like this! Haven't we suffered enough? Do you have to be so cruel?"

"You must die in there, Lieutenant Price Wesson," Diablo replied, pulling Locklin's revolver from its holster. "Both of you! However, I am going to let one of you die the easy way."

Diablo had the rapt attention of both army officers as he broke open the Colt .45 and removed all but one cartridge. As he snapped the cylinder shut, Nachise and Bando pulled their revolvers, cocked them, and pointed them toward Locklin and Wesson.

"There is one bullet left in your gun, Major," said Diablo, turning the weapon in his hands to grip the barrel. "You two brave soldiers can work it out between you who gets a bullet in his brain, and who dies the horrible, lingering death."

Bando and Nachise, as usual, flanked their chief on either side. Wanting to give him ample space to make the throw, they both moved along the pit's edge till they were some ten feet from him. Calculating the fifty-foot distance to the rock from where he stood, Diablo swung his arm pendulum-style a few times, then gave the revolver a high toss.

Major Boyd Locklin rose up on his knees and caught the gun with both hands. He now had resolved himself to the fact that he and Wesson were doomed, but he desperately wanted to take the vile Diablo into eternity with him. He didn't know where the single cartridge was positioned in the cylinder, though he wanted to use it to shoot Diablo.

Diablo, of course, was aware that the thought would cross Locklin's mind. He had covered himself by having his subchiefs ready to shoot the major off the rock if he even looked like he would try it. It would take Locklin three or four seconds to break the gun open, locate the cartridge, position it correctly for firing, and snap the cylinder into place. In that time, Nachise and Bando would shoot him off the rock. Locklin would never get his shot off.

Sitting down again and holding the gun, the major pondered the situation. Maybe...just maybe he could do it fast enough to put a bullet in Diablo before the subchiefs could shoot him. Even if the wound he inflicted on Diablo was not fatal, the impact of the slug would knock Diablo down...and standing where he was on the slope at the pit's edge, he could do nothing but fall to the six or seven diamondbacks that were positioned directly below him at that moment.

"Well, brave white eyes soldiers," said Diablo, "who is going to die the easy way?"

Pale of face, Price Wesson looked at Locklin.

Suddenly the major knew what he would do. The odds were too heavy against him that he could move fast enough to assure himself of a shot at Diablo. His mission was to rid the world of the bloody devil. He was heavily handicapped at best, but there was one way to cut down the odds—the old military element of surprise. In his pockets were two fist-sized stones. One of them had Diablo's name on it.

Lifting the revolver above his head, he looked at Diablo—while memorizing the Apache's exact position—and said, "I'm going to lay the gun between us. The man who can stand it no longer and wishes to die quickly can pick up the gun and use it."

Diablo was laughing and saying something to his comrades as Locklin laid the revolver between himself and Wesson and whispered, "Talk to them. Keep their attention on you while I get one of these rocks out of my pocket. They'll shoot me, but at least I'll take the wicked devil with me."

While Locklin casually turned himself so as to keep the Indians from seeing him extract the rock from his right pocket, Wesson called out, "I am begging you Apaches, as human beings, to let us live. Have you no compassion in your hearts?"

The rock was in Locklin's hand and his head was down. Visualizing Diablo's position, he summoned all of his strength and poised himself for the throw.

The Apache chief placed his hands on his hips, threw his head back, and laughed. "Compassion? What is that, white eyes?"

Bando and Nachise were laughing hilariously, heads thrown back, eyes closed.

Boyd Locklin had to catch himself from falling off the rock after hurling the stone with all his might. It struck Diablo a perfect blow between the eyes. Stunned, his head popped back. He reeled, clawed the air, and fell over the edge, landing hard.

The subchiefs had ceased laughing and were in shock as they looked down at their venerable leader, who lay stunned on the pit floor, shaking his head. Diablo had landed on two rattlers, which were now in pain and striking at him angrily. Others were slithering toward him, black eyes unblinking and ugly tongues flicking.

It was a moment of absolute terror for Bando and Nachise, who seemed to have forgotten the two soldiers atop the rock. Still holding their guns in hand, they knelt at the lip of the pit. They heard the choleric hisses and rattles and saw the snakes writhing, jerking, and striking in nervous anger.

Diablo's head cleared enough that he realized what was happening. Ejecting a wild scream, he examined the bloody spots where the fangs had broken skin. Rising to his knees as more snakes struck him, he blindly seized one at midbody and raised it up to throw. But he was too slow. The serpent's mouth opened at the same time it curled its body around his wrist, and in that splint second before it struck his face, he saw the black tongue jutting out and the tiny dark spots at the points of the curved fangs—the holes through which the snake would shoot its venom.

Wailing in terror, Diablo ran mindlessly a few feet and fell. The snake on his wrist struck him again, this time directly in the left eye. More diamondbacks were slithering toward him. Rising again, he flung the snake from his arm, stumbled over a rock, and hit the ground once more. Another rattler was there to sink its poisonous fangs into his flesh. He crawled a short distance and was struck again by a big rattler, but Bando and Nachise knew he would never move again.

Like they were in some kind of trance, the subchiefs turned and climbed the steep slope, totally ignoring the men atop the rock. Mounting up, they led Diablo's horse in the direction of the creek and vanished from sight.

Boyd Locklin choked on his dry throat and said to Wesson, "That'll be all for Diablo's army. They'll go back to the Chiricahua Mountains now. White folks in this area won't be bothered for a long time."

Wesson ran a dirty sleeve across his mouth, but said nothing. He was looking at Diablo, who lay face-down with snakes crawling all over him. "What a horrible way to die!" he said, eyes bulging.

Pointing to the gun between them, Locklin said dully, "If you want to use it, go ahead."

The lieutenant looked at him. "You mean after watching what

we just did, you would still let me die quick and easy and face a horrible death like that yourself?"

Locklin swung his glance to Diablo, looked back at Wesson, but did not reply. . .

CHAPTER TWENTY-TWO

Colonel Wayne Stover and his men were solemnly riding past the tall, sandstone bluffs that hid the pit, heading back toward Fort Grant. They had given-up on ever finding Locklin and Wesson.

Speaking to Lieutenant John Frame and Sergeant Bifford Caley, who rode beside him, Stover said, "I hate this. How am I going to face Linda Locklin? She's such a great soldier. I wish—"

The colonel's statement was interrupted by the roar and clattering echo of a gunshot. Quickly, he pulled rein and raised his hand for the column to halt.

"That was a revolver, sir," said Frame, "and it came from somewhere in those bluffs."

"Let's check it out," said Stover.

Weaving among the bluffs, the colonel and his men soon found that there was open territory the army had never known existed. It took them less than five minutes to find the pit.

"Look, sir!" exclaimed Biff Caley. "On that rock! It's Major Locklin! And he's alive!"

Boyd Locklin was draped atop the rock, barely clinging to it. His head lay listlessly on one arm. At first he thought he was hallucinating when he heard Sergeant Biff Caley's voice call his name. Was this what happened when a man died of dehydration? Did he hear familiar voices just before expiring?

When it came the second time, it was all too real. Lifting his head, he stared northward, blinking against the brilliance of the low-hanging sun. He saw what looked like a thousand horsemen outlined against the sky. Letting his gaze trail downward, he focused on Biff Caley, who was standing at the very spot at the pit's edge from where Diablo had fallen to his death.

When Locklin worked his way to a sitting position, the one

hundred and ten men lifted a rousing cheer. The major raised a hand, waved weakly, and managed a smile. Leaning over the edge of the tall, slender rock, he set his gaze on the lifeless form of Lieutenant Price Wesson, who lay at its base, covered with slithering snakes. Near Wesson's body lay the revolver. There was a bullet hole in his right temple.

"Major!" called Caley. "Hold on! We'll get you out!"

The top half of the sun's fiery rim was still in view above the western horizon when one of the sentries in Fort Grant's tower shouted across the compound that Colonel Stover and the search unit were coming in.

Thirty seconds later, Linda Locklin was bounding up the tower stairs. When she reached the platform, she squinted into the sun, raking the land with her gaze, and said to the sentry who was looking through a pair of binoculars, "It looks like the whole bunch is returning. Can you tell if they have my husband and Lieutenant Wesson?"

"I'm trying to figure that out, ma'am. Should be able to tell shortly." After a long pause, he said, "Looks like...yes, I'm sure of it. They've only got one extra man. He's riding double in front of Sergeant Caley."

"Well, can you tell who it is?"

"Not quite, ma'am. He's got his head down."

"Is he wearing a hat?"

"No."

"Well, is his hair dark or light?"

"Hard to tell, ma'am. He's riding in Caley's shadow. If he'd just—There! He sat up! It's the major, ma'am. It's Major Locklin!"

"Let me see, please," said Linda, opening her hands.

"Sure." The sentry smiled, handing her the binoculars.

Placing the binoculars to her eyes, Linda focused on the weary face of her husband. "Yes, it's him! Oh, thank God!"

Bounding down the stairs, she passed through the gate, which was just swinging open. Pausing to wipe away a tear, she lifted her long skirt calf-high and ran toward the approaching column of riders. "Boyd! Oh, Boyd! You're alive! I love you! I love you!"

Other books by Morgan Hill:

Ghost of Sonora
Dead Man's Noose
The Last Bullet

A Deadly Choice...

Clay Bostin's fortune changes quickly on the Nebraska plains. Left to die in excruciating pain by marauding Indians, he is rescued by an wagon train and nursed back to health by lovely Rachel Flanagan. Soon afterwards, the Cheyenne attack, and Clay is chosen to replace their fallen trail boss. Now it's his fate to protect the pioneers from the relentless assault of the Cheyenne warriors. What will happen if brutal Black Hawk reaches the beautiful girl?

ISBN 1-59052-278-8

Bandit or Freedom Fighter?

In the veiled and shadowed history of the West, there rides a mysterious horseman. His headless shoulders testify to his death at the hands of the law—in a state that forbade Mexicans like him to own property. A state that turned a deaf ear to the rape and murder of his beautiful young wife. This is the Ghost of Sonora. Was he man or myth? Was Joaquin Murieta the Napoleon of Banditry, as the California Rangers have charged, or *El Patrio*, the great liberator of the Mexicans of California? Here is his story. You make the decision.

ISBN 1-59052-134-X